"What a beautiful tearful roller-coaster ride this has been! Paula delved deep into the innermost feelings of the human heart to write this spellbinding, suspense-filled historic romance novel with a cliffhanger ending. I can hardly wait until the second book comes out so I can find out if Naomi gets the happy ever after she yearns for!"

—ELIZABETH BENNETT
Educator, Sephardic Believer in Yeshua Ha'Mashiach

"I could not put it down! 'I am Naomi,' I told Paula after she read a few pages. She nodded and continued reading until I exclaimed, 'Tía Vida was my grandmother!' You will relate to the characters when you read Naomi's sweet poignant journey from poverty of spirit to faith."

—CORRENE EHRICK
Foundation for His Ministry, Sephardic Believer in Messiah

"Casa de Naomi is the story of a woman's personal growth as she experiences romance and falls in love while she hides who she is. The author has given us insight into the life of the immigrant—displaced, despondent, dependent, the humble, trembling soul foisted into a world where expectations run high…more than a book of romantic fiction…she has given us a novel filled with deep feelings, strong convictions, and poignant life experiences."

—MARIE ODEN
Founder/facilitator, Shuvah Yisrael Writer's Group, writer

D1736031

"Casa de Naomi is a very believable story of a Sephardic Marrano who hides her Jewish blood in the mid-twentieth century. I could see Naomi and Chaz figuring out how to be newlyweds. I indentified with Chaz as he tries to please his woman. This story will resonate with all readers especially those who want to step into the shoes of the Jewish descendants of the Inquisition."

—JUAN DAVID ALCALA BENNETT
Author, *The Walls of Spain*

"Mrs. Michelson's passion and empathy for her characters made them come alive. I appreciate the extensive research she has done on this unique population, which afforded her richly detailed story the resonance making this a rewarding read."

—BARBARA ASHLEY
Author, *Amazons, Rebels & Spies*, as well
as nine books for young readers

CASA de Naomi

The House of Blessing

PAULA ROSE MICHELSON

TATE PUBLISHING
AND ENTERPRISES, LLC

Published by Tate Publishing & Enterprises, LLC
127 E. Trade Center Terrace | Mustang, Oklahoma 73064 USA
1.888.361.9473 | www.tatepublishing.com

Tate Publishing is committed to excellence in the publishing industry. The company reflects the philosophy established by the founders, based on Psalm 68:11,
"The Lord gave the word and great was the company of those who published it."

Book design copyright © 2011 by Tate Publishing, LLC. All rights reserved.
Cover design by Kellie Vincent
Interior design by April Marciszewski

Published in the United States of America
ISBN: 978-1-61346-138-9
1. Fiction: Jewish
2. Fiction: Sagas
11.11.10

DEDICATION

To the One from whom all blessings flow.
God said, *"... all people on earth will be blessed through you."*

In loving memory of Elisabeth Rose Bennett
(Alcala-Narro) Leatherwood, a Sephardic Jew
who returned to Spain to serve the Lord.

ACKNOWLEDGMENTS

Every author knows her journey of creativity requires the assistance and support of a few committed and unique individuals. My journey affirms that experience.

I would like to thank Correne Ehrick, my *Sephardic* friend, who listened to my ideas, prayed for the work to be completed, and shared her life with me. Your unique ability to support my creative process has been a source of light as I worked through the research, which birthed this saga. I am indebted to you for giving me the papers that document your family history, affirming that Jews escaping the Inquisition came to America and settled in the Southwestern United States.

Hilario and Patricia Camacho, thank you for sharing your personal journey from Spain to America. When I hear Hilario cant during worship, I rejoice because God brought you from darkness to light and to the reality of your Jewish heritage. Thank you for your friendship, faith, and the material that you entrusted to me.

Trish, thank you for pouring yourself into this work as an act of worship to our *Messiah*. I am eternally grateful for your knowledge of Spanish, your commitment to excellence, and your desire to assist me without any thought to your reward.

Marie Oden, although we are hours away, you made yourself available to me though e-mail and prayers. I am grateful for the continued gift of your support and insight. Thank you for forming the writers group at *Shuvah Yisrael*, where I realized that though I sit in a solitary room while I write, I am never alone.

To Marlayne Grion, who put me in touch with Tate Publishing, thank you for listening to and supporting this endeavor. As an author, your wise counsel has proven invaluable.

To my dear friend in *Messiah*, Kathi Macias, who gave her time, talent, and mentoring skills, which helped bring this work to fruition, I send a heartfelt *todah rabah*—thank you very much.

To Barbara Herzog, my dear friend and published author, whose wise counsel never failed to inform my writing and whose thoughtful critique made each rewrite better, thank you is not enough, but since words fail, it will have to suffice.

To the myriad of authors, writers, teachers, and believers who sought God on behalf of this work, may all of you experience the blessings that you so lavishly bestowed on me.

I wish to thank Janey Hayes at Tate Publishing for her affirmation of and faith in the The House of Blessing books, and Hillary Atkinson, my editor, for bringing my vision to completion.

Finally, I saved the best for last! I would like to thank God for my husband, Ron, without whom this book would never have been completed. Ron, the day I met you was the day my forever began! How fortunate for me that I married a man who loves to write and enjoys encouraging me. Without your continued assistance in every phase of the development, and editing of this book, I would have faltered. Thank you for always making yourself available, no matter how busy or tired you were. You truly are the place where my *House of Blessing* resides!

SEPHARDIC VOICES

For the past several years, I have been working on the novels that comprise *The House of Blessing Casa Saga* of which this is the first volume. I found most *Sephardic* Jews reticent to speak or write about their families experience during the Inquisition because until twenty years ago, the Decree of Expulsion was still in effect. They feared revealing themselves for they were taught that to do so in a country of only one faith—that of the Catholic Church could place them in peril. After much research and discussions with a few Spanish Jews, as well as dialogues with those who teach history and literature, I discovered that only a few knew of and understood these people's lives, religious practices, and personal histories. This disconnection occurred due to the ongoing pressure within *Sephardic* families to remain hidden within a culture that has been hostile to their existence. This started with the signing of the Decree of Alhambra, which began the Spanish and, later, the Mexican Inquisitions. This decree was in effect until March 31, 1992. Because of this, it is only now that a few brave people are willing to step forward and share their stories.

It is my pleasure to introduce you to three *Sephardic* believers in *Messiah*. Each has allowed me to share with you how they moved from where they were to owning their Jewish heritage. They hope that as you read their words you will believe that people are still dealing with feelings of generational fear, which make it imperative that they keep their progeny in the dark about their religious heritage.

Corrine's Voice

I was born in 1929 and raised in downtown Los Angeles. My religious training was in the Catholic Church, as all in our family had done for years. In 1984, my son David, who had research our history told me that we are Jewish. I paid no attention to him. In 1974, I found myself drawn to Jewish things. When my grandmother died, my mother showed me her baptismal certificate. I noticed that her godmother's last name was Gold. I asked my mother about that, as Gold is a very unusual last name for a Spanish person to have because godparents are usually family members. She told me that her cousin had told her when she was a child that they were Jews but not to tell anyone. It was then I remembered my grandfather singing in a strange language out by the chicken coops, and my mother saying, "He sings like a cantor!" The realization that we were not what we seemed to be created within me a hunger to know more. Since then I have invested my time and energy to learn all I can about my Jewish roots. That investigation has made me aware of the charges the Inquisitor made against my family, revealed the possibility that they may have come over with Columbus, and the knowledge that they settled in what is now the southwestern United States. Today, through much work on behalf of my family, I have acquired the documents to prove what I am saying. Were it not for the Decree of Alhambra and the Spanish Inquisition, we would still be in Spain, but due to that decree and its effects upon my family and the Jews still hiding, I am willing to state that what man meant for evil, God used for good! For in *Messiah Yeshua*, I have found my Jewish *Messiah* and have been able to own who I am as both a Jew and a believer in my Kinsman Redeemer.

—At seventy-four, **CORRINE EHRICK**
began to worship as a Sephardic Messianic believer.

Betty's Voice

When I was in my early twenties, my parents took me on a trip to visit relatives in Saltillo, Mexico, where my grandfather Miguel Narro was born and raised. They were rich and very Catholic. They had disowned my grandfather when he accepted *Yeshua* as his Savior and became a

Protestant pastor. Many years later, my great-aunt Rosario (Rosary) confided to my mother that there had been two *rabbis* in the Narro family. After that, my mother wore a Star of David that she had bought. She told my son John David that we were Jewish. My grandfather refused to eat pork, but we never knew why. No one ever talked about our Jewish heritage. However, now I know that some believed we were Jewish and other family members denied it. My father, David Alcala, most likely had Jewish ancestry also since Alcala is a *Sephardic* Jewish name. My great-grandfather Ambrosio Alcala was born in Alcala de Henares, a city in Spain that had an imposing Jewish presence and two *synagogues*.

—ELIZABETH ALCALA-NARRO BENNETT
is a Sephardic Jew whose children bring the gospel
to those in Spain. She worships at a Messianic congregation.

Janice's Voice

There was a stirring in my heart to follow my mother's influence and learn about the Jewish people. I remember my fourth grade class in parochial school, where Sister Demetrius instilled within us the fact that the Jews did not kill Christ, but it was our sins that put him on the cross. Between my schooling and Mom's love for the Jewish heritage, there was birthed within me a tenderness toward the Jewish people. As I reached what some would call middle age, this stirring intensified until I needed to know more. For years, I told people that I was Basque. However, I never went to the town whose name I bore. Then I met a woman whose son was a missionary in Spain. I asked him if he could take me to Ulibarri and he agreed. In 2008, I made the trip to Spain. We traveled throughout the Navarra region until I finally stepped onto the soil that had been home to my family centuries before. Imagine my surprise when I discovered that there was a strong Jewish presence in that region. Could my mother have been trying to tell me something all those years ago? I will never know for sure. However, my journey of the heart allowed me to look at my heritage and history with new eyes. When I returned home, I told my children, "We have a Jewish heritage." They rolled their eyes. Months later, my son called and said, "I was waiting for the metro and was approached by a scholarly man who looked at my badge, which identifies me by my last name. He read

'Mireles' and asked me if I knew about my name and my heritage. I was able to give him the information you had shared with us. I was stunned when he gave me additional information, which proved to me that what you had said was correct! I called you, and I told my brothers and sisters that what you had said was true."

—JANICE MIRELES-ULIBARRI
has been involved in Messianic Worship since 1994
and served as a volunteer in the Israeli arm in 1999.

HISTORICAL NOTES

The Spanish Inquisition began with the signing of the Decree of Alhambra on March 31, 1492, which was in effect for five hundred years. That decree instituted *pureblood laws,* which forced the Jews to leave Spain before midnight of the above date, become a Catholic *converso* (which was the title the church gave them, meaning *convert*) or *Anusim* (*the forced ones,* as they called themselves), or die.

Prior to the signing of the decree, the crown moved the Jews into towns expressly set aside for them. This made it easy for the office to monitor the conversion of those Jews who had not married Catholics and subsequently converted or convinced those in high office that they believed in Christ. During that time, fervent priests were preaching against the Jews; many who feared death became Catholic and were assimilated into that faith. Others allowed themselves to be baptized and acted Catholic while practicing their Jewish faith at home. The records show that Jews who did not covert and could not, or would not, leave watched their homes and towns razed and torched before the officials killed them.

The church appointed the office of inquisitor and his assistants. Their work involved the unification of Spain under the Catholic Church. While the office hunted the hidden Jews, some Jews who followed the Laws of Moses, as they called the Old Testament, sought Jews who had fallen away from Judaism and called them back to that faith. The inquisitor's office labeled those working to bring Jews back to Judaism *Judaizers.*

During the trial of *Judaizers,* the church sought repentant conversions. If a person was unrepentant, the office stripped him of his rank and worldly possessions, tortured him for information, and killed him. If the person repented, the church occasionally showed mercy and allowed him to serve as a cleric. A penitent forfeited everything he owned, was incommunicado for life, and forced to wear a penitent garment, which reflected his reduced status, making him a target of ridicule. If the church deemed the penitent unsuited for service, he incurred everything listed above, was placed under house arrest, and never allowed out of the sight of someone associated with the office of the inquisitor. Jews who became Catholic during this time were called *New Christians* as a means of differentiating them from those who had no Jewish blood.

Since the majority of the population was illiterate and poor, they viewed this as God's recompense for what they assumed was the Jewish belief in their superiority. It took little encouragement for those working within the office to find many who were willing to falsify their witness to curry favor with those in power. The Inquisition's purpose was to rid the country of all dissidents, including Moors, Muslims, and gypsies. Records show that some Catholic Spaniards used it to acquire the wealth, property, and power they coveted from other Catholics who practiced Catholicism hundreds of years before the Inquisition began.

It is sad to realize that the place where Judaism flourished after the Jewish diaspora from Israel became an extremely hostile environment toward them for hundreds of years and horrifying to note that Hitler's Third Reich used the *pure blood laws* that Spain had instituted against the Jewish people when Hitler implemented his final solution.

When we study the Inquisition and its effects, it is important to mention that the Spanish Inquisition came to the new world. The first governor of New Spain, Luis de Carvajal y de la Cueva, was a *converso*. The office of the inquisitor brought him to trial and found him guilty of *Judaizing*. He died during his incarceration. The office arrested the members of his family, and they faced the reprisals mentioned above. The only member of this family to survive the Inquisition was Leonor de Caceres, a distant niece of the governor's. She recanted her Jewish faith at fourteen, was placed within the house of the inquisitor, and when she reached marriageable age was married to a devout Catholic.

Throughout the world, many people are interested in discovering if their heritage is Jewish or, as the Spanish Jews say, *Sephardim*—a word derived from Sepharad, a root word found in Scripture. In the Southwestern United States, many people of Spanish and Mexican ancestry, as well as Caucasians and some Plains Indians, wonder about the artifacts they have, customs they practice, and stories they heard that suggest a Jewish heritage. Some use the name *Sephardic, Ladino, Anusim, Marino,* or *Converso* when they refer to themselves, and that leads many knowledgeable people to believe they are Jewish. Since the Jews lived in Spain for hundreds of years and married Catholic Spaniards, many believe that if you scratch a Spaniard, you will find a Jew. Others, both here and in Spain, have noticed that their last names are the names of Jewish towns razed during the Inquisition. Whether here or in Spain, whether people know they are Jewish or just suspect, the Spanish Jews have learned, over centuries of percussion, to hide who they are as a means of survival.

On March 31, 1992, five hundred years to the day the Edict of Expulsion was signed, King Juan Carlos of Spain and Queen Sofia, his wife, stood in the main synagogue of Madrid. The king wore a *yamulke*—a skullcap. Chaim Herzog, the president of Israel, flanked him. What he said reveals the Spanish attitude toward the heinous acts the Jews experienced. "May hate and intolerance never again cause desolation and exile. Let us be capable of building a prosperous and peaceful Spain based on concord and mutual respect. What is important is not an accounting of our errors or successes, but the willingness to think about and analyze the past in terms of our future, and the willingness to work together to pursue a noble goal.[1]"

Although the king rescinded the edict, he did not apologize for the expulsion because to do so would be unfaithful to Spanish history, which continues to view the country's unification under Christian rule a most noble endeavor. However, history records that as of March 31, 1992, those who are Jewish may now live openly in Spain.

As you read the *Casa Saga*, please remember that our heroine's story occurred while the Decree of Alhambra was still in effect. Before you begin, imagine what it would be like to grow up in a world where you were taught that who you are and what you believe might lead to your being arrested for life or killed and that what you experience could happen to your family. Those choices are the reason our heroine sets out on the journey you are about to experience. As she does, she thinks about America and silently repeats a line of Emma Lazarus's poem, which says, "Give me your tired, your poor, your huddled masses yearning to breathe free, the wretched refuse of your teeming shore, send these, the homeless, tempest-tost to me..."

A Safe Haven

Naomi knew she was in trouble the moment the immigration official had told her, he was taking her to Ellis Island. No immigrants had disembarked there since the end of World War I. Someone had told her that the authorities could remove a passenger from a ship because of a problem with their paperwork. Yet even when she sat where the man had pointed and closed her eyes, she refused to believe that her situation was as dire as it appeared.

Her mind brought her back to the moment her life had changed forever. She could still hear herself scream, "Abuela Sosa, please do not be dead," sobbing while she had tried to shake the old woman awake. The next thing she remembered was that the old woman's daughter-in-law had packed her meager belongings into her suitcase. Unable to stop herself, she demanded, "You have no need of me anymore? I gave you a year of my life! Your *esposo*—I mean, your husband—promised he would help me enter America and search for my uncle if I took care of his *madre!*" As she uttered the words, her sorrow had mounted, for the kindhearted old woman had treated her as if she were her very own kin. However, that was certainly not true of the daughter-in-law, who seemed unfazed by the old woman's death as she dispassionately closed the lid to the girl's suitcase and stared at her. *Why is she in such a hurry to rid herself of me before the doctor examines* Abuela *Sosa and declares her dead?* She remembered the secretive phone call the woman had answered, worried that the family had somehow discovered that the last name she had given was not hers, felt a knot in her stomach, and knew her worst fears were going to come true.

A swell hit the boat broadside and her thoughts returned to the present. Nevertheless, she refused to open her eyes to gauge the rough sea or look at the Statue of Liberty because she believed that immigration would never let her stay in America now. Only when the boat docked and the man grabbed her arm to hurry her onto the wharf did she open them.

They entered a building and turned down a dark corridor. The man pointed to a chair in a stark office. She nodded, entered, sat down on the hard, wooden chair, and clutched her worn, brown, leather suitcase to her chest. An official took a man into a room. Before the door shut, she heard his interview begin.

She believed hers would be next, closed her eyes, and tried to think about her answers. But all she could think of was that her bright plans of coming to America to find her uncle were for naught. She remembered leaving her family in the middle of the night without an explanation or a good-bye and tears threatened to fall. *I was a fool to agree to work for no wage because Mr. Sosa promised to help me achieve my dream when we arrived.* She thought of all she had left, Mr. Sosa's promise, and admitted, *He lied to me!*

Her thoughts returned to Abuela Sosa's death. She could almost hear the old woman say, as she had the day they first met, "Many get *to* America. But getting *into* America can be difficult."

I should not be here, she told herself while she tried to still her fidgeting. *My entry into America should have been easy. Everything was attended to at the American Consulate before we left Spain—my documents, my medical history... I filled each paper out with the utmost care!*

She looked around the waiting room. She was the only one there. Aware of the stories of the chosen few who were allowed to enter the country, she tried to think of anything but the future she feared and remembered reading that the original buildings had burnt to the ground and nonflammable materials had been used when they rebuilt the facility. *It must have been an awful fire. Still...*

When she heard the door to the office open, she looked at the wall clock and realized that at least an hour had passed since she sat down. An official took the man they had interviewed away. He left the door open at another man's request. Hoping she might hear the men she assumed would decide her fate, she leaned forward in her chair, saw them pace back and forth, and listened to their conversation.

"Too bad the grandmother died," she heard the large man say, his voice filled with what she prayed was sympathy for her plight.

"And just before the boat was to enter the harbor," the small man agreed.

"Still it's not our fault. She has no sponsor. We must send her back to Spain."

"But she says she has no people," a man she could not see said.

"Sad yes, very sad."

"I tried to call the lady but was told she was out," the small man said.

Naomi saw the large man wait while the man she had not seen left the office. Then he turned to his associate. "I told you not to speak about that!"

"It doesn't make any difference. I left a message, but there's no one to help the girl." He looked at his watch. "We can't wait any longer. It's already five thirty. The office should have closed half an hour ago."

The large man glanced at his watch. "You're right. We can't wait any longer. Ask her to come in."

The teenager was certain they were going to send her back and muttered, "Oh, *Adonai,* I cannot go back there!" When she heard her own words, she thought, *Perhaps in America I should speak with* Adonai *in English,* so she pled, "Oh, God, please help me ... I cannot go back there!"

An old woman sat down next to her. "Would you like to stay in America?"

"*Si!*" Naomi wondered where the old woman had come from and why she had asked her such a question. She feared that the woman might not understand her, so she switched to English. "I mean, yes, I would. I would love to stay."

The old woman smiled. "I will arrange it for you."

Naomi gasped. *Maybe God is watching out for me after all!*

The small man stuck his head out of the door to the office, caught Naomi's eye, and motioned for her to enter as he left.

When she stood, the old woman rose as well. "Say nothing," the old woman whispered. "Let me talk." They walked into the office together.

In seconds, Naomi and the old woman stood before the large man. He frowned. It seemed to her that the lines on his face were so deeply etched that he had never heard of the word *smile. This man has the power to send me back to a life I wish never to see again,* she told herself while she tried to steady her wobbly legs.

The man pointed toward the chairs, which faced his desk. "Sit down please. We have very little time."

He fixed his dark eyes on the old woman. "Since you did not answer your phone, I thought you might be done with this business."

"You know how it is with me, Victor." She reached into her over-sized purse and handed him a sheaf of papers.

"*Sí, claro.*" Victor seemed to smile with relief as he replaced the girl's official papers with the documents the woman had handed him. "Still looking for that special one, eh, Tía?"

"But of course."

He reviewed the documents. "I see you are still using the same lawyer."

"Yes. He is able to help me in my work."

Victor turned his attention to Naomi. "This lady will vouch for you so you can stay here. Would you like to stay in America?"

"*Sí,* I would like to stay very much." She peeked at the old woman. *She looks just like* mi tía *Rosa, the same stark white hair, the same small frame, the same dignity of bearing, the same edge to her voice, and, I am certain, the same caring heart.*

She looked back at Victor. Relief welled up in her chest. "Thank you." She wanted to say more but did not trust herself to utter another word because she feared a slip might cause him to send her away.

Victor nodded, pulled out the necessary forms, picked up his pen, and said, "March twentieth, nineteen fifty-two," while he entered the date.

He turned toward the girl. "What is your name, child?"

"Naomi Baruh."

Victor nodded and wrote her name on the form. She was amazed that the official did not question her about her last name since she had assumed that was why she was there.

He turned to the old woman and asked some questions. When the forms were completed, he opened his desk drawer, took out his official stamp, and legalized her documents. Then he buzzed for his secretary. When she arrived he said, "Make copies for La Señora."

He turned toward Naomi. "I would like to introduce you to your sponsor—your Tía, or as we Americans say, your auntie. You are a very fortunate girl. Do what she tells you and all of us will be happy that you have decided to stay with her."

"*Sí*… yes, I will." She knew that she had never owned a promise as bright as the one this new land offered.

Victor's secretary returned with the copies. Naomi watched as the man checked them over, placed them in a legal binder, and handed it to the old woman. "Here you are. Do not to lose them on your way home." He nodded toward Naomi.

When Tía nodded, Naomi wondered if the two of them had spoken in some sort of secret language. Before she could ask her sponsor or Victor what he meant, Tía placed the binder in her bag, stood, and motioned for her to do the same. "There will be no problem. I will take the same precautions I always do." Tía shook Victor's hand and smiled at her.

Naomi felt they had ulterior motives and believed her concerns validated when Victor let out a sigh, which sounded like a sigh of relief. But before she could find out what was going on, Tía led her out of the office.

Once they were outside, the old *tía* patted her purse and glanced at her watch. "We must hurry or we will miss our boat!" She grabbed Naomi's hand and ran in the direction of the ferry.

They arrived at the ferry as its whistle blew and the captain hollered, "Hurry up and get aboard!"

The old woman paid their fare, gave their tickets to the attendant, rushed Naomi up the gangplank, and pointed to the top deck. "Let's go up there. You will be able to see where you are coming from and where you are going to."

Naomi scurried up two flights of stairs and waited for her sponsor. Tía joined her and pointed to draw Naomi's attention toward Ellis Island. "This used to be the port of entry for all who sought freedom. Now it is the last hope for those the system will not let in. Always remember, today that system did not win—at least not as far as you are concerned."

Naomi stood at the rail and watched the island diminish. When the wind whipped her hair into her face, she turned, saw the city of New York with its skyscrapers, and smiled. Aware that she was about to realize her dream, she clutched the rail, and looked upon America, the land of freedom and opportunity, for the first time.

When the boat docked, all sorts of sights and sounds assailed her, but she closed her eyes so that nothing would distract her and took a deep breath of free air. "Thank you, *Adonai*," she whispered. The wind blew her prayer of gratitude past her sponsor's ear and out to sea.

With a wide grin on her face, she opened her eyes. Before she could see much of the goings-on at dockside, the old woman grabbed her hand and pulled her along. "Hurry up. We have to make our bus."

When they reached the bus, its doors had closed. Tía pounded on them and demanded, "Stop—open the door and let us in."

"Sorry," the bus driver said as he opened the door. "I was about to leave. With the motor going, I couldn't hear you." He nodded toward the elderly woman who sat on the bench seat behind him. "If it hadn't been for this lady here, I would have driven off without you and the girl."

"It is lucky for me that you have a passenger who pays attention!" Tía unleashed a withering gaze upon him, and Naomi was grateful that the lady was not angry with her. Her sponsor took her hand, walked past the woman, and nodded. "Thank you, Teresa, *mi amiga.*"

She took Naomi to the back of the bus and motioned for her to sit down. The girl took the seat and asked, "Where are we going?"

"Home to *mi casa.*" She fiddled with something under the dolman sleeve of her coat. "Just sit back and relax. I will let you know when we need to get off."

Naomi watched as the bus wound in and out of dense traffic. The old *tía* noticed her curiosity. "I am taking you to Spanish Harlem. Most of the people who live in New York have shortened the name. They call it Harlem, but we Spanish settled there and named the place, so we call it by its full name that honors us and our presence there. Although other groups have settled there and many Spanish people have moved, it is still, in my opinion, the center of Spanish life."

Naomi said nothing since she did not understand how each ethnic group in the city differentiated themselves, nor did she care. Her only concern was to see where they were going should she need to flee, so she watched the road. As the miles ticked by, she thought about the procedure at immigration and realized the man had given her no card of any sort. She remembered her uncle had written that everyone needed one and she began to worry.

The old woman pointed to a building. "See, there is Zabar's, my favorite place for sweets."

Naomi looked where her sponsor pointed and told herself, *She seems nice. I have no reason to worry.* She turned to look at the road and tried to get her bearings as the city rushed by. At each stop, she looked at the old woman questioningly.

"Do not worry. We are almost there."

"Good." Naomi smiled, eager to forget the events that had forced her to accept the old woman's help. "I want to begin my life here as soon as possible."

"You all say that."

"What do you mean? And what was that man at immigration referring to when he asked you if you were not done with this business yet?" It seemed to Naomi that Tía stared at her. Her concerns about her lack of a card and the mysterious discussion between Victor and the old *tía* escalated.

Before she could ask a question, the old woman smiled. "We can talk of this once we get to *mi casa*."

When Naomi did not respond, her sponsor turned to pat her hand. Naomi glimpsed a manacle around Tía's wrist and knew she must flee. She began to stand. The old woman felt her move, grabbed her hand in a vice-like grip, pulled her into her seat, and handcuffed their wrists together.

Naomi froze. Her heart beat so fast she feared she would pass out. She opened her mouth to scream. *No one would do this to someone who is here legally. If you scream, you will end up back at immigration and you will be deported.* Forcing herself to act calm, she closed her mouth and said nothing. When the lady sitting behind her asked her a question, she bit her lip, shook her head, and tried to look relaxed. Aware that she was trapped, a feeling of resignation washed over her as she upbraided herself for having mistaken the old woman for kindness itself.

She stared at her sponsor, spotted a Catholic church through the window behind the woman and was horrified. *Spanish Harlem,* she thought, *I left Spain for religious freedom but have to hide here just as I did there.* Fear of the religious community's reprisals if they discovered her faith, coupled with the situation she now faced, caused her to flush scarlet. When she did she realized that the old *tía* could see her thoughts and feelings when she looked at her face.

Tía smiled, nodded at her, and cooed, "Now we will have lots of time to talk."

Naomi glanced at her handcuffed wrist. "All right," she said in an attempted show of bravery, which she feared fooled neither of them. "We will talk." She grasped at her last shred of courage, lifted her chin, and squared her shoulders. "Then we will see about this!"

"Good." Tía stood to get off the bus and dragged the girl along as she hid the handcuffs with her scarf. "It is a short walk from here to *mi casa*. Trust me. This will work out well for both of us."

They left the bus stop, turned right at the first corner, walked a block, turned right again, and continued past three houses. Naomi's eyes darted in all directions, frantic to find anyone who would help her. There was no one on the street.

"Here we are." The old woman opened the latch on the weathered gate, which led to her *casa*, pulled Naomi in, and shut the gate firmly behind her. Naomi heard the latch close and knew she had given up much more than she had gained. She wished to be anywhere but where she was and shivered with apprehension while the woman dragged her up the path. Because of the deep twilight, she slowed her steps and strained to see where she was going. Frustrated by the girl's dawdling, the old woman urged her on. Naomi quickened her pace on the path of irregular and oddly shaped bricks, which had lost some of their mortar. Forced to forge ahead, Naomi struggled to keep her footing and was surprised to see a familiar object off to the left side of the yard. A large kettle, like the one her *mamá* used to wash their clothes, stood proudly in a place of discarded importance, weeds growing around it. The sight of a familiar object reminiscent of home calmed her down enough to wonder, *What an odd thing to see in the front yard.*

Tía pulled her up the porch stairs. Once they were on the landing, the old woman opened her mailbox and retrieved her mail. Naomi sneaked a furtive glance at the place and realized the shutters and front door were as weathered as the gate. Aware that behind that foreboding door lay the unknown, she looked at the handcuff that encircled her wrist and grimaced.

"Come." Tía pulled Naomi to the door's threshold. They stood under the porch light while she dug in her purse for her keys and muttered, "I know they are in here." She found them, selected a key, and worked it into the lock. "What is your name?" She opened the door and motioned for the girl to enter.

"Naomi, I ... I thought you heard ... that."

"No, I did not. I had only one thing on my mind—I had to get you out of there before someone came in and questioned you."

"Oh! You ... you ... were afraid for me."

"Now let us understand each other. I have an obligation to help young women like you!" The old woman pulled the girl across the threshold and locked the door behind her. "I have done so before and will most likely do this again. Those I help work for me or for someone else in the community until their debt is paid. Then I help them find a job or a husband."

While Tía spoke about saving young girls—her *niñas,* she called them—from deportation, Naomi understood a little about what she had agreed to and her heartbeat slowed. Her thoughts drifted to the letter from her uncle and her plans to find him once she had arrived safely in America. She placed her free hand in her skirt pocket and felt the letter's edge, worn rough from her family's continual folding and unfolding of this breath of freedom from across the ocean. She could not remember a time before the letter from her *tío* for his description of the bright promise of America had given her family hope. Whenever life became bitter and difficult, her parents would pull it out and read it to the family. Then they would commit to each other, "Next year in America!" instead of the customary "Next year in Jerusalem!" as every Jew says at the end of the Passover meal. For, to them, America was the promised land. Naomi fingered the letter's edge and silently promised, *I will find you,* mi tío. *I will find you as soon I am able.*

Tía continued to talk while she dragged Naomi through the vestibule. The girl stumbled, righted herself, and noticed the parlor on her left. When Tía stopped to put her mail on the sideboard, Naomi looked around. *No one would ever suspect that a house so unkempt on the outside had such comfortable furnishings within.* She wondered at the absurdity of her looking at the place and thinking as she had, rather than trying to find a way to flee, and reminded herself that although she was in America; nothing had changed. Resigned to the situation, she tried to find something positive, saw that a baby grand piano held the place of prominence in the sparsely furnished room and smiled in spite of herself when memories of playing the piano for Abuela Sosa surfaced. She reconsidered her assessment of the place and added the word *grand.* When her consciousness flooded with memories of the many times she had played for the Sosas' blind grandmother, she reminded herself, *That was another time, another place. Abuela Sosa is no more.* Images that had brought her comfort as she traveled the world with them flashed before her eyes. In an attempt to stop them, she reminded herself that the promises they had made they had broken. *Now those bright hopes will only bring you pain. It is best you think about this situation since it seems worse than the one you just left.*

"Come." The old *tía* pulled her through the living and dining rooms while she searched her ring. When they crossed the kitchen's threshold, she found it and unlocked the handcuffs. She eyed Naomi. "This was just a precaution!" She threw the handcuffs down on the battered kitchen table.

Naomi looked at the cold steel.

"Sit down!"

Naomi obeyed, felt her will disappear, and wondered if the old *tía* viewed her as a tool to mold to her demands.

The old woman put the kettle on to boil. "I will make some tea and we will talk." When the teapot whistled, she set the leaves to steep.

While they waited, she made a phone call. "*Hola*, Flora. Please tell everyone at the market that I am sorry I was unable to hand out paychecks. I had to go to immigration. Tell them I will be in tomorrow." She placed her hand over the receiver and looked at Naomi. "What would you like to eat?" Naomi shrugged. When she did not answer, the old woman turned away and continued her conversation.

The girl took a moment to take in her surroundings and discovered that the cheerful gingham wallpaper and spotless kitchen helped her feel at home in spite of her fears. She noticed that the kitchen tiles were reminiscent of an advertisement she had seen in a recent magazine. Believing that only the needy trafficked in others' misery, she sighed with relief.

"What would you like to eat?"

"Whatever you have will be fine." It seemed to Naomi that the woman had decided to treat her as a guest instead of the prisoner she knew herself to be. Her emotions heightened; she remembered how foolish she had been to trust Mr. Sosa and admitted to herself that she had been naive to accept this woman's help without knowing what she had agreed to. Aware that she had placed herself in peril, she hardened her heart as she sat on the edge of the chair. The meal ordered, the two of them, captor and captive, waited for it to arrive. Alone in this strange new land, Naomi tried to fight off her fear of this unknown woman and the situation as she reminded herself, *There was no other choice.*

"Naomi," the old *tía* said at last as her gaze swept over the girl. "Tell me how you came to be at immigration."

"Well…" Naomi stalled. *How much do I tell this woman? Do I tell her the truth, and if not, what should I leave out or make up?*

"Naomi!" her sponsor snapped, her voice demanding an immediate answer. "Do not think about what to say. Just tell me, in the simplest way possible, how you came to be there."

Naomi swallowed. It seemed best to tell the truth, so she began, "I came with the Sosa family. I was the companion to their blind grandmother."

"That is an unusual job for one so young to have. By the looks of you, I would not think you more than twelve."

Naomi strained to sit taller in the chair. "I am fifteen."

Tía rose to fill their cups. "How does a girl as young as you find a job with a family coming to America? You had not been a companion before, had you?"

Naomi watched the old *tía* bring the cups to the table, took her first sip, and gulped down courage. "I was in need of employment." Aware that the warm feelings she usually associated with tea did not exist here, she continued, "There was this family with a blind grandmother. They required someone to tend to her every need as well as read, play the piano, and help her enjoy the tour. They thought I might do."

"But you are so young. Why did they pick you?"

"I do not know. Perhaps it was because I agreed to work for no wage."

"I see." Tía's gaze swept over the girl.

Aware that what she said might have led the woman to think her easy to manipulate, Naomi added, "They pledged to help me find my uncle once they settled here. Then they changed their minds."

The old woman waved her comments away. Feeling them dismissed, she went against her upbringing and added, a note of pride in her voice, "But it was Abuela Sophia who chose me for herself!"

"I see you found favor with her?"

Mortified by her outburst, Naomi cast her eyes down and quietly admitted, "Yes."

"Then I am certain you will find favor with me also."

Since she did not know how to answer, she thought of her needs. "Excuse me. May I ask some questions?"

"If you must."

"What is your name and how long will it be until I can leave?"

"Those are the same questions every one of you asks." Tía poured another cup of tea for herself. "Those I have business dealings with call me La Señora. You are to call me Tía as all my girls do. Vida is my given name, but few have permission to use it. It breeds familiarity. Do you understand?"

"I suppose so."

Tía looked at the girl, motioned for her to say more, and waited.

A moment passed before Naomi understood what the old *tía* had implied. When she did, she asked, "This is a business arrangement, right?"

"Correct, a business arrangement. But nonnegotiable since you must stay here or be picked up by immigration and deported."

"I understand."

"Good. Now, so that no one will suspect what we are doing, it is best for you to call me Tía, as Victor said. This will make it easy for others to believe that I really am your aunt. Our little ruse will make sense to immigration and the community, should they choose to investigate our situation." She eyed the girl. "I have given you something you could not get without my help. Now you will give me payment."

"All right." Naomi's heart raced at what she might have agreed to. "How do I pay you?"

"Since you are fifteen and a minor, you will work for me until you are twenty. That is a good age for a woman to be on her own. Before then, I believe someone might take advantage of you. During these five years, you will be able to pay me back for what I have done for you. At the end of that time, you will have your freedom, the skills you need to make your way in this country, and five hundred dollars—one hundred dollars for each year you are with me, a good amount for a young woman to begin a new life with."

Even as Naomi nodded, she wondered what the old woman would ask of her and wished that the woman who looked like her *tía* Rosa was actually her sweet aunt. However, she knew that the resemblance was only an illusion. "I have nowhere to go and no one who cares. I will give you what you ask."

"Good. Then welcome to *mi casa*." She picked up Naomi's suitcase. "Now come." She walked to the bedroom across the hall from the kitchen, opened the door, and gestured for Naomi to enter. "Many have been happy here. You will be too."

Naomi looked around the sparsely furnished room that was to be her home.

Tía pointed to the wardrobe. "In there you will find everything you need." She walked to the wall cattycorner from the bedroom door, pulled aside the yellow drapes, and flipped on a light switch. Naomi looked through a lovely pair of French doors that opened onto a large patio. A fountain, much like those in Spain, with chairs around it, as well as a loveseat and a few scattered side tables, were directly in front of her. Off to the right was a wrought iron dining set, which could accommodate eight. She drank in the beauty and serenity of the place and her breath caught for a moment. The old woman's unspoken words were clear; she would be able to sit by the fountain and gaze at the garden below.

"As you can see, I have chosen not to treat you as a servant but as a guest in *mi casa*. I ask that you do what I require and respect my privacy, as I will yours. And you must at all times remember your place. Now, I will leave you to change into something acceptable for one who works for me to be wearing. When you come back to the kitchen, we will eat and discuss your duties."

Naomi sat on the old iron bed, took a moment to think about her situation, and wondered, *What have I gotten myself into?* Aware that this question might lead to fearful thoughts, she roused herself and looked around the room. *I am grateful to have a place of my own,* she admitted. Surprised that the simple act of admitting how she felt caused her to shudder; unwanted memories of the bitterness she had experienced in Spain assailed her. She knew that her situation could be much worse, tried to find something positive to think about, and told herself, *I should have some privacy here.* Then she cautioned herself, *Remember to do nothing that breeds familiarity.*

Aware that she needed to return to the kitchen as soon as possible, she stood and walked to the large oak wardrobe. She ran her hands over its beautifully carved panels. *Why is something this fine in a servant's quarters?* she wondered. She opened the large, double doors and peered inside. There were no uniforms, just hangers that held ordinary garments. Each dress was modest but none would reveal her station. Keenly aware that her sponsor had chosen colors and styles that would not cause her to appear a servant and yet not allow her to think more highly of herself than she should, Naomi forced a tentative smile. *This Tía is more like mi tía Rosa than I thought.* She assumed that she understood the old woman's hidden message, appreciated her thoughtfulness, and decided to call Tía Vida, her *tía*. Pleased with the realization that she would not be humiliated in front of others she took off her clothes, folded and placed them in the bottom of the wardrobe. Then needing to assure herself that her uncles letter was safe, she took out her skirt, felt for it, then placed it on top.

When she returned to the kitchen, she wore the mustard-colored dress with the white collar. Because of the formality of their agreement, she waited in the hallway for an invitation to enter. She saw her *tía* at the sink with her back to the hall, holding a phone to her ear, and heard her say, "Yes, Victor, we arrived home without incident. Do not worry. Naomi understands everything. Yes…yes, I see. No, she will not run away. I scared her just as I do every girl I bring home. Yes…I did…I used the handcuffs, just as you told me to. Do not worry. She is safe."

When her *tía* hung up the phone, Naomi cleared her throat.

Tía turned in her direction and waved her in. "Let me see you."

She stepped into the kitchen and waited.

"Good, very good," her *tía* muttered. She walked around the girl and nodded toward a chair. "Sit down, Naomi."

Naomi acquiesced and was pleasantly surprised when her *tía* sat down across from her. "Naomi, I know our arrangement forces you to delay your plans. However, if you are as clever as I think, all that you learn here will serve you well when you leave. Understand?"

"Yes. I understand."

"Now, this is our first night together. I always try to help my new *niñas* feel at home on their first night, so we will eat together and we can talk. You can ask me questions about this situation. After tonight, you will find your position in my home will not allow you to treat me with familiarity, nor will we dine together."

As Tía finished her last sentence, there was a knock at the door. She stood, walked to the pantry, and brought out some dishes. "Naomi, I believe our meal has arrived. Answer the front door."

Naomi rushed to the vestibule, turned on the light, opened the door, and saw a young woman who wore a bright orange dress with a matching sweater. She held a sack, which Naomi assumed was their food. The girl looked her over and giggled.

"So you're her new girl." Her lips curled slightly in obvious disdain. "Let me look at you!"

Naomi stood still, frozen by the brazen attitude of one she did not know, a girl who acted superior to her for no apparent reason. "Come on.

Turn around," the girl ordered. "You aren't much to look at, so scrawny, with that wild, curly, hair and those big, sad eyes." She patted her shiny, straight pageboy hairdo, which was so popular. While the girl stared at her, Naomi remembered that her *mamá* had said, "Only a harlot wears her hair like *un hombre!*"

Not through with her insults, the girl raised her voice, "I heard La Señora brought another *beggar* home. I also heard you're Spanish! No wonder you can't answer! None of you knows enough to learn English before you come here." The girl glared into her eyes and demanded, "*Cómo te llamas?*"

Naomi saw no reason to offer her name in response.

"No wonder you had to leave Spain. You're too stupid to know your own language! Probably nobody wanted you around. What's the matter, cat got your tongue?"

La Señora stepped out of the shadows of the living room, into the light of the vestibule. She narrowed her eyes and clenched her jaw. Everyone who knew the old woman feared this look. However, the delivery girl did not notice, nor did she hear the tension in Tía's voice when she exclaimed, "Shame on you for such rude behavior!" She walked to where the girl stood and snatched the bag out of her hands.

The girl shrugged. Then she realized she had to say something and mumbled a halfhearted, "Sorry." She turned to leave.

"Come back here! I'm not done with you!" La Señora's icy cold voice stopped her in her tracks.

The girl turned back, her look of arrogance replaced by one of fear.

"Apologize to Naomi!"

The girl stood her ground.

La Señora looked at her watch then back at the girl. "Rochelle, I hired you. Now I am firing you! Pick up your things from my store and do not come back, not even to buy something. I do not want to see you again. Do you understand me?"

"But, Señora, look at her!" the girl whined. "She's just a *little mouse!*"

The old woman glanced at Naomi. "That may be but this little mouse has more dignity and courage than you will ever have. I am sorry I wasted my time on you. Now, leave!"

As the girl turned away, the old *tía* put her arm on Naomi's shoulder in a comforting gesture. "This will not happen to you again," she promised. She watched Rochelle take the stairs two at a time. "Sometimes it is impossible to help the neediest among us."

While they headed to the kitchen, Naomi considered all she had seen and heard. She believed the old woman could make what she said a reality and smiled. "*Gracias,* thank you. I have never been safe anywhere before."

"I suspected that was the case," her *tía* said as she unpacked their meal.

"Why did you think that?" Naomi asked, surprised that she felt comfortable enough to ask.

"Am I a fool? No one as young as you leaves her home and family and travels with others unless there is something painful that continues to occur." Vida looked at Naomi and smiled. "I do not know your story, but I sense that you have run from something. Perhaps here you will find something worth running toward."

Naomi nodded as they sat down to eat.

During their dinner, her *tía* confided, "All I will teach you has a purpose and a plan. Even the clothes I have selected for you to wear."

"These?" Naomi tried to sound grateful while she glanced at her apparel.

"Yes, my little mouse. I want you to be safe and grow into whatever you are to become. I chose these garments so no attention will be paid to you."

Tía waited for Naomi to respond. When the girl said nothing she asked, "Have you ever watched a flower grow?"

"Well, no … not really."

"I have," her *tía* said, eyes bright with remembering. "A beautiful flower needs to be protected. These clothes are part of your protection. While you are with me, you can develop your unique talents. I will give you as much encouragement as I can. However, to the rest of the world you are to appear as invisible as I can make you. Then when it is time for you to bloom, you will become visible. Do you understand?"

"I think so." Naomi wondered if her *tía* might care for her since she had gone to so much trouble on her account. "I will do as you ask. And I will try to show you how much I appreciate all you have done for me."

Tía sighed and stared off into the distance. "You all say that when you first arrive, but confinement in this house will probably make you resent me, as well as this imposed situation. If that happens, be sure that I do not see you looking forlorn or hear words of regret. Understand?"

"*Sí,* yes." Now Naomi knew that her *tía* and Victory had placed themselves in peril to rescue her. "I understand!"

Visibly shaken by the girls affirming response, *tía* said, "Yes well…Now let us eat and get to bed. It is already after eight, and our day starts early."

When their meal was over, Tía stifled a yawn while they cleared the table.

"I will finish here. Please go to bed."

"But I have not given you your instructions."

"Do you have them written down?"

The old woman eyed Naomi closely. "Can you read English?"

"I can! It is one of the reasons Abuela Sophia chose me."

"Good." Tía reached into the pantry and pulled out a yellow binder. "Everything you need to know is in here. Read it all tonight, but be sure to get some sleep."

Naomi took the binder. "I have done well on little sleep before."

"I am sure you have." Her *tía* yawned as she left the kitchen. "You have probably learned to do well with little of everything. I pray that God will allow me to rectify that in some small way while you are here. After all, everyone deserves to feel valued."

Naomi stood at the kitchen's threshold and watched her *tía* walk down the hall. When the old woman reached her bedroom door, she turned back, looked at her, smiled, and said, "Naomi, welcome to *mi casa*, and welcome to America!"

Hiding in Plain Sight

Naomi's loneliness was so pervasive that she searched for a way to escape her isolation, thought about the times her *mamá* had taken her and her sisters to church to light their candles, remembered how they had successfully masqueraded as Catholics, and wished she could do the same. *It is better this way,* she told herself, her loneliness assuaged by the fact that she did not have to explain to a friend why she had an aversion to all things religious. Yet sometimes, when the church bells rang, she felt closed in by her isolation, and wished her *tía* would release her from her pledge. Then she would remind herself that if her sponsor thought she was not as she seemed, she would be out on the street, picked up by immigration, and deported. Many nights she lay awake in her room as feelings of guilt overwhelmed her. In the quietness of the *casa,* she would think about the choices she made that lead her to live a life in the shadows. She wished she could undo the decisions that had forced her into this difficult situation.

She tried to remind herself that her *mamá* had called it "hiding in plain sight" and taught her at an early age how to blend in. Although she had fled Spain in search of freedoms the Jews did not have there, her lot was very much like theirs. Yet when she remembered the stories of the Jews forced to become Catholic or die during the Inquisition, she breathed a sigh of relief, for she believed that no one in America would do such a heinous thing. As a hidden resident of Spanish Harlem, she knew her omission placed her in daily peril. She feared telling her *tía.* She feared not telling her *tía.* She was unable to own who she was. For as long as she could remember, no one had ever stepped from the shadows of their faith into the true light of day. No one had ever spoken of who they were or whose they were.

Naomi was pleased that she did not have to live a life of two faiths, as her *tía* put no store in "such foolishness," as she called it. Hiding here was easier. Yet sometimes, when she heard the church bells ring, she would think of her desire to be involved in life outside the *casa*. If she had spoken with someone, she might have confessed that each time she heard them, her heart leapt for joy. Just as suddenly, the memory of her shameful secret would resurrect itself. Aware that she was not Catholic but Jewish, she would curl into a ball for protection and remember the painful feelings of rejection she had experienced. Tremors would seize her body as she ruminated on the times others had shunned her family on her account. In her mind, the fault was the church's because it was through her participation in the life of the church that she had heard many things that affected her and left her no alternative but to flee.

The words of the nuns followed her across the ocean. "Jesus could never forgive or love a Jew. The Jews killed Him. They are an abomination before God." Though those who had spoken the words were far away, and she sometimes wondered if she had remembered their words correctly, she assumed they were her adversary, for she did not know that there is one who is unseen who wars against the elect. Although she knew that what the church had taught was a lie, her mind hammered the words at her until she found herself thinking, *Jesus could never love me. My people killed him!*

When she was young, her family had stayed in one place. As she matured, it seemed to her that they moved from town to town. At fourteen, which was well beyond the age when most took their first communion, she looked at her image in her *mamá's* chipped mirror, and noticed that her looks were singularly different. *My face carries the map of Israel. I need to leave.*

She searched for, and finally found, a way to correct the situation. Eager to stop the guilt she felt for leaving without a word, she consoled herself, *When I go, my family will have a normal life. And when mi tío and I have saved enough money, we will send for them.* Whenever her longing for her family became unbearable, she would remind herself, *They are better off without me.* In the silence of her room, she would struggle to stifle her feelings of loneliness, loss, and isolation. Whenever her desire to contact her family overwhelmed her common sense, she would weigh the options between the better life they had and the personal hardship she suffered. Then she would shore up her resolve by reminding herself that only by leaving had she been able to give them the life they deserved. She believed her misery to be a small sacrifice to make for those she loved. Yet during *Shabbat*, the Jewish Sabbath, when she took time to meet with God, she found no comfort. *This isolation and inability to fulfill my plan is what comes to those who pretend to be what they are not—beloved of God.*

She counted each day that passed and hoped that the end of her obligation would hasten. Though her *tía* was kind to her, she yearned to be free. As the months became years, she saw her dreams diminish while Tía's needs became her priority. Although the old woman had spoken to her about the blooming process, now a few months shy of twenty, Naomi noticed no changes. She was still the same size and had the same feelings, and longings.

However, as the end of her servitude drew near, she experienced a surge of hope. Driven by her desire for freedom, she tried to learn all she could about the outside world, which she felt ill prepared to venture into since her *tía*, true to her word, had kept her hidden within the house.

Naomi set Tía's breakfast tray down on her bed. Tía picked up her newspaper and noticed its rumpled pages. "I see you are becoming interested in other things."

The young woman realized her *tía* knew she had read the paper before putting it on her tray and blushed. "I will be leaving soon. I have to learn something about this land if I am to make my way in it."

"I suppose." Tía waved her away. As an afterthought, she added, "In my office are books that will assist you. Read them if you like."

"Yes, Tía." Naomi exited the room, closed her sponsor's door, smiled, and whispered to herself, "She will keep her word to me."

The next morning when Naomi brought in her breakfast tray, Tía smiled at her. "All the other girls I brought here were content with whatever they learned with in the *casa*. However, since you wish to know more, I will give you some additional information about this land and how to manage your way in it."

Setting the tray on the bed, Naomi responded to what she assumed was Tía's wordless invitation and sat down on her bedroom chair. Aware that she had done the unthinkable, she stood immediately.

Tía observed her reaction and chuckled. "You have done all I asked of you and done it well. However, to become a student you will need to sit and listen. You may want to write things down so you will have your notes to refer to later on."

"Good." Naomi grinned.

"Why so excited?"

"Because I thought I would leave here as I came."

The old woman rose from her bed and motioned for Naomi to follow. She entered her office and sat at her desk. "None of you believes me when I say I will follow through with what I promised."

Naomi sat down across from her. "Tía, I came to you with nothing. You sheltered me. You gave me a way to remain in this country. If that was all you did for me, it would have been enough."

"Yes...well..." Tía fought back tears. She opened her desk drawer and picked up a document. "Now we begin."

When their session ended, Naomi headed to the kitchen to wash up the morning dishes. *I never knew she could be so kind.* She glanced at the clock and realized that her *tía* had spent an inordinate amount of time explaining the Bill of Rights.

"But, Tía," Naomi remembered asking, "why do I need to know such things?"

"It is one of the foundational documents of this country. It is important that you know what you have so you do what is necessary to keep this country the free place it was intended to be." Naomi thought about how she had come to this place and silently admitted, *Freedom is hard won and easily lost.*

The outside world beckoned as it always had. Instead of pretending that she did not notice, this time Naomi allowed her desire for freedom to engulf her. Her feelings of claustrophobia surfaced and her situation seemed to hem her in on all sides. She struggled to fulfill her obligation—for fulfill it she would because it was her desire to leave knowing that she had done all she had promised. Tía kept her word and taught

Naomi a little about the world outside. Yet, it did not occur to the young woman that her eminent departure was on Tía's mind until one evening when she stayed out late, entered the *casa* and said, "Naomi, I have something for you. Come and see." She pointed to a baby-blue valise.

Naomi hurried toward her.

She smiled. "I have a new suitcase for you!"

"But, Tía, I have a suitcase."

"That is old and worn. You are to begin a new life in a new country. I intend to send you off with a new suitcase. I want you to put it in your room. You can look at it and plan. Plans are what take us from what is to what is yet to be. Without a plan, nothing happens. Always remember that."

"*Gracias.*" Naomi took Tía's gift and turned toward her room.

"I...I...wish you would...stay with me." Tía's voice was so unfamiliar in its hesitancy that it did not sound like the old woman at all. Naomi stopped but did not answer, nor did she act on her urge to run to her *tía* and throw her arms around her. "But...I know you must...go."

Naomi turned and looked at the old woman. "Why did you treat me differently than the others?"

"Because...you *are* different."

Naomi nodded. "Tía, being here has been the greatest blessing and yet the most difficult thing I have ever had to do. I thank you for all you have done for me and for what you taught me. But I must go."

"I thought so." The old woman fought to regain her composure, and forced a smiled, though it was tremulous at best. "Of course you must go...after all...you have plans. Soon you must be on your way."

"Thank you for understanding." She turned toward her room and counseled herself, *This is not the time for false hopes—for my family's sake, I must forge ahead.* She entered her room, put the suitcase down, pulled out a sheet of stationary from her side table, and sat on her bed. The blank page looked intimidating. After all this time, she was surprised to find herself wondering how to begin her letter. She wanted to let her *tío* know that she would come to him soon. Yet she fell asleep looking at the piece of paper. Her subconscious mind seemed to dictate,

Dear Tío,

My time of servitude and hiding is ending. I look forward to meeting you in the light of day and enjoying the freedom of this country where we do not need to fear being who we are.

Your *sobrina*,
Naomi

No, she told herself, *use English. Sign it, your niece, Naomi!*

A Change in Plans

A painful wailing interrupted Naomi's sleep. She assured herself it was only a dream, turned over, and pulled the covers close. A moment later, she heard someone calling. She was on her feet. It was not a dream but her *tía* sobbing. "Help, call the doctor!"

"I am coming." Naomi threw her bedroom door open and ran down the hall. When she reached Tía's room, she paused for a split second to pray and collect her thoughts before she turned the knob. She opened the door and froze. Her benefactor lay crumpled at the side of her bed.

Naomi rushed to her side. "Do not try to move me. Call the doctor!"

Knowing there was not a second to lose, Naomi ran to Tía's office and dialed doctor's number. When he answered, she exclaimed, "Tía has fallen! Come at once!"

Doctor Apayo arrived in what seemed like minutes. He examined Tía and spoke with her privately. When he came out of the room, he told Naomi, "I usually discuss my patient's situation with a relative and no one else." His gaze settled on her. "But you are as close to her as a daughter would be if she had one. She will not recover. She suffers from severe malnutrition, which caused her legs to bow as a child. That, coupled with the deleterious effect of her rheumatoid arthritis, makes it impossible for her bones to hold her weight anymore. At one point, an operation might have helped, but she refused to have one, saying her *niñas* needed her. These issues and her intermittent wheezing in the cold weather necessitate complete bed rest. Though, as I said before, she will not recover."

Naomi noticed his look of concern and wondered at the timing of the unfortunate fall. "What does she need?"

"She needs someone to live with her, someone to take care of her." The doctor's gaze intensified, leaving Naomi no doubt as to his thoughts.

"But, Doctor, I am to leave here shortly."

"I heard that. However, can you not consider staying for her sake? She helped you when you needed help. Can you not be generous and do the same for her?"

Naomi wanted to yell "no." Yet, as much as she longed to go, she knew her heart might cause her to stay. "Have you told her what you told me?" she asked in hushed tones as Tía called for her.

"Of course," the doctor said as they walked toward the door. "Now hurry. She calls because she needs you."

While the doctor showed himself out, Naomi hurried to her *tía's* room, opened the door, and entered. "Tía, do not worry. I am here."

"Good," the old woman whispered. She motioned for Naomi to come close. "Did the doctor talk to you?"

"Yes." Naomi fluffed the old woman's pillows.

"So you know, the doctor says I need a companion to help me," she rasped, her eyes appealing to the young woman for her assistance. "I am getting along in years and this fall has weakened me. I want you to stay with me." She took a deep breath and continued, "Years ago you told me how you cared for the blind, old grandmother. I know you have a caring heart and will make it worth your while to stay and tend me. Since you have a desire to educate yourself, I will arrange for you to go to school so you can become an American citizen. If you decide to stay, I will leave you my savings, this house, and my business. I will make sure that you will have a good life and can make a living. I am giving you this opportunity because though your heart has not always been at peace with what we negotiated, you held to your commitment. I know that if you commit to my care, you will stay and complete your obligation. Many will commit to staying, but few will follow through on their word. I know that you will. Think what this will mean to you in the future. After all, what are a few more years if, after I am gone, you can have a life of ease that you would never have access to without this inheritance?" Vida closed her eyes and it seemed to Naomi that she had fallen asleep. She was about to leave when the old woman roused herself and muttered, "Think about this offer and let me know what you decide."

Naomi left the room, feeling as if she were in a stupor. Aware that she needed to think about the ramifications of accepting the offer, she sought solace, walked through the kitchen, and sat by the fountain. Over her years of isolation the solitude of this place, which reminded her of her family in Spain, had given her a great deal of joy. She ended each day either sitting by, or, in harsh weather, looking at the fountain, for it was the one place where she could have a few minutes or, on rare occasions, an hour to herself. This time, she did not sit for an hour or two. Instead, the night passed and the sky filled with the soft rays of morning. Still she did not move. Even the cheerful birdsong, which greeted her every morning when she awoke, went unnoticed. *My dream is almost within my reach*, she thought. In the next breath she wondered, *Can I put my plans aside again or will I have to give up my dream?* Her conflicting thoughts were impossible to sort out. Then she remembered all her *tía* had done for her and admitted, *I owe my tía everything. How can I say no to her?* She knew she could not leave and hesitantly, half-heartedly, agreed to stay.

Even as she did, she tried to find another solution. It was through her process of letting go of childhood dreams that she allowed her feelings of longing and personal need to wash over her. Overwhelmed, she cried out and put her hands over her eyes, aware that the very thought of choosing to stay was more than she could bear. Spent, she lowered her head and sought God. She prayed and sat still while she waited for tears to come. No tears fell. None came. Since the children in Spain had ridiculed her and her family, she had been unable to cry for herself. Even when she had worried about her looks being unacceptable, she had not cried. Now she felt there were no more tears left. For she had cried them all long ago. She shivered and reached for the old woman's lap cover to throw over her shoulders. As she pulled it tight, she heard a thud.

Gripped by fear, she bolted from her chair and ran into the house. It was still somewhat dark inside, but she knew her way and was in front of Tía's door in an instant. She entered and flipped on the light. Tía lay prostrate on the floor next to her bed. Naomi hurried to her side and rolled her over. She saw the look of humiliation in the old woman's eyes. It was a telling moment for both of them. While Naomi struggled to get her *tía* back into bed, she realized, *I could no more leave her than I could leave myself.* She pulled the covers around her benefactor. "Yesterday I stayed with you because of our agreement. Today I stay because you asked."

"Call my lawyer…and have him come over," Tía croaked. "Documents must be drawn up."

Naomi nodded and closed the door. She walked to the old woman's study, felt the weight of responsibility heavy on her shoulders, and silently prayed, Adonai, *help me. If you are listening, help me to do what I must.*

The next morning, Naomi was in the vestibule dusting the sideboard when Mr. Ralph Martinez, the attorney, and Padre Paul, the priest, greeted each other while standing at the threshold to the door. As she walked toward the door, she watched the play of their shadows through the opaque glass and heard ever nuance of their dialogue because the transom was open.

"Why in this day of modern conveniences does La Señora still keep with the old ways?" she heard the attorney mutter. "Still no doorbell."

"One should not change anything that still works. Better a caring heart and an offering to Our Blessed Mother Church."

Since she had spoken with each of them, Naomi knew they were aware of the old woman's condition. Over her years in the *casa*, she had heard a lot about these men and assumed that each hoped the lady would select him to manage her estate since she was, obviously, unable to do so for herself. Others had informed her that each of them had tried to curry favor with La Señora and the general population of El Barrio, and each had worked hard to acquire a manner of meekness. From observing them when they visited Tía, she knew that each valued his own wisdom, each believed that he alone should manage the old woman's funds.

Perhaps, she mused, *the attorney has decided that everyone needs his services in the end, even those who fear God. And the priest, no doubt, he believes his services at the end of one's life are even more important than those of a lawyer.* She could almost hear them thinking, *Whom else could she trust but me?* She was aware that her musing was not appropriate, so she took a deep breath and pulled the door open. Nodding a humble greeting, she gestured for them to enter. As she did, she reminded herself that they considered her little more than a necessary nuisance and knew that never in their wildest dreams could they have imagined how her presence in Tía's house was about to change all their plans and hopes.

She watched the two men as they stepped into the shuttered semi-darkness of the *casa*. "Tía is resting for a moment," she explained as she led them into the parlor. "Her strength left as she was preparing to see the two of you. But she will be all right in a while." She motioned to a silver tea service, which she had set out for their visit. "May I pour you some tea?"

The padre looked at her in apparent amazement. Since she had never before spoken to them beyond what was necessary, Naomi wondered what was going through his mind.

"Dear," the old padre began as he took a sip of tea from a delicate china cup, "where did you learn to make tea that is so rich—almost like coffee?"

Naomi glanced up from the cup she was pouring for herself and smiled. She knew that neither of these men had ever concerned themselves about her before, and that was to her advantage. "Why, Padre, you flatter me. Thank you for being interested in such a small thing as this little service, which I have done for you when you visited La Señora. This tea is made like one would make espresso. You may know it better as sweet tea because after I poured your tea, I added sugar and cream both in large portions. I learned to make it this way from *mi mamá* while I was yet a young girl in Spain." She lowered her eyes so he would not see the pleasure she derived by giving him a small tidbit of her history. She remembered the times she laid out tea for these men, yet they had never before spoken to her or asked any questions. Since he did not respond, she looked up to see if he understood. Noting the look of confusion in his eyes, Naomi almost lost control of the tight rein she kept on her emotions. Although the situation was a serious one, she felt like laughing at the absurdity of their role reversal: she, a servant, acting like a grand dame, and he, the priest, seeming as confused as she had been when she first arrived at Tía's *casa*. Fighting to regain control, she coughed to stifle her natural reaction and smiled sweetly as she lowered her eyes.

"Are you from Spain then, my child?" the old padre asked.

"*Sí,* I am." She smiled and struggled to sound appropriate while she reflected upon Tía's wise words, *Men will want you or want something from you. Watch what they do and make certain it matches what they say. Be very careful, even of those I have trusted. They may try to take advantage of you, for they will see you as a young* niña *and pretend to take care of you but may be busy taking better care of themselves!* Resolved to do as the old woman had taught, Naomi stood and nodded, as if Tía were there by her side reminding her that these men might have ulterior motives. "Pardon me, I need to check on Tía and see if she is ready to receive you."

The men had stood the moment she did. When she turned away, they looked at each other but said nothing until it seemed she was gone. Because Naomi had thought that might be the case, she hesitated outside the room and listened as they spoke.

"What," ventured the attorney, "has happened to the girl?"

"She is no longer a girl but a woman," Padre Paul answered.

"All right, she is now a woman. So what of it? We are here at La Señora's bidding not to assist this—this pretender! She is nothing! No one with a good reputation will have anything to do with her! She has remained hidden in this *casa* since she arrived. Except for us, few people even know she exists. If tomorrow she were to leave, no one except La Señora would miss her!"

"That is true. How old do you think she is?"

"Probably close to twenty."

"How would you know that?"

"I and my father before me have been involved in La Señora's work for many years. We prepared the papers that allowed the girls detained by immigration to stay here. Without someone to vouch for them, the government sends the girls back to their place of origin. With our help, La Señora brought some of those *niñas* into this country. The paperwork was always the same, always set up for a fifteen-year-old Spanish female. Strange," he mused, "once La Señora brought this *little mouse* home, she never brought another *niña* to her *casa*. After this one arrived, La Señora would only go to immigration once she had arranged for the girl to have a job and a place to live. I asked her about this change several times, but she never explained her reasons. It was as if she was looking for something and found it in this one. But I will never understand what she sees in the girl, or woman, as you call her."

When their conversation ended, Naomi raced to Tía's room, checked on her, and returned. Instead of ushering the men to her benefactor's room, she remembered that the old woman's training had made her wiser and listened to see if either of them would unwittingly reveal anything else. Silence greeted her, so she stepped out of the shadows and motioned for the men to follow her.

Quietly, with reserve and decorum, the priest and attorney moved forward. When they did, Naomi wondered if they suspected that she had overheard them. *No matter,* she told herself, *perhaps it is good for them to be unsure about what I know or where they stand with me.* When they reached Tía's bedroom, Naomi knocked, then opened the door. "Tía, the two men you asked me to invite are here to visit you." She waited for her *tía* to motion for them in. When she did, Naomi turned to withdraw.

"No, Naomi, come here," the old woman wheezed. "Sit in this chair. Stay next to my right hand, listen, and remember, for in the days to come you will need to know all that is said today so that nothing will be taken from you when I am no more."

The priest and the attorney exchanged glances. The padre nodded, removed his vestments from their pouch, and put them on. He lifted his voice in prayer and began to perform the last rites.

"No, I am not ready for this!"

"I understand, but we must proceed."

"Not yet! I have matters to discuss with my attorney!" The old woman turned toward Mr. Martinez and began to speak. Within the hour, Tía had attended to everything as she promised. Naomi watched as she signed the legal documents. The attorney glowered while he placed the papers in his briefcase. He seemed bewildered and annoyed by the proceedings, but he told La Señora, "The final papers will be mailed to you once they are recorded." His voice broke with feigned concern as he asked, "But surely, La Señora, do you think it wise to give your power of attorney and leave your estate in the hands of one so young and unschooled in the ways of the world?"

"I most certainly do." The old woman chuckled, obviously pleased by her attorney's reaction. "I have every confidence that, unlike many, Naomi will do all I have instructed. And when I am gone, she has agreed to continue my work."

When Naomi heard this, she struggled with the awareness that there was more to her agreement than Tía had told her. Nevertheless, she steeled herself and refused to show these men any sign of concern. She smiled and silently prayed, *God, if it is your will that I remain here indefinitely, then give me your* shalom—*your peace.* She forced herself to smile at Tía and stood to usher the men out. At that moment, she sensed a whisper in her heart that said, *When you were on the patio, you surrendered your life to this.*

As the unlikely trio left the old lady's room, Naomi said, "You have both shown my *tía* a great kindness today."

Mr. Martinez smiled. "The pleasure was mine." He took hold of her hand and tried to press it to his lips.

The priest watched as the attorney's attempt at flattery elicited little response from the young woman. "I think it is time to go. I fear we have overstayed our welcome." He took Naomi's hand in his and looked purposefully into her eyes. "I will come whenever you need me."

"Thank you both." She walked them to the door. Once they were gone and the door firmly closed behind them, she exclaimed, "I refuse to spend my time with those hypocrites!" She brushed her hands against her skirt as if ridding herself of filth, patted her hair into place, and returned to Tía's room.

As the two men walked away from the *casa*, Mr. Martinez stopped and took his time lighting his pipe. "Strange that such a *little mouse* should have the entire estate," he said at last. "She has no connection to our dear friend. Perhaps we should try to have La Señora's will overthrown. The girl must have taken advantage of her for this situation to come about."

The priest readily agreed and they began to discuss how they might correct La Señora's error in judgment.

"Look," the lawyer finally said, "it is not good for the *little mouse* to have such a great inheritance without someone to protect her."

"That is true, but what can we do? We do not know the child. Since we never paid attention to her before, why would she listen to us now?"

"Undoubtedly she will not, but she will pay attention to her heart. Let us be a blessing to the *little mouse* and find someone who will marry her. In this way we can be sure she is protected and not led astray by a world she knows nothing about."

"I think that would be best. Having her safely settled would help me sleep better at night!" These words confirmed the priest's approval. Since they both agreed that the work of the Tía's must continue, all they had to do was find the right man and their problem would be resolved.

Naomi viewed her future as one suddenly filled with possibilities. Tía prodded her to call the school and find out where and when she could attend citizenship classes. Naomi got the information and arranged with one of Tía's married *niñas* to come in for three hours twice a week. She told her benefactor about the arrangements and was shocked when the old woman railed at her. She ran from her room crying so hard that she did not hear Tía's apology.

Later that day, Naomi checked on her *tía* and found her fast asleep. She slept through that day and most of the next. Naomi feared the old woman would not awaken this side of the grave. It was twilight when she picked up the phone to call the doctor. Before she had begun to dial, she heard the faint tinkle of the bell. Glad that she had put it on Tía's nightstand, she rushed to the old woman's room. Aware that her nerves were frazzled, she paused to collect herself, then opened the door. Tía *is now my American* madre *and I will treat her as such,* she reminded herself. "Madre Vida." She smiled as the term of endearment escaped her lips. She believed her greeting was appropriate since she was the only daughter the old woman would ever have. "Please forgive me for upsetting you."

"No, *mi hija*… my daughter, you have done nothing which needs forgiveness." She patted her bed, silently inviting Naomi to sit next to her. "You did not yet know all that I need you to do for me. I did not turn things over to you so you would stay here and watch me. I need you to make sure that my business continues. Now that I am refreshed, I will tell you that you are to be as me at immigration and help the little *niñas* as I helped you. All the information you need is in my desk. Mr. Martinez will draw up the paperwork for you when you need it. In addition, there is the market, which you must manage. Many who work there depend on these jobs. I need to know that you will make certain they will have work, not only for themselves but also for their children if they need it. *Comprendes, mi hija?*"

"*Sí, sí*… yes, but how will I do all this?"

"We will call for assistance from my friend Myra. She will send a girl to you who you will train to take care of me. There is too much for you to do all by yourself. At night, you can take care of me. During the day you will serve me best outside the *casa* by taking caring of what is ours." Naomi's eyes widened as Madre Vida spoke about her new responsibilities. With each utterance, she became more overwhelmed. Her fear was evident to the old woman, who pointed an arthritic finger at her and insisted, "You can do this! I have chosen you because I know you will succeed! Do you believe me?"

Naomi nodded, surprised that she truly did believe the old woman. "Yes, Madre Vida, I do."

"That is good." She pulled the edge of her sheet over the blanket so the soft fabric was against her tender skin. "I am hungry and thirsty. Please bring me something to eat before I fall asleep again."

Naomi ran to the kitchen, put together a simple meal, and it brought to her. She set the tray on her bed and turned to leave. "But, child, where is your meal?" Dashing to the kitchen, Naomi fixed another tray as she pondered the strange turn of events.

When she entered the suite, the old woman smiled. "I am glad you have chosen to stay." *So much freedom ... so much responsibility,* Naomi thought. *How can I handle everything and discover who I am?*

The old woman looked up from her cold beet soup, sweetened with a slight zing from mild chilies, and studied her daughter's face. "What is troubling you, Naomi?"

"Forgive me, but I am concerned. I do not know how to do any of the things you want me to do."

The old woman chuckled. "You will learn." She mopped up her bowl with some bread and added, "Just as I did."

"Just as you did?"

"Yes, exactly as I did." Madre Vida shared how her own adopted *madre,* Esperanza, had taught her the very things she would teach Naomi. When Naomi realized that Vida had felt as ill prepared as she felt now and made it through, she relaxed.

"Listen, why do you think I never brought another *niña* here after you? Why do you think it was only the two of us? I know you were aware, since some of my grown niñas stopped by to visit, that many girls were here before but none since you came. Even in town, they would ask about you, but I kept you sheltered with me always. Never did I farm you out. Did you never wonder why? Did it never seem odd to you that I never treated you as I treated them?"

"Well ... yes, I did wonder about that. But I have always been treated differently no matter where I went, so it did not seem so unusual."

"Then you know that you are one who was set apart. I do not know why, but my good fortune is that I found you and was able to get you for myself. I have watched you. I know you. You can do all I ask of you. You will bring blessing upon my name long after I am gone. And the people here will come to know how much you care for them as you do what I tell you to do. Now I am tired. You must let me rest."

Pondering this strange turn of events, Naomi took Madre Vida's tray from her feeble hands. The old woman smiled up at her. "I was one such as you. Tía Esperanza gave me this work in trust. I learned to do it and you will as well. Now leave me, for I must sleep."

Naomi walked into the kitchen, set their trays on the counter, and hurried to Madre Vida's office. She entered, looked around, and realized it was now hers, as was the success for the work Vida trusted her to continue. She walked to the massive oak desk and sat down in the chair the old woman had sat in a few days before. Knowing her *madre* as she knew herself, Naomi reasoned that the top drawer held information she needed. She opened it and took the items out one at a time. There were timecards for the employees at the market, files for expenses and vendors, and legal agreements for those who rented space there. She found a file titled *Immigration*, opened it, and saw the papers Mr. Martinez had drawn up for Madre Vida. She set them aside. Under those, she found a file with her name on it.

She took it to the kitchen and brewed a cup of tea. As the sun began to set, she flipped on the outside lights, stepped onto the patio, lit the torches, sat down, and opened the file. When she scanned its contents, she saw a diagram that would lead her to a book, which Madre Vida mentioned as *important*. She hurried to the office and found a unique book bound in red where the diagram showed it would be. Eager to look through the file, she returned to the patio, sat down, and placed the book on the table, intending to look at it later.

When she flipped the page and read, "*Detener* … stop. Go no further until you read *The Book of the Tías*," whatever illusion of independence she had vanished almost as fast as it had come. She picked up the book and leafed through its pages. "It seems I received my freedom so I could do what these women require of me," she mumbled. Yet as she read, she found the entries fascinating. Esperanza, who had begun the work, wrote the first entries. Those that followed were from Madre Vida. As Naomi read her adoptive *madre's* entries, she saw the date when Vida first mentioned that Naomi would be her successor and realized that it had been written it shortly after she arrived at the *casa*. Madre Vida's last entry to her was a paraphrasing of the last words Esperanza had written to Vida, the girl who would continue her work. Aware that they applied to her as well, Naomi spoke them aloud. "Be fearless. Those who have come here need your assistance." Though she spoke the words firmly, she was not firm in her resolve and stayed up all night trying to figure out how she could realize her plans and continue the work she had benefited from.

As the shops prepared to open for business, Naomi yawned, and stretched in an effort to clear her mind. She could not stop herself from thinking, *My letter seems different, as if Madre Vida chose me not because I was convenient but because of some inner quality she knew I possessed. She hinted at this when she wrote,* "I searched for you until I found you. I sheltered you and kept you safe. You have received more than anyone else has. I expect you to do what those who are behind you ask you to do and what those who are coming need you to do. I have equipped you to do all I have given you to do."

Moved by the letter, which had been written years before she heard the words spoken by the woman herself, Naomi wondered, *What did she see in me all those years ago—a frightened, scrawny, wide-eyed girl with nothing to offer? What made her choose me?* She assumed she would never know. Yet she held *The Book of the Tías* in her hand, bowed her head, and accepted the commission. Her fate sealed, she admitted, *I will never find you,* mi tío, *because I will never look for you. My heart is committed to meeting the needs of those, like me, who face deportation.* She knew that the letter she had tucked into her skirt pocket so long ago would go unanswered. *Here is a mission God equipped me for. I will not walk away from it … not for* mi tío, *not even for my family!*

Her future sealed, Naomi remembered fleeing Spain because she had feared others would discover her to be a Jew in a country that allowed only one faith, that of the Catholic Church. She remembered Madre Vida hiding her in the *casa* and feeling safe. As she thought about her journey, her old worries found voice, and though she would never tell a soul, she remembered that the last name she had given to Mr. Sosa, Victor at immigration, and the one Madre Vida had given the attorney which would appear on her adoption papers was not hers. Aware that she must return to immigration bearing that false name, she found herself more fearful of deportation than before. Realizing there was no one she could take her troubles to, she got on her knees and prayed, "Oh, God, help me to help others as my *tía* helped me. Allow me to know you and guide me always in the way I should go." She felt a heavy weight lift from her. Infused with the joy, which comes when one casts their burdens upon God, she felt the strain she had been living under vanish. *By agreeing to take the role of* Tía *and praying to God for his wisdom, I have again become as I was before the ruinous poison of the Jewish curse caused me to flee seeking a safe haven,* she thought.

If only—the memory of her childhood wish, quiet for all these years, stirred, *if only it had happened sooner!* At that moment, she felt as if she could again hear herself, as a child, praying to God. She had wanted others to think of her as a true daughter of Spain rather than a Jew. She had asked God for that blessing. However, her request had gone unanswered, and the children had continued to call her names, chasing her home as they yelled at her that she had killed their Christ.

Naomi cried out, "Oh God of my fathers, God of Abraham, God of Isaac, and God of Jacob, help me do as I am asked! Keep me safely hidden in you and I will serve you all the days of my life." She sobbed, aware that by accepting the role of Tía, she had become visible and all the terrible things that happened to her before could happen again. For one such as she, who had mastered the art of being invisible, putting herself in a situation where many would scrutinize her was unsettling. Yet she was committed to assist those fleeing situations too painful to describe.

Emboldened by a renewed faith in the Lord and her position in the community, she asked, "What can they do to me now? As Tía's chosen one, I have wealth and a good reputation with Madre Vida. No one would dare question me about my ability or my heritage. They will know Madre Vida choose and trained me and that will be enough for them." She realized the protection wealth would afford her and smiled as she stood, blew out the candles, and went to bed.

Becoming a Blessing

Naomi was finally able to leave the confines of the *casa*. Though she rushed from citizenship classes to the market, visited Victor at immigration, and allowed some married *niñas* to take her shopping for a wardrobe befitting her new station, she savored her freedom. Yet as busy as her days were, the time she valued most was her daily meeting with Madre Vida. There was much for her to learn, and her American *madre* knew what and how to teach her. Every night she and her mentor would have their meeting in the old woman's room while they ate their dinner together. Sometimes she was with her for hours. At other times the old woman's fragile health caused them to end their sessions as soon as dinner was over. The time they spent together had a single focus, to prepare the young woman for the world outside and the work she would carry on. Though Naomi was grateful to be able to study to become a citizen, she knew that what Madre Vida taught her would allow her to fulfill her obligation. Although she wanted to understand all she was told, it never failed that just as she began to grasp what the old woman was saying, Madre Vida would wave her away. "That is enough for tonight. You think about what I have taught and tomorrow you can tell me how you applied the lesson."

"Are you never pleased with me, Madre Vida?"

"My child, I know the doctor told you everything about my condition so you know this will most likely be my last spring." The old woman wheezed. "I must do everything I can to prepare you." Naomi gasped. Madre Vida turned, locked eyes with her, and willed her protégé to act, as she must. "When I was given charge of Tía Esperanza's affairs, little notice was taken of me. I was able to learn as I went through the tasks of each day. But did you not notice the cunning looks that crossed the faces of our good padre and Mr. Martinez when they learned that you were to become my own daughter? Surely, you could not judge, as I did, that you may be in danger from the men I hoped would assist you. Learn what I teach you so that you and our work will flourish. And you, in due time, will find another to take your place. Remember, do not put your trust in men, but trust in God alone."

Naomi nodded, aware that she had noticed these things. However, these concerns paled when she thought of Madre Vida's life ending. *Do something to help Madre Vida,* she scolded herself. As she did, she knew there was nothing to do except keep faith with the pledge she had made so she forced a smile. "Do not worry, Madre Vida, I will do as you have taught me." Before she finished speaking the words, she remembered herself as an adolescent telling her *mamá* in Spain the same thing. In the next heartbeat, she thought about the night she fled rather than deal with that life. After all these years, Naomi's feelings of shame drew her back to Spain as nothing else had. Then just as quickly, her mind brought her back to the present.

Madre Vida watched the telling play of emotions cross her daughter's face. "I see that you understand. Let us use our time to prepare you and give you what is necessary for success. In success, there is much pleasure, especially when it means the lives of the little *niñas* are changed. People you have never met will have better lives because you helped these girls stay here. Is that not something to strive toward?"

Eyes alight with unshed tears, Naomi nodded and said, "Yes." As she did, she found herself rejoicing, *Me, the girl who was a curse, now a blessing. What magic is this?*

"I see that you understand." Madre Vida glanced at her bedside clock. Aware that this was her benefactor's signal for her to say good night, Naomi stood, kissed the old woman on the forehead, and left the room.

What would it feel like to be a blessing? Naomi wondered while she walked through the house. *Would it be evident to everyone? Or would it be like the last time* mi mamá *was with child? Oh, do not draw attention to yourself. If you do, others will discover you are a liar and a thief,* she told herself, for though she had agreed to become all her American madre was teaching her to be, she still feared exposure.

Whether it was the responsibility of their mission's success or Madre Vida's words that caused Naomi to have a sleepless night, she was not sure. All she knew was when bird song roused her, she stayed in bed, lulled to sleep by the chirping she loved so much. It seemed that only a few moments had passed when she heard someone. *It must be Maria,* she thought. She glanced out her French doors, and noticed it was still early morning twilight. *Perhaps I had a bad dream.* She listened intently and heard the sound of distraught wailing. Aware that something was terribly wrong, she jumped out of bed, opened her door, heard the sound of fervent praying, and looked toward Madre Vida's suite. Maria stood in a pool of light at its entrance.

Naomi raced down the hall, thought of her adoptive *madre's* words to her, and silently prayed, *Madre Vida, please do not be*— Before she completed her prayer, she remembered herself screaming, "Abuela Sosa, please do not be dead!" She forced her mind back to the present and shuddered. *No!* she told herself, *I cannot let someone I love die again!*

When she reached Maria, the young woman was wailing as tears streamed down her face. *Madre Vida is already dead,* Naomi thought. She reached out to Maria. The young woman turned toward her but did not seem to recognize her. Not knowing what else to do, and not able to look inside the suite, Naomi pulled her close. Maria sobbed. "Tía always liked to wrap her neck with as many scarves as possible. She told me it kept the chill from her old bones." She pointed to the bedpost. "But look what has happened."

Naomi forced herself to look into Madre Vida's room and gasped. Vida's face was ashen gray and looked more like a death mask than the caring woman Naomi knew her to be. Steeling her resolve, Naomi scanned the ornately carved bedpost and saw where Vida had gotten her scarves caught. "She is dead," she said gagging on the words as she spoke them. *She strangled to death,* Naomi silently admitted as tears welled up. Aware that Madre Vida would frown on such behavior, she dashed them away as she told herself, *There is much to do before you can grieve.*

She turned toward Maria, steeled her heart for the task ahead, and demanded, "Why are you here this early?"

Maria gulped back a sob. "It was our secret. Tía did not want me to tell you. She feared you would get up every night to tend her."

"Maria, tell me what you are talking about!"

"She was…I mean…always got cold…at this hour. She wanted a hot water bottle…for her feet. She said it helped to warm her old—"

"We need to call the doctor! He must come and tend her!"

"But…she…is dead," Maria sobbed hysterically.

"I need to call the doctor now! I do not want her to be attended by strangers." Naomi took two steps and turned back. Maria stood riveted at the threshold of the suite and continued to look at Madre Vida's corpse. Her sobs echoed throughout the house.

"Come with me." Naomi, took her to the kitchen and brewed some chamomile tea. "Drink this. Calm down and tell me why you were in Tía's room at this hour."

"But I already told you," the young woman wailed as she sniffled and wiped away her tears.

Blinking back her own, Naomi forced herself to calm down. "I had trouble hearing what you said…tell me again."

"Oh, forgive me." Maria glanced at Naomi for support. Naomi nodded, so Maria continued, "Tía always had me come in at this hour. She said her feet were cold, so I brought her a hot water bottle because she told me she could not sleep when her feet became chilled. It was a little secret between us. She didn't want you to know. She feared you wouldn't leave her to do, as she put it, *the things of first importance*. This time, however, she was as you yourself saw her. I believe she is with the angels now."

"*Sí*…she is gone from us." Feeling removed, yet overwrought by the situation, Naomi stood and walked to the office. She dialed Dr. Apayo's number. When he answered she said, "Madre Vida is gone from us…please come." She returned to the kitchen. Maria was crying while she rung her hands in despair. Not knowing what else to do, Naomi's training took over and she focused on the young woman's needs.

News of Tía's passing brought all who knew her to visit the house. The door to the *casa* was seldom still. Many came the day she died. Others paid their respects during the six days that followed. Life for Naomi and those in the little *barrio* of Spanish Harlem that extended into the surrounding suburbs changed. Everyone felt the disruption. Although people had seldom visited the *casa* before, it seemed that they now traveled hours to pay their respects to her family, of which Naomi was the sole representative. Those who knew her before marveled at the change they saw in the young woman's bearing and demeanor. Many who came identified themselves to her as a member of Las Niñas. Each woman would say no more than this as they reached into their purse or pocket and handed her a small wad of money or a few coins. Naomi was shocked that anyone would think of money during such a time. One woman noticed her look of disdain and pulled her aside. "Listen, this is not for you," Justine said. "It is to continue the work for the *niñas. Comprendes?*"

"*Sí.*"

It appeared to Justine that Naomi did not know what she meant when she said "yes" so she insisted, "Come, I will show you!" She took Naomi to the office, closed the door, pulled out the blue companion volume to *The Book of the Tías*, and placed it in Naomi's hands. "Open it." Naomi opened the book and saw columns of names and numbers. She looked up with tears in her eyes, aware that she was finally grieving her loss. She was unable to speak.

Sensing this Tía's state of mind, Justine explained, "We all paid. Each month after we left, we all gave a little so others could have a good life. But you are her chosen one. I fear you will pay with all of your life rather than a few coins here and a dollar or two there as we have. May God bless you, my sister, for continuing Tía's work." Naomi forced a wan smile.

"I live only a few blocks from here." Justine picked up Tía's phone-book and pointed to an entry. "Here, this is my phone number. Call me whenever you need my assistance. I will help you as I did our *tía*. And always remember that our *tía* said, we would become a blessing." She turned, reached the threshold, and realized that Naomi had not budged. Since Maria was staying at the *casa* for a few weeks, Justine opened her mouth to call her. Before she uttered a syllable, she thought of all this Tía's life of service entailed, decided to befriend her, and asked, "How can I help you?"

Naomi blinked but did not respond. She took Naomi outside and settled her by the fountain. Naomi looked at her surroundings and hoped they would prove as restorative as they had in the past. However, she was unable to relax and fiddled with a loose thread from her sweater while her agitation mounted. Justine noticed her behavior. "Be at ease. It is two o'clock. People are working, busy with their children, or cooking dinner. No one will come to visit until this evening. Rest. I will bring you something to eat and drink. Then you must sleep. I will stay the night, as I told *mi esposo*, Bobby, I would."

Naomi nodded, grateful to yield to the woman's care. Freeing her mind as best she could, she leaned back into the arms of the wicker chair. She took a deep breath and closed her eyes. Confronted by sorrows that haunted her, she silently admitted, *Madre Vida died before my training was completed. The very morning she died my adoption papers and my citizenship papers arrived in the mail. But there was no one to thank or to share the moment with.* Finally relaxed enough to think of other things, she listened to the birds chirping, closed her eyes, and thought, *The sunlight filtering through the trees does feel nice.* She breathed in the sweet smell of newly mown grass, remembered Spain during harvest, and drifted off to sleep. She heard it before she knew what she was hearing. It grew louder and louder. She felt as if her body would rip apart. The fear of the unknown gripped her. *No, I am not afraid of the unknown. I am afraid of people finding me to be less than they need me to be.* She broke into a cold sweat and ran her fingers through her hair. Sensing she had forgotten that she was in America and needing to feel safe, she told herself, *These things could not happen to me here, not in America. You are safe. You are a woman of means with a mission to accomplish.* Almost awake, she searched to find a way to make her fears vanish. Since she had lived with the fear that others would discover her secrets, she knew that was the problem and pledged to die rather than reveal her faith or her illegal status. It took less than a heartbeat for her to calm. When the last vestige of her fear had passed, she forced herself to think of the future and silently proclaimed, *I will be a blessing!*

She roused herself, walked into the kitchen, took a cloth from the drawer, moistened it, and patted her face and neck. She was hungry, opened the refrigerator, and looked inside. Trays and casserole dishes were stacked on top of each other and crammed in so tightly, she wondered if she would be able to get anything out without having to remove everything. When she scanned the countertops, she saw cakes, pies, fruit, and gifts piled up, and realized how much the community had loved Madre Vida. Aware that others would go without, Naomi called, "Maria, Justine, come, *amigas*; let us gather much of this and take it to the mission. There are many there who need to eat, and we have too much."

"*Sí*, it is so." They sorted what they should keep and what they would take to the needy.

"Just like Tía," Justine said.

"No, just practical."

When they heard Naomi's comment, the women insisted, "Yes, just like Tía!"

Naomi soon discovered that Madre Vida had been right to choose her because she found the work absorbing, rewarding, disheartening, and all consuming. Ten years passed so quickly, one would scarcely notice if it were not for the continual flow of teenage girls through her *casa*. If anyone had asked Naomi about the girls' comings and goings, they would have discovered that Tía did not mind because her work with Las Niñas defined who she was. Although most women nearing thirty would be looking for a husband, Naomi busied herself with her work, her friends, and their children who grew older and dearer to her as the years rushed by. She participated in their lives as if they were her family. Whenever she did think of her real family, she would remind herself, *Here in America, this is the only family I will ever lay claim to.*

Since the day she slept in the garden after Madre Vida's death, she had kept her secrets. Now as she sat in the garden, watching Justine and Bobby with their children, and Maria with her husband and two stepsons, she was at peace. *Only in America could women from such different places become* amigas, she thought as she watched Carl and Miguel, Maria's stepsons, throw their football back and forth.

Justine's youngest, Roberto, came over to sit in her lap. But before he did, he demanded, "Tía, tell me about the time you loved me the most!"

Naomi smiled at him. "Roberto, I have always loved you."

"But, Tía, remember it was right here on your patio!" Roberto stomped his foot for emphasis. "My mother has a picture of it taken on my third birthday when I was still a little boy."

"I remember that birthday. I was sitting on this very chair and you came up to me, lifted your arms, and hurled yourself into mine. I caught you and said, 'My, what a fine *bebé* you are, my Roberto.' But that was a long time ago." She tousled his curly hair. "Now you are a big boy, six years old."

"*Sí*, I am *un hombre*."

"I can see that you are!"

"Look, Tía!" Julie twirled around the patio on her toes like a ballerina. "Look at what I can do."

"Every Sunday the same old stuff." Alex picked up his mother's car keys and headed for the door.

"Alex, these comments of yours are not necessary," Justine called after him. "Apologize at once!"

Alex held his head high while his eyes glared with all the *machismo* pride he could muster. "Sorry, Tía, it's not your fault you have so many *bambinos* around."

"I give up!" Justine looked at Carl and Miguel to see if they heard Alex's comments. "What is a mother to do? He is too old to spank, taller than me by a head, and running wild as can be."

"Now calm yourself," Naomi chided. "He is a man. It is hard for him to be around the little ones all day long. Relax, Carlos and Maria's boys are too far away to hear what he said. Besides, Alex is a good person. Do not worry, he will be—"

"I know," Justine and Maria interrupted, "a blessing."

"A blessing—who wants to be a blessing?" Alex stormed out of the *casa.*

Maria and Justine looked at Naomi.

"Let's pray," Maria suggested. The two of them bowed their heads and prayed. Naomi stood and cleared the table. *What a blessing to have this family,* she thought, as she did every Sunday, *truly a gift from God.* If the others had realized she was not praying with them, they would not have thought it odd. For they knew it was her inner strength and capabilities that placed her in the position Tía had trained her to fill. They, as all who lived in the *barrio,* were aware of Naomi's ceaseless efforts to enlarge her ability to assist those in need, not just at immigration, but also within their community.

Many had heard her say, when giving someone a hand without making it feel like a handout, "Today I help you. *Mañana* you will help someone else." Usually those in need would hear this and stare at her as if she were crazy. She would smile, pull out the little green book from the oversized black purse she had inherited from Madre Vida, open it, and have the person sign a pledge that he or she would do just what they said when the time came. Once they had done as she asked, Naomi would put the book in her purse, look the person in the eye, and ask, "*Comprendes?*" Then she would wait until they said, "*Si, comprendo.*"

Those who watched her do this with the most down and out reprobates laughed behind her back. Yet over the years, stories had come back to her, some in letters, and some as one hears news through the network of the *niñas,* who were married or in business. Each time a story would reach her ears, she would smile and remind herself, *You will be a blessing! A curse can become a blessing.* Her smile would light up her inner most being, and she would think about all that happened to bring her to this place and tell her heart, *What a blessing it is that Madre Vida chose me and gave me this life of purpose.* Then that unexplainable feeling would cross her mind once more, and she would wonder if God had not brought her to immigration, into Tía's care and to *Casa de Vida* for such a time as this.

An Arranged Marriage

As Naomi's reputation for caring and good works continued to increase, so did her visibility within the little community. Many took note of her, a self-possessed woman with a sizable dowry and a thriving business. Suitors tried to win her but none knew her well enough to claim her attention. None could draw her heart away from its single focus. Both Padre Paul and the parish's attorney, Ralph Martinez, tried to introduce her to good men who would look after her and be happy to manage her estate with their assistance. After many failed attempts at matchmaking, they concluded that although the *little mouse* was no longer timid, she would never marry because she was married to her work.

Early one April morning, the priest rushed toward the rectory, heard hurried footsteps behind him, and turned back. "Padre Paul," the attorney rasped as he hurried toward him. "A word please, Padre."

"I am on my way to take a rest from the duties of the morning."

"But, Padre, I have good news that I know you will want to hear since it concerns our *little mouse*," Ralph said with a wink.

"I am always interested in good news."

"Yes, I know you have the welfare of the entire parish on your mind. That is why I came to you first. I know how much Naomi's situation has weighed on your mind." He redirected the priest's steps.

"That is true," Padre Paul said as they walked along together.

They reached an eatery the attorney frequented. "Would you like a coffee, my friend?"

"*Sí, gracias*, a coffee and a talk, eh?"

"This place makes good coffee. Let us sit on the patio away from the crowd. I have something to discuss with you in private."

His curiosity aroused, Padre Paul raised no objection when the attorney pulled him inside, lead him to the patio, and selected a table. The good padre ordered the coffee Mr. Martinez recommended. Once their coffee arrived, he drank slowly and settled into his chair. Since the attorney seemed to be taking his time, the priest looked around. *It is comfortable out here.* He took another pull of his espresso and watched the pigeons descend upon the remains of a meal on a nearby table. *They behave as some people do.* He believed Ralph had brought him to the eatery to hatch another scheme. As he considered how to sidestep becoming involved in another failed attempt at matchmaking, he remembered he had told the attorney that he was no longer interest in wrestling control of the estate from Naomi. When the attorney had questioned his decision, he had informed Ralph that he believed Naomi had proven to be as competent as she was caring. While he thought about their heated exchange, he sighed. He knew that though the attorney had heard him, Ralph would still try to involve him in his schemes.

"Padre, that sigh sounds like it has come from a man who has a great weight within his spirit. Are you burdened, my friend?"

"Many things concern me. I have burdens and worries for some who are in my care."

"I know what you mean. I am concerned that we have not acted well for Naomi's sake, and this weighs heavy on my heart."

"I understand. But what can we do? She is a woman now set in her ways. She needs no one."

"That is true. However, that does not mean that she is complete. We know a woman needs a man just as we need our faith in God."

The priest frowned. "What are you suggesting?"

"Oh, have you not heard?" Ralph asked with a wide-toothed grin. "One of Naomi's reprobates has become a philanthropist."

"And how did this come about, my son?"

"It seems that Naomi gave him a few dollars when he was in a bad way. I understand she had him sign her pledge book. The rest of the story is as unlikely as her own is. I have heard it repeated that he said from that day to this, he kept his pledge. In making it the *cornerstone* of all he thought and did, he was blessed beyond his capabilities or understanding. All this man now asks is that he may approach the lady with a proposal of marriage."

"This must surely be of God. But why would she marry now? She is able to accomplish all she wants without a man. What would motivate her?"

"Ah, Padre, one should never underestimate the desires of the heart once it is fanned," the sly barrister said. "We do not need to promote this union, but let us introduce the man to Naomi and see what God will do. After all, it is not good for a woman to be alone, and as Naomi ages, who will take care of her? Not everyone can be as fortunate as La Señora was when she selected the *little mouse* to care for her and carry on her work. After all, Naomi has done well. Does she not deserve a portion of her life for herself?" The priest was about to answer, but before he could, the attorney added, "And this man, Chaz, has a connection to our lady like none of the others that have visited her before."

The priest considered everything the attorney shared, believed the matter settled, and stood to leave. "I see that you have been thinking about the lady's situation a great deal. She will at least want to meet him and hear his story. Perhaps this is the man." That said, he turned and walked out of the eatery.

The attorney followed on the priests heels, reached his office, and called Naomi. When she answered, he asked her to meet the man her actions had saved from, as Chaz himself had put it, "A life without meaning."

Ralph had them meet at his office so the man could explain the effect Naomi's words had on him and the extraordinary change he experienced once he had signed her pledge book.

"It was as if I was one dirty and thrown away by life, lying in the gutter, defiled by the refuse of the world," he told her. "Then a miracle happened to me. Do you know what that miracle was?"

Mesmerized by this man, Naomi silently shook her head. Chaz's eyes never left her as he stood, walked over to her, bent down, and softly whispered in her ear, "It was you. You saw me as I could be. What you said to me, the pledge you made me sign, the words you made me say, were the first positive words I ever took to heart." Naomi turned her face and looked directly into his eyes so she could see if he was lying.

Chaz smiled at her. "You changed my life, and this life of mine, it is yours if you will take it."

Shocked, Naomi pulled away. When she did, she thought, *Never have I been drawn to anyone as I am to this man.* Her feelings frightened and amazed her. *How could you feel anything for this* hombre? *You do not even know him.* Yet she had to admit that just as some people had come to meet her because of the stories they heard about her, she had decided to meet Chaz because of the things she heard about him. Even before he asked to meet her, many had asked her if she knew of him. They were always surprised when she answered, "No, we have never met."

"No," they would say. "How can you not have met him when he says that what happened between the two of you changed the course of his life?"

"If he has something to thank me for, let him do what I do and help others," she would respond. "That is thanks enough." However, in her heart, Naomi knew that everything she had heard about this man filled her with joy. During their meeting, she believed the feeling was mutual. *Oh be happy with what you have,* she cautioned her heart. Yet, schooled in the denial of her own desires as she was, she could not stop herself from wishing for a fuller life, a life where she would receive those things that she knew would complete her. She looked at Chaz and sensed a yearning within her that prior to their encounter she had never felt before. She wondered if the metamorphosis she witnessed outside her French doors each spring, when caterpillars spun their cocoons and emerged later in the season as beautiful butterflies, could be hers. Though she yearned to find out and become all Madre Vida had spoken of on her first night at the *casa*, she forced herself to asses this situation from a practical viewpoint. Her heart would have none of it, and against her better judgment, she found herself wondering, *Could I become all God created me to be?* Aware that her life was one of service to others, she upbraided herself, *Be happy with what you have.*

Minutes ticked by. When Naomi did not respond, Chaz said, "It is hard to know what to say when you do not know me. Why not spend some time together? That way we can get to know each other."

Even as Naomi agreed to his seemingly innocent request, she thought, *Will I still be able to accomplish all I have committed to do if I give my heart to him?*

"Good. I will court you so you can decide if I am worthy of your hand in marriage." Naomi gave him a tentative smile. "There now, that was not so hard, was it?" Chaz took her hand and led her out of the attorney's office.

When news of their courtship reached those in the *barrio*. Many who knew Naomi spoke of her worthiness to her suitor. Chaz squired Naomi around Spanish Harlem and courted her in a manner usually reserved for the very rich. Their courtship proved that he was motivated out of the tenderest of feeling for his intended. Naomi had never needed anything fancy to wear. She considered herself a plain woman and believed it best that she accomplish her tasks without drawing attention to herself. Now as Chaz wooed her, she allowed her friends to take her to the local dressmaker who, according to Justine and Lucinda, could make lovely clothes for only a few dollars more than store bought.

As the days flew by, Naomi discovered Chaz's love through the flowers he sent and his note that accompanied them. There were the daily outings Chaz took her on which he had planned expressly with her in mind. Every time they parted, Naomi thought about marrying Chaz. Each time they came together, she discovered Chaz had found another new and enjoyable way for them to spend time together. Since he knew that his intended never left the *barrio* except to rescue a girl, he found new places to visit within the community. He took her on walks, out to dinner, or to a play. Each time Naomi saw Chaz, she felt herself fulfilled.

Six weeks of courting ended abruptly when Chaz asked Naomi for her hand in marriage. She knew his proposal was inevitable and throughout their courtship, she found she could think of nothing else. Being a person who weighs her options, she had forced herself to think about living without Chaz and his attention. She looked at her calendars pages filled with all the things they had enjoyed together and smiled when she remembered his many kindnesses. She thought of the months that had lengthened into years before he came and a calendar filled with nothing but obligations and realized that living without Chaz meant denying what she felt. She believed Madre Vida would have frowned upon that. This belief coupled with the promise of fulfillment lead her to realize, *I cannot go back to being content with the way things were before Chaz came.* Her heart knew that everything she thought was true, so when Chaz proposed, she did not need to ponder but said, "Yes, I will marry you."

It was no surprise to anyone, least of all the attorney, when he opened the paper and found their wedding announcement in its pages. Overjoyed to have accomplished his desire and pleased that he had found the woman a worthy husband, Ralph waited until he knew the priest was free, hurried to the church, found Padre Paul, opened the paper and read, "Naomi Blanco is to marry Chaz Romero—"

"Yes, it is true." The padre wiped happy tears from his eyes. "I know because I am officiating at their nuptials."

Naomi's wedding day was the best and the worst day of her life. When her voice trembled with emotion while she pledged herself to Chaz, she feared the very edifice they stood in would crash down upon her. She felt herself a fraud. *How,* she asked herself, *can I pledge to love, honor, and obey without telling him about myself?* Yet, she stifled her worries and exchanged vows and rings. Then she lifted her veil to reveal herself to him, knowing all the while that he did not know her at all. Chaz looked at her and smiled. She smiled back. As she did, she hoped that the joy that infused the moment with the bright light of promise would become a reality.

They held the reception at the *casa.* Naomi was happy to have it there since it helped her absence from her husband's side go unnoticed. Throughout the evening, she acted the happy bride and host. Yet her eyes never met her husband's as she rushed to attend to everyone's needs except his. It was late when the festivities ended and everyone left.

They were alone.

Naomi looked at Chaz and knew she was worried. What she had only partly admitted to herself during their wedding was now a glaring incrimination. By omission, she had lied to him. Her feelings of remorse drew her back to memories of her childhood before the family had begun their nomadic life. She thought of those *Yom Kippur* observances when her *papá* had locked all the doors to their small *casa* and shut the windows tight while everyone in the family scurried to the basement to fast and petition *Adonai* for the forgiveness of their sins. She remembered how they stood while he read the extensive list of the sins of commission and omission, which all Hebrews pray through when they observe the Day of Atonement. It seemed to her that this memory could not have surfaced at a worse time. As she tried to shake off her concern about *Adonai's* condemnation, she thought she could almost hear her *mamá* say, "Hurry, let us finish before our neighbors come looking for us and find us huddled in the basement like someone who has something to hide!" She remembered the first time they had honored God this way with nothing to hide their secret but a tent that stood between them and whoever might be listening. She shuddered, and caught her breath, afraid of what she had done and how it would play out for her. For the first time since she had left that life, Naomi felt the judgment of God heavy on her heart and admitted, *Before I worried about how Chaz would react if he knew I was not Catholic. Now I wonder how we can have a life together if I cannot tell him about myself.*

Chaz felt her withdraw. "What has happened that there is a chill between us? Have I done something to make it so?"

"No. The problem is not yours but mine. Forgive me," she called as she fled. "I fear that I will lose you and it worries me more than I can bear."

He watched her run away and remembered the priest meeting with him to prepare him to deal with his bride who, Padre Paul had observed over the years, had never allowed anyone to really know or manage her. Because he believed no one had shown her love without an ulterior motivate, he counseled Chaz to be gentle with her so that Naomi would learn to trust him. Chaz believed the priest was right because Naomi had never revealed herself completely to him or, as far as he could tell, her dearest *amigas*. As she fled, he remembered telling the priest, "I will wait until she is ready because she is worth waiting for." No sooner did that commitment flood his consciousness than he remembered the priest asking him what he would do if she were skittish, and he reaffirmed his commitment. Chaz closed his eyes and visualized the padre smiling. He believed the priest knew that he would take good care of his bride. It was then that he remembered the old man had said, "If she runs from you, it is because she is reserved and fears letting anyone in."

When his thoughts returned to the present, Chaz realized he did not know where to spend the night. He found himself feeling as if he were a guest in the *casa*. He picked up his suitcase, which contained all he had chosen to bring to Naomi's house at this time, and walked to the door she had closed. He was not happy that he had purposefully not told Naomi everything about himself. But early in their courtship, he had realized that if she understood his work and his world, she might deny him her hand in marriage. And that he would not allow. With that resolve in mind, Chaz reached the door Naomi had closed, knocked, and asked, "*Querida* beloved, where should I put my things?"

Naomi opened the door and peeked around its massive bulk. She was startled to see her husband standing in the hall holding his suitcase. Her face flamed crimson as she shyly whispered, "*Perdona*."

Chaz saw her jaw tighten as her color heightened, revealing her raw emotions. Concerned that his being a head taller than her might make her feel more threatened than she already seemed, he stepped back a pace.

"*Amor,* be patient with me. I am new at this and not certain of what to do, as I have no one to explain things to me. Please give me some time and I will come to you."

"You take all the time you need," Chaz said with great forbearance. "I will wait."

Naomi was surprised. She had not expected her husband to grant her request.

Chaz waited, suitcase in hand.

Naomi looked from Chaz to his suitcase and back again. "I ... planned for us to be together ... tonight ... and ... for the rest ... of our lives."

Chaz forced a smile. "We are together, just not yet in the same bed. Do not fear. All good things come to those who wait. And I promise to stay here and wait because you are worth waiting for." Naomi breathed a sigh of relief, entered the hallway, and beckoned him to follow. Chaz waited for her to take the lead, followed her down the hall, and remembered telling the good padre, "Just for now, our marriage will unfold as Naomi allows it to."

Naomi stopped at Madre Vida's room, which to her looked like a grand suite with its fine linen and opulent furnishings of a bygone era. She smiled tentatively and motioned for Chaz to open the ornately carved door as she stepped back. He smiled at her, opened the door, turned on the light, and peered within. He was surprised to see a room like this in a home where women dedicated themselves to rescuing others. He turned toward Naomi and noticed the look of pride in her eyes. "Why do you not occupy these rooms?"

"These rooms belonged to Madre Vida. I planned to wait until I wed to bring you, *mi esposo,* here to the very best I have to offer. I am not ready to be here but you, Chaz, must live here until I am."

Chaz placed his suitcase in the room and turned toward his bride. "Do not fear, beloved. Waiting makes everything more special. You will see; in a little while you will be here with me." He took her hands in his. "Until then remember we are husband and wife, *comprendes?*"

Naomi looked into his clear brown eyes, which she believed held no subterfuge and nodded. "*Sí, comprendo.*"

"Oh," Chaz chuckled. "Do I need to have a pledge book for you to sign?" They laughed at his remark. It seemed to them that their laughter brought them together as their vows, yet unfulfilled, could not. "We have a shared history, a shared commitment, and we will have a shared life," Chaz said. "Do not worry. All will be well with us."

"Yes," Naomi agreed. "All will be well with us."

Commitment and Confrontation

Naomi awoke to early morning bird song, stretched and sighed with joy as she thought about the previous night and the kindness of the man she had wed. She could still hear his assuring words and that, coupled with the refreshing sleep she had gotten, brought her the peace she had lacked the day before. Aware that this was a day that only happens once, she bounded out of bed, and threw on her white cotton tunic. She rushed into the kitchen to make her husband a hearty breakfast. Since her favorite pan was already on the stove, she turned on the flame, poured in some oil, and hummed a tune while she cut and added onions to simmer. She took the other ingredients she used for her special Spanish omelet out of the cupboard. Setting them aside, she cracked the eggs into a bowl, took her whisk out the drawer, heard the sound of footsteps, turned in their direction, and froze.

Chaz crossed the threshold and gazed at her. "Good morning."

"Oh, please, sit while I make us something to eat." She ran her fingers through her long tresses and tied them at the nap of her neck.

Chaz smiled as he came up beside her. "Permit me." He loosened her hair and ran his large fingers through her unruly mane.

Naomi turned toward him, noticed a smile, then a grin.

"So lovely." His hands cupped her chin and raised her face toward his. "So very lovely."

Could there be something lovely about me? Naomi wondered. Chaz drew her lips to his. Before they touched, Naomi pulled away. "I need to pay attention to my cooking, or I will burn our marriage breakfast." She nodded to a nearby chair. "Sit and I will tend to this. Then we will have the whole day to be together, just the two of us."

Chaz sat down and watched his bride cook their first breakfast.

When she noticed that his eyes followed her everywhere, Naomi became flustered. She knew she needed a moment to collect herself, grabbed a vase from the cupboard, raced into the garden, and returned with it filled with flowers. Chaz took the vase from her hand, placed it on the table, and lifted her hand to his lips. He gazed into her eyes and kissed it. He reached for its mate and repeated the behavior as he drew circles within her palms. Though their meal needed her attention, Naomi could not bring herself to stop Chaz. "Come, let us be together." He placed his strong arm around her slight frame. "Then we will eat." Naomi knew that Chaz was claiming the rights of a husband and turned off the flame. He took her hand in his and led her down the hall.

When they reached Madre Vida's room, Naomi froze. A look of fear crossed her face. Almost as quickly as it came, it disappeared.

Chaz pushed the door open with one hand and drew her close with the other. He gathered her into his arms and placed her upon the bed. He watched to see her many thoughts as they played upon her face. Finally, he saw her relax and asked, "It is good?"

"*Sí,* it is good," she said, a smile on her lips. He bent down to kiss her and was startled when the phone rang. He looked up, saw Naomi reach over and grab the phone. "Forgive me," she mouthed. "But a *niña* might need my help."

"I understand." He moved away but stayed close enough to listen.

Naomi spoke with Victor. Their brief conversation finished, she hung up the phone, and ran down the hall. "I must go," she called over her shoulder.

"Dear, what is the problem?" Chaz followed her. He stood in the doorway to her bedroom.

Always modest, Naomi pushed this concern aside, pulled a dress from her wardrobe, and threw it on. "There is a *niña* at immigration.

The family that brought her to America refuses to keep her. Their son is of marriageable age and wants her, so she is to be sent back." After a quick search, she found her shoes and put them on. She brushed and braided her hair, wrapped it into a coronet, and pinned it into place. She grabbed the large black purse she had inherited from Madre Vida. "I must get there before she is sent away!"

She hurried to her office. Chaz followed upon her heels. She opened the desk drawer, found and shoved the necessary papers into her purse, and rushed to the front door. As she turned the knob, she looked at her husband. "Chaz, I am sorry this happened today, but we have our whole lives together. This girl may have only today. If I do not help her, I will have broken faith with the Tías. Do you understand?" She stepped onto the porch, turned, and smiled at him. "Be patient, my beloved." Before he could answer, she hurried away.

Chaz saw her round the corner and reminded himself, *She is worth waiting for.* He walked into the kitchen, cooked and ate their marriage breakfast by himself. Once that sad meal was finished, he stood on the porch and waited for his bride to return. Lunchtime came and went. There was still no sign of Naomi. By one o'clock, he was worried. He had never asked how many hours it took to rescue a girl. Now he wished he had. He found himself looking at the corner every few minutes and wanted to upbraid himself. Instead he thought, *No bride should expect her husband to be happy with strangers in their* casa *the day after they wed.* In an attempt to squelch his negative attitude, he turned his mind to the *niña* Naomi had gone to get.

Finally, unable to stop himself, he looked at the corner Naomi would turn. She was walking down the street with a girl in tow. When she opened the gate, he stepped off the porch, forced a smile, and rushed forward. "Here, let me take that." He took the bundle from his beloved, which he assumed held the girls clothes. When he glanced in the girl's direction, he was startled. He had never seen one as fair yet self-possessed. It appeared to him as if the girl's eyes assessed him. Aware of the morays he had pledged to abide when he wed, he put his arm around his bride's waist. The couple mounted the porch steps together. The unity and conformity of their steps was not lost on the girl who followed them. She saw the porch swing, sat down, and placed her feet on a nearby Adirondack chair. While her gaze swept the patio, she reached under her hat, pulled out a tendril of her luxuriant blond mane, and twirled it around her finger. Naomi turned and saw the girl sitting in the dappled sunlight. "Lola, please stay there. I will prepare a place for you."

The girl nodded. Naomi whispered to Chaz, smiled at him and entered the *casa*. He turned back to attend to the girl as his wife had requested. The girl moved her legs so that her skirt opened to reveal her long lean limbs, she looked at him, rolled down her socks, and watched him assess her every move. Chaz turned away, entered the house, and caught up with Naomi. "She cannot stay here!"

"Oh, she must. They always do. That is what immigration expects. Should they come looking, they must find her here."

"I have heard there is a grandmother's house out back. Put her there."

"What bothers you so? You knew all about this work before we wed. What is the problem?"

"Can you not understand?" Chaz shouted at her in frustration.

"I have no desire to disrespect you!" Naomi explained as she raised her voice to match his. "But I made this commitment long before we met! You knew it was for me a commitment I would not break! Not even for you." She searched her husband's face. Instead of seeing the understanding countenance she had hoped for, she saw how angry he was. She knew his anger was her fault but refused her inner counsel, which told her to recant what she had said. Overwhelmed by the situation, she teared up, ran to her bedroom, and slammed the door shut. *It was my work and his that brought us together,* she reminded herself. *If I give up this work, I will not be the one he fell in love with.* Her body racked with sobs, she spent her tears and fell asleep.

Chaz returned to the girl. He was certain she had heard everything he and Naomi said since they had spoken loud enough for those walking by the *casa* to hear them. Lola glanced up at him, bent over seductively, and with slow, deliberate motions rolled her socks up to cover her shapely calves. Then she turned and smiled her radiant greeting at him. "Follow me." He picked up her bundle. He took the lead. They walked through the house, across the upper patio and garden. Then they redirected steps toward the stairs terraced and flanked with plantings and took them to the lower patio. Neither of them said a word. When they reached the grandmother's house, Chaz reached above the doorjamb, found the key, and opened the door.

The girl peeked into the dimly lit room and teetered on the uneven Spanish tiles. Afraid she would fall, she wrapped her arms around him and gazed boldly into his eyes. A look of salacious pleasure crossed her face. She watched his countenance and saw a spark of desire, then repulsion. Since she had dealt with men like him before, she knew she would win. When he said, "Do not touch me," she heard his disapproving tone. As he cast her grasping arms away, she noticed his manner was aloof. But it was only when she watched him put her bundle in the house and retrace his steps as quickly as possible that she knew she would have him.

Chaz returned to Naomi's *casa* and headed for some wine to calm himself. As he poured it out, its bouquet filled the room while he wrestled with his demons. He downed the glass in a hurry and felt his world slowly right. He poured another and headed for the back patio. He stopped, admitted he feared the sight of the girl and her effect on him, grumbled to himself, and headed to the front porch where he sat down. He made the trip from the porch to the bottle several times. By dusk, he felt ill. He saw his reflection in the front window. "I look like I did when I was on the street!" He pulled up his trousers, which had slipped down low on his torso, tightened his belt, and straightened his spine. Because he knew that he could not allow himself to become a drunkard again, he walked into the kitchen and poured the dregs down the drain. Remorse flooded his mind as he stood at the kitchen sink and looked into the garden. He had thought of that place as a lovely refuge and planned that he and Naomi would enjoy each other's company there. Now looking at it brought impure thoughts to his mind. Aware that if he acted as the girl wanted, he would end up on the street again, Chaz threw the bottle into the trash. He heard the glass shatter, walked to the vestibule, picked up his jacket, and left.

Angry with himself for his reaction to the girl and frustrated by Naomi's defiant response to his demands, Chaz knew he needed the absolution of confession and headed to the church. By the time he reached the confessional, the line was long. Aware that he was possibly the neediest, he waited. Because it was less than twenty-four hours since he had wed, he believed that people were staring at him. He wanted to be inconspicuous, so he hunkered down.

He heard laughter. Then someone called his name. When he did not answer, Eduardo came up from behind and slapped him on the back with the flat of his hand. "Chaz, *mi amigo,* what brings you here so soon? Too rough on your *esposa* on your wedding—"

Chaz clenched his right hand into a fist and rounded on him. He landed a right cross and heard the sound of cartilage as it broke. Eduardo groaned and reached for his bloody nose, his look of friendship replaced with one of pain.

Everyone hollered expletives and glared at Chaz. Padre Paul heard the commotion from inside the booth and asked the woman within to pardon him. He opened the door and saw Eduardo holding his nose. Since everyone was yelling at Chaz, he looked at him and realized the man's countenance was a confession. Confronted by a sight he had not seen before within the sacred walls of the church, the priest stood. With as much dignity as he could summon, he approached the men. As he did, he nodded to his assistant, Esteban, and pointed toward the confessional. The young priest hurried to take Padre Paul's place. "Esteban will be with you momentarily," Padre Paul announced loud enough for everyone to hear. Once the priest saw Esteban close the door, he took each man by an arm and guided them to his office. "Tell me nothing until we are alone!" He walked by Luna, his secretary. "If anyone asks for me, tell them I am in a meeting."

They arrived at his office. He ushered them in and shut the door behind them. Because of the altercation, he had the men sit on the window seat, which he had insisted be built large enough to accommodate an arguing couple. Then he watched each of them intently. Once Chaz's furry had abated, he looked at Eduardo and saw that his eyes had swollen and blood was caked between his nose and upper lip. He applied gentle pressure where the nose looked crooked and felt the cartilage give. "*Sí, mira,* it is broken!" He turned toward Chaz, and in his most restrained voice asked, "My son, why do you do this in the house of God and why to your very own *amigo*? Did he not stand up for you at your wedding?" Chaz's lips moved, but the priest could not hear him. He leaned closer and overheard the bridegroom's impromptu confession. As he spoke with Chaz, the man's anger and fear were reconciled as he said the prescribed penance. Then Chaz fell asleep. Padre Paul nodded to Eduardo and they left his office together. "I will take you to the emergency room." As they walked by Luna's desk, the priest nodded toward his office. "Chaz is not to be disturbed, nor is he allowed to leave."

The miles ticked by. Finally, unable to stop himself, Eduardo asked, "Padre, why has this happened and what will happen now?"

"My son, we will speak about this only once, you and me. Then we will act together as though you never heard any of this. Do you understand?"

"*Sí.*"

The priest parked the car and looked at Eduardo. "Our friend has his hands full. He has one woman whom he loves, but she does not yet know how to love, and another who excites him, but by whom, thanks be to the Blessed Virgin, he is repulsed. We must pray that Chaz and Naomi stay pure and true to their commitment before God. We must also find a way to get that girl, Lola out of their house, the sooner the better."

"But Naomi will not allow her to go!"

"That is the problem. Of course, Naomi will want the girl to stay. But we must find a way to entice her to do what will be good for everyone."

As Eduardo nodded his head, his face contorted into a mask of pain. True to his *machismo* upbringing, he forced a smile and exited the car. "Do not worry. I have been to the emergency room. I know what to do."

The priest waved good-bye and headed back to his church. Aware that no one could hear him, he said, "Never has anything like this happened before. I had hoped to go to Rome. Now I will be happy to stay where I am. What will I tell the Bishop if he questions me about Naomi's relationship with the church and her love of our Blessed Virgin? I wanted her settled with a good man to love and look after her. Since she would not allow me to find an appropriate man for her, I had hoped this Chaz would do. Yet already there is a problem. This one caused because of the woman herself and her tender heart!" Even as Padre Paul heard his words, he remembered that he had waved the rules so he could marry the couple and hoped the Bishop would not want a report. As he parked the car in the church's parking lot, he muttered, "What to do? What to do?"

When he stepped from the car, the padre gazed longingly at the church, turned, and walked the few blocks to Naomi's *casa*. The front door was slightly ajar. He assumed that Chaz had forgotten to shut it, walked into the vestibule, and listened. Since he heard nothing except the sound of his own breathing, he did not wait for someone to invite him in but walked to the kitchen. He stood at the sink. His gaze wandered beyond the back patio to the area where the grandmother's house was and remembered visiting that place once when one of the *niñas* had come down with an illness that required isolation. The movement of a woman child drew his gaze to the garden. His eyes riveted on her. Once he saw the girl pick flowers and place them into the décolletage of her bodice, he realized that she was a wanton by the way she used the things of the garden to draw attention to an area where a modest woman would never want anyone's eyes to roam. He understood Chaz's attraction and repulsion, for even her simplest movements were unwholesome. *Still,* he thought, *who am I to judge, a person who enters a house illegally?* Later, he might tell himself as he struggled to find an explanation for his behavior, *I needed to see what kind of child could turn a man's head, especially a man who was just married.* However, he knew he would never forget looking at the girl with unmasked revulsion when he realized that though the sunlight glinted off her skin, and her blonde hair flowed in the breeze, something was wrong. "She is one who can look pure and innocent yet lead men to hell," he said as he hurriedly retraced his steps. "Chaz is right! The girl is trouble and must be sent away as quickly as possible or Chaz cannot stay in this *casa!*"

The priest took his own advice and left so quickly he almost ran into the street. Even as he hurried back to the church, he realized that he would not feel fully himself until he entered his office. When he did, he found Chaz waking up. By the way the man slurred his words, the padre knew the wine was still affecting him. He sat next to this misunderstood bridegroom and applied a cool compress to his forehead. "I have been to the house. I have seen her. You are right to be concerned. She is one who can make a sane man lose his mind. Her look of innocence is misleading. But Naomi cannot see her as a man does."

"How do you know these things?" Chaz groaned.

"I was not always a priest. I too have looked at a pretty girl. Upon occasion, I have seen one such as this Lola, this type, so innocent, so charming, so dangerous. Men can lose their minds over such a one. We will find a way for her to have a place but not with you and your wife. Let us pray." The padre bowed his head and asked God to grant Chaz patience, wisdom, and restraint while they waited for an answer to their prayers.

Both the priest and Chaz agreed that he could return home now that prayer and a plan fortified him. Chaz walked home haggard but more lighthearted than earlier. He remembered the priest had said, "Do not pay attention to her. Think only of your wife and fulfill your marriage vows. You must consummate your union as soon as possible. Then you will not have a wandering heart."

When he rounded the corner and looked at Naomi's *casa*, Chaz saw his bride waiting on the porch for him and was pleased.

"*Querido. Querida.*" They greeted each other as their eyes met. "Forgive me!" they said as they came together and hugged.

"I was getting worried. Where have you been?"

"I went to see the priest." His eyes searched her face for understanding.

"Why does such a little thing bother you so much?"

"Beloved, I want to have you, yet you put me off. How can you become comfortable with me while there is another in our *casa*?"

Naomi blushed. "Oh, forgive me. I did not understand. Is that what bothers you? Well, then, put her in the grandmother's house."

"I have. But, beloved, she has an effect upon me that is not wholesome. Believe me, I cannot be around her. She is not a good girl."

"Nonsense. How do you know?"

"How do I know? I am a man! That is how I know! Even the priest knows! After he heard my confession and helped Eduardo with his nose, which I think I broke, he came here and saw her. He agrees she must go. He will help us find a good, safe place for her."

Greeted by silence, Chaz looked at his bride. He hoped to see understanding in her countenance. Instead, he saw the figure of a strange woman wearing his wife's clothes as she turned and walked away from him. Startled by the transformation, he watched as she entered the house. "Please, for our happiness, listen to me." Chaz noticed that she held her body rigidly straight like one grievously wronged. He thought he could say something that would help her understand what he had meant to say, so he followed her inside. Before he had time to gather his thoughts, desperation overcame him, and he begged, "Please, beloved, do not withdraw from me in anger."

Naomi turned toward him, pain etched upon her face. Quietly, her voice a controlled whisper, she said, "It is me and the girl, whichever girl I choose to bring here, or there is no marriage, and you should leave now!" She turned away from him.

Chaz followed her.

She walked into her bedroom, slammed the door shut, and shot the bolt.

Chaz knew there was only one noise that sounded like that. "There is no talking with her!" He walked to her door and pummeled it unmercifully with his fists. Finally, his anger spent, he stopped. His hands were raw and bleeding. He walked to the kitchen sink to run some cool water over his lacerated skin. Before he turned on the water, he was startled to hear a soft voice caress the back of his neck.

"Smart of you to stop trying to get her to see your side of things. Leave her alone and she'll come around to your way of thinking soon enough," Lola cooed. "Let me see those hands." She held out hers. Chaz looked at the girl while fear and desire played across his face, revealing his inner torment. He gave her his hands, palms up. She did not make a compress for them or use any soothing ointment, rather she began to suckle them.

Unable to stop himself, he moved closer to her. "How old are you?" he asked, his voice a hoarse whisper.

"Old enough to know what pleases a man like you," she said with a laugh.

He was ashamed he had asked such a revealing question and wished to turn away but found he could not. As he watched, the girl pulled the scarf from her neck and ran it over his wounded skin. Aware that his words and actions had led her to believe that he was hers for the taking, he knew he must put a stop to her assumption and forced himself to move away from her. But she moved closer to him. Now his hands, which had throbbed from the beating he had given them, were aflame with excruciating heat. But he knew the heat had nothing to do with the pounding he had given those hands moments ago. "Leave me alone," he cried in anguish. He pushed her away.

"Okay," Lola said with a seductive lilt to her voice.

Chaz watched as she slowly pulled her scarf away, sauntered to the garden, and turned back to look at him. "I will for now," she said, using a tone similar to the one he had used with her.

Chaz followed her. He grabbed her scarf, careful not to make contact with her flesh since he was aware of the searing need for her that the mere touch of her set off in him. Yanking at the scarf, he turned her toward him. His eyes locked on hers with firm determination. "If you do not stay away from me, I will take the key and lock you up in the grandmother's house, *chica!*"

"Good," she cooed. Her laughter bubbled up under her full-throated voice. "Then you will know exactly where to find me!"

Shocked into silence, Chaz watched her sashay across the patio and down the steps. "Oh, Mother of God! Help me now!" he exclaimed. As he did, he remembered the priest's words.

Lola heard him and laughed. She turned back, saw him grimace, and knew her laughter had found its mark. She reached the lower patio and looked up. He stood where she had left him. His were eyes vacant, his face devoid of expression. "I already smell your life's blood being offered up to me on the defiler's altar of immorality," Lola whispered. She sashayed to the grandmother's house and turned to look at Chaz once more. "You will choose to follow me of your own free will, or I will make you suffer."

Guilt and Yearning

Chaz sat by the fountain. *How could you be interested in a girl you revile?* He closed his eyes to ward off any more distractions from the girl. The smell of smoke on the breeze brought him up short. *Ah, they are barbecuing.* He breathed in the aroma of meat and beans cooking on an open grill, remembered his family and the *rancho*.

"Un hombre's *work has never been to make things right for a* mujer," Chaz heard his padre and Abuelo Gravile agree, as if it were yesterday. They were sitting around the table after dinner, their bellies full of tacos and beans. The men smoked their cigars and bet on the card game they played every night. At times like these when they would make such statements, he would look from one to the other and wonder if what they said was true.

"Sí, *this is true*," his grandfather, Gravile had nodded when he noticed his grandson *Chaim's* questioning look. "Women were put here by God to please and care for men. It is their duty, their job!"

"*And, if they do their job well, we will give them a reward!*" his padre had said with a deep-throated chuckle. His grandfather choked on the cigar smoke he had inhaled as he guffawed in response to his son's joke. Chaz smiled as he remembered how his grandfather's eyes had glistened. He realized that he had not understood what was so funny.

"*You see,* Chaim, *women were made to please man,*" his grandfather had said. "*That is what makes them happy. Show me an unhappy woman, and I will show you a woman who has never had her husband's pleasure foremost in her mind!*"

Chaz had wondered if his grandfather was making things up as he sometimes did, so he looked at his father. "Padre, is this true?"

He remembered his father winked at his grandfather. "Sí, *women derive their pleasure from men. Men derive their pleasure from many things. But women need to be married in order to fill their lives with joy!*"

Chaz kept that memory in mind and walked to Naomi's bedroom door. "Beloved, please come out. It is getting late. We should do something for dinner." He waited. No answer. He was aware that he had begged earlier in the day. He had never done that before. Since he believed there was nothing more that he could say, he turned away.

Naomi hurried to her door and opened it a sliver. "Forgive me, beloved," she whispered.

Chaz was so lost in his thoughts that he did not hear her. Naomi watched him walk away. *What else can I expect, a deceitful woman married to a virtuous man.* She shut her door and turned away from all her heart longed for. *How could a marriage, which was supposed to unite us, cause us to lose the growing regard we felt for each other? I must let him go . . . but I cannot. He cares for me. I need someone to care for me,* she admitted as she reached the safety of her maiden's bed and cried herself to sleep.

A few hours later she awoke, looked at her bedside clock, realized that Chaz would be asleep, and walked to the kitchen, intending to fix something to eat. She turned on the light, saw the vase Chaz had taken from her hand and placed on the table, remembered that intimate moment, and her heart skipped a beat. Then, just as quickly, guilt washed over her. She walked toward the vase and looked at the wilted flowers, untended by a loving hand. Aware that other flowers would bloom in her garden because of the way she tended her plants, she chose to believe that one act of neglect could not kill their fledgling love if it was tended. Confronted with her duplicity, she reminded herself of all those who continued to love even when their love was rejected. Until that moment, Naomi had been unaware of her steadfast belief that true love could continue even in the face of neglect. She clung to her belief and told herself, *It is not too late! I will find a way to show Chaz the love I intend to share with him!*

She sat down to think about how she could show her husband that she had not meant to put him second and saw an envelope with her name on it. Her hand trembled as she picked it up. Her unspoken prayer was that the missive was from Chaz and that it was one of forgiveness and understanding. She tore the envelope open and found a snapshot of herself. Startled by a picture, she had never seen, she wondered where it had come from. A scrawl in the bottom left corner read, "Here is a picture of the lady, as you requested." Further inspection showed it was dated eight years ago. Again she wondered who would want a picture of her and why. Her fingers played with the envelope as she pondered that answer. She glanced at the torn flap, saw some words written on it and read, "It pains me to cause you sorrow. If you would like, I will go. I do not want to go, but if you would like, I will."

Aware that she had created a situation that she could correct, she rushed down the hall to the bedroom where her bridegroom lay. She threw herself at his door and sobbed, "Do not leave me! Life is not better when you are gone. Let us work this out together!"

Chaz opened the door and pulled her to himself with kisses and words of endearment. He picked her up and looked at her with unbridled longing. "We will have no more of this, *comprendes?*"

"*Sí*... yes, I understand!" She gazed into his clear brown eyes. He smiled and kissed her lips. Naomi smiled back. She looked at her surroundings, remembered Chaz had agreed to wait to consummate their union, and realized she had placed herself in a situation fraught with peril. She smiled at him, aware that she was prepared to surrender. Chaz turned and carried her away from the bedroom.

"But where are we going?"

"Away from temptation and dishonor."

He carried her to the kitchen, placed her in a chair, opened the refrigerator, pulled out some boxes, and opened them.

Naomi watched him and gasped, "Look at all this food!" She wondered at the thoughtfulness of the man she had wed. "Never in my life have I seen so many choices for just two people! Whatever were you thinking of to do such an extravagant thing?"

"I did not know when you would want to eat, but I knew that I would wait until you were." He tried not to laugh at the look of consternation on her face. "I was hungry when I bought this. And I thought that if you are stubborn as I am, I might be hungrier still before we shared this meal. So I prepared a market feast. Besides, once the people at the market knew it was for you, they suggested all these things. It is good to be married to the woman who owns the place." He chuckled, and placed their meal on oven plates to heat. "If we must argue, could we do so when we have full stomachs?" His stomach growled. He laughed. "This is painful."

Naomi's stomach let out a growl. Struck by the absurdity of the moment, they both laughed. Their laughter broke the tension between them. They smiled at each other and remembered that once before laughter had helped them overcome difficulties.

Within moments the food was heated and on the table.

"This was a very good idea!" She took large portions of everything and piled them on her plate. They ate in silence. Once she was full, Naomi smiled at Chaz. "Thank you for thinking of this."

Chaz looked at her, filled a tortilla with spicy rice, and rolled it up so he could take a mouthful. Before he did, he nodded. "*De nada,* it was nothing."

"Nothing indeed!" She began to tidy up, reached for a bag from the market, saw the name of her market, and blushed.

Chaz gulped down his last bite. "What is it that makes you color so?"

"Oh … it is … nothing."

"Naomi, there are no little things that concern you. Tell me why you blush."

She struggled to gain control of her emotions and finally said, "You will think I am silly."

"There is nothing silly about you or what you think. Tell me."

Naomi looked at him with the eyes of an innocent. "What will those at the market think of me? I did not make your meal." Before he could answer, she turned away. "You must be ashamed of the wife you married."

"Naomi, I did not marry you because you were perfect. I married you because my heart told me that you belong to me." Unable to articulate all his words meant to her, Naomi turned and stared at him. Chaz took her face in his hands, and kissed her eyes and mouth. He muttered sweet endearments, which she had never thought to hear. He pulled away for a moment and looked into her eyes. "You are my treasure! Who cares what those at the market think? All anyone needs to know is written in my eyes, which always follow you, for I love you."

"Oh." Naomi sighed as joy engulfed her.

"Besides, do you not own the market?"

He saw her look of surprise and swatted her backside in a playful way. She responded in kind and as she did, she realized the freedom and blessing of a husband who chose to forgive and understand her.

It was a little after midnight when she snuggled into her covers. Before she let herself fall asleep, she thought about their meal, Chaz's words of affirmation, and realized, *Never in my life have I had an evening like this one. What fun it is to be with him. We fit together well.* She stifled a yawn and silently prayed, *Please, God, let this be true. Do I not deserve this little bit of happiness? For my whole life, I have never asked for myself. I have always come or gone, as others needed me to. God, I need and, most importantly, I want our marriage to work.*

Chaz stood on the front porch and smiled to himself. He took his cigar out of its wrapper and rolled it between thumb and forefinger. As he did, he thought about the evening, which for him had ended all too soon. His imagination stirred, he applied too much pressure, and the cigar snapped in two. Aware that he had broken his *evening pleasure*, as he had come to call his daily cigar, he tossed the pieces aside, reached into the house, and grabbed his jacket from the coat tree. *How late do they stay open?* he wondered. Then he reminded himself, *Xavier's shop never closes.*

Swinging his jacket over his shoulder, he walked to the tobacconist's. He whistled a tune he had sung to the cows all those long, lonely years ago. The haunting refrain brought him up short. He thought about being out on the range with the herd at fifteen and sang, "I'm back in the saddle again, out where a friend is a friend." He walked a few paces and remembered the next line. "Where the longhorn cattle feed on the lowly gypsum weed, back in the saddle again." His quick, determined movements brought him back to the life on the *rancho* with his family.

"No one in this family has ever owned land," his Abuelo Gravile had told him when he was a teenager. "It is better to own your own soul and be free to go where you want when you want." That had been his plan, to be a *vaquero* like all the men of his family. He tried to remember the rest of the words to the song as he thought about what it meant to be a cowboy. He neared the shop and admitted to himself, *I have not sung that tune since I stopped breaking wild horses on the rancho in Texas. I wonder what brought it to my mind now.*

He entered the tobacco shop and nodded at Bridgette.

She was sitting by the cash register, knitting, and as was her custom, she looked up to see who had entered before she said, "*Hola.*"

"*Hola*, Bridgette." Chaz walked to the humidor, which held his favorites. "Xavier's not here tonight?"

"No. He went to play cards with his friends. You used to go not so very long ago."

"*Sí.* But there are things that I must attend to first."

"How can you attend to these … these things, as you put it, if you are here and she is not?"

Chaz ran his fingers over the leather of an old whip that hung on the wall. He knew it was a reminder of a previous life lived by some long forgotten *vaquero.* Then, he remembered why he had come and reached for a cigar. "I know how to gentle a horse so as to not break its spirit," he muttered. He looked at the whip. "But I do not know how to treat a wife who was been kept apart from the world. This is a mystery I must solve." As he turned toward the cash register, he nodded toward the whip, as if the *vaquero* who had owned it could somehow shed some wisdom on his situation.

"*Perdóname* for overhearing your remark, my husband's friend, but there is no difference."

A look of surprise crossed Chaz's face. He pulled up a chair and sat down across from Bridgette. "How can you, a lady, say such a thing? Naomi is not a horse but a woman!"

She glanced up from her knitting. "Your wife will be lucky if you are gentle with her. And you, my husband's friend, will have a wife worth keeping. I grew up on a ranch. I know from the tone in your voice when you speak of the horses you have worked with, when you and Xavier have spoken of such things, that you were a good trainer. Think of this when you and your wife are together. We all know that La Señora never let Naomi out of her *casa* until she became ill. Naomi never dated or, even as far as any of us knows, ever thought about a man until you came for her. Treat her gently. Show her where you want her to go. Then give her time. She will follow, for I know her heart yearns for you."

"How do you know this?"

"It is obvious to all who look. She glows when she is with you. Have you not seen it to be so?"

"Perhaps it is just her way."

"No! It is not her way! Nor has it ever been the way of the Tías of Las Niñas. None of them, as far back as any of us can remember, ever married. She loves you or she would not have done so. My *abuela* told me a long time ago that none of the Tías wed because they had to keep their home free of men so they could focus on the girls. There was also the concern that if one of them married the man might develop the … the wandering eye. You understand?"

Chaz had already peeled the wrapper from the cigar. Now he placed it in his mouth and moistened it. He thought of what she said, picked up a match, and looked at her. "*Con su permiso?*"

"No! Go home. You can solve nothing here. Go home to her!"

Chaz stood and pulled out some bills to pay for his smoke.

Bridgette pointed to the door. "Don't! Just go!"

He placed three singles on the counter. "How do you and your grandmother know so much about the Tías? I thought they and everything they have done is a secret."

"It is, but all of Spanish Harlem knows. Yet we say nothing so as not to draw attention to this work and make a problem for the good women who surrender their lives for these needy ones. We have always known. Many of us have had the girls work for us. Some have married into our families." When she saw his look of concern, Bridgette explained, "Our Holy Mother Church says we should do good works in the Blessed Mother's name."

Pleased that he understood, Chaz turned to leave. "And you, Chaz, are the first man in such a situation as this, so we are all praying for you."

Glad to have the walk home to think of all he had heard, Chaz clenched his cigar between his teeth, remembered the way it felt to gentle a pony and how, in the end, the horse would respond out of love for him. He realized he could accomplish all he wished if he applied that knowledge to his marriage. He smiled to himself and took the porch stairs two at a time. *Yes, I will work this miracle with my wife. I have the skills and know how to use them to win her to a life filled with love. Her life has been one of service. I will show her the fullness that life can become when love enters.*

He opened the front door, paused, noticed the stillness of the *casa*, walked to Naomi's bedroom door, and whispered, "I will be gentle with you my beloved. You will let me guide you and I will lead you in a way that will be a blessing to you all the days of your life."

A Day Away

Dear One,

    The days grow warm. Let us go to Central Park and picnic together. Wear something casual, bring a jacket and a hat. I will be ready for our day together by ten.

Until then, all my love,
Chaz

He slid the note under her door, smiled to himself, and thought, *Life can be so very beautiful. You will see our lives will be joyful.*

When the full light of morning illuminated her room, Naomi knew she had overslept. For the first time in her life, she realized that not adhering to her schedule did not matter. All that mattered was the joy she felt as she greeted the new day. Then just as suddenly as this feeling had come, she admonished herself, *Do not be a fool. A pleasant evening and some fun does not mean much, just a brief moment in time. Do not expect more!* She glanced at her bedside clock and realized that Chaz must be waiting for her to fix his breakfast, so she put aside her musing and crossed to her door.

    She glanced at the floor, noticed a folded piece of paper, and realized it was from her husband. Her heart caught in her throat. *He is leaving me,* she thought. Tears fell unabated as she picked up the missive and crumpled the paper. She was about to throw it into the trash when she saw something drawn on the back. Hurrying to her nightstand, she smoothed it out, and saw the heart he had drawn with her name in the center. A surge of hope filled her. She turned the sheet of paper over and read what Chaz had written. She was thrilled. She had never been to the Great Park, and he wanted to take her. Happy that he really did want her, she hummed a merry tune and rushed to her wardrobe in search of what Chaz had called *casual clothes*. Her eyes darted from one choice to another. Nothing seemed right. Eyes downcast, she left her room and went into the kitchen to make breakfast.

Chaz was already dressed and sitting at the table. He looked up from his mug of coffee as she entered. "Naomi, why are you not dressed? Did you not see my note? Will you not come with me?"

Naomi's eyes sought his. "I want to come, but I have nothing *casual* to wear."

"Is that all?" He laughed.

"What is so amusing about this situation?"

"Do not worry about this. It is my fault."

"How can this be your fault?"

"I knew that you have always been here. I should have realized that you would not have clothes to play in."

"*Play!* I have never had time for play!"

"*Bueno,* I will teach you how to play. First, we will shop for some clothes for you. Hurry and get dressed before we lose the morning. I first went there in the morning, and I want you to experience it as I did."

Naomi smiled, elated by everything Chaz said. Yet because she feared he was speaking down to her, she insisted, "I am not a child!"

"It is true, my dear wife, that you are not. Because of the circumstances of your life, I fear you have never been a child. So allow me to teach you the joy of having a play day, just the two of us." He winked mischievously. "We will both be as childlike as we wish!"

Naomi looked at him with all the love her heart could hold and turned toward her room.

"Good. Just put on anything so we can be on our way. We will shop for whatever you need. Once that is done, I will see about lunch."

The day was as wonderful as Chaz had hoped. He discovered that taking Naomi out of her world of responsibilities and purchasing things for her that she liked but would never buy, gave him pleasure. He purchased jeans, a blouse, a sweater, and a good pair of walking shoes. However, it was his extravagant purchase of a beautiful yellow hat with red roses embroidered on its brim and a coordinating scarf that spoke to Naomi's heart. He had seen her glance at it longingly when they entered the store. However, schooled in practicality as she was, she chose a nondescript hat instead. Chaz intervened when he noticed that even as she stood at the checkout counter, her eyes still admired the hat that she had refused to try on. He smiled at her, took the plain hat from her head, walked over to the hat tree, and placed it on a peg. Grinning at her expectantly, he took the hat she had admired off its peg, placed it on her head, and turned her around to look at herself in the mirror. "This is how you should look!"

She stared at him.

"Why do you look at me like that?"

"Why do you want to buy me such a frivolous hat?"

Chaz smiled and put his arms around her. "My wife, you looked at this hat when we entered the store. You continued to look at it even when you had that ugly hat on your head. Why not get what you want for a change?" Naomi's eyes sparked with joy and she nodded her approval. Chaz motioned to the clerk. "Can you remove the price tag? My wife wishes to wear her hat now." When the clerk nodded, Chaz took Naomi's hat from her head and handed it to her. She removed the tag and handed the hat back to him. Chaz smiled at Naomi and placed it on her head. Aware that this hat was one that should grace a beautiful person's head, Naomi felt loved. As Chaz turned her toward the full-length mirror, she heard him say, "This is how you should always look!" She felt undone by his comment because she heard a longing in his voice she had always assumed no one would ever feel for her.

"Thank you ... I ... I love this hat. It makes me look like a fine lady and a little girl all at the same time!"

"It makes you look like you should. We should never be too grown up. It is hard to shoulder worries unless we take time to refresh ourselves as children do." He paid the bill, and held out his hand to his bride. "*Es que mi pequeño* ... come my little one." They walked into the morning together. When they reached the street, Chaz noticed that Naomi's eyes darted back and forth. He understood her unspoken dilemma. "Now, about food, do not worry. We will get something at the park."

She smiled up at him and yielded herself to his plans. Since she had taken over Madre Vida's work, Naomi had never let anyone take charge of any aspect of her work or life. If she were truthful with herself, she would have admitted that she had been in charge of the *casa* since the day she arrived. Now, greeted with the ability to have a day where she could experience freedom from her commitments, her spirits lifted. She felt unfettered and chuckled.

"Why are you laughing?"

"I am happy for you to take the lead. Even if I wanted to go to this park, I would never know how to get there. Except for my work at immigration, I have never gone anywhere outside of the *barrio*. I lack the courage to leave the neighborhood. You cannot imagine how happy I am that you are in control of this day."

"Good, men should always take the lead. I am glad that you are pleased in this. Now let us enjoy our day!"

Naomi knew that if anyone had asked her about her special days she would have had to admit, "The days I treasure are few." Yet if they had asked her to name them, she would have been hard-pressed to think of any. Perhaps after a moment she might have said, "There was the day which…" She would most likely have stopped as she tried to remember what days were meaningful. If she did remember a special day, she found she thought of it because of some service she had performed. Of course, there were the days of blessing, which followed Madre Vida's death. If anyone had asked her about them, they would have noticed the trace of unshed tears as she admitted, "Those blessings are so mingled with pain that I cannot separate the two."

Now, as she and her husband headed back home, Naomi knew she would treasure this day in her heart. All they had done seemed to meld together in her mind. She felt it would be almost impossible for her to tell any of her friends who might ask what they had done. The one thing she did admit to herself was that she had never felt so fulfilled.

When they entered a subway car, Chaz directed her to the empty seats in the back. He smiled at her as they sat down together. It seemed to her that they were stealing a few more precious moments before they would have to resume their roles, she the head of Las Niñas, he a well-known and sought after philanthropist. She noticed how hard he tried to make their day away last and believed he felt as she did. She lay back in his arms with a sigh.

When several moments had passed, Chaz asked, "Why so quiet, my wife?"

"I want to put the memory of this day in my mind like a snapshot so it will be there always. I do not know what I liked best, the rowing on the lake, the kielbasa and sauerkraut, or the birds as they sang their sweet song to us while we lay on the blanket and the sunlight shone down. I have never spent a day like this. Thank you."

He smiled at her, she said no more until they disembarked, and Chaz lead her up the stairs. Before they emerged into the sunlight of their neighborhood, she pulled him aside. "I did not know that life could be this sweet."

Chaz heard her voice quiver and smiled. "I too have had a wonderful day." They stepped onto the sidewalk. "When we have children, you will be able to experience things like this through their eyes and I know you will enjoy it." A gust of wind came up and caused her scarf to waft in the breeze. Chaz tucked it around her neck. "But never will you be able to see what I have seen today."

"Why would what you saw today be different from what I will see if we have our own *bebés*?"

"Naomi, to see a flower open in season is a pleasure. But when a flower has been forced to be dormant for such a long time, to be able to help it to open unexpectedly out of season is a miracle!"

"Am I your miracle then?" Her joy of the moment mingled with the blessing that was Chaz.

"Yes, that is what you are to me." He reached for her hand. They turned down her street and saw the *casa* that awaited them. Chaz smiled, happy to look at the place he thought of as *Casa de Naomi*, the House of Blessing.

Gifts of Love

"Oh, *la casa* needs some attention. Why did you not tell me?"

Chaz squeezed her hand and smiled. "*Amor,* because this is your home, I have always seen it as a thing of beauty. After all, the one who lives within its walls cares for and loves all who cross her path."

"I know that you love me, but look at the shingles, the front door, and the porch. They all need repair."

"These things can be taken care of. Do not worry. Because the property across the street fronts on this and the main street, I plan to buy it, restore its exterior, and build out office space for my charity. While the workers are there, I will have them fix whatever you want. Perhaps you would like to have a new *casa*. My workers are at your disposal. What is your pleasure, my beloved? Tell me what you want and I will make it happen."

"You have made arrangements to buy the place?"

"I hoped to do so. However, I have been unable to find the owner. No one knows who has the deed to the place. From the looks of it, no one has lived there for many years. Do you know who owns the property?"

"Yes, you do."

"I own this property? How is it possible that I own this place since I have not bought it?"

"It is all legal, my husband. One of the Tías bought the place many years ago in case one of us should marry. She knew that a man around the house all day was not a good thing, especially with the *niñas* there. When she purchased the place, she reasoned that if one of us married, a man could pursue what men do. She knew that a man should not be forced into a harem of woman, as she supposed a man might look at the situation we Tías are committed to."

"This is wonderful!" Chaz picked Naomi up and caught her to his chest.

"This rundown rubble of a shed that might have once been called a house is wonderful? What, my husband, is so wonderful about this?"

"Do not look with the eye but with the heart. Can you not see it as I do?"

"I do not know how. *Mi mamá* taught me to be practical. In this I find assurance."

"I know this about you, but feeling secure is not a life. It is a mere shadow of what life can be. Come, let me show you." Chaz took her by the hand and led her up the path to the little house. He put his hands to his forehead to block the sun's glare and tried to peer into the front window. Years of dirt obscured his view. He tried to see into one window then another.

Naomi almost laughed when he tried to wipe away the years of grime with the sleeve of his jacket. "Do you really want to see this place?"

Chaz turned toward his bride and smiled. "*Sí,* one should always visit whatever inheritance one has been given."

"Wait here. I will bring you the key."

"Wonderful! And bring back a flashlight."

"I do not have one. Will a candle do?"

"Yes, but hurry before we lose the light."

Naomi hurried across the street and noticed the sky was beginning to color. Though she loved to view sunsets, she kept her thoughts on Chaz and his house. *Everything pales when I compare it to the day I have spent with Chaz,* she thought. Mi esposo *has given me more than a wonderful day. He has given me a sense of myself that I have never felt before. Now I will give him a place for him to be himself, away from the* niñas *and me.*

She hurried through the vestibule, crossed the kitchen's threshold, and smelled something sweet and spicy. Lola stood at the stove where several pots simmered. The teenager looked up and saw Naomi. "I hope you don't mind me cooking. I got hungry, looked for something to eat, and decided to make dinner. I thought you and Chaz would come home hungry. I'm starved, but I'll wait until the two of you are ready for dinner."

"How thoughtful of you, Lola." Naomi pulled out a kitchen drawer, found the key, and picked up a candle and matches. "The food smells good. We will be over in a few minutes. Take some time to freshen up.

When I get back, I will set the table on the patio. Then we can sit down and eat dinner together. Now please excuse me, I must get this key to Chaz. He is waiting at the house across the street."

Chaz fished out a pencil stub stuck in a windowsill, dug into his pockets, and found the receipt from the morning's purchases. He whistled as he walked the property and scribbled notes about the dimensions and condition of his house. By the time Naomi crossed the street, he was beaming. He had already decided it was, as he had suspected, the perfect location for his office.

"Here." Naomi placed the key in the palm of his hand. "This is what you have been waiting for."

Chaz looked her up and down. He allowed his gazed to intensify as he looked at her face with a desire that she had assumed no one would feel for her. "No, you are what I have been waiting for all of my life. This key will allow me to work close to you. I am thankful for the property, because I had thought I would need to find office space far from you and travel time would eat into our lives. But never forget you are more valuable to me than anything I will ever own, be given, or achieve. Naomi, you are my whole life, as I hope I am yours." He bent down and kissed her passionately. Naomi felt her body ignite with pent-up longing. She gazed at her husband, and sighed aware that she did not want her world to return to what it had been before his love and kiss claimed her. *I never want things to be as they were before,* she happily admitted to herself, as she stood encircled by Chaz's loving embrace. Chaz had the odd sensation that somehow, in a fraction of a second, Naomi had changed. He pulled away and looked at her. "What is it, my love? Have I done something to offend you?"

"No … no, just the opposite. You have given me … such joy. Never did I ever allow myself to think that someone would feel this way about me!"

"Then what is the problem, beloved?"

"Well," she blushed, "that kiss!"

"Oh yes! That was a wonderful, marvelous, fabulous kiss." He remembered how her lips felt on his and the feelings that one kiss had evoked within him.

"Yes," Naomi agreed eyes downcast.

"If you agree that it was a fine kiss, why are you withdrawing from me? After all, you kissed me back and with as much fire as when I kissed you!"

"Yes, that is true." Her color deepened. "Do you not remember the day we wed when I allowed you to kiss me lightly, without feeling, so the custom could be upheld?"

"How could I ever forget that at the very moment when we should have experienced *la gran pasion,* which only those who truly love each other can ignite, the kiss felt more like one I would give my old *abuela* when I said good-bye."

"Exactly."

"Exactly what? What are you talking about?"

Naomi gazed at her husband. Her heart in her words, she admitted, "I did not know I was ready to give you all my love in that way."

"*Amorcita,*" Chaz said while he drew her close. "What has made you so fearful of me?"

Naomi's body trembled from the touch of him. "I am not fearful of you but of myself. Always I have been in control of my life and my feelings. Now I have given you the most precious thing I can give, my kiss, which I have saved to give to the one I would love forever. Never have I kissed anyone like this! Never have I loved any one like this. Never will I kiss or love another in this way. This kiss, this love is only for you. I have saved it all of my life. Please treat it as precious and do not let me be dishonored or disgraced."

"Do not worry, beloved." Chaz put the key into the lock and opened the front door. "I will never love or kiss another. This I swear by all the saints as an oath and a promise, which I will never break, for I know it would be a sin to treasure so lightly that, which you have held in trust for me. I promise you will never regret the gift of your love or the seal of its devotion, your kiss." He smiled at his bride, aware that in some strange, beautiful, and inexplicable way what they said meant more than the words the priest had spoken over them. To finalize their marriage ritual, he swept her up in his arms, carried her over the threshold and into the once grand splendor of the parlor of the dilapidated old ruin of a house. While he set his bride down on warped floorboards, he whistled. "This was once a fine home." To help Naomi see the house as he did, Chaz pointed to the dingy but beautiful tiles on the fireplace and the elaborate crown molding. "See, it is a good house." He saw an old ladder, opened it, hurried up its rungs, and extended his hand toward his curious bride. "May I have a light?"

While Naomi struggled to light a candle, she silently prayed, *God, please keep him safe and do not let him hurt himself.*

Chaz reached for the candle she held in her hand. "Naomi, give me the light."

"Chaz, I cannot get the match lit."

"Here, let me help you." He took the match from her and struck it against his belt buckle. It flared. As Naomi brought the candle's wick to it, it lit. They gasped as one small light illuminated portions of the dim, musty room. Chaz blew out the match and tossed it aside. He held the candle high and looked at the ceiling. "This needs to be repaired, and the roof needs to be checked for leaks." Aware that his mind had strayed from his bride, he blew out the candle, climbed down from the ladder, and smiled at Naomi.

"You are happy with this … this rundown old ruin?"

"Yes. I am well pleased. It will be good, and our life together will be good. Wait and see."

"Yes, I will wait and see."

Chaz handed the candle back to Naomi. She grasped it and remembered the lovely aroma of the meal Lola had made. "We must hurry. Lola has made dinner and is waiting for us to join her."

"I told you I do not want to be around the girl. She is trouble."

"Well, she has gone to some trouble to make a lovely meal for us. I promised we would be there soon. After all, what can one meal do to you? You, a man of property, are not afraid of a little one such as she, are you?"

"Just one meal!" Chaz insisted as they walked across the street. "One meal! That is all!"

Naomi squeezed his hand and they mounted the porch steps together. "Yes, my husband." She opened the door, flipped on the light, looked at Chaz, and laughed.

"What is so funny?"

She pointed toward the mirror. "Look!"

Chaz glanced at his image and chuckled. "I looked like a chimney sweep."

"All that poking around the old house has made you happy and filthy. Beloved, go shower."

"But have we not made Lola wait too long already?"

"Do not worry. I will make some iced tea and a salad while you wash up. Then we will eat."

Chaz entered the suite. His gaze lingered on the bed, which he hoped they would share tonight. Aware that Naomi waited for him, he showered, dressed, and combed his hair. Ready to join his wife, he picked up the record and remembered his plans to share the song with Naomi on their wedding night. When he thought about that difficult evening, he was glad he had waited. Because their time away from the *barrio* had brought them closer, and the kiss they shared had sealed Naomi's pledge to him, he knew it was the right time to give her his gift.

He stepped onto the patio, set the record next to the player, spotted Naomi, and heard her call, "We have iced tea out here." She motioned for him to join her on the loveseat. "I have already filled your glass."

He smiled and walked toward her.

Lola smiled at him, then turned toward Naomi. "Excuse me. I will get our dinner on the table."

Naomi nodded at the girl and patted the seat next to her in a wordless invitation to Chaz who joined her. As an afterthought she said, "Lola if you like, I will help you."

"No, you're newlyweds. I fear I've come into your lives at a time when the two of you should be alone. I'll have dinner with you and clean up so that the two of you can have some privacy. I may be young, but I understand about a man and a woman." While she spoke words that she hope would ender her to her sponsor, she tried to catch Chaz's eye.

Before Naomi could respond, Lola had turned toward the kitchen. It seemed that as quickly as she had left, the girl was back with several dishes on a tray, which she placed on the table.

Chaz looked at the table then at his bride. "Before we begin our meal, I have a gift for you."

"A gift for me?" Naomi's voice overflowed with emotion.

"I bought a song for you … for us." He hoped that she would understand what he implied and searched her face. Satisfied, he put the music on and led his bride to the imaginary dance floor. "I believe this song is one that you have never heard. It was popular in the fifties. I selected it for you because it speaks of us. Listen to the words and you will know, beloved, how much I understood about you even though we did not know each other as well as we do now when I selected this gift. Even the things that you had not shared with me, somehow I knew about them."

Naomi smiled and struggled to quiet her racing heart. She wanted to experience the song the way Chaz envisioned she would and took a deep breath to calm herself. She saw Chaz's eyes fill with expectation and worried that she might not have the reaction he wanted. However, as suddenly as they had come, her concerns evaporated. *It feels as if an angel has sent a message to my heart*, she thought as the song filled the garden and she discovered the exquisite beauty of Chaz's love for her while they danced together.

You ask how much I need you

"I did not know how much I needed you until you found me," he said, his breath hot against her skin.

Must I explain? I need you, oh, my darling.

Oh, never let me go, Naomi thought as she smiled up at him.

Like roses need rain,
You ask how long I'll love you.

"What fragrance are you wearing, my beloved?"

I'll tell you true.

"None." She felt him hold her closer and sighed.

Until the twelfth of never,
I'll still be loving you.

"I never thought it would be like this."

Hold me close; never let me go.

Naomi looked at him and her body quivered. "I did not know that anyone could make me feel this way."

"You are trembling. Are you cold?"

"No, it is the nearness of you that makes me tremble." She closed her eyes and realized, *Romance is more than something lonely people make up. Chaz is teaching me this as we dance together, as he speaks his heart to me.* And she loved him even more for it.

Just as Naomi was ready to believe this joy would never end, the music stopped. However, Chaz danced and hummed the tune while they glided to the record player. He started the song again and sang,

"You ask how much I need you, must I explain?" He nuzzled her ear and whispered, "I need you, oh, my darling, like roses need rain. You ask how long I'll love you; I'll tell you true." Naomi loved their dance, but the part she knew she would treasure forever was when Chaz held her so close she felt they were one and said, "Until the twelfth of never, I'll still be loving you." Each word burned into her mind and with each utterance, she knew they would live within her heart forever.

Although a bride, Naomi had never allowed herself to imagine that such a wonderful world could exist. When the music stopped, she floated through the rest of the evening. They sat out until the night deepened. Then they went inside arm in arm. Chaz escorted her to her door, took her in his arms, and kissed her. "Come to me, my beloved. Come to me soon."

They parted.

He walked down the hall.

She watched him go and was about to stop him when he turned and said, "Until the twelfth of never, I'll still be loving you." He entered his suite and closed the door. She stood alone in the hallway. For the first time in her life, she knew that she no longer needed to be alone. *He wants me and adores me. He is waiting for me and is mine by marriage. Why, are you not going to him? You want to,* her heart cried. She was aware of her desire for him, a desire she had tried to deny since the day they had spoken their marriage vows.

The unrelenting shame of her heritage raised its ugly head. Naomi forced herself to turn away from her heart's desire. As she entered her bedroom, she thought of it as a cell of penance because she knew there would never be a time when God would forgive her if she pretended to be other than she was. Tears would not come as she tried to reason with *Adonai* and sort out how she could have what she wanted without revealing who she was. When the hall clock stuck two, she found peace in the realization that she had lived this way all of her life. *Surely, Chaz will not realize that I am not as he is, and even if he does, he loves me and will make allowances for me.* Unable to believe her fantasies could become real, she decided to do as her American *madre* had taught and made a plan. *I will see how Chaz reacts to what I do on Friday, Saturday, and Sunday. If all goes well, I will go to him.* Finally, some semblance of peace restored, she fell asleep.

Preparation

It was Naomi's market day. She dressed, tied her new sunhat under her chin, picked up her carryall, and prayed, Adonai, *help me to fulfill my commitments and let Chaz see me as a wife worthy of his love.* Although she looked forward to visiting the open air market, she hoped to return before Chaz missed her.

Preparation for her Friday night meal and her Sabbath rest had always been the highlight of her week. However, when she stepped onto the porch she realized that this day was different. She wanted Friday night to go well and hoped that Chaz would find it in his heart to affirm his love once he knew about her. Yet she feared he would not and that thought threatened to overtake her joy. She remembered her prayer, hurried along, and heard her *mamá* saying, "This day begins our week, and our joy is to celebrate it as God told us to." Even Naomi's ever-present fear of discovery could not dampen her joy as she wondered how God would answer her request.

She walked by the old church, looked at its towering structure, and reminded herself, *God does not live in buildings, no matter how grand they may appear.* As if on cue, she heard her *mamá* say, "God lives and speaks to us through his feast days. That is why we must honor and keep the Feast of Shabbat. We cannot now keep all of the feasts, but, *mi hija,* my daughter, we must keep this one. It is first among them and the one that brings us back to God every week! Promise me that you will be faithful in this!" She remembered she had answered, "*Sí,* I will try." And her *mamá* had exclaimed, "Do not try; do!" Her bittersweet memory brought a smile to her lips.

When she reached the vendors' stalls they were still setting up, so she stopped by those she always visited before she began her shopping and planned to visit the others when her marketing was done. Since none of them had taken in a *niña* or become involved in her work, she viewed these people as her friends. Because they were the only friends she had who looked at her as if she were just another woman, she enjoyed visiting with them as any shopper would.

Keenly aware that she wanted to return home before Chaz missed her, Naomi looked at the clock across from the baristas, noticed that it was a little before eight, and said her hellos. She scanned the tables, walked to the one selling vegetables, and purchased baby carrots, broccoli, and onions. While the vendor counted out her change, she reminded herself, *Tomorrow night at sundown, I will light the candles. I will say my silent prayer to God as I face east. I will circle my hands around the candles three times, as all the women of our family and faith have always done, and,* she vowed, *I will watch and see how Chaz reacts.*

Hurrying toward the booth where she bought her protein for the main course of her Sabbath meal, she wondered what Chaz would like to eat. *This is the first* Shabbat *meal I will cook for him. I want it to speak of my love for him.* She saw fresh sea bass and thought, *This would be sweet and succulent served cold on Friday night.* She wondered if Chaz would like fish and heard her *mamá* saying, "When it comes to food, men like meat with spice, nothing too fancy, and always something to drink." She smiled for she knew that her memory served her well.

Carmen spotted her, reached under her table, pulled out two packages, and called, "Naomi, I have your beef for you. As always, it is wrapped and priced. There is no need for you to wait at another vendor's table. It is already here as promised!" Afraid that people were watching, Naomi quickened her pace. When she got there the woman whispered, "And it has been butchered by a *kosher* butcher as you requested. Besides, you know it is the best beef in town!"

"Because I will cook my first Sabbath meal for *mi esposo,* I wanted to see what the others have. I want it to be special, so I have tried to select the things that he would like best."

"I heard you were married a few days ago. So I have added, at no extra charge to you, some beef liver." Carman bent over, picked up a small package, and winked. "Organ meat carries the strength of the animal within it. I know that everyone here has prayed to the Blessed Virgin and asked that your husband will be a strong man and that the Madonna will strengthen your union." She handed the packages to

Naomi. "Here, a gift for you and your *esposo*. Think of it as a wedding present." Naomi placed them in her carryall.

"Why do you always order two packages of meat instead of one?"

"*Mi mamá* always insisted we do this in case we needed to feed more people than just our family. I have continued to do as she did." She pulled out her wallet, counted the amount, and handed the bills to Carmen.

Carmen pushed the money away. "No! No money today!" Naomi smiled, put her wallet in her carryall, and turned away. "Go, and may God bless you and give you many fine children!" Carmen called after her. When people turned to see who Carmen had addressed, Naomi felt that she had become a spectacle and hurried away.

The church, with its spires and stained glass windows, came into view. Aware that the shortest route home required her to walk by the church she knew she must take it if she was to return before Chaz missed her. The edifice appeared to overshadow everything else, and memories of early evening twilight on Friday nights in Spain surfaced. She smiled as she saw in her minds eye how her *mamá* would gather her and her sisters together, make sure they were dressed in their very best, walk with them to the church, and have them light their candle. She could almost hear her admonish, "Always remember we use their practice to hide our own. When you light your candle, pray to *El Shadai,* and he who is unseen will hear you even though we are in a place that does not know him."

When she turned the corner and looked at her home, she breathed a sigh of relief. She opened the gate, thought about her mother's faith, and told herself, *I can do this.* However, when she entered the house, she admitted, *I am not as brave as* mi mamá. She forced a smile and walked to the kitchen to make some tea.

Lola stood at the sink and turned when she heard footsteps. "I see that you're back. Chaz looked for you, but you were gone. I suggested he have something to eat while he waited for you to return."

"I forgot to tell him that it is market day. I will go to him now."

"Don't worry. He's busy with the old house across the street. Already there are men over there to see what he wants done. Besides, I told him you'd be back soon. Why not have a cup of tea and relax? I'll fix a lunch for you to take over to him later. If you like, I can make a meal for both of you to share."

"*Sí,* that would be very nice." She took the cup of tea Lola handed her, sat down, sipped it, and relaxed. "Good … very good." She drained the cup and held it up for the teenager to refill. "Sometimes I think of this as liquid energy."

Lola looked at Naomi quizzically but choose to keep her thoughts private as she responded, "*Sí,* I have found this to be so." Hoping to endear herself to her benefactor, she mimicked her vocal patterns while she offered to put some cheese and crackers out for Naomi to nibble. Her offer refused, she turned to unpack Naomi's purchases. "*Señora,* we always had our market day on Saturday. Why do you go so early in the week?"

"That is a custom I learned from *mi mamá.* My mother always said the earlier we go to the market, the better the selection would be. I have always found this to be true. I have even found that it is best if the housework is finished before the weekend begins. That allows me to have some time to rest."

Lola turned toward Naomi. "I have heard it said that there are many in some areas of Spain who believe as you do." She refilled her cup and glared at her sponsor. "Do you believe in the Virgin birth?"

It seemed to Naomi that the teenager's tone conveyed that she was the mistress of the house and Naomi the interloper. *This girl is too inquisitive,* Naomi thought. She smiled and praised God for the Blessed Virgin.

"Good! I was afraid I was in a house with one of *those* people."

God, how many times do I have to pretend that I am not as you have made me to be? Naomi drained her cup and placed it in the sink. "Lola, since I have committed to help you, as I have helped many others in the past, let us get along. We all have our own ways of worshiping God, and we have own habits. We should not look at each other as if we were a fish that needed to be filleted and its bones and scales thrown away. Let us look at each other and see what is good. Can we agree on this?"

Lola frowned. Her mind began to scheme, but she smiled ingratiatingly. "Forgive me for judging you. I regret that I caused you to think that I didn't appreciate all you've done for me. Be at peace. I'll always stand up for you because when there was no one else, you stood up for me."

Naomi turned away. "That is not necessary."

"Oh, one never knows what may become necessary. Life can play tricks on all of us." The teenager waited for a response. When none was given she sauntered out the back door, picked up her magazine, sat down on a chair, and thumbed through its worn pages.

Naomi began to clean the vegetables. A few minutes later, she heard Lola singing the song Chaz had given her. Though the teenager's rendition sounded crass, she found herself unable to ask her to stop. The more she listened, the more the song's message of love seemed tainted. That upset her. She knew that if Chaz heard it, he would have stopped Lola. However, Chaz was not there. And Naomi feared that if she asked Lola to sing the song as it had been sung the night before, the teenager might rebel against her authority.

Forcing herself to think of all she had to do to prepare this first Sabbath meal for Chaz, she poured oil into a pan and heated it. She planned to use one of her mother's favorite recipes, which she knew from heart. While she waited for the oil to heat, she remembered her *mamá* saying, "Some spices create satisfaction or contentment, others create heat." Naomi was aware that her mother's words were true and now more than ever before, she wished she were there. When the sautéing was done, she added the beef and cooked the mixture for ten minutes. Adding a bay leaf, salt, pepper, and cumin, for flavor, she lowered the flame, and let the ingredients cook for five more. She removed the empanada dough and hard-boiled eggs from the refrigerator and began to cut the dough into circles. Each time Naomi cut the circles to just the right size, she remembered how her *mamá* had praised her. It had been a long time since she had heard the words and she usually worked at a snail's pace so she could savor her memories. But that was not the case today as she hurried to finish the task, peeled the hard-boiled eggs, and cut some into small pieces. By the time that was done, her filling was ready, so she spooned a teaspoon on top on each circle, placed a slice of egg on top, added a slice of green olive, and crimped the edges. She placed her main course aside until the oven reached three hundred and fifty degrees and put the additional eggs in the refrigerator. Her mind drifted to all the ways eggs were used for the *Shabbat* meal and the next day when *Torah* laws forbid Jews to cook. She looked at the leftover filling and remembered how her *mamá* had loved it when her *papá* teased, "How is it that the Lord—blessed be He—could create the world in six days, making everything perfect, and you always have leftover filling," as he took a big spoonful and smiled.

She opened the package that contained the liver. *Carmen meant to give me beef liver but handed me chicken instead and wings and thighs as well.* Pleased with this unexpected Sabbath blessing, she cleaned the chicken pieces and livers and placed them on a paper towel to wick the moisture away. The heat in the kitchen and the memory of chopped liver, made with *schmaltz* the way her English friend Rhoda Sternberg had taught her to make when she had traveled with Abuela Sosa, reminded her of how fortunate she had been. Using her friend's recipe, she cut an onion, placed it and the small pieces of chicken skin in the skillet, and covered them with a glass lid. This allowed her to watch everything simmer and see when the mixture turned a golden brown so she could remove the skillet from the stove. She pulled out the slotted spoon, the *schmaltz* jar from the refrigerator, and placed them on the counter. *I never believed I would meet Jewish people who were able to talk about their belief in God and own a Bible without being afraid of reappraisals,* she thought. *What wonderful cooks they were.*

Chaz entered the kitchen. "*Amor,* why have you cooked so much? Have you invited guests?"

"No." She pushed a wayward tendril behind her ear and returned to her task.

"Then why do you cook so many things at once?"

She turned to answer him and smiled. The sunlight from the kitchen window illuminated his rugged good looks, and she was proud that he was hers.

"I do not want to spend time in the kitchen during the weekend, so I do as much as I can on Thursday in preparation. And, of course, now I have an additional reason to not be in the kitchen."

He picked up a big spoonful of her empanada filling and looked at her questioningly.

"I have kept it on a flame, so it is still hot. Better blow on it before you taste it."

"Am I a mere child? Do I not know how to eat?"

"No, indeed you are not! Do you think I would marry someone who could not stand toe to toe with me?"

"Good!" He gulped down the mixture. His face flushed red. "Water!" he croaked.

Naomi filled a glass with water and handed to him. He gulped it down. Once he had regained his normal color, she asked, "How did it taste? Not to spicy, I hope."

"No," Chaz rasped. "It is just as good as my *madre* used to make on the *rancho.*"

"Good." Naomi laughed in spite of herself. "Are you certain it is not too hot?"

"Oh, I like things hot!" He smiled at her.

"I guess you do."

"*Sí*, I do!" Both of them laughed while she turned to her cooking. Chaz nuzzled the back of her neck. "My wife, I like you like this!"

"Good, I like us like this too!"

Lola overheard their discussion and walked into the kitchen. She saw the couple together and feigned surprise. "Naomi, how can I help you?"

When Naomi turned away from Chaz, the teenager saw a look of frustration cross his face.

"Lola… Lola… Lola," Naomi called three times, each time raising her voice.

"Forgive me, Naomi. My mind wandered back to my home."

"I understand. We all have those moments. I have found that I do not have many bouts of homesickness if I keep busy." She pulled out a dust cloth. "Here, dust the furniture and think about what you are doing rather than the family you miss."

"*Claro que sí*. Where should I begin?"

"Start in the living and dining rooms. Do not dust my office or the little bedroom across the hall from here." The girl looked at her questioningly, so Naomi explained, "You will know the room because there is a box inside the door near its lintel."

"After I dust, do you want me to sweep the floor?"

"Only after I tell you how I want that to be done."

"Is there a special way to sweep the floor?"

"There is a special way to do all things."

"What makes the way we do things special?"

"When we do things in love, then they are special. Do you not agree?"

"Perhaps."

Chaz looked at his wife with newfound respect. "Truly, everything done with love is special?"

"Why, yes, my love. Have you not found this to be so?"

Chaz scratched his stubble. He remembered the times when his mother or father had told him that they were going to discipline him.

"Because we love you and want you to grow up to be a fine man." Now a grown man with a sordid past, he had to admit that the hard things his parents tried to teach him, which he eventually learned on the street, would have been a blessing if he had listened to them and done as they asked. He knew that if he had done that, they would have seen him with eyes filled with admiration rather than the low regard they had held him in until the last few years. "You are wise beyond your years. How did you learn so much while being sheltered in this house?"

"Chaz, one does not need to be in the world to understand human nature." She placed her hand in his. "See how my hand fits inside yours? In just this way, goodness, love, and beauty fit inside those who seek to build their lives on the principals in the Bible."

"How does one build his life upon something only the priests understand?"

"Anyone can understand that God is good. He has given us the ability to love each other because that is the way he wants us to live."

"You are speaking foolishness. God wants us to do as the priests direct and not to think too highly of ourselves." When Naomi did not respond, he continued, "This is an unusual discussion. No one knows what God wants or even how to please him without going to the priests. They are our link to God. Everything else is an illusion. Do you not agree, my wife?"

"You are right, of course…" Before she had finished her sentence, her heart warned her, *We may never agree about anything concerning God.*

"Naomi, I am finished with the dusting." Lola entered the kitchen. "Please show me how you would like the house swept."

"Sweep the house from the threshold of the front door to the back door."

"Tía, why am I doing this work in this manner? Both my mother and her mother before her swept in the opposite way. Is there a reason for this?"

"Yes there is," Naomi said. Frustration colored her tone and she knew it. Their continual need to understand why she did everything the way she did caused her to silently admit, *I wish I could tell them that in my mother's casa we never swept out the front door because we had fastened our Mezuzah to its lintel. Since it contained a portion of scripture only someone who wished to disrespect God's word would do such a horrid thing.* Instead, she answered, "Many times I swept the dirt out the threshold just as someone came to call. If you sweep as I ask, this will not happen." While she uttered the words, Naomi was painfully aware that though she was in America, she still needed to answer as all Jews trapped by the Inquisition and forced into Catholicism did.

Lola nodded, took the broom and dustpan into the vestibule, and began to sweep. "I never thought about things as much as you do. I see there is much I can learn from you."

"I do not know much, but I have had time to ponder things within my little world and see how to make this *casa* run smoothly. After all, that is our duty as women. Now hurry or you will be at this task all day."

A few minutes later, Lola walked into the kitchen and saw Naomi simmering something. "What are you doing?"

Naomi jumped at the sound of the girl's voice. "You startled me! I did not hear you come back. Have you finished?"

"Yes." Lola showed her the debris in the dustpan. "Where should I put this?"

"Go out the back door, turn right, and then right again. At the side of the house, you will see a large green trashcan with a tight lid. Put the sweepings in there."

Lola walked out the back door, found the trashcan, and threw the sweepings out. She sauntered back to the porch and smelled something unusual. Since Naomi was cooking, she stepped inside and watched as Naomi used her slotted spoon to strain the thick, honey-colored *schmaltz* into the jar. "

"What are you doing?"

Startled by Lola's question and the teenager's presence in her kitchen, Naomi almost dropped the jar. "Oh … nothing … really." She put the lid on the jar and placed it on the counter.

"I have never seen this done before! What have you made?"

Naomi looked from Lola to the jar and took a deep calming breath. "I rendered chicken fat. It is an odd thing to do, I will admit. But doing this allows me to serve the same dishes we all make. However, those who eat mine notice that they are a different."

"But this is a Jewish custom! You are a *converso!*" Lola shouted. "You are a Jew. *Santos, perdónenme.* The saints forgive me! I am in the house of a Jew!" the teenager cried hysterically.

Naomi squared her slim shoulders and looked into Lola's eyes. "You have been out in the sun too long. *Santa* Sarah, help Lola to not have so many worries about me that I may be able to—"

"To what?" The teenager yelled. "To make me a Jew?"

Chaz rushed into the kitchen. "What is the matter? What has happened?"

Lola pointed an accusing finger at Naomi. "She is a Jew, a *converso!*"

"Lola, what did my wife do that made you so hostile toward her? Nothing except rescue you from immigration. She is a saint. You do not deserve her efforts on your behalf. You need to pack your things now and leave."

"No! She cannot leave! Immigration will pick her up. If my friends find out that I did not do as I pledged, they would not assist me in my work. Lola must stay!"

"How can you have someone stay here who so distrusts you as to label you one who is to be avoided at all costs?"

"What she thinks of me does not matter! Her effect on this work does! I realize she must leave. But we need to have a place for her to go before we send her away."

"That makes sense. Do you know of someone who needs a girl?"

Naomi thought for a moment. "The seamstress who lives down the street has need of a girl. She will be back on Sunday. Until then, Lola will stay in the grandmother's house. I hate to ask it of you, Chaz, but you will have to take some food down to her and leave it at the door."

"Tía Naomi, please, please forgive me. I did not mean what I said! I'm sorry!"

Naomi looked at the girl for what she hoped would be the last time. "Lola, I have never known someone like you, so young, so beautiful, and so fearful. What did I say to cause you to react this way?"

"You prayed to Saint Sarah. Everyone knows she is a saint many *conversos* have taken as theirs because she was the wife of Abraham."

"Lola, this saint's name was chosen for me because my mother had me, her first child, when she was old. She told me she prayed to *Santa* Sarah for God to bless her as he had blessed Sarah in her old age with a child, the child of promise. When God did this for her, she told the Virgin Mary that she would have me select Sarah as my saint's name. I selected this name because *mi mamá* asked me to, with tears in her eyes, as she told me the story of the miracle of my birth. She said I was her gift from God."

"Oh! Forgive me," Lola cried. She threw her arms around Naomi's neck. "I did not know!"

Naomi placed her hands over Lola's and pried them off her. "I can forgive you. I can even try to understand you. But, I cannot have someone here who looks to find the worst in someone who has committed to help her. I do not know what happened that made you this way, but I know that what is going on inside of you, your lack of trust, might—no, I believe—*will* affect my work. Your behavior makes it impossible for you to stay. On Sunday, you will go. I cannot allow you to jeopardize the work even though I believe that you are the neediest *niña* I have brought to this *casa!* It is settled. I will speak with Dora and arrange things."

Lola stared at Naomi.

Chaz placed his hand in the small of his wife's back, glanced at Lola, and pointed to a chair. "Wait there."

Lola glared at him and sat down.

Chaz guided his wife into the living room and settled her in the Queen Anne chair. "Stay here. I will sort this out with Lola." He draped a quilt over her, and noticed that when she looked up at him, her expression seemed pained as if she had become aware that there are things that happen in this world that are hard to face alone. "Do not worry, *querida*." She curled into the softness of the fabric. He watched her eyelids flutter shut and hoped she would drift off to sleep aware that he was concerned for her. He realized she was defenseless when the sordid things of this world confronted her and found himself praying that she understood the many roles he would play in her life. When Chaz saw her body relax, he turned toward the kitchen and Lola.

Naomi felt him move and mumbled, "I have something important to tell you."

"I will be but a few moments, my love. Let me deal with the girl then I will come back, all right?"

"*Sí.*"

Chaz entered the kitchen and poured a cup of coffee. "I do not know what game you are playing between my wife and me, but it is over! You have disrupted our lives. If you speak of your strange ideas, you could undo the work Naomi and many women before her pledged to continue." He tilted a chair over on one leg, rotated the back to face the girl, sat down, and looked at her.

"Do I frighten you so much that you need to place the back of the kitchen chair between us?"

"You are not frightening at all! What makes you believe that anyone is interested in or believes what you have to say? My wife is an exceptional woman. Her good deeds and the work she does with the *niñas* speak for her. You? There is no one to speak for you. You were to be sent back to Spain because the family you were with could not control their son's desire for you." Lola's anger flared. She did not utter a word but stared at Chaz with hard eyes. "I see the shock on your face. Did you think we did not know your situation before Naomi went to get you?"

"If she knew, then why did she come for me?"

"Because she made a promise for all of her life to help women who were to be sent away because they came to this country with no one to vouch for them. In her mind, all of you are like her own children. Do you know how much it hurts when children are ungrateful?"

"Yes, I know this. I raised my brother and sister after my mother died. I did not have a childhood. But I made certain they did!"

"And what happened?"

"The usual, I guess."

"What do you mean 'the usual'?"

"For the ones like me, life robs us of our joy. So I took joy from others whenever I could. Those like Naomi have so much. They need to share it with those like me, for I have nothing, less than nothing," she said as tears streamed down her cheeks.

Chaz stared at her.

"Why do you not offer to help me?"

"You are very needy. But what you believe you need, I cannot give. And what would be of benefit for you to know, I believe you will not value."

"Oh, you speak in riddles!" Agitated she stood so fast, she had to grab her chair before it toppled.

Chaz pointed toward the back door. "Go to the grandmother's house. Stay there until I come for you."

Lola walked out of the kitchen, down the path, and around the old tree. She turned back, noticed the reflection of the fountain in Naomi's bedroom windows, and stood on her tiptoes to see if there might be a way for her to enter undetected.

"I did not realize Naomi's bedroom has doors that open onto the patio. It must be lovely in the heat of the summer for them to be opened to let a breeze in." She walked to the hated grandmother's house, entered, slammed the door shut, and screamed, "They will all understand that what I have done is for their own good. When I find what I am looking for, I will unmask that fraud!"

Suddenly aware of the benefits of being alone, she smiled to herself. She found a pad of paper and pencil she had seen, sat down and tried to remember all of the things she had learned over the course of many years of inquiry. When her memories returned, she could almost hear the priest say, "If a Catholic were really a Jew, there would be evidence of their rituals. They would always have a good reason for everything they did and everything they owned. Those reasons seemed to support their claims to be Catholic. But we never see those things in homes that are not inhabited by *conversos!*"

Lola taxed her brain, and the teenager's old habits resurrected themselves. *It is as if I could still hear the voices of my relatives and my teachers* she thought, pleased that she had remembered the way to unmask a Jew. This information had helped her sidestep trouble before, and she knew she was in trouble again. As she thought about how she had manipulated the hatred of her countrymen to her advantage, she told herself, *Here, in America, it is no different. They may think this is a . . . a melting pot, but if someone pretended to be what they are not, I am certain the only thing that would melt was the illusion that this person was somehow as good as a saint!*

It was dawn before Lola finished her list. She read it over and sighed with satisfaction, elated to discover the things that set her off were part of the list the priest had given her. *No one can ferret out a Jew as easily as I can,* she thought. She placed her list and the copy of the Decree of Alhambra, which she had brought from Spain, in her new magazine. *No one would be interested in looking inside this,* she said to herself, proud that her plans were so easy to hide.

Revelation

Chaz leaned over and blew a gentle stream of air onto Naomi's face. "You do not want to sleep the rest of the day away do you?"

She awoke with a start and jumped off the chair. "What time is it?"

He stepped back. "Well, what time is it?"

He looked at his watch. "It is only two o'clock. Why are you upset? There is nowhere we have to be and no plans that need our attention. Come and sit down."

"No! Not now! I have no time. I have much to do, and the day is running out! Why did you let me sleep so long?"

Chaz headed for the front door. "I will leave you alone so that you can get your temper under control and do whatever it is that is so important to you. Call me at Xavier's when you are ready for me to come back. But be warned, I will not live with a woman who cannot handle her emotions. Do we understand each other?" He turned and looked at his wife.

"No, please do not leave! I promise I will not behave this way again. It is just that I have so much to do and now the time has been wasted!"

"We have all the time in the world. Relax." He walked back to where she stood.

"That is the problem. I had to work today and may be a little tomorrow. Then I would have been able to relax and spend time with you. I have always ordered my life in this way. I take Saturday as my quiet day. And of course, on Sunday afternoons, *mis amigas* and their families come for a late lunch. I had planned a special dinner for our first Friday night together. But now …"

Chaz took her heart-shaped face in his hands and kissed her lips. "There is only one thing that counts." He gazed into her eyes.

"Yes, and that is?"

"That is that I will love you until the twelfth of never, remember?"

She smiled and leaned into him. "I remember." Even as she spoke, she pled with God, *I am home in him! Please do not let anyone to take this blessing from me.*

"Love is the best medicine, eh, my sweet?" He kissed her brow. She nodded and picked up the quilt. "That is beautiful. My *madre* had a quilt like that. The wife of the *patron* who employed her gave it to her as a wedding gift. It was handmade, a real treasure." He took hold of her hand, looked at the quilt and then into her eyes. "Much as this one is."

She folded the quilt and put it on the display rack. "The quilt is very lovely. More beautiful still is a love strengthened by difficulties. This is the greatest gift we can give to each other."

"That is true." He took another kiss from her lips. Naomi looked up at him. He sensed her unspoken question and smiled. "Do not look at me so. I told you that I would love you till the twelfth of never. This means at all times, no matter what."

"How can you want to kiss me, let alone speak of love, when you were angry enough to leave?"

"I did not want to leave you. But I had to get away from your behavior. You acted as if you were someone other than yourself. I had to give you a reason to become who you are. I must admit, I admired the fire within you when you were angry. But I did not want it directed at me."

Before she could stop herself, Naomi asked, "Why?"

"That is a question worthy of an answer. First, let me share with you that I would never let you treat me the way I have seen some men treated. I think that when a man puts up with unreasonable outbursts from his wife, he loses his self-respect. And as you know, I understand how that feels."

Naomi eyes filled with tears. "Yes, when I heard of your interest in me, I did not remember you. However, I must tell you that while we courted, I remembered you being on the street. I know that you worked hard to get where you are. I agree that no one should make you feel as you did then. After all, my problems are not yours."

"*Querida* dear, your problems are mine. But I cannot help you when you are so angry that I am unable to ask you questions, which, when answered, will help me help you, *comprendes?*"

"*Sí, comprendo.*" She wrapped her arms around him. "It never occurred to me that you would try to help me."

"Naomi, did not your *padre* help your *madre* in all things?"

"I do not think so. I have tried not to remember those times."

"It sounds to me like things were difficult for you as a child." He kissed the top of her head. "But now the two of us are together, and we will make our own choices, which will show how much we love, care for, and need each other. If we affirm our love in this way, we can do almost anything. If you will trust me and not choose to live in fear." The words and the way Chaz said them caused Naomi to turn away. Chaz placed his hands on her shoulders. "There will be no more hiding. We are married. We will share everything together."

"What do you mean?" she asked with a forced lightheartedness that she feared he would detect.

"I mean we must learn about each other so that we do not hurt the one we love. Do you agree?" He turned her toward him and looked into her eyes. "I could get lost in your eyes."

"They are just like everyone else's."

"No." He drew her close and looked into her azure blue orbs. "Naomi, there is nothing ordinary about you or your eyes. When I look at them it is like looking into the clear water of the Mediterranean."

"What a lovely thing to say."

Wanting to know what was going on at the *casa,* Lola snuck back and stood where no one could see her. *Lucky for me that I grabbed my new magazine to look at,* she thought as she flipped through its pages. The heat of the day beat down upon her, and she got thirsty. She knew there were ice-cold Cokes in the refrigerator, listened for voices, and heard none. It seemed the way was clear, so she snuck in, put her magazine on the counter, and reached for the refrigerator's handle. Before she could grasp it, she heard the couple approach, scurried out the back door, and listened for its loud bang. To her immense relief, it shut noiselessly. Suddenly aware that she had left her magazine behind, Lola worried that they would find it.

Naomi reached the kitchen's threshold and saw the partially prepared meal. "I have so much to do. I do not know where to begin."

Chaz tied a kitchen towel around his waist. "Where should I begin?"

Naomi put the jar of *schmaltz* in the refrigerator, glanced at him, and laughed. "You look, you look…" She hiccupped.

"What is so funny?"

She hiccupped, took a deep breath, and began, "You look like someone who is dressed up for ..." She hiccupped.

"Why do you make fun of me when I am trying to help you?"

When her hiccups had stopped, she said, "Because this is not who you are. I married a man, and that is what I need you to be."

"Then how can I help you?"

Naomi frowned, then smiled. "Go to the market and ask for Flora. She has a daughter who is good with housework. Tell her I need her to come and help me after she gets home from school."

Chaz removed the dishtowel and threw it on the counter. "What is her daughter's name?"

"Flora, of course, but everyone calls her Florita."

Chaz smiled and walked toward the front door. Naomi noticed his determined gait and realized he had undertaken her request as if it were a mission of mercy.

Once the front door had shut, she hurried to the kitchen, and put away the things that had triggered Lola's outburst. She picked up the towel Chaz had thrown on the counter, felt something underneath, pulled the towel aside, saw a magazine, and knew it belonged to Lola. When her fingers bent around the evidence of the girl's uninvited visit, she felt a piece of paper, pulled it out, and eyed the pages. *These papers are old. Why would a girl like Lola be interested in this? I do not want any more surprises from her,* she told herself as she scanned the first page. Her eyes riveted on the words, *The Decree of Alhambra.* It was almost impossible for her to breathe when she realized that the document she held was responsible for the Inquisition. *See what fear has done to us,* she thought. She forced herself to read, "The Royal Edict of the King and Queen of Spain, the Alhambra Decree, 31 March 1492," aloud. As she continued, she found the decree held her attention as few things had. Aware that no one would hear her, she said, "This document changed the lives of all the Jews that lived in Spain or in any place Spain ruled. How could something we have never seen have so much power over us?"

Holding the reality of that time and the penalty for her faith in the God of Abraham, Isaac, and Jacob in her hands, Naomi realized that this was her heritage. She sobbed, pulled herself together, and told herself, *None of their stories ended well. But mine, mine,* she insisted with firm resolve, *will be different!*

After reading most of the text, she surmised, *There is nothing in this document that can harm me.* When she had finally convinced herself that her family was not at risk, her eyes fell on the words that made her people a target. She sat down and read the decree with morbid fascination. Finally needing to hear her thoughts, she said, "These words changed my family's lives forever." She continued down the text and realized, *They caused others more fortunate than us to go to an early grave.*

She knew the work was a fabrication filled with misinformation and the taint of Jewish racism when she read, "The Christians follow the Jewish religious practice such as circumcising their young, giving them books from which they may read their prayers, declaring to them the fasts that they must keep." She thought, *All neighbors share such things.* She turned back to the decree and read, "Joining with them to read and teach them the history of their law, indicating to them the festivals before they occur, advising them of what in them they are to observe." It even covered gifts that the Jewish people had given their neighbors such as teaching them about unleavened bread and meats ritually slaughtered. It pointed to instructing them about the things they must refrain from such as eating and other things in order to observe the law and persuading them as much as they could to hold and observe the Law of Moses. At the end of the document, these words—*The Jewish people had tried to convince the Catholic population that there is no other law or truth except for this one which is found in the Law of Moses*—robbed her of all hope. Naomi placed her head in her hands, moaned, and rocked back and forth as she had seen her *abuelo* do whenever he prayed, hidden in the dark corner of the basement facing east. She crumpled the pages in her hands and cried out to *Adonai,* as she recited, "*Sh'ma Yisra'el Adonai Eloheinu Adonai echad,* Hear, Israel, the Lord is our God, the Lord is One." It was the most comforting prayer she knew, the one she had prayed every Shabbat of her life. Her years of hiding in plain sight overtook her need to hear the words, and she finished the prayer in silence while she wept bitter tears.

"Florita will be here soon," Chaz called.

She stood, turned toward the vestibule, realized he had just opened the door, dashed her tears away, and picked up the decree. "I will be back in a few moments," she called. As she hurried through the back door, she forced herself to breathe normally, tried to collect her thoughts, and struggled to regain her composure. She opened the French doors, entered her bedroom, and thought, *I must not let him see me like this.*

Chaz searched the *casa* for her. Unable to find her, and thinking she had not heard him, he stood in the hallway, and repeated, "Florita will be here soon."

Huddled behind her door, Naomi said, "Good. Now, my hero, go visit Xavier because there will be much to do. *La casa* will be in turmoil. Go visit your friend and come back at dusk."

"How can I go without a good-bye kiss?"

She emerged from her room, turned toward him, and planted her feet firmly apart, certain that he was too far away to notice how her lips trembled or see her tears fall. "Chaz, let me finish my work. Later we will kiss." She pointed toward the front door.

He turned and walked to the vestibule. "If anyone told me that I would allow myself to be thrown out of the house by my bride, I would never have believed them."

Once he was gone, Naomi entered her room, looked at the document, and tried to understand the implication of finding this edict in her kitchen. She turned it over, found the list, and read it as her heartbeat doubled.

- They keep their Sabbath from sunset Friday until sunset Saturday night.
- They will do no work during their Sabbath.
- They clean their homes before their Sabbath.
- They wash themselves before their Sabbath.
- They wear clean clothes on their Sabbath.
- They read and study their holy book and pray to their god.
- They light no lights or fires on their Sabbath except for their special Sabbath candles, which they light during a ritual prayer.
- They do not cook on their Sabbath.
- They sweep their homes from the front to the back door.
- They keep a sacred paper attached to the lintel of their home in a special box made expressly for that purpose.

- They choose their children's saints' names from those found in the Old Testament.

- They will not eat certain foods together such as dairy and meat.

- They will only eat animals butchered according to their law.

No one would understand why I have this, she told herself. She clutched the papers to her chest, hurried to her office, closed and then locked the door as an added precaution. Taking the key from its hiding place, she opened the safe, rolled up the edict and the list, and placed them within its confines. *I hope the removal of this document and list will put a stop to this evil work.* Yet, even as she locked the safe, she wondered, *Why would someone choose to jeopardize all I have pledged to do?* The name *Lola* flashed across her mind, and she realized that she knew more about the teenager than she had ever wanted to. Drained from stress, she entered her bathroom and splashed cool water on her face. *A person has to be shaped from birth or maybe even before then to become involved in such things.* "I never knew anyone like this until now," she muttered.

She walked into the kitchen as the hall clock chimed, waited until the last one struck, and realized, *More than an hour wasted.* Hurrying to the sink, she intended to work like two people. Since the serenity of the garden had always calmed her, she glanced outside, hoping that it would work its magic upon her once more. Instead, she saw the flutter of Lola's scarf as the teenager moved into the shadows of the grandmother's house. *She has probably used those papers to her advantage wherever she has been.*

There was a knock on the front door. "Naomi, I'm here. May I come in?" Florieta asked.

"*Claro que sí,* of course, Florita. I am glad you could come." Naomi assumed an air of confidence she did not feel, walked toward the vestibule, and looked at the willowy young woman who had been a chubby girl the last time she visited.

"My mother said Chaz had come to the store and asked me to help you with some housework, so I brought some music. These will make the time fly. Working with music makes it feel like I'm almost not working at all! Don't you agree?"

"I do not know."

"Haven't you ever played music when you've had to do housework?"

"No. I never thought about making something fun. I have only thought about getting the work done. Could you work with the music playing and still do a good job?"

"Yes! Mother says my work is better when the music is on. I seem to work at double speed!"

"Then let us try. I too could use a little more fun in my life, especially today."

"Good." Florita walked the record player, shuffled through the records, and remembered her mother saying, "Naomi is a sweet woman, and we all love her. As much as she would like to approve of your rock 'n' roll, I do not think you should bring your music into her home. Naomi is still a bride. So take some of my music for her to listen too."

After a moment had passed, Naomi asked, "What is taking so long?"

"These are what my mother told me to bring. She thought you'd like them better than mine."

"These are not yours?"

"No, mother said you'd like hers better." Florita grimaced. She held out the records for Naomi to view. "You pick."

"What am I looking at?"

"Look at the titles and tell me which one you'd like to hear."

"I have never listened to records. You choose."

"All right. What type of songs do you like?"

"I have no idea, Florita. Just pick one so we can get started."

The girl held up a blue and black vinyl record. "How about this one?"

"All right. Put it on and let us begin. Chaz will be home soon, and I want to have the house in order."

Florita placed the record on the player, put the needle on the record, and turned the machine on.

Naomi watched the teenager and thought, *How fortunate for me that Florita could come. She knows what to do. I could leave and be confident that she would clean the* casa *as if I had done it myself. What a blessing this one has turned out be.* She walked into the kitchen and remembered her *mamá* saying, "When we do something to help someone else, what we do becomes a double blessing if we do it in the way they want the work to be done. It blesses the one who receives and the one who gives. I think this pleases God." While Naomi pondered her *mamá's* wisdom, the turntable rotated and the music filled the air as the sound of a male voice interrupted her thoughts.

> *Lady of Spain, I adore you,*
> *Right from the first night I saw you.*

How is it possible that this person sings my heart's desire, she wondered. Her mind raced ahead of the music tugging on the heartstrings of her of unspoken yearning.

> *My heart has been yearning for you.*
> *What else could any heart do?*

These words remind me of things I have willed myself to forget. Now I rejoice in remembering. So enthralled was she that the words became a backdrop for her revelation. She did not consciously hear them again until the singer sang the refrain. Without knowing it, she whispered, "Be happy with what you have and do not long for what is unattainable."

Florita came into the kitchen and overheard her mumbling. "Did you say something?" When Naomi did not answer, she asked, "Do you like the song?"

"Yes."

"If you want, I can get the sheet music for you. When I walked by the music store I saw the score in the window. I can hurry there and come right back."

"I would like that." Naomi pulled out a few dollars from her purse. "How much will it cost?"

"I don't know. I've never bought sheet music before."

Naomi had always been careful with money. However, feeling as she did, she placed a ten-dollar bill in the teenager's hand. "Florita, buy the music and I will get busy here." While the teenager ran her errand, Naomi opened the refrigerator and took out the second package of beef she bought every Thursday. She smiled to herself and hurried to make the filling. When she finally placed her empanadas in the oven to bake, she breathed a sigh of relief, and realized how right she had been to do as her *mamá* had taught her.

It seemed only a short while later when Florita ran into the kitchen gasping for breath, and placed the money and the receipt on the table. "I…ran all…the way there and back. Here." She handed the score to Naomi. "Oh, by the way, Mr. Morales, the shop owner, sends his regards. He told me that although the songs not new, when he heard it playing he bought the sheet music and put in the window knowing you'd be by once you'd heard the song, you being from Spain and all and now in love. Well, he was sure you'd be in to get the music soon."

Always one who like to remain in the shadows, Naomi thought it odd that she found the teenagers bright-eyed chatter endearing. Although she wished she could hug the girl or say something affirming, she chose to keep herself apart, and said a polite, "Thank you." She went to her office and sat down behind her desk. *This room has been a place of revelation for me,* she thought. However, she had never used it for any personal self-discovery. *Perhaps it is a sin to spend time on thoughts like these.* About to chastise herself further for being a self-absorbed fool, her eyes found the words on the page calling her. Settling back into the soft, well-worn leather of her office chair, she read them and realized that until the moment the song's lyrics had ignited her desire, she had not fully understood her need for fulfillment.

I have been waiting for this, she thought while she clutched the sheet music to her chest. However, she believed that what she wanted could never be and told herself, *Chaz believes he has a love for me that will last forever. He thinks he will never leave me no matter what comes. However, I have only given him the shadow of myself. Because of this, I have settled for less than I want. But I have received much more than I deserve.* Tears glistened in her eyes as she looked at the music and thought about the words that had evoked such an emotional response from her. *I will put this where all secrets are safe.* She unlocked the safe and placed the score within. Tears of longing fell as she thought of things that she feared would never be. She wiped them away and placed the music along with an unspoken prayer in the safe. It now held her shame and the fullness of her heart.

She walked to the linen closet, took out fresh bedding, her best tablecloth with its matching napkins, and towels, and set them out for Florita. Upon entering the kitchen, she took down her china and stemware and placed them on a tray. She carried the heavily laden tray into the dining room. When Florita entered the room she asked, "Can you manage the bedding and set up the dining room table? I need finish my preparations for our special Sabbath meal."

"Don't worry. I've done this for you before. This won't take any time at all. Then, if you like, I'll help you prepare your meal."

"Thank you, but I want to do all of the cooking myself."

"Mother told me you'd say that. She said you like your own seasonings and rarely have anyone help you when your making a special meal. She mentioned that on Sunday afternoon you have the store deliver. But since it's your store mother told me that they use your recipes."

"Your mother speaks of me a lot it seems."

"Why not? You're a woman to be emulated."

As a foreign speaker, Naomi was loathed to ask, yet she knew she must so she said, "Emulated ... what does that mean?"

"To be emulated means that you're pointed to as an example for others."

"I do not think I am someone who anyone should point to in this manner." She shuddered at the very idea that others would try to be like her, a woman in hiding.

"Well, my mother says you have a house where anyone could show up and get a meal and probably a bed for the night if they needed one."

"I do what I do because I have grown up to be who God created me to be. You will see, Florita, with a little help from God and some caring people, the same thing will be true of you." As Naomi spoke, she thought about Lola, and her eyes riveted on the grandmother's house. She glanced at her helper. "Florita, there is something I need you to do for me. But I hate to ask you to do this."

Florita saw where Naomi was looking and pointed toward the old building. "Have you hidden something out there?"

"I brought a new niña home from immigration. Chaz took one look at her and said she was no good, but I did not listen to him. Now she seems to want to find out something bad about me. Chaz sent her to the little house out back. He told her to stay there until we send her to Dora's, which we cannot do until Sunday evening since Dora is out of town until then."

"You're helping someone who doesn't appreciate what you're doing? Mother was right. You're a saint!"

Naomi shook her head, took a step back, raised her index finger, and wagged it at Florita. "Do not say these things! It is a sacrilege to think this way! Do you understand?"

"Yes. Please forgive my sudden outburst. I won't say anything like this again."

Naomi looked at Florita, who was sweet and innocent for all her adult behavior. "Forgive me. It is just that *mi mamá* taught me to never treat the things of God lightly."

"Oh, yes! The church is big on that too! I didn't mean to offend you. I know that you're a woman of faith. My mother has often spoken of you as a role model. Whenever I would tell her something was too difficult, she'd tell me about you. She and her friends admire you a lot."

"I am not here to be admired. I am here to make sure that ... that ..." *What should I tell this child?* Naomi asked God. Thinking her prayer foolish, she said, "That this house is put together and my husband has something to eat tonight!" She threw out the unusable batch of empanadas. "Please fix a tray of food and take it down to the grand-mother's house. Leave it on the little table and come back quickly."

"But the flies will get into the food."

"That is true. Place a towel over the dish, knock on the door, and then come back as fast as you can. I do not want you to speak with her because I fear that *tu madre* would hear something she says coming from your mouth! Do you understand?"

"Completely." Florieta opened the refrigerator and pulled out things for the girl's plate. "I will fix something for her to eat for tonight and tomorrow. I will knock on the door and leave as fast as I can. Don't worry. I've handled nasty girls at school."

"I am not worried. I am scared! The things that she says, if you listen to her long enough, they seem to make some sort of sense."

"Don't worry, Naomi. Whatever that girl says about you, everyone will ignore it. We all know you. You're safe here in Spanish Harlem. All who live here have heard of your good deeds."

"No one is good before God!"

"That is so." Florita believed that she was in the presence of some-one who truly understood God and added, "That is why we are lucky. We have forgiveness."

"*Sí, sí* ... lucky." Naomi sighed, a faraway look in her eyes. *But where,* she thought, *is there forgiveness for me?*

She returned her task. The time seemed to fly as she found herself going through the motions while her mind drifted back to her child-hood in Spain. *Yes, it is just* mi mamá *always said, "There is a reason God placed a description of what a wife should be in the book of Proverbs.*" She heard the words of her *mamá* as if it were the first time she had spoken them to her and her sisters, "This has been written so we will know how to do what is best and when to ask for help."

Chaz, has probably never read or thought about the Bible, but I remember mi mamá *made all of us—Deborah, Esther, Rebecca, and me—memorize the words from a page that a* Tía *of ours had been able to save* from *the time of the great difficulty by hiding it in the lining of her wedding dress. Mamá said, "Tía put it there as a preparation for her wedding day, should God choose to bless her in that way. I remember* Mamá *held up the holy writing and said, 'We have only a small piece of what was written in God's book, but we should learn the words and try to live by them so we would walk close to the God of our forefathers.*

Of course, we girls wondered how our mamá *had come to have this important piece of God's Word. When we asked, she refused to tell us. Then at some point, she decided we needed to know more about our history and the situation that had occurred during the terrible times. She shared with us that the Catholic priests had burned all* Jewish Bibles *and other writings. But* Tía Rosa, *a woman fully devoted to God, and the* Jewish *way of life, found a small portion of God's word. Since she never married, she passed the writing down to each new generation of girls. In this way, she had hoped we would know how to please God.*

I remembered what the scripture said, Naomi thought, as she mumbled, "She is clothed with strength and dignity; she can laugh at the days to come. She speaks wisdom, and faithful instruction is on her tongue. She watches over the affairs of her household and does not eat the bread of idleness. Her children arise and call her blessed, her husband also, he praises her. Many women do noble things, but you surpass them all. Charm is deceptive, and beauty is fleeting, but a woman who fears the Lord is to be praised."

Florita returned from the lower patio, heard Naomi mumbling, and asked, "What are you saying?" "If there's something else you want me to do, you need to speak louder."

"I was not speaking to you. I was remembering something *mi mamá* had all of us girls learn when we were young. They are words that I have spoken sometimes. Now that I am married, I find them most useful. I know they will help me understand how to be a good wife."

"Oh! Don't worry about that! From the way your husband acts, you must be a wonderful wife!"

"Why do you say such things?"

"Well, no one I've ever known has had her man come looking for help. If one of the women in the *barrio* needs help, they make do, or ask each other. No, Chaz, he truly loves and cares for you. That must mean you're a good wife!"

"Florita, if it only was as easy as you think!"

"Naomi, sometimes adults complicate what is easy and deny what is difficult. Take Chaz. He loves you, right?"

"Right, but he will love me more when he finds the house in order and a meal ready for him when he comes back, *comprendes?*"

"You sound like my mother."

"Is that so? Maybe it is because we older women have learned a few more things than you young ones!"

Florita turned back to her work in earnest. Soon the preparations were finished. Naomi glanced at the clock. "I did not mean to keep you so long. You will have to hurry home if you are to help *tu madre* with her preparations for dinner as she tells me you always do." She had Florieta open her palm, and placed some singles, and three five-dollar bills in it. I have given you extra this time because I heard that you have been saving for a sweater. Now you will be able to buy it. Just make sure that you give your offering to the church."

Plans Realized, Plans Begun

When Florita opened the door, her mother's outstretched hand greeted her. "But I wanted that sweater," the teenager whined. She put the money into her mother's palm. "You know the orange and green one I showed you the other day."

"I understand." Flora put the money in her purse. "But your sister's *quinceañera* is a week away. How can we think of ourselves when we still have to make the last payment for her dress and incidentals? After all, Florita, you had a beautiful coming out. Now it is your sister's turn."

"When I had my *quinceañera,* you never asked Alicia to give any money toward my party!"

"She was a child and could not help. But you, you are a woman and will be treated and behave as a woman must. I have not raised you to think of yourself but of others. Did you see how our own Tía puts those before her who have no regard for her or the work they benefit from?"

"I know you want me to be like your boss and always think of others, but it is just a sweater!" Florita ran to her bedroom and heard Alicia practicing the "Habanera" she was to sing for her fifteenth birthday. She admitted to herself that since she shared a room with her younger sister a portion of this room was all she had, so she opened the door. Her sister waved to her and returned to her practice. Florita listened and thought, *Why are things difficult for me and easy for you?*

She turned, ran to the back door, hit the screen hard, and stepped onto the patio. The door slammed shut. Flopping down on the hammock, she hid her face in a pillow, and tried to understand why her mother wouldn't let her spend the money she'd earned to buy the sweater.

"Hey, what's up?" Alicia asked.

"Nothing."

She pulled the pillow from her sister's face. "Florita, the way you said that makes me think it must be something."

How is she able to confront me with a tender look and a voice so sweet that I know God chose to bless her rather than me? "Well, if you must know, it's about the sweater I pointed out to you after Mass last week, the one in Blanche's window."

"I know the one! When I saw it, I thought you must have it! I can see in my mind how beautiful you will look when you wear it to my name day party!"

"I earned the money to pay for it. Mother made me give it to her. She needed it for your *quinceañera!*"

"That's awful! Mother shouldn't worry about my party; it'll take care of itself!" She pulled some bills from her pocket and handed them to Florita. "I've saved this. Here you take it."

Florita pushed her sister's hand away. "I can't take this! And don't fib, I know you've saved this money for the Academy of Performing Arts. Our parents have planned for you to become an opera singer! It would be a sin if you weren't able to get the vocal lessons you need. No sweater is worth their being disappointed."

"You, my sister, should have that sweater! I planned that you would wear it with your new needle-worked skirt at my party. Don't you think they would look lovely together? Besides, our parents will agree once I have explained everything."

Florita shook her head.

"Have you ever heard our parents contradict my suggestions?"

Florieta gazed at the bills. "No. They never have. But their plans for you are important! Besides, our parents know you've saved this money. You could get in trouble if you give it to me."

"They won't have a problem about this." Alicia pressed the money into her sister's palm.

Florita put the money in her skirt pocket. "How do you do that?"

"Do what?"

"How do you get them to believe that what you say is what they want to do?"

"Well... it must be because what I say seems right to them."

"I wish I could have some of your magic rub off on me."

"Don't wish that! Right now, I'm their darling daughter. But if I ever went against their wishes, they'd treat me like everyone else."

"You're just saying that to make me feel better."

"You think I'm wrong? Wait and see what happens when I sing my own music at my *quinceañera* instead of the music they've selected. They've made me practice with that old vocal coach, Señora Blanca, for almost a year. I hate the sound of that music! But I have a surprise for them! I've written my own music. When the time comes for me to perform, Cousin Carlos and his band will help me show them that I am out from under their authority at last!"

"What do you mean?"

"I've written to our cousins in Mexico and sent them my music. It's all planned. They've learned the set and will assist me in this big surprise!"

"This doesn't sound like a surprise! It sounds like a disaster! I don't know why you have to use your party to announce your musical plans. Our parents could be humiliated." She stood and wagged her finger at Alicia. "Be careful what you do because you might lose their love, and that would affect you for the rest of your life!"

"But it's no fun always being the good one, the one that all of the plans and sacrifices are made for. You're lucky! You get to grow up normal. I always have to worry about everything. Didn't it occur to you that it's harder to be good and, 'sing like an angel,' as *Mamá* says I do, than it is to be normal? I have to set myself free from their dreams so I can have my own. You understand, don't you?"

"I think you're making a mistake. I know what it's like to be the one who is not admired. I wouldn't wish this on you. But if you choose this for yourself, I'll help you if I can. But before you do anything, I think you should talk to the priest."

"The priest! He's worse than our parents. He told me it's my sacred duty to use this gift to honor God. Can you believe that? I would rather die than be forced to sing only church music! Why, that would be worse than doing as our parents have dictated! I think I wouldn't be able to sing a note if I were trapped into a life of opera and sacred music! Do you know what I mean?"

"I understand. I'll pray for you. I'll also pray for our parents. Alicia, our parents would overlook all of this if your music is good. Is it good?"

"You'll have to wait and see." Alicia turned and walked away.

Florita sat on the stump, which served as a makeshift table for the family for as many years as she could remember. *How can I help my sister realize that this choice might lead to a life she's not prepared to live? There must be someone who can tell me how to help Alicia, but who?* As she ran her finger over a smoothed groove, she remembered La Señora's death. "*Well, what we know about the little mouse? Not a thing,*" her mother had said when she discovered that La Señora had chosen Naomi to take her place. "*Why did she leave us in the care of a foreigner? She knows less than anyone who works at the market! She seldom left that house except to go to the open-air market until* Tía *got ill. How could* Tía *have done such a thing?*" Then one day her mother announced that she had spent time with Naomi and could see that the old *tía* had chosen wisely.

How long has it been since that time … let me see Alicia was five, so it must have been ten years ago. I wonder how it was for Naomi when she came from Spain and a family that loved her to America and lived with mother's boss. I've heard that the old woman was hard to deal with, though everyone held her in high regard. I wonder what caused Naomi to leave her family and come here without anyone to rely on. As Florita pondered Naomi's life, she realized she was the perfect person to speak with about Alicia's situation. *It is as if God whispered her name in my ear,* she said to herself as she entered the kitchen.

Florita's mother smiled at her. "Time to set the table."

"I'll be right there." She ran down the hall and picked up the telephone. "I need to call Naomi. I didn't finish a chore, and she paid me for the work. I need to see if I can go back tonight and finish the job." While she dialed the number, she silently prayed, *Naomi, you must have some wisdom for me.*

"*Bueno,* hello," Chaz said.

Florieta assumed the male voice belong to Naomi's husband and said, "*Señor* Chaz, it's Flora."

"Flora, is there a problem?"

"Nothing's wrong. I just need to speak with Naomi."

Chaz smiled at his wife. "Flora needs to speak with you." He handed her the phone.

She waved it away. "Tell her that since three people are out ill, inventory will not be taken until Monday."

Chaz placed his hand over the receiver. "Wrong Flora, my love."

Naomi took the phone. "Florita, is there a problem?"

"Naomi, when I got home, I realized I didn't finish my work."

"You are mistaken. You did everything just the way I like."

"Naomi, please, I need to come back and talk with you tonight. I have a problem and need some advice."

"Let me see if I can make time for you." Naomi looked at her husband questionly.

Chaz winked and mouthed, "Play along! She smiled, he raise his voice and said, "Naomi, I just remembered Xavier and I have tickets for the ballgame."

"Tonight? But I planed we would spend the evening together."

He silently applauded. "He surprised me with them since we both enjoy the game! It is an *amigo* night. Let us eat early." He nodded toward the phone. "Then I will go to the game." When he saw his bride look at him strangely he whispered, "By the time you have finished your visit with the girl, I will be back."

"Thank you," Naomi whispered. "Chaz will be out. Can you be here at seven? It is a school night and I want to make sure that you get back home at a reasonable time."

"Thank you. I'll be there at seven."

"Oh, one more thing, Florita, do I need to call *tu madre* and make an excuse for you to come here?"

"No ... Naomi. I ... told my mother I had to return and ... and finish the work you paid me for."

"Good. I would not like to lie to your mother for you. I have too much regard for her."

Florita walked to the kitchen, reached into the cupboard, and pulled out the bright Fiestaware dishes that the women of her family had collected. She liked to set the table because the hodgepodge of cobalt blue, paprika red, adobe brown, avocado green, sunflower yellow, and cantaloupe orange made this dinnertime chore enjoyable—but not tonight. The lie she had told, the clandestine meeting she planned weighed heavy on her heart, and her stomach knotted. *This must be what it feels like when one strays from God*, she thought. Since she had acted in a worldly way, she tried to use the world's mindset to rectify her concerns and admonished herself, *You don't really believe in the condemnation of the priests! You're a modern woman!* The more she tried to convince herself that her lie was justified, the worse she felt. She set the table, sat down, laid her head on her arms, and let her long, loose hair cover her face. "Not feeling well?" her mother asked. She pulled Florita's hair from her face and felt her forehead. "You may have a fever. You have been running around so much, what with graduation and your sister's party. And now going back to Naomi's tonight."

Florita turned her face away. "I have to go, but I won't be gone long. Besides I'll feel better after I finish my work."

"All right, you go, but come back as soon as you are done."

"Yes, I will." *I have told so many lies, I must be very far from God now.*

Flora put the food on the table. "Everyone come to the table. Dinner is ready." The family sat down for the evening meal. This was the only time when they were able to eat together. Flora had established the order of things and allowed no variance. Patterns set, Florita sat in the same chair she always had. She received plates of food from her brother, the oldest, and handed them to Alicia, the youngest, as she had since her sister was old enough to sit at the table. She took directions from her mother, as was her custom, and watched her family as they ate their meal and spoke about the joys and cares of their day. Yet, for some strange reason, she felt set apart. *I never believed that I mattered*, she thought as the discussion ebbed and flowed around her. She thought about Alicia's plans and realized, *What I do can make a difference.*

Her mother glanced in her direction. "Still not feeling good?"

"I'm all right...really." She moved her food around her plate.

"I don't think so." Flora reached over and turned her daughter's face toward the light. "Your color is off. I can feel you shaking. I think you have a chill. You're not going out tonight!"

"I've got to go back! If I don't complete the work, Naomi may never ask for me again. Anyway," she fibbed, "it's just my woman's time."

"Is that all?" Flora motioned for Florita to get up from the table. "Here, sit in your father's recliner." She picked up the newspaper he had left scattered on the chair. "I'll get the hot pad." She hurried down the hallway and returned with it in her hand. "This always works." She made Florita as comfortable as possible and smiled at her. "You'll feel better soon."

"Flora, are you coming back to dinner soon?" her father asked. "We are all waiting for you!"

"I am coming right now."

Florita snuggled into her grandmother's afghan, flushed with a feeling self-importance. She tried to think of how she should begin her conversation with Naomi. The more she thought about the situation, the more she realized it was one thing to feel important, another to do something of value for others. Aware that her life had a purpose outside of herself, Florita promised herself and God that the information she shared with Naomi would not be gossip.

When the meal was finished, her mother stood to clear the table and smiled at her. "I think you're feeling better already."

"I'm fine! That old heating pad does the trick every time." She glanced at the clock. "Let me help you clean up before I go." She stood, folded the afghan, and put it back in the place of honor.

"No." Flora nodded to the bowl of chicken soup she had warmed up for daughter. "You sit down and have some of this. It will warm you up."

"Thanks." Florita walked to the table and looked at the bowl of soup. "How did you know I'd like this?"

"Do not be silly!"

"I'm not being silly." She gulped down the soup. "I just want to understand how you knew what I'd like."

"That is a gift God gives to a mother. It is a certain feeling, which lets her understand her newborn *bebé*. That gift stays for always if there is love between the little one and her *mamá*. It stays all their lives. You will find out about this someday. Just wait and see!"

"No! I don't want to have children! I want to do something different with my life!"

"It is always good for a woman to be able to do something to help out ... that is until the babies come. Then hopefully you can stay home. But if not ... not. It always works out. After all, look at me."

"Yes, look at your *madre*. She raised all of you and worked at the market all day," her father said. "She is a wonder!"

Oh, it's impossible! I've live with them all of my life and they still don't understand me! Before she let herself get too worked up, her thoughts returned to the discussion, she would have with Naomi. *How can I ask questions without being nosy?* She remembered her mother had said, "Do not pry into other people's lives; it is impolite." *What should I ask? What do I say?* She had no idea. For when it came to things like this, she had never spoken to anyone outside of her family before. *I don't know how to do this,* she admitted to herself. Then again, she reasoned, *Maybe the problem is all the lies I've told. No. I think its fear. If Naomi tells my mother why I went to her house, my parents will be angry!* Just the thought of her parents being upset with her made Florita sick to her stomach. Since she did not want her mother to see that she was upset, she hurried to finish her soup. Then she laid her head on her arms.

Her brother Desi bumped her elbow. "Excuse me."

She looked up.

He bent over and whispered, "Alicia told you her plan, didn't she?"

"Yes."

"Don't worry. We'll think of something."

"I hope so." She looked at the clock. "It's almost seven. I better hurry or I'll be late." She grabbed her purse and sweater and hurried toward the door.

"Wait," her mother said. Florita turned back. Her mother motioned for her to come into the kitchen, took hold of her face, and turned it to the light. "I think you are growing up, my daughter. You are becoming responsible and thoughtful. These are traits I admire."

"Thank you, Mother."

Her mother handed her a plate of sweets. "Bring these to Naomi. I made them for her just the way she likes. Naomi says that my desserts are the best she has had since she left Spain!"

"And she is right," her father said. "After all, you learned from my *madre*, who learned from hers!"

Flora silenced her husband with one of her looks. "Give her this with my thanks for letting you come back to complete your work."

Naomi's *casa* was only two blocks away, but it seemed to Florita that the walk took forever. *How do I do this, God?* she asked. She did not expect an answer and received none. With each step, her concerns mounted. She tipped the plate but did not notice until she rounded the corner of the first block and looked down. Aware that one of the cakes was about to fall off, she stopped, uncovered the dish, and used the tip of her finger to nudge it into place. She anchored it firmly with the plastic wrap and thought of the women she knew who had something unique about them that her mother and Naomi called a *blessing.* For her mother it was her ability to make the most wonderful desserts. She was known to bring them to special people and those who were down and needed, as her mother would say, "A sweet moment in their life to remind them that given enough time, things always get better." For Naomi it was her life of service to Las Niñas. Each woman made a difference. *I wonder what God wants me to do, that is if God will continue to be interested in the life of a sinner like me.*

She turned the corner, found herself back on Naomi's street, walked past three houses, and noticed that the twilight was deepening. She entered the yard, closed the gate, walked up the steps, and headed for the front door. As she raised her hand to knock, Naomi said, "Florita, sit in La Señora's chair." Florita looked to the place where her voice had come from. Naomi sat on an old wooden swing, almost swallowed up by the night. She turned toward the chair and realized it was a seat of great honor. Her mother had told her, "Never sit in it unless instructed to do so." The teenager had heard it rumored that Naomi never sat in the chair. She thought she had misunderstood and turned back to look at Naomi. The porch light shed just enough light to allow the teenager to see the woman's concerned countenance. Although Naomi's gaze seemed to affirm her, Florita knew she had lied and assumed that this was a test. She shook her head at the chair, which was elaborately woven and massive. "I'll pull up one of the smaller chairs over." She turned toward the Adirondack set.

"Florita, you are wasting valuable time! Sit where I have told you to!"

"Yes, Naomi." Florita perched herself uncomfortably on the edge of the seat.

"Now, what can I do for you?"

"Yes…well…well…you see, Naomi, I need some help with a problem. I thought you'd have some wisdom for me to share with my sister." *There, it's out. I've done it. It wasn't that bad after all.*

Naomi smiled. Her eyes grew soft with understanding. "What sort of problem does Alicia have that sends you out at night and causes you to tell *tu madre* a lie?"

"Oh…she's headed for a big problem with our parents and she doesn't care."

"What are you talking about?"

"I…don't think I…can do this. I've lied to God, my mother, and now I think I'm about to lose my courage."

"Courage is a very good thing to have. Are you motivated by a problem that makes you think you need courage?"

"I guess so. I mean, I think coming here to see you about family matters takes courage, don't you?"

"That depends." Naomi handed Florita a glass of iced tea. "Who are you being courageous for and why?"

"It's for my sister!"

"I understand. Your sister has a problem that you want to fix, correct?"

"Yes! You understand. That's it exactly!"

"Florita, does Alicia know she has a problem?"

"Of course not!"

"Then are you not being a little premature?"

"If I wait until she does what she's planned, things will change for her and not in a good way."

Naomi took a sip of tea and looked at the teenager. *I thought I noticed a change in her today but believed it was just the beginning. I was wrong. She is already an adult.*

"Tell me, Florita, what has Alicia done?"

"She hasn't done anything yet. But she told me that she's going to use her coming out party to declare her independence."

"How will she do that?"

"She'll sing her own music, not opera or holy music but the stuff we hear on the rock 'n' roll stations."

"I see." Naomi tried to imagine how the Santoro family would react. She could still hear Flora gush, "I have a daughter who sings like the angels! We are truly blessed by God!"

"I understand your dilemma." She stood and lit the candles on the porch. Florita saw her move from candle to candle and smiled as the once-foreboding porch was illuminated. "This is a private matter, one that is very close to your heart." Naomi sat down. "I will not tell anyone what we talked about or why. Does this sound good to you, Florita?"

"Yes. Thank you. I've been so worried about Alicia and the lies I've told. I'm afraid I've put my mortal soul in danger."

"I am not a priest, but I am certain the good padre will rebuke you and give you a way to restore your relationship with the church, yes?"

"Yes. I've been so nervous. I don't know where to begin or what to say."

"Well, what are you planning to do?"

"I don't know. That's why I asked to speak with you. Alicia thinks that performing her own music will be a declaration of her independence."

"But you do not think this is a good idea?"

"A good idea? How is this a good idea?"

"You are very worried about your sister."

"You know how it is. You grow up with someone. You think you don't care about them. At times they're a nuisance. Then you hear that they plan to do something foolish, and you know if they go through with their plan, their life will be changed forever—and not in a good way. What would you do?"

"I do not know. I have never been in your situation."

"But I have come to you for answers! I want to help my sister make a good life, but I don't know what to say."

"I understand." Naomi looked into the distance. Florita waited for her to continue, but Naomi was lost in her own thoughts. Then she heard the sweet, melodious whistling sounds of the resident bluebird, remembered the first time she had heard him sing, and smiled. She thought back to her life before Spanish Harlem. "Do you want to know how I came to be here?"

"Yes. I'd like to know." Florita took the plastic wrap off the sweets and offered them to Naomi. "Everyone says you don't talk about these things. Many want to hear your story, why tell it to me?"

Naomi picked up a sweet and took a bite. "It never seemed very important before." She took another bite. "Your mother sent these delicacies to me to make amends for you, yes?"

"Yes."

"I think you should also have one. You can taste the sweetness on your tongue as we speak of difficult things. It is always good for words of truth to be sweet upon the tongue. Then, when we have another sweet, we remember what we have heard and understand more about our choices and responsibilities."

"Oh, I see." The girl selected one and devoured half of it with her first bite.

"Have you not eaten tonight?"

"I was too upset to eat much. Now I'm hungry, but that doesn't matter. What matters is to find out how to help Alicia."

"I understand that you are very worried and wish all these things would go away."

"How were you able to understand that I was here for Alicia's good and not as sort of a busybody big sister?"

"I have eyes, and they see that you are in pain. I have ears, and they hear that you are worried. Never have I known you to keep things from *tu madre*, so I think this is serious. If not, I would not have told you to come after you lied, *comprendes?*"

"*Sí*, I understand."

"So it seems you care enough to put Alicia before yourself at all costs?"

"At this moment that's true."

"And if you do this, this, whatever you think you must do, when will you give your sister back her life?"

"I'm not trying to take control of her life!"

"Really? Then what would you call it?"

"Caring, I would call it caring for Alicia."

"Let us suppose that someone wanted to care for you in this way. How would you feel?"

"Well … I guess I'd be upset."

"You are right. Anyone would be upset if someone else tried to be in charge of their life. I learned a long time ago that most people care more about what you can do for them than what you think they should do, *comprendes?*"

Florita frowned. "Yes, that's true."

"I do not enjoy being with people who talk about how others should live their lives. Rather, I treasure the ability to live my life in an authentic way. Do you understand what I mean?"

"Authentic? What does this mean to me and Alicia?"

"Nothing or everything. It depends on what you choose for it to mean."

"Now you are talking in riddles and treating me like a child."

"I know that you are not a child. A child would not be worried about her sister." Naomi refilled Florita's glass. "You are a young woman, raised in a home where there is love enough for all of you. Because of that, you have learned to return that love. That is a wonderful legacy."

"I guess so."

"Florita, in this you and your sister are alike. Neither of you values what you have. However, if you had lived where I did and felt blamed for every bad thing that happened to your family, you would know how much your parents love you. You would ask them for help. But I know this is not what you want to hear." Naomi weighed the girl's need and what she hoped would help. "When I look back on my life and the lives of those who have been helped by Las Niñas, I have learned a few things. I will share them with you since they are the only wisdom I have. No one can live the life of another. No one can understand the thoughts of another. People who seem gentle on the outside are often strong inside. Those who demand things from us are frightened. They believe no one cares about them. To help your sister, you must allow her to be herself. If she has to have a hard time to learn a good lesson, it will help her grow strong. Your family will be able to deal with this and move on because in your home there is love. With love, all things are possible. Without love, nothing of value ever matures. If you step into this situation that has you so worried, would you not rob your sister of learning an important lesson?"

Florieta frowned and thought a moment. "Now that you've put it that way, yes, I guess I would. It seems that I need to let my sister live her own life, even if it means facing hardships."

"You can see that now. Let me ask you another question. If your sister always did what you though was best, she might never grow up and become her own person. Do you plan to take care of her for the rest of her life?"

"No! Absolutely not!"

"Good." Naomi rose from the swing. "Then I think you know what to do."

Florita placed her glass on the tray. "Nothing. There's nothing for me to do. Alicia needs to make her own choices and learn from them. Is that what you are trying to tell me?"

"That is it exactly, Florita. Now if you think about all you have put yourself through since Alicia told you her plan, what do you think life is about?"

Naomi stood, walked to the door, and waited. The teenager hurried to open the door. "I don't know. Maybe it's that life is messy."

"That's a good way to look at life. It is messy, especially for those who try to keep it all neatly tied up like a gift." Seeing Florita's look of dismay, Naomi stopped to collect her thoughts and continued, "Life is a gift." She motioned for the girl to follow her through the vestibule. "What we have been given is a true and precious gift when we give it away to someone or invest it in something other than ourselves."

"That's what I was trying to do ... to be like you."

"Florita, I have never reached out to help anyone until they needed help. I think it best to realize that no one will appreciate you if you step into their life and correct something for them that they believe works."

"But I want to be helpful."

"Is this what you really desire?"

"Yes. I've felt this way all my life."

Naomi flipped on the light, put the tray down on the sideboard, and turned back to look into the teenagers eyes. "*Mi mamá* taught that the eyes are the mirror to the soul." She retrieved the tray, headed to the kitchen, and motioned for Florita to come with her. "Are you sure about this desire of yours?"

"It's been my motivation for as long as I can remember."

Naomi indicated to Florita that she wanted her to walk beside her. "Do you know what motivates me?"

"No, but I'd like to."

"What I really like to do is bless others. Is that why you wanted to speak with me?"

Florita looked at Naomi in joyful amazement. "It's as if you heard my heart!"

"That is often the case as one grows older. It will happen to you someday, I suppose." They walked through the front rooms and reached the kitchen. "Come in." She motioned for Florita to join her at the window and pointed to the backyard. "Do you see what is out there?"

"I can't see anything! It's dark outside."

"That is true. Just as we cannot see what is hidden by the darkness, we cannot see what will happen in the future, no matter our feelings or our fears." Florita thought this was a rebuke. Her face flamed crimson. Yet for some inexplicable reason, she turned toward Naomi. Naomi seemed not to notice the teenager discomfort, as she put her arm on Florita's shoulder as one would a daughter. "You, *amiga mía,* should come to my *amiga* group. We gather here every Sunday at about two in the afternoon. This is a small group of my closest friends. All of us are just like you, women who care about others and try to make a difference."

"I thought you were going to say I should try to become a blessing."

Naomi waited for Florita to say more, but the teenager opened her mouth as if to speak, closed it again, and fidgeted. While Naomi watched the teenager, she remembered how on edge she had been when she first came to the *casa.* The fleeting memory of Madre Vida signaling for her to say something more showed her what to do. She mirrored that behavior and Florita relaxed. The teenager smiled at her, took a deep breath, and admitted, "I've always wanted to be invited."

"I see you have heard about us, *sí*?"

"Everyone speaks of your group, but why would you want me to be part of it? I'm still in high school."

"*Mi amiga*, what you have to offer, and who you are, is unique." She walked Florita to the front door. "You do not need to be a high school graduate for me to see what will come to others through you. Besides, over the years many have come, both those who are growing and those who have needed other women to support them in their choices. Tell your mother I insist that you come! Will you do this for me?"

Florita walked home with a new firmness in her bearing. She could still hear Naomi ask, "Will you do this for me?" *Of course, I should have said yes right away,* Florita thought.

When she looked at the front door of her home, she noticed that her mother stood at the threshold watching for her. She glided past her and into the living room.

"What has happened to you? You left here so pale that we worried for you. Now you enter our home as if it were a palace and you a royal princess."

Florita turned and laid her head on the nape of her mother's neck. "Oh, Mother, Naomi is so wonderful."

"It seems that cleaning Naomi's *casa* has become an event in your life."

"Not at all. It's just that while I was there we talked a little about life and choices, and she invited me to her *amiga* group!"

"You mean the group that meets on Sunday afternoons?"

"Yes! She told me to tell you that *she insists that I come.*"

"I told you that you were growing up." Her smile left no doubt as to her approval. "How wonderful for you to have her for your mentor. All the girls who attend Naomi's group turn out to be such wonderful people. Just think of it, Naomi's *amiga* group!" Flora exclaimed. "Dominic, *esposo mia*, come and hear the good news!"

He rushed to the living room. "What is all the commotion about?"

"Nothing," Flora winked at Florita. "It's just that we have good news!"

"Well, tell me the news!"

"Florita has been invited to join Naomi's *amiga* group!"

Florita's father sat down on the nearest chair, dumbfounded.

"What is your problem, old man?"

"No problem. It's just that all our little ones are growing up. Soon it will only be the two of us again just like in the beginning."

"Stop thinking about yourself! Our beautiful Florita has been invited to become a part of the *Blessings Club!*"

"Mother, the name of the group is *Las Amigas.*"

"You know the name of the club. I know that the women in this club bless others wherever they go."

"Just think of the honor Florita has brought to our home." Her father took the corner of his old robe and wiped his tears. "That Naomi would choose to take an interest in our daughter speaks highly of her." He stood, walked to Florita, placed his hands on her head, and, to the best of his ability, gave her a blessing as he had seen the priest do.

Desi hurried into the room. "The *Jai alai* match is going to start."

Dominic glared at his son. "Do you not see something important is going on here?"

"But, Father, last time I didn't tell you the match was on and you were upset with me. This time I tell you the match is about to start and you're upset with me."

"And your point is?"

"My point is, I can't figure you out!" When his father did not respond, he stormed out of the room.

Flora nodded her head in the direction of her retreating son and touched Dominic's shoulder. "*Esposo mío,* he is hurt. Go speak with him."

"No. This moment belongs to Florita. No match or childish attempt to get my attention will work. This is Florita's time."

Dominic walked to the map that had hung behind the living room couch for as long as anyone could remember. "Come, Florita, look at the world with me." Florita knew that if she joined her father, her triumph would disappear as they studied the map together. Dominic pointed to indicate where she should stand.

Here we go again, she thought. "I don't want to play this game tonight, Father."

He gazed at the map. "Come, my chosen one." He waved his hand toward her, beckoning her to join him.

"*Papá, no puedo.* I can't. I have homework to do."

Her father looked at her, turned towards the map, and waved his forearm from the far left to the far right. "See all of this."

"I see the map. It's just where it has always been. And here we are looking at it, just as we always have."

"No. Not so." Dominic nodded to his wife and smiled. "Flora, *esposa mia,* please go get the box."

Her mother's smile matched her father's, and Florita would later admit it was then that she suspected they were up to something. She did not know for sure, however, until her mother returned with a small, ornate box. Flora handed it to her husband. He placed it in his daughter's right hand. "This, my sweet daughter, is for you."

Florita looked at her parents, then at the tiny jewel of a box. "And here is the key." Her mother handed her a small charm. Florita sat down on the couch. Her eyes traveled from the key, to the box, and then to her parents.

"Go ahead, open your surprise," her father insisted.

"Yes, it is time for you to know we have not only thought of Desi and Alicia but also of you!"

"This is a night full of surprises." Florita gulped back happy tears.

"Come, Papá, let her open this by herself."

"Yes, you are right, Flora." They turned to go.

"Don't go. Come and sit down by me. If I am going to open a gift from you, then I want you to be here."

"Well then open your gift!" They sat down on the couch, one on either side of her.

"I will. But right now I want to hold this in my hands." She looked at the proof that her parents had thought about and planned something special just for her. "Do you understand?"

"Of course I do," her mother said.

"You do?" her father asked. "What do you understand?"

"Well, I am not really certain. But I want to understand."

They looked at Florita who gulped back happy tears. "I didn't think you'd made plans for me. I'm surprised." She placed the key into the lock, opened the box, and saw a piece of paper with her mother's handwriting on it. She opened and scanned the noted.

Her mother smiled at her. "Please read the note out loud for all of us to hear."

Florita looked at the two of them and sniffled. "Our beloved daughter, we know you have a special gift of caring for others." Her voice caught in her throat, and tears threatened to fall, but she continued, "Because of this gift, we do not know where life will take you. We have set aside money every month since we realized you might need to leave us. We want you to know that wherever you are to go in the world, God will guide you, and we will try to provide for you."

"I thought Naomi was the only one who understood me and only because of our talk tonight."

"Do you think we could live with you your whole life and not see what a caring person you are?" her mother asked.

Florita looked at the two of them with tears on her face. "Now I know that you understood my heart even before I did and always approved of me, I've everything I ever wanted." She folded the note and placed it back in the little box.

"But there is more!" her father insisted.

"There is? What more could there be?"

"Turn the box over," her mother said.

She turned the box over and saw a small black book in a plastic cover attached to the bottom. The word on the jacket said *Passbook*. Embossed below it was the name of the local bank. "But, Papá, you told us banks were not for us."

"That is true. Banks are for those who make plans, long-range plans. And we have been making those plans for you ever since you were in the third grade."

"Why then? What happened in the third grade?"

Her mother chuckled. "*Ay, mi hija,* do you not remember how upset you were when your teacher yelled at another student for no reason?"

"Yes, I do. I still believe it's important for people to stick up for each other!"

"That is what you told me that day when you showed up at the market. I was in the middle of my shift. But you insisted I go back to the school with you and speak with your teacher. I could not leave and told you so. Do you remember what you did?"

"I don't, besides that was a long time ago."

"You sat down on the floor by my feet and told me that if I did not fix this, you would not go to school. And you, my daughter, have always loved school. That was the moment we found out what was important to you."

"Well, it worked, didn't it?"

"Yes. What you did made a difference in that girl's life and possibly in the lives of many of the students who had Señora Fernández as their teacher. That very day we opened your savings account."

"Go ahead," they said. "Take out your passbook!" Florita pulled the book from its plastic sleeve. By the looks of it, they had visited the bank often.

"Open it and see what we have set aside for you!" her father exclaimed.

She stared at the passbook, remembered the times she thought herself of no importance to her parents, looked at them, and uttered a heartfelt, "I'm sorry."

"Sorry! What do you have to be sorry about?"

"I always felt I was an afterthought. I never did anything out of the ordinary. You never made a fuss over me. You know Desi has lots of friends. And Alicia, she sings like an angel. Me? There never seemed to be anything special about me."

Her mother moved closer to her. "You have been our secret joy."

"Really?" She looked at her mother, then at her father.

"What your *mamá* says is right. You see, there are times when we can help nurture a gift. Like your sister, Alicia's singing. At other times, talents are helped along through activities. Like Desi's sports. But yours had to be nurtured by God and would bloom when and where he chose."

"Dominic, you made this sound complicated." Flora took her daughter's soft hands in her large calloused ones. "*Mi hija*, only God can grow a tender heart. All your father and I could do was watch, wait, and prepare for you to bloom."

"It is as your mother has explained! And there was one thing more that we did, remember, Flora?"

"Yes, I remember."

"What did you do?"

"I told you about Naomi. We decided that she would be a good person for you to know. I managed to have her ask you to help her over the years in the hopes that something like this would happen."

Florita smiled and hugged her parents. "Thanks for knowing me before I knew myself." She looked at the passbook and realized that she did not care if there was only one dollar in her account. The fact that her parents had cared enough to make plans for her was all she had ever wanted. She smiled and opened it to the first page.

"No, go to the back of the book," her father said enthusiastically.

"I will." She wondered how many times they had gone to the bank and turned to the last page. "This is enough to buy a car! How did you do this?"

"If you look at this last year's entries, you will see there are some large amounts," her mother said. "Many in the neighborhood watched your nurturing ways. They knew that this was your last year of high school, thought you might be called away, and because of that, some of them gave us money to keep for you."

Florita looked at the large sums deposited to her account and began to cry. "But none of them can afford to do this!"

"Daughter, these people understand more than you know. Someone with a gift like yours may be called to go to other places. Just as Naomi came to us, you might need to leave. Everyone has come together to increase the amount we were able to set aside for you. They will never tell you who they are. The money was given to help you go where God calls you. *Comprendes, mi hija?*"

"Yes, I understand." Florita's tears fell unchecked.

Dominic stood, reached in his pocket, handed his hanky to his daughter, and clapped his hands together. "Now you understand about the map?"

"Yes," Florita said through her tears. She stood next to him. He smiled and nodded at her. They turned and looked at the old map. "You were trying to prepare me for the world outside Spanish Harlem, right?"

"Florita, we do not know where God will call you, but this is always your home," her mother said. She stood and placed a kiss on her temple. "*Comprendes?*"

"*Sí, comprendo.* Now I understand many things." Florita unfolded her father's handkerchief and blew her nose amid tears of joy.

"Now, Florita, do not share this with anyone. Not even your brother or sister. This has been a discussion between adults. Children do not always need to know what adults plan, understand?"

"I understand and I'll say nothing."

Dominic noticed the time, sprinted across the dining room, and turned into the hall. "Desi, how is it going with the match?"

Her mother headed to the kitchen, turned, and faced Florita with tears in her eyes. "I know that you will always do what is right."

Startled by her mother's words of affirmation, the teenager thought about the money she had taken from her sister, walked to her bedroom and gave the money back. "I have found something that means more to me than money can buy." She hugged the girl, smiled, and nodded toward the record player. "Perhaps you should practice some more."

Naomi watched Florita until the teenager turned the corner. Then she stepped across the threshold, closed and locked the door. She walked through the living room and entered the narrow hallway that led to her office. As she entered, she remembered how she felt the first time she entered the room after Madre Vida had died. She sat down, picked up the red volume that she kept close at hand, and opened it. Before she picked up her pen, she thought about all that had transpired. When she began writing, Naomi knew this entry would be different from any she had written because she had never invited a teenager to join her *amiga* group. Once she was done, she reread her entry.

She pulled out a new frame with a matching canvas and searched her flower files. *The entire community would think it odd, but I continue to view these women as* Madre Vida *viewed me. They are buds that unfold and become beautiful flowers.* Naomi thought of Florita while she flipped through the pictures. She envisioned a purple thistle and was delighted to find it amongst the others of the same color. *Florita, this is you.* She examined the lovely photo. *But there is more to you than this,* she thought and resumed her search. She found a cluster of delicate yellow tea roses and a white Shasta Daisy with a large black center. As was her custom, she placed the photos side by side and reviewed them.

Pleased with her selection, Naomi believed her search for the essence of the girl realized. She worked with great skill and dexterity as she cut around the flowers and placed them on the canvas in an artful arrangement. *There … a portrait of Florita the woman, the girl has already become.* She applied the bonding agent, and watched, as the paper and fabric became one. Taking out a purple card that coordinated with the largest flower in Florita's botanical arrangement, she placed it on her desk, and stopped for a moment to collect her thoughts. *This time I have someone more like me than all the others,* she finally admitted. Pen in hand, Naomi wrote:

Florita Santoro
Commitment Date: June 5, 1967
Completion Date: _____

She placed her finished project in its fame, walked to her gallery, and hung the new floral piece. She sat down, looked at the portrait which hung in the position of honor, and thought, *Florita, you have a caring heart. None of the others has spoken as you have. You are the one who will take over this work.* A sigh of relief escaped Naomi's lips. *I wonder why Adonai brings these women to me,* she thought while she put away the materials she had used. *I have no great wisdom to give. In many ways, I have lived a sheltered and restricted life.* She reminded herself about her fledging Tía and prayed, *Thank you, Adonai, for Florita.* She smiled and turned out the light.

She knew Chaz would return home soon, decided to make a snack for him, and walked toward the kitchen. Her senses prickled. She stopped short and listened, frozen with apprehension. She heard an odd sound. *A sudden wind must have come up for the trees to make that noise.* Still feeling that something seemed amiss, she entered the kitchen, grabbed the heavy iron skillet she kept on the stove, and flipped on the light.

Startled, Lola bolted for the door. Naomi dropped the pan, grabbed the kitchen broom, wedged it between the counter and door, blocking Lola's only route of escape. "You were told to stay away from the house. Why are you here?"

"Oh…well…I was lonely…I thought, I would come and listen to the radio. There were no lights on for quite a while. So I thought you were out."

"Really? Do you go into places where you are not wanted when you think people are out?"

Lola looked at the floor. "Forgive me. I know I was wrong, but it's awful being cooped up like I've been all day."

"Lola, go back to the grandmother's house and stay there! If Chaz comes back and finds you here, he will put you out even though it is dark! Believe me, you are here only because you agreed to stay where he put you until we could move you on Sunday!"

The Promise

Chaz entered the house and called, "Naomi, the moon is lovely. Come let me show it to you."

"Leave now," Naomi whispered. She walked into the dining room, kissed Chaz, heard the back door close, and hoped that he had not noticed.

"Where were you?"

"Since nothing was open, I walked around and looked in shop windows."

"That sounds boring." Naomi turned away.

Chaz took hold of her hand. "There will be no more turning or pulling away from each other. Besides, I have brought you a surprise!" He placed a pink box on the table.

Naomi looked at the cardboard box tied with twine. "How did you manage to get baked goods at this hour?"

"You are not the only one who has connections here! I stopped by the pastry shop—just to look—and the owner—"

"Marcos."

"Yes, Marcos came back to frost a wedding cake, saw me at the window, and invited me in. He offered me a coffee, and before I knew it, he told me about your sweet tooth. Then he asked me why I was walking around at night without you. I told him I might be in trouble and he gave me some *petit fours* hoping they would get me out of the 'dog house' as he put it." Chaz opened the lid.

"Oh, but this is awful!" Naomi scooped up some icing with her finger.

"Why is this awful?"

"I cannot continue to eat like this." She sat down and picked up the small, icing-encased *Tarta de Zanahorias* in her hand. Between bites of carrot cake, she confessed, "I will grow as fat as an old *abuela*."

"You have not eaten any sweets since our wedding day."

"Florita brought sweets from her mother. I ate two already plus this cake, which is one of my favorites." She stuffed the rest into her mouth.

"I will help you." Chaz stuffed a cake into his mouth.

"Chaz, do you also crave sweets or are you just trying to make me feel better?"

"I would only do this for you."

"You mean you do not like sweets?"

He walked into the kitchen, turned on the faucet, and gulped the water. He stood and laughed as water dripped down his chin. "I always thought these old faucets were the best."

Naomi handed him a towel. "I can see that they are better for some things than others."

He took the towel from her and smiled. "Naomi, never let it be said that I did not try to protect you from all things. Even the sweetest things in life can have a bad effect if taken too liberally. I would protect you even from this if I could. Now about Florita, is there anything I should know?"

"She needed a woman's advice, nothing more. Since I invited her to *mi amiga* group, I will see her on Sunday."

"Good." He took her hand and pulled her into the backyard. "Come, before we miss the beauty of the night!" She stepped onto the back patio, looked at the sky, felt Chaz place his arms around her, and sighed, sheltered in the circle of his love. He drew her so close she thought she could hear his heart beat. "God has made all of this for us to look at so we can believe he exists!"

"You believe that God exists?"

"Of course I do! Do you mean to tell me that you have doubts about this?"

"No, not at all. But I did not know that you thought about these things."

"Did I not tell you that my great Uncle Hilario is an archaeologist?"

"*Sí*, you told me during our courtship about him. He is the man who digs in the dirt to find where we come from and how we lived long ago, right?"

"Yes. His work and the evidence he showed me when I was a child led me to believe that God exists, and on a night like this, I am amazed that anyone could doubt it!"

Naomi laughed and turned to face him. "Are you sure that it is not the sweets that make you talk like this?"

Chaz held her tight. "The only sweet that could have this effect on me is the one I hold in my arms."

"You may think that now, but if you found out I was different than you thought, I fear there would be trouble between us." She walked into the kitchen.

"Why do you have to question what I say?" Chaz followed her, noticed the time, and knew she was heading to bed. Before they parted he asked, "Can you not try to trust me?"

Naomi did not respond.

Chaz walked into the suite, closed the door, and sat down on the chair. He knew he needed sleep but could not quiet his mind. When night became dawn, he rose from the chair, and looked at the bed aware that it had been a long time since he had lost sleep over the concerns or behavior of another. While he showered, he remembered that it was Friday, Naomi's special day. As he dressed, he decided to see how the day went before he tried to figure out what had upset her, and opened the bedroom door. Driven by the aroma of fresh brewed coffee, he headed for the kitchen, entered, and saw his bride. She wore a bright green and white gingham dress with yellow, purple, and orange embroidered flowers at the neck and hem. She stood in front of an elaborate espresso machine. He pointed to the plume of steam that the machine had emitted. "That smells good. I have to admit I prefer espresso to coffee!"

Naomi handed him a demitasse cup of the brew. He downed it in one gulp.

"Do you prefer this to sweets?"

"Sí, I confess that is true!" He handed the cup to her and nodded toward the espresso machine.

"You want more?"

"Sí." He grinned. His eyes roamed her body. "I want it all!" When Naomi turned to refill the cup, Chaz reached into the cupboard and took out the largest mug he could find. "Use this!"

"But, Chaz, do you not know that when you drink all of this at one time you could get ill?"

"You have your addiction and I have mine!"

She filled the mug to its brim. "I see that in this matter we are much alike."

He sat down and looked at his wife. "Naomi, once you stop looking for similarities and differences between us, you will be much happier."

"You are right. I will try to do better."

"I have not said this because I think you need to change or do better, as you call it. I love you as you are."

Naomi looked into his clear brown eyes and wanted to believe every word he uttered. However, since she had deceived him, she knew his words were not for her, but for the person he thought she was.

Chaz sensed there was more to say and pointed to a chair. "Naomi, sit down."

"*Un momento*, the sausage is almost done and we have artichokes with eggplant for breakfast."

"What? No toast or muffins to spread some thick jelly on?"

Naomi turned back to the stove. "No sweets today, my love. There were too many yesterday. Remember?"

Chaz stood, came up beside her, and laid his hand on her shoulder. "Naomi, you are the only sweet I will ever need."

"Really?" She fixed his plate.

"Yes, really." He laughed, took his plate out of her hands, picked up the sausage, and took a big bite.

By the time Naomi sat down across from him, he had devoured the sausage.

"Where were you taught to eat like that?"

"What I was taught is not important. What matters is who I am now. All you need to know about me is already before you. It is who we are now that matters the most. Do you not agree?"

"Well…I…" Naomi wondered how she could answer the question and not reveal herself—not just yet. "I think what we are now is connected to who were in the past." Then, before she could stop herself, she said, "Even if it is a past we wish we had not experienced. I think our experiences shape us and, in some ways, mold us." Before she finished her last sentence, tears threatened to fall. Chaz was transfixed by the abrupt change in his bride. Naomi stood to refill his mug. "This is a silly conversation. It is too beautiful a day for us to talk about such things. Yes?" She forced a smile.

"Yes."

She handed him his espresso. "What are you going to do today?"

"I am meeting with the architect to draw up plans to modernize this house. I do not want to take away from the charm, or change the structure, but the *casa* needs to be updated."

"A dishwasher would be nice and maybe a new roof. Perhaps we could replace that old gate in front with the rusted hinges."

He picked up a pad of paper and a pencil. "Tell me everything that you want done to the place."

She shared her heart's desire. Half an hour later, she stopped.

Chaz looked at the list. "Are you sure you have told me everything?"

"Well … yes."

"No, I think not!"

"I have asked for too much already."

"Naomi, I will tell you if what you ask for is too much. You are to tell me everything. That is the way our marriage must be. Do you understand?"

"Yes."

"Good." Chaz looked at her expectantly. Naomi smiled back, pleased with all the plans. "Where would you like me to begin?" She shrugged. "What is the most important project?" He waited for a response and was surprised when she did not answer.

Their breakfast over, Naomi stood to clear the table. "Start with the gate."

"The gate is the last thing we should work on."

"I see that it makes no sense to you. But please start with the gate."

"My wife wants the gate attended to first! It will be done for you just as you asked." Chaz walked toward the vestibule.

"Good. I have never liked that gate!" She followed him, remembered how she had first come to the *casa*, brushed aside a tear, and handed him his briefcase. "Will you be back for lunch today?"

Chaz noticed that though her hand shook, she tried to vanquish any sign of sorrow. Since it seemed that she did not want to draw attention to her distress, he answered, "Do not count on me. I have to meet with the supervisor overseeing the build-out. Between the two meetings, I could be gone all day but plan to be home an hour or two before dinner."

"*Bueno.* We will have a special meal tonight." She stood on tiptoe and gave him a timid little kiss on his cheek. She saw his color flush red and was surprised when he took hold of her with both hands, pulled her swiftly away, and gazed into her eyes.

"Naomi, I cannot wait much longer. When will you come to me?"

"You have been patient. I should not have made you wait so long. This has been hard on me also." She looked at him, reminded herself of his many kindnesses to her, their talk the night before, and told herself it was time to become more than just a paper wife. "As you know, Friday night after dark and Saturday are my alone times, Sunday morning I prepare for my *amiga* group. And Sunday night…" she sighed as she looked into his eyes with the promise of longings fulfilled, "Sunday night there will be no more waiting for us! I will be with my husband then and forever after."

"Truly?"

"Yes, truly. I *promise* I will not make us wait any longer!"

Properties and Priorities

Chaz had never been so frustrated. The more he tried to focus on what the architect said, the more his mind wandered. "You have asked me the same question three times!" Mr. Louzada exclaimed. "Are you ill?"

"Not ill, just thinking."

"My time is valuable. Perhaps it would be best if you come back another time."

"I am focused now, just not on this project." Chaz picked up a cylinder and rolled out an old set of blueprints. "What do you make of these?"

The architect looked them over. "Interesting, the place is old. If I were to work on this project, we must agree to bring the house up to current code specifications. Otherwise, nothing will pass inspection. Since this is critical, that is where I would begin. Of course, you probably want to have modern amenities added and the house restored." He flipped through the elevations and returned to the front blueprint. "Your wife's house, I take it." He checked and rechecked some barely visible figures on the last page and smiled with satisfaction. "It is the one on the side street before the park where the bus turns right, correct?"

"How did you know that?"

"As a boy I had occasion to visit the place. And the old *tía* asked me to visit there several times while I was completing my degree. I thought the house was in need of repair, but La Señora, as those in the neighborhood called her, would not let me touch a thing. She just wanted to know how to keep the plumbing running and questioned me about the house's ability to stand. Once I assured her the house was solid, she had no further need of me. She was a strange one, that old woman. There was a younger woman who was never far from her. The quiet one tended to her every wish. Now that I am married, I often think about that woman. My wife could take a few lessons from her."

"What made her think you would drop everything you were doing to inspect her place? You were not in the trades. How was she able to get you to visit when you were busy with your studies?"

"My friend, are you not married to Tía Naomi?"

"Yes. I am."

"Then, *amigo*, let us skip these formalities!" The man extended his hand in friendship. "My given name is Armando."

The architect grasped Chaz's hand while Chaz stared at him. "Are you somehow affiliated with the work of the Tías?"

"You might say that. My *abuela* was one of those girls. Did you know that the old lady was really difficult? My grandmother often told me to buckle down or she would leave me with her *tía* for a day or two! 'That,' she said, 'would teach me to mind!' I don't know how your wife was able to be with her all those years, living in the background, unable to even go out. You know what they called her down there, my friend? They called her *the little mouse!*"

"I can assure you that she is not a little mouse now! I intend for her to have everything she asked for. But there is an odd stipulation."

"What stipulation, my friend?" Armando opened his humidor, took a cigar, and handed the box to Chaz. "They're the best... from *Cuba!*" While the architect waited for Chaz to respond, he clipped off the end, and moistened the wrapper.

Chaz glanced at the selection and placed the humidor on the man's desk. "She asked that the gate be taken care of first."

"Of course she has." He lit his cigar. "All the girls lost their freedom once that gate closed behind them. Do not get me wrong, La Señora did them a great service. But she made sure they all repaid her. In fact many still pay." He smiled as he drew the tobacco into his lungs. "My wife hates that I do this, but there are so few pleasures left for a man with seven children and a mother-in-law at home."

"You mean the girls pay?"

"*Sí.* How else do you think the Tías have been able to help those in need? The girls are grateful, as they should be, and because of that, they help with a few dollars every month. This allows Naomi to continue the work." Chaz listened while the architect explained the situation his wife had lived in and its effect on the girls. Several hours later Chaz stood to leave. "Now, my friend, the girls, even your wife, have been sworn to secrecy. What Naomi does must remain a secret. Otherwise, immigration would stop her efforts and the girls would face the wrath of the system without an ally. What I have told you must stay in this office."

"That makes sense. But my wife must know that I understand and support what she does."

"She keeps what she does a secret to protect you and many others. The work she does is dangerous, and she does it under the watchful eyes of immigration. I am sure Naomi keeps the details a secret to protect you and many others."

"I know she is an American citizen because she showed me the papers so she has nothing to fear."

"That is all very fine, my friend. Still, we do not want to create any reason for the officials to look her way. *Comprendo?*"

"I think you sound like your grandmother. Perhaps she was worried about deportation. Maybe she did not have a green card." Chaz reached for the door.

"Listen, my friend, I have been where immigration holds people until they are deported. Many of those who are to be deported have lived in this country a long time. That does not stop our government from sending them back from where they came. It is nothing new, this sending people away. Your wife pledged to fight this! She needs all of those who have been helped to give. However, she is the one who takes all of the risks. She is a hero!"

"I knew she brought girls home from immigration, but I had no idea that she was involved in something this dangerous."

"Do you think she came to this job unprepared? That Tía of hers taught her a lot of her tricks. And if I am any judge of character, she probably has connections at immigration."

"She does. I remember she got a call while fixing our wedding breakfast. She could not tell me much about what was going on because she had to rush off."

"They all are like that."

"What do you mean they all are like that? Does your wife rush off and endanger herself for others?"

"That is not what I meant. I meant to say it better."

"Then I suggest you succeed!"

"What I meant to say is that all of the Tías are mysterious." Afraid he had given his new friend more information than he had intended, Armando was glad that Chaz did not respond. When he finally ushered Chaz out of his office, as he did with all his well-heeled clients, he breathed a sigh of relief. *Why do I never remember to do as Yvonne suggests,* he silently rebuffed himself. He remembered she had said, "Armando, just because you have found someone who knows something about the details of what you do or you find you have mutual friends, does not mean that you must tell them everything. Guard yourself or others will think you a fool."

Armando shrugged his shoulders, walked to his desk, rolled up the blueprints, and placed them in the cylinder. *La Señora's house,* he thought to himself as he covered the exposed end with a metal disk. *I will make this a place where Chaz and Naomi can live and have their family and friends over for many years.* He tucked the cylinder under his arm. *I need to look at the surveyor's report and check with the title company before I work on this project.* He called the cab company he always used and requested his favorite driver.

By the time Armando had reached the curb, Sid was waiting for him. Before the cabbie could open his door, Armando was already seated. "County Recorders Office and hurry." He leaned back in his seat and watched the city speed by. *I will give them a home that will grow with them, yet not feel too big. It will be a two-story house with a balcony and bedrooms upstairs for Chaz, Naomi, and their family. The work Naomi does and the* niñas *she brings to the* casa *can use the downstairs. And, of course, there will be a playroom for the children.* He took out a pad of paper and scribbled some hasty notes.

Chaz walked down the subway stairs. El Barrio, Spanish Harlem, he thought, *When I left I thought I would never come back here! But, living there is not as unusual as meeting in someone else's office.* Still he knew that meeting Armando at his firm had allowed the architect to feel comfortable. That comfort, plus his familiarity with the house, and Naomi's American *madre* made for an informative conversation. Chaz put his money in the slot, took his ticket, and entered the next car headed his way. He found a seat in the back and tried to collect his thoughts.

He looked at the passengers and noticed an old woman who held the hand of a young boy. "Tatarabuela ... *mia* great grandmother, why do I have to go back so soon?"

The old woman picked the boy up, placed him on her lap, and wrapped her arms around him. "It's your home. You'll see, *mi pequeño*, everyone likes to go home."

"Tatarabuela, have you forgotten I am an *hombre?*"

"I have not forgotten." The old women chuckled and smiled at him. "Still, even a fine *hombre* like you has to go home."

"Really? Why does everyone like to go home? Wouldn't they rather stay with you?"

"Now, listen don't try to wheedle your way into staying with me another day. We promised your *madre* you would be back by lunchtime today. Remember?"

"Yes. I remember."

When they reached their destination, Chaz noticed she could not manage the boy, his suitcase, and her shopping. "Excuse me, Señora, with your permission, I can help with these."

The old woman was a good judge of character and sized him up quickly. She was about to nod when her great-grandson said, "You told me never to speak with strangers."

The old woman chuckled and patted the boy's head. "You are a blessing and a comfort to me, Ray, but we have too much for the two of us to handle. This man ..."

"Chaz."

"Yes, Chaz has offered to help."

"But, Tatarabuela *mia*, I can take care of you." He picked up a grocery bag.

"Forgive my great-grandson's bad manners." She turned to the boy. "I know you can, but this man will assist you." Once the boy had discovered which bag he could handle, Chaz picked up the suitcase and the other bags from Zabar's. They walked up two flights of stairs, and emerged into a cloudless, bright, sunny day.

"Where are you going?" Chaz asked.

The woman gazed down the street. "What time is it?"

Chaz rearranged the packages and looked at his watch. "It is eleven and a few minutes."

"Oh!"

"Is there a problem?"

"No problem, just a little delay." She nodded toward the boy. "I will have to keep him busy for a while. His mother is not home yet and I have lost my key."

"There is a little coffee shop across the street. If you will allow me, I would like you to be my guests while you wait. I am sure they have something for the boy as well."

"That sounds like a good plan."

Since his schedule was full, Chaz had little time to spend with his bride today and found himself wondering why he had offered to assist them. Then he remembered Naomi's pledge book. *Ah, Naomi, if you only knew how much what you did for me continues to influence my actions! No wonder I am so in love with you. I was a bum. Now look at the transformation and all because you had faith in me when no one else did!* He opened the door of the baristas and motioned for the old woman to enter. She did, followed by the boy. The patrons saw her and stood. They walked down the aisle to the back. When they sat down, the patrons sat, and resumed their conversations. "I thought you were a visitor here. But it seems that everyone knows and respects you enough to stand when you enter."

"I am no one of any consequence. They do this when I come. I think they stand in awe that a woman my age that can get around and take care of her great-grandson as I do."

"It's like old times seeing you here again," the barista said when he came to take their order. "Would you like your usual, Teresa?"

"That would be nice. Can you bring a treat for my *una preciosa*—my precious one—since he has been such a good boy?"

"What would he like?"

"Maybe a—"

"Maybe a Coke and a cookie?"

"Yes, a Coke and a cookie." Teresa placed her hands on the youngster's head, closed her eyes, and said a prayer. Then she turned toward Chaz. "Excuse an old woman's foolishness, but I never miss an opportunity to pray over him. I believe when he sees what I do, he will remember to pray when the time comes for him to stand up for God."

Chaz took a pull from his espresso. "Does God need people to stand up for him?"

"I believe he does." Teresa assessed him. "So, you are Naomi's husband. I heard that you are a good man. God knows that woman could use someone in her life to look out for her for a change."

"I think you are right. But how do I look out for someone who is so—"

"Competent?"

"Yes, that is the right word."

"My people too are very much that way. Give her time and be patient. She will come to you a little at a time. At least that is the way it was for *mi esposo* and me. I do not think things have changed much in the last eighty years. Have they?"

"No." Chaz took another pull. "Sometimes it seems that I have married someone whom time has not touched. I believe if I had met her in Spain as a child she would be just as she is today, so fresh, strong, yet very naïve."

Teresa looked across the street where the old jewelers' clock stood, still keeping perfect time. "We must go or we will be late!" She stood, picked up her shopping bags, and struggled to pick up the boy's suitcase.

Chaz put his hand on the suitcase. "Here, let me help you."

She smiled at him as he picked it, and the bags, up.

"Come on, Tatarabuela!" Ray dashed for the open door.

"Oh, no, you don't!" The barista shut the door.

Ray stomped his foot. "Peter, I never get to win, do I?"

Peter winked at Teresa and opened the door for her. "No, my little man, you will never run out of here without your great-grandmother to watch out for you. Not as long as I am able to keep you safe."

They walked while the heat of the day beat down on them. Chaz saw the old woman pull out a hanky and wipe beads of perspiration from her neck and face. "Excuse me, I do not want to be impolite, but if you would like, I can hold the boy's hand so you can take off your hat and jacket. There is a slight breeze, which might refresh you. But you are so covered up that you cannot feel it."

"That is very thoughtful of you, Chaz, but we are almost there. Besides, my people are covered even when it is hotter than this."

"Who are your people?"

"I thought you knew." She nodded toward a strange-looking building.

"Me know? What should I know?"

"No wonder you were so kind to me. You did not realize that I was different than you."

"How different? We are both of the same people, yes?"

"*Sí*, that is true."

"Then how are we different?"

Teresa pointed ahead. "See that tree over there, the one with bark peeling off of it?"

"Yes, I see the tree."

"That is my childhood home. It is now the home of my granddaughter and her family. Mine is one of the families that originally settled this place. Yet many here treat us not as friends but as a curiosity—or worse still as a threat."

"I was with you and saw them all stand up when you came in. What was that about if not a sign of respect?"

"Tatarabuela, *nuestra casa*... we're home!" Ray raced up the steps and rang the doorbell.

"Yes, we are home!" She looked at Chaz. "Come with me." When they had mounted the stairs, the old woman sat down and motioned for Chaz to join her. "I will tell you about us."

The front door opened and Ray ran inside as a young woman came out. "Alisha, this is Naomi's husband. I had too much on my hands. He was kind enough to help me with these packages and the boy."

"I told you not to go to Zabar's today, didn't I!" Alisha kissed Teresa. "But, no, why listen to the voice of reason when you want to believe that you can still do everything you have always done!"

"All right already, that is enough! I have always gone to Zabar's on Friday before I come here. Why should I stop doing what I am able to do? Remember, I am not dead yet! Am I?"

"No, Bisabuela, far from it!"

Teresa pointed to the groceries and the boy's suitcase. "Take these inside and let your *madre* know that we are here. Then bring us some ice tea. That's a good girl." While the young woman did her grandmothers bidding, Chaz thought that this family was very different from his. Though the exchange between the two seemed warm, he found them rigid in a way he had not experienced before. Perplexed, he wondered about the old woman's prayer over Ray because that was another thing he had never seen before.

"Now, I will answer your questions and the way you react will let me know if I will see you again."

"You like a bit of drama in you life. All right, I will play along!"

"On the contrary, I dislike drama. That is why I tell you about us so you will never feel that I have tricked or played games with you."

Alisha placed their drinks on the table.

"Teresa, I do not understand."

"Oh, but you will." She smiled at her granddaughter and took a sip of ice tea. "Many years," she began as if she were telling the story for the hundredth time as one would an old fable, "many, many years ago my people were in Spain and that was a bad time for us! However, some of us were fortunate enough to leave before the killing began. Before we were forced to become Catholic."

"Are you speaking of the Inquisition?"

"Yes. That is what I am talking about."

He stood. "I should leave."

"If you leave, we will never meet again. My access to your community is difficult. But you can always visit me here. I would very much like that. I would like to be a friend to the woman who has helped so many, but she has always shunned my family and me. We are, you see, Jews. Yet the miracle is that we too believe in *Messiah Yeshua*, or as you call him, Jesus the Christ." Uncertain if it was the heat of the day or Teresa's revelation that made his head ache, Chaz knew he had to avoid anymore stress if the surprise he had planned for Naomi was going to happen. Hoping to ease the pain before it escalated, he picked up his glass and put it to his forehead. While Teresa shared her history, he looked at her through the liquid and tried to understand why what she said should matter to him.

"See that tree?"

"Yes. What of it?"

"That tree has stood there since before I was born. It will be there long after I am gone. If a tree can stand for so long and not decay, why would anyone think that our faith in God will not withstand more than even that tree can?"

"I agree. Faith in God stands forever. But how can a Jew be a Christian?"

"That is a very long story. Come back some Friday after lunch and we will talk some more. Remember when we entered the coffee shop and they all stood up when I came in?"

"I think I will always remember that moment."

"I will tell you a secret. Many people think they stand to salute my advanced years. But I think they stand to let me know that they recognize a woman of faith."

On the walk back to the *casa,* Chaz spoke his thoughts aloud so he could hear his own counsel. He seldom did this. However, as founder and head of a philanthropic organization, he had discovered the validity of voicing his concerns before he arrived at a decision. The CEO of Crossroads called it the Socratic Method when he had overheard Chaz mumbling. Chaz called it common sense. Between the architect's comments and Teresa's revelation, he was certain that common sense was in short supply. However, having heard his own thoughts, by the time he rounded the corner, he knew that *Naomi* did not need to know about Armando and the information he shared, and she most certainly did not need to hear about Teresa!

Armando headed to the pay phone in the lobby of the Hall of Records and wondered if they knew how much land they owned. He dialed the number. No one answered. "Oh, come on, Chaz! Pick up the phone!" Several people looked at him in a manner that let him know they found his outburst unacceptable. He tried again, then hung up. He had asked the cab driver to wait and hurried to the curb. By the time the cabbie saw him and pulled up Armando was mad. The man opened his door intending to walk around the cab as he always did, per this man's request. But frustrated by the delay, the architect opened his own door. "Sid, just get behind the wheel and drive!" Sid headed to the address Armando gave him. Though the architect urged him to hurry, they crawled along. Armando glanced at his watch, then at the traffic.

Chaz turned the corner, saw Armando open his door, jump out of his car, and trip. He hurried toward Armando while the man grabbed the rickety old fence. Chaz grabbed hold of Armando's arm. "Are you all right?"

Armando brushed weathered paint chips from his hands. "Fine … fine."

"Good. Have you something to show us already? Or have you come to speak with Naomi and find out firsthand what she would like?"

"Neither." He picked up the duplicate records he had dropped, assessed the property, and spotted a table and some chairs on the porch. "Tell Naomi to come out here. I have something important to share with both of you!"

"If it is about the house, Naomi has asked me to handle everything. There is no need to bother her. Besides, this is the day she bakes for the week."

"House! House! Who said anything about the house! This is about the land!"

"The land. This piece of land? It is nice. But there is not much of it."

"No, you are wrong! There is a lot of land here!" Armando turned and pointed in all directions. "There is an acre of land!"

"No! Really? An acre? Where exactly is this land?"

Armando sat down on a chair. "Call your wife and we will talk!"

Chaz pulled Armando off the chair. "You better come with me. Naomi will never believe that you left your office to visit us in the middle of a workday unless she sees you." He opened the door. "Naomi, we have unexpected company!"

"What? Chaz, I cannot hear you!"

"Come with me." Chaz dragged Armando into the kitchen. "Naomi, Mr. Louzada the architect has come down from the city to tell us about an acre of land that he thinks we own. He is very busy. Can you come into the dining room and hear what he has to say?"

"I will be there in a moment." Naomi worked her fingers though her hair, slipped on her espadrilles, turned towards her husband, and realized they were staring at her. "The two of you, out of my kitchen!"

They walked into the dinning room and closed the door.

She took off her apron, rushed to her room, reapplied her lipstick, and dabbed on some perfume.

"Naomi, what is taking you so long?"

She rushed to the kitchen, took a pitcher of iced tea out of the refrigerator, and placed it and some glasses on a tray with. "Coming." She carried the tray into the dining room and put it on the table.

The architect stood and took her hands in his. "Naomi, it's been a long time since I was here."

Naomi looked at him. "I remember when you came to see the house for Madre Vida, but that was twelve or thirteen years ago."

"*Sí, exactamente!* The last time I came, you were still the *little mouse* who hid in the shadows. Now look at you, a lovely lady, with a good man. You are to be congratulated!"

"I am the one who should be congratulated." Chaz drew his wife to him and settled her at the head of the table.

Naomi shook her head and stood. "It is not proper for me to sit in the chair reserved for the man of the house."

"Normally I would agree with you, but Armando is here to speak with the owner of this property. Since that is you, it is fitting for you to sit there."

"But, Chaz, this is our property."

"What can one do with such a woman?"

Armando rolled out the copies he had made of the lots that compromised Naomi's inheritance. "*Amigos mios,* let's not quibble over such small matters when there is much to discuss!"

Naomi pointed to the copies. "What is all this?"

"Because, I wanted to research the boundary lines of your property to see if there were any changes in the building codes, I went down to the hall of records. As you know, the city has been growing in this direction. I needed to find out if there were any new building restrictions, or if a new survey of the land would be required."

"Why did you need to do all of that for some minor changes to the *casa?*"

"I know it has been as it is for many years. Yet, if you look over the original blueprints, it was once a small home on an acre of land. These front rooms and La Señora's suite are much grander than the rest of the house because one of the Tías paid to have them added when funds became available. Now, with you married and because of the important work that you do, I figured that we could make some changes. We could increase your comfort, and perhaps add a second floor to prepare for some children, should God bless you in that way."

"I see. Chaz, is this what the two of you talked about?"

"I gave him your list and he said he would be happy to do the work for us. I never mentioned structural changes or adding a second floor. But it sounds good to me."

"Gentlemen, this house is held in trust for the *niñas* who need to come here. It is to be a refuge for them. Many who have been helped have come back to visit. What do you think would happen if they came, and found another house, something different? Do you think they would knock at a new or different house? Are you aware that some who leave Spain without a permanent destination have heard that if things get difficult they are to come here? What would happen to these girls if the house changed? Can you imagine a girl, frightened, unable to stay in this country without my help, not able to be understood, and not able to read English, finding a house that no longer looks like itself? How would she find me? How could I help her? Armando, this is a very nice plan. I do thank you for all the thought you put into our comfort and living arrangements. But the house, from the front at least, must continue to look as it does!"

"Yes, yes, Naomi. But actually I didn't come here about the house."

Naomi stood. "Then why are we meeting?"

"I know this is difficult for you to grasp, but you own not just this house, but those on each side, the ones that back onto them, and the house across the street. That house is on a double-deep lot. It's zoned to allow for a home and business combined. You own an acre of prime New York City property!"

"This does not change my decision."

"But, my dear, just think of the money you could make if you sell and reestablish your work further from here. I checked. There is a very nice community thirty minutes commute time. With the subway, you would never notice the difference. This land has been rezoned. Think of all the people who need to live close to downtown. Your one acre is possibly worth a quarter of a million dollars. You could expand your work and that is why—"

"Is that what you want? You want to uproot the work that has gone on here for more than three-quarters of a century? You want me to be the first person in the *barrio* to betray my commitment to the others who have ignored voices like yours that have tried to get us to sell? Do you not realize we who have chosen to stay here and continue this way of life have done so because we want to preserve your history and heritage?"

"But, Naomi, look at the facts."

"All right, Armando, let's look at the facts. The other parcels that you mentioned, house those who have worked here. They will be available for others to use in the future. This is a community! I thought you knew that when you came here all those years ago. It seems I was wrong. Madre Vida told me to listen to what people say and make sure it matches what they do. So let me ask you, do you have any interest in a real estate company? Or do you plan to give this sale to one of your *amigos* so they can make a lot of money from a lucrative venture?" Naomi looked at Chaz for assurance. "Also, who would be the architect for this project?"

"What are you accusing me of?" Armando stood and reached for the papers he had intended to show them. "I came to bring you a blessing!"

"No. You came to fatten your wallet and those of your friends." She ushered him to the vestibule and pointed at the front door.

He opened it and turned back. "If you change your mind, you know were to reach me."

Chaz watched him hurry away. "We will find another architect—one who wants to fix the house, not our lives!" He closed the door and reached for his bride. "I am proud of you. I have to admit that when I heard some in this community called you the little mouse, I was concerned. Now I know I have no fear for you in that regard. I think they misunderstood your calm, quiet demeanor and assumed they could manipulate you any way they wanted. I am certain those who tried never tried again. Am I right?"

"Yes. I had to learn to stand up to everyone when Madre Vida died. Even the priest and our attorney thought I had tricked her into adopting me. They tried to arrange for me to marry someone they could control. In that way, I think they believed they could get control of the estate."

"The estate? What are you talking about? There is no estate."

"There is a large estate. Why do you think Armando was called when things needed to be done?"

"I thought it was because his grandmother was one of the *niñas*."

"That is correct. Once a woman comes into this house, our commitment follows her, and should she marry, her family's as well."

"That is why there is the market and these other houses."

"Yes, even your house, my love, remember?"

"Of course I remember. I must say that it was a surprise to discover that someone planned for me before I was in the picture."

"That is true but it was an older and much wiser Tía than me who realized there might be a need for this one day. She bought the place so it was there for me to give to you."

"How fortunate for me to live in a home where I am loved, not only by my wife, but by someone who cared about me, and planned for me, before I was born!"

"Now you understand about Las Niñas. Now, about Armando."

"Say no more. We will find someone else!"

"No. We will use him. He is probably going to get in trouble with his *abuela* Trudy for acting this way. However, he will call back and make amends. We will use him. That is one of the benefits we knew we would have when we helped his family pay for his education."

"Does he know about this?"

"Of course he does. Why do you think he left his studies and came here whenever Madre Vida asked him to?"

"When he spoke with me about that, it seemed she never had him do any work. Why make him come down here and give him nothing to do?"

"She did not ask him to come because we needed him. She had him come so she could make sure that the money she invested in his education would yield a good person. After all, Chaz, it is one thing to help someone, but Madre Vida and I look for the circle to be completed. That happens when the person we help, helps someone else. So far, the only person Armando has helped is himself. If we will give him another opportunity to help others, I believe he will learn that community and commitment are more important than a big office, and a cabbie available whenever he wishes."

"For someone who has never left this little place except to go to immigration, how do you know so much about Armando?"

"Did I just speak to the wall? Were you not listening?"

"Well since you will not tell me, I will assume that though you live here, you have spies everywhere."

"Spies, no. People who keep me informed, yes!"

Heartache and Heat

Chaz followed Naomi into the kitchen and wiped the sweat from his brow. "It feels like a sauna in here." He leaned against the wall and watched his wife in her element. She smiled at him, took out the mixture of noodles, cottage cheese, eggs, and sugar she had prepared for baking from the refrigerator. Pleased to have a unique dish to serve him during their special meal, she remembered her friend in England who had taught her how to make the noodle *kugel* connection that she made every Ere' of Shabbat, ran butter around the oblong Pyrex pans edges and bottom, then poured the mixture into the pan. After dotting it with more butter, Naomi placed it in the oven to bake at three hundred fifty degrees. Although the heat was escalating, it did not faze her.

She looked in Chaz's direction, stopped for a second, kicked off her shoes, and pushed them under the table. Then she turned to check the pots simmering on the stove. Chaz glanced at her discarded shoes and saw her straining to reach the top shelf. He raised his arm and reached into the cupboard. "Tell me what you need and I will get it for you."

"Why do I need your help? I have a good system!" Curling her toes, she used them to fish her shoes out from under the table. She put them on, stood as erect as possible, and reached as high as she could. "See, with my high heels on I am able to reach everything."

"What I see is that you have always needed to make do. Now I am here and my job is to take care of you. Instead of looking for a pair of shoes, you are to look for me when you need help."

Naomi moved to the sink and washed the glasses from their meeting with Armando. "I am not used to depending on anyone."

Chaz took a towel from the drawer and dried the dishes. "We are a team now. You understand about teams?"

"No."

"But surely in your home where you grew up there were others who looked out for you, nurtured, and cared for you."

"Look, Chaz, since you seem to need to know, I will tell you about this, but only this time. I do not like to dwell on things of the past. Do you understand?"

"I understand that you do not want to tell me even though you say you will. However, it is important that I know what keeps hurting you. Does it come from the time before you came here?"

"Yes. But not in the way you think. Sit down, and let me tell you how it was with me, and my family." Chaz sat down while Naomi checked her pots, cut some cookie dough from the frozen roll she had made the day before, placed them on a cookie sheet, and put them into the oven to bake. Wiping her hands on her apron, she sat down across from him. "Have you ever been singled out as someone who does not fit in?" Chaz looked at her questioningly. "What I mean is, have you ever found that your family was treated badly because you were with them?"

"There were all those times I was drunk and acted out. That was hard for my family, especially my parents. They had set me a good example but I did everything they told me not to do."

"So what happened?"

Chaz grinned at her. "What happened? *You* happened!"

"Yes, I understand. But what happened before that?"

"Before that, I realized that I had to leave. I did not want them to be hurt and I knew that what I was doing would cause them pain. So late one night, after everyone was asleep, I left. I never said good-bye."

"It was painful for you, yes?"

"Yes. It was hard to leave my family like that."

"This is also my story. I did not leave because of drinking. My family always watched my behavior. We girls did not drink except on specific feast days. However, my unusual looks caused others to treat my family and me badly. My father and mother were always telling us that we needed to pack up and move to another town or find another opportunity."

"Why would what you looked like cause such a reaction?"

"Look at me and compare me to the other women of Spanish heritage that you have known. Do I not look different to you than they do?"

Chaz's eyes assessed her every curve and he smiled. "They were jealous of your exotic looks."

"*Mi mamá* told me that. But when you see your family moving from town to town, and hear others muttering nasty words, you eventually know who you are, and what others think of you."

"And who are you, Naomi?"

"First, let me tell you who I was."

"All right then, who were you?"

Afraid that she would cry before she could utter a word, Naomi took several gulps of air. "I was a curse. Wherever my family went, all was fine until people saw me." Hoping she would feel reassured, Chaz stood and sat down in the chair next to her. "Then everything would fall apart and we would need to move again." She put her head in her hands and sobbed. "I was a curse! Because of me, my family was cursed!" He rubbed her back and watched her mop up her face while he wondered how she had been able to cope. Her iron will returned. She sniffled and pulled herself together. "I have never spoken to anyone about this. I will never talk about this again! Do you understand me?"

"Naomi, if this is too painful for you, you should stop."

She gritted her teeth. "No, you have a right to know this, this truth of mine! At the age of twelve when girls have their first communion and receive lovely gifts, my family used whatever excuse they could so I would not experience rejection. Finally, at fourteen, when people began to wonder why they had waited so long, I left. That was the best thing I could do for them—allow them to have a better life, God willing, without me."

Chaz teared up with concern. "My dear, where did you go? How did you manage?"

He truly cares. He really does, she thought. Naomi took her hand from his, used it to caress his check, and smiled. "You are a sweet surprise to me. I never dreamed there would be anyone in my life. But you, *mi amor,* are a gift from God." Tears streamed down her face. She stood, reached into the pantry, took out a tissue, and dabbed at her eyes. "I got a job as a companion to Abuela Sophia. She let me call her that when her family was not around. They were wealthy and wanted her with them when they traveled throughout Europe. Their plan was to settle in

America. It was my good fortune to help this blind woman who having never seen me was not offended by my looks. Because of her blindness, I believe she saw my heart. With her I had a season, though brief, of peace and revelation."

"What do you mean?"

"Because she was not blind in the things that mattered, she taught me what it was like to be valued and appreciated for what I was. She did not compare me to others. I have always been grateful to her for that. Anyway, on the night before we were to dock in America, she died. The doctor said it was congestive heart failure. The family said they were sorry, but they did not need my services anymore. I think you know the rest."

Naomi stood, looked at Chaz, and wiped away her tears. "I will never speak about this again, do you understand me?"

"Now that I understand where you have come from there are no more ghosts between us."

"Good." Naomi moved back to her pots.

"You truly are a blessing. You bless everyone who knows or meets you and in many ways you have blessed those who will never know or even hear of you." Chaz walked over, placed his hands on her head as he had seen Teresa do earlier that day, and imitating her, he prayed a blessing over his wife.

She sniffled, and turned looked at him with all the love she had. "You understand. Then I am grateful that we had this talk."

Chaz nodded and took her hand. "Now I understand why you were chosen for this work."

"Madre Vida did not know these things."

"Naomi, you wear your heart on your sleeve. You think that no one sees who you are. But those who care, we see who you are."

The timer buzzed. Naomi put on her mitts. "I have to get these out now, or they will burn." She opened the oven door and removed the cookie sheets.

Chaz glanced at the kitchen clock. "I am more than two hours late! I missed my lunch meeting with the foreman and that man is hard to get a hold of."

"I am sure he will come back to check on the work."

"That reminds me, can you make me a sandwich before I go?"

"Nothing makes a woman feel more wanted than having her man ask her to stop what she is doing and make him a sandwich." She opened the refrigerator and pulled out the fixings. "What would you like in your sandwich?"

Chaz eyed his selection. "Honey, just make it easy on yourself. Something simple will be fine."

Hearing voices coming from the front yard, Chaz walked to the front door, realized he had left it open, and noticed that the crew was huddled around the foreman. He walked into the kitchen as Naomi put the top slice of bread on his sandwich. Grabbing his lunch, Chaz headed for the door. "Thanks, *Nomi*. Derrick is back. I will eat this at the site!"

Not hearing a response, he turned to look at his bride, and saw emotions of surprise, and sorrow flash across her face as tears fell. He retraced his steps. "What did I do? Did I hurt you in some way, *cariña?*"

She smiled up at him while tears streamed down her face. "No, you brought back a sweet memory to me, one I have not thought about since I left my family."

"Really?" A sweet memory caused you to react with tears?"

"When you get to know me better, you will find I cry for some of the strangest reasons. Right now I am crying over a happy memory."

"Really?"

"Really." She turned toward the front door, put her arm through his, and walked him to the vestibule. "You see, Chaz, *mi papá* did many things, worked at many different jobs, but his trade was construction. When he could work in his trade, he was the happiest he could be. During those jobs, he was able to come home for a break, while there he would, if *mi mamá* was not around, he would ask me to make him a sandwich, like you just did. No one else would do that for him, as *mi mamá* had him on a diet. However, he was *mi papá* and I knew he needed more food than my mother gave him. She was stingy because she worried about money. When he asked if I would fix a sandwich for him, it was just like the one I have made for you. Many times, he was too busy to sit down. So, he would pick it up, head for the door, and holler back, 'Thanks, *Nomi*.' When my younger sister, Beca, started to talk, my name was too hard for her to say, so she called me *Nomi*. The people who have called me *Nomi* have been those that are closest to my heart." With tears on her face, she pointed to her heart. "Just as you are with me here, so are they, and somehow when you called me by my family name, it was like you became one with all of us, as if I had been meant to be with only you! Can you understand?"

Chaz stared at her, aware that in his wildest imaginings he could never have fantasized a reality more wonderful than theirs. "Yes, I understand." They stared at each other for a moment. When Chaz laughed, he broke the spell. "Odd as it seems, I am glad I made you cry. Each of us needs to keep our good memories close to our heart."

As she wiped joyful tears away, Naomi heard the noise, looked at the property across the street, and pushed him outside. "The men are back. You need to go."

"But, sweetheart, I cannot leave you now."

"Why not?"

He drew her into his arms. "I don't want to lose the magic!"

She looked at him, the full force of her love visible for him to see. "We cannot lose this. God has chosen us for each other. I know you are the one God intended for me from the beginning of time. You are my destiny! Now my life has really begun!"

Moved by the force of her profession, Chaz, bent down to kiss her.

Just as his lips drew close to Naomi's, she hollered, "Chaz, the soup! It smells like I have burned our soup!" She ran to the kitchen.

He followed upon her heels and grabbed her hand. "Let it burn! It is too hot for soup!" She turned to look at him. He kissed her passionately, turned on his heels walked to the front of the house. When he reached the threshold, he turned and saw her standing in the dining room looking at him. "That was the best sandwich I have ever had!" Hand on the door, he stopped once more and looked at his bride. "What time do you go to church today?"

"Why, are you planning to go with me?"

"That is exactly what I plan to do. Take my wife to church for the whole community to see what a lucky man I am!"

She stared at him and wondered what to say. She wanted him to feel included but needed him to stay at the construction site so her secret would remain one until she was ready to tell him about herself. *Oh*, she silently prayed, *wait for Sunday night.* "I go about four for the lighting of the candles. Then come home to an early dinner. But I know you are busy. I can go by myself. I always have."

"Naomi, you worry about too many things. I will be back in time to get cleaned up and be turned out well so that you will be proud to have me escort you."

She could hear him whistling as he crossed the street and was almost completely undone when she realized he was whistling the tune he had gifted her the other night. As she entered the kitchen, she thought, *Yes, until the twelfth of never, I will still be loving you!* Pulling her heart away from musings that she feared would be her undoing, she looked at the soup, and realized that it was, as Chaz had said, "too hot for soup" while she poured it down the drain. Almost finished with her Ere' of Shabbat preparations, she hurried to wash the dishes, aware that for the first time in her life, she was thinking about a man rather than God on this most special feast day.

Hurrying into the dining room, she replaced the tablecloth with her second best, took her candlesticks out of the breakfront, and looked at them lovingly for they represented the freedom she sought to worship *Adonai*. Placing them at the foot of table where she always sat, she looked at the varied colors within the olivewood. There was only one place in the world were they were made, Israel! *If I had not been traveling Europe with the Sosa family, I would have never been able to buy these treasures.* Her eyes sparkled with the memory of the freedom she had experienced during that brief time. She remembered how worried she had been about spending the money she found in her uncle's envelope to buy the candlesticks. Then she had envisioned lighting them. Her heart heavy with the loss of her family, yet filled with the promise of love, Naomi was brought back to the present as she looked at all she had accomplished, and reviewed what would be available for them to eat on Saturday. Satisfied that she had done everything she had set out to do, she walked to the kitchen, hung her apron on the old peg inside the pantry, and walked to her room.

After showering and toweling herself dry, she combed her hair, and rubbed moisturizer into her skin. She attempted to use the mascara as Lucinda had taught her, thought of Chaz, and poked herself in the eye. Her hand trembled. All she could think was, *Oh, God, he really loves me.* Aware that no one had loved her like this before, she tried to apply the mascara once more, hit her eye with the wand, and threw it in the trash.

I will not try this again! Chaz loves me as I am! I do not need to pretend to be someone else.

Strengthened by her husbands love, she walked to her wardrobe, pulled out one dress after another in rapid succession, held each one up, and looked in the mirror. *Nothing seems right.* Naomi worked quickly but at the end, she realized that nothing she owned could match the way she wanted to look for her husband. *I just bought these. They are the nicest clothes I have ever owned.* Startled by this new awareness, she looked at herself in the full-length mirror. *Have I changed that much?* She traced the line of her high cheekbones with her eyes while she fixed her hair. "Come on now, Naomi," she said as her mother in Spain had when she needed her to do something quickly. "Just find something that will do for today!" Then, just as if she were again that little girl, *mamá* was trying to teach, she heard her *mamá's* voice, as if she were standing next to her. "Naomi, do not reach for the obvious. Look in the hard place. Remember, the revealed things belong to man, but those that remain concealed, they belong to God. And blessed will you be, *mi hija*, my daughter, if you search for those things with all your strength, all your heart, and all your might."

"*Sí, mamá mía*," she answered as if her *mamá* was with her. Then she heard herself asking as she had when she was a child, "What is to be revealed that has been concealed?"

"I do not know," she heard her mother's voice answer. "Only you know that, my daughter." Startled by her mother's revelation, Naomi sat on her bed amid the dresses she had pulled out. *I love him. I did not mean to care for him this much, but I do. I want to please him, but I do not know how! Yes, that is my problem. It is not the clothes! It is because my heart is happy and confused.*

She stood, picked up the dresses, and put them away. When she held the last dress in her hands, she wondered, *Why did I pull this out? It is much too warm to wear.* Since she kept her winter clothes on the other side of the wardrobe, she moved a garment aside to make room for the dress and was surprised when she touched plastic. *What is this? I have never covered my clothes this way.* She took the opaque plastic wrapped garment bag out of her wardrobe, looked at the silk-wrapped hangers, and realized that someone had placed it there for her to find. A second later, she saw a bow that held a note. She sat down on her bed, realized this was a gift, and pulled the note from its envelope. *This is from my niñas,* she thought as she read:

> Dear Tía,
> We thought you would like this.
> Your Niñas

Overcome with emotion, she realized, *I would have never looked there in the summer!* She remembered her talk with her imaginary mother. *Your words guided me there,* mi mamá. As she unwrapped the gift, she thought, *They should not have done this. But since they did, I hope whatever they bought will be appropriate for church.* She removed the garments, held them up, and gazed at her finery. Laying each garment on her bed, she discovered that each had a piece of paper attached. She looked at all of the outfits, found herself drawn to the lovely azure blue dress, picked it up, and saw a note. "Perfect for church, wear your red shoes and purse." The second was an almost sheer nightgown and robe. The note, "The best marriages begin in the bedroom," made her blush. Mi mamá *would disagree. She told me the best marriages begin in the heart.* The last item was something she had never owned: a bathing suit. *I am not going to wear this,* she told herself. She noticed that the yellow eyelet suit was modest and knew Chaz wanted to go to the beach on days like this. She could almost hear him saying as he had last week, "I will teach you how to swim. It will be great fun. You will see the beach! You! Me! Hotdogs! Believe me; you will love it!" *Well,* Naomi thought as she put the bathing suit and nightgown back in her wardrobe, *if you love it, Chaz, I am certain I will also.*

When she closed the wardrobe's door, Naomi noticed the time. *See what daydreaming does to you?* she scolded herself as she hurried to dress. Finished, she glanced at her reflection and realized whoever had shopped for her had better taste than anyone she knew. The material itself, although pure cotton, was smooth and very soft, as if there were no threads holding it together, just air. The color was a dark shade of azure blue, which brought out the color of her eyes. Putting on her dressy red sandals, she changed her daytime purse for the lovely red one she saved for special occasions. She glanced in her mirror and smiled. *I really like this!* She checked her hair and makeup. As she did, she thought of the many times her mother had suggested she wear this color. "No," Naomi remembered saying all those years ago. "It will call attention to me. Please choose another color!"

"But," her mother would say, "why can you not let me show the world what a lovely girl you are, Naomi?" And so it would go every time her mother had to sew something for her, the same conversation over and over again.

I love this, Naomi admitted. *Mi mamá, you were right! I should have listened to you, but I was so afraid.* "Forgive me," she said aloud. Then she picked up her purse and left her room.

As she walked into the living room, Chaz emerged dressed and ready to go. He smiled as he walked to the vestibule, picked up a florist's box, removed a small corsage, of red tea roses, and white baby's breath. He motioned for her to stand before him and pinned it to her shawl collar. "I knew you would look lovely in that, for you are truly lovely to look at!"

"Am I really? I never thought so before today."

Chaz wrapped his arms around her slender waist. "There will never be a day when I will let you forget just how lovely you are. That blue is your color. I hope you wear it often."

"*Muchas gracias.* But, I have to admit, I did not pick this out."

"I know. I did.

"You did? But this is from *mi niñas.*"

"They asked me to accompany them so they could be sure they selected things that I would like for you. When I held up this dress, all of them asked the shop girl if she had it in a different color. They insisted, 'She'll never wear this!'"

"'Nonsense,' I said, 'Naomi is to be my wife. She will not be dressing to draw attention to herself but to please me.'"

"And do I please you?" Naomi cast her eyes down, afraid to look into his.

He lifted her chin until her eyes met his. "*Sí, muchísimo.* Yes, very much."

Aware that she needed a moment to collect herself, Naomi reached into her purse to pull out her scented hankie. "I forgot something. I will be but a moment." She rushed to her room and grabbed the delicate lace hankie she had sprinkled with rosewater as Madre Vida had taught her. Then she stopped and twirled around the room as she had seen Julie do ever since she was a little girl. Regaining her dignity, she straightened her outfit, and turned to leave.

"I am getting forgetful! My mind is so preoccupied I am forgetting important things." She unlocked her French doors, flung them open, went into the bathroom, filled the sink with cold water, soaked, and rung out thin oversized bath towels. She took the straight-backed chair from its place, rushed outside, and draped the towels over its back. Mounting the chair, she attached the towels to the makeshift line she had devised years before.

When she stepped up to the vestibule's landing, Chaz looked at her questioningly. "Is everything all right?"

"It is now."

He kissed her hand and they left arm in arm. "Good." They walked toward the church where they were married. This was their first outing in the community as man and wife. Chaz noticed that Naomi seemed nervous and asked, "Are you sure everything is all right?"

"Yes, of course. When I got to my room I realized that I had forgotten to prepare for the heat."

"The heat?"

"As Armando told us earlier today, different parts of the house were built at different times. My room was added later, and from what he did not say, I assume it was built without a permit, which means no one inspected it. That explains why in the winter, it is cold, which I can handle by wearing warm pajamas and bundling up with lots of down comforters. But in the summertime, if I forget to open the patio doors, and place damp towels in front of them, my room will become like a sweat box, impossible to sleep in."

"That works?"

"Yes. But only because the overhanging eves keep the wet towels moist for hours."

"Is that what took you so long?"

Naomi forced a smile as she thought about the ordeal of going to church and pretending to be someone different than she was. "Of course it really only took a moment, didn't it? I would not want to be late today of all days."

"No, you were not late, Naomi. It must be me. We were both ready at the same time. But I found it hard to wait for you."

"But, Chaz, it only took a few minutes and now I will be able to sleep there tonight."

"Too bad. I would have been happy to have you share my room with me instead!"

Saints and Sinners

When they reached church, some friends called them over to chat. A few moments later, the choir began to sing and they said their good-byes. As they mounted the church stairs, Naomi said, "Everyone made such a fuss over us. I feel uncomfortable when people gather around us as if we are the reason they are here!"

"*Nomi*, I know you prefer to live in the shadows, but now that we are married, you have become visible."

I do not know how much more visible I could become than I am today, Naomi thought as she tried not to shudder. She gritted her teeth and forced herself to say, "Yes, Chaz."

They entered the church. She followed her husband down the aisle. He sat her in one of the front pews and joined her. Aware that she was under the watchful gaze of the priest, she silently prayed, *Oh,* Adonai, *please help me.* The service began. While the priest's voice droned on, she found comfort in the memory of her *madre* telling them, "Follow what they do. And remember, you are there to honor *Adonai*, your God!" She nodded to herself, began to pray, and felt her body relax.

At the conclusion of the Mass, Chaz placed his hand on hers as they stood. He turned toward her. "Padre Paul gave us a lovely Mass today."

"Yes." They walked back through the pews. "Do you come to church often?"

Chaz tried not to laugh. "Naomi, I must confess. I never go to church. I did this for you."

"But, Chaz, I only come to light the candles and pray. I, like you, do not go to Mass."

When they stepped into the sunlight, Chaz turned to look at her. "You are not saying that to make me comfortable, are you?"

"No, I am saying that because it is true. I find the Mass very difficult. It is so long and drawn out. Besides, I always have so much to do."

"Good. It is settled. We do not need to go to Mass again."

"Well, yes that is true. But I do need to light my candles."

"*Como desee*, as you wish." They reentered the gloomy old building.

Chaz followed Naomi to the place where the votives were. He remembered being concerned that he had married a devout woman. However, as he watched her, he thought how well suited they were for each other. Then, just as quickly as that thought had come, he remembered the rumor that many who gave their lives to the service of others walk so close to God there was little room in their lives for someone with flesh and blood. When she looked at him, the vision of her took his breath as well as his fear away. But it was not until she lit her candle that he saw her transformed, illuminated by the soft light and thought, *Madonna, she is truly beautiful!*

Finished, she grabbed his hand, and they left the church. Naomi smiled at him as he looked at his watch. "Come, let us have a coffee." He led her to the barista's shop. When they entered, everyone stood. Naomi stepped back. Chaz took hold of her hand and drew her into the place. "*Nomi,* they do that whenever a woman comes in. Right, Peter?"

Peter nodded toward Naomi. "No, we stand to honor her! Welcome to our establishment, Tía." He motioned to a table and shooed those sitting there away. "Come, sit here! It is the best table in the place."

"No, no, that is not necessary. This table over here will do."

"Nonsense!" He settled them at the table and took their order. "I have been waiting a long time for you to visit. I owe you a debt of gratitude."

"You owe me nothing."

"Yes. I do. Angie, *venir a tu papá*—come to your papa!" He bent down and held his out his hands. The toddler came to him. "Look at her! Isn't she beautiful?"

"She is lovely. But I have never laid eyes on her, or you, so I am certain you owe me nothing, nothing at all."

He picked his child up. "Señora, are you not the lady who paid for Lupe Montoya's education?"

"I had a little to do with that, though not much."

"Well, then, see my child, she had a cleft palette. Lupe gave her a free surgery because you told her to give back as she could from what she received." With tears on his face, he sat down in a vacant chair. "We have been waiting a long time to thank you." Naomi stared at the man as he gathered himself together.

"Ramona, come. I need help out here." Peter turned his child toward Naomi. "See, this is what I want you to be like when you are grown!" Ramona came around the corner just in time to witness, "this foolishness," as she called it. "But this is the woman!" Peter exclaimed.

"Thank you for visiting us so that we could give you something from what we received." Ramona smiled at Naomi as she walked behind the counter. She tried to push out a beautifully wrapped gift box the size of an end table with her foot. "Peter, will you help me? The box is cumbersome, remember."

As they pushed it toward Naomi, she eyed the box. "I cannot take this. Give it to the doctor."

Peter and Ramona smiled at her. "Naomi, the doctor has received her gift. A cousin of ours works at the parking garage where she parks. We arranged free parking for her for a year. But you, *señora*, our angel who walks in our midst, we did not know what to give you. We spoke with your girls, one thing led to another, and all of those that have been touched by your work, whom we or the girls were able to contact, got together and made this for you."

Angie pulled her thumb out of her mouth and said, "Open, open, open."

Peter chucked as he rumpled her hair. "That's her new word for the day. Hey, Angelíca, today is the *open* day, *sí?*"

The little girl looked at the large box intently, toddled over to it, and looked up at Naomi. "Open, open, open."

"All right." Naomi removed the wrapping and took off the lid.

"What is it?" Chaz asked.

"I do not know." Naomi separated the tissue, smiled at the couple, and turned to Chaz. "Look, look at all this lovely detailed work."

A chorus of voices called, "Take it out so we can see!"

Looking up, Naomi saw that many of her *niñas,* as well as some of their children, and grandchildren had gathered inside the place. Others stood outside using their hands to block the glare while they tried to peer inside.

Maria jostled her way through the crowd outside and walked in. "All right, bring in the table top!"

"Chaz, what is going on?" Naomi watched the customers clear their tables and put them together.

"How would I know? I was in here earlier today. But I had no part in this."

Four women came in carrying a quilting board. They set it down on the hastily cleared tables, put down a clean white cloth, and placed the quilt on top. Naomi gazed at the beautiful handmade quilt and smiled. She opened her mouth to say something but words failed her. Her eyes sought her husbands. He smiled at her reassuringly. "I never expected anything," she began tentatively. She glanced in Chaz's direction, saw him looking at her, pride welling up in his eyes, and continued, "This is so beautiful! I will always treasure it and those who made it for me!" Her eyes moved from one square to another while she read the notes embroidered in the material and touched the needlework. "My mother and I used to quilt. I have not made one since I came to live here. Not enough free time."

Julie came forward. "Look, Tía, this is mine! Do you like it?"

Naomi looked at the needle-worked picture. "How did you do that?"

"Mother helped me! Remember she took a picture of me as I danced on your patio? We sketched it onto the square. Then I embroidered it. Do you like it?"

Naomi smiled and gave Julie a hug. "I love it." She looked up and saw the throng. "Thank you all so much. This is something I will always treasure!" When Julie stepped aside, another, and then another, and yet another woman, child, grandchild, or beneficiary of her work took her place so they could show Naomi their square and share a moment with her.

They left the barista's much later than either of them had intended. Naomi looked at the pre-twilight sky and a touch of anxiety threatened to steal her joy. Chaz struggled to manage the large bulky box and glanced at the sky. "Sunset in about an hour, my love." They waited for the light to turn green. "Am I to understand that you believed that no one knew about you, or any of the things you did that they benefitted from?"

"Well, I ..."

Maria pulled up in her station wagon. "Need any help?"

Chaz set the box down. "Yes."

"Good." She hopped out of the van and got her two boys to help load the box into her car. "I'll have the boys take this round to the back and put it by your French doors. Have a nice walk!"

"*Boys.* Those boys are as big as linebackers. They picked that box up as if it were full of feathers."

Naomi took Chaz's arm in hers. "It is not the strength of a man that is important but the integrity of his heart."

"Naomi, I could not have put it better." They crossed the street. "Integrity is everything!"

When Lola realized that Naomi and Chaz had left, she entered Naomi's room. *How nice of you to leave the doors open for me.* She looked around the sparsely furnished room and laughed. *This certainly looks like the room of a chaste woman!* Her eyes searched for her sponsor's hidden secrets, anything that would reveal her real identity. *That vivid blue outfit you wore caught my attention. I might have missed you if you hadn't stood on the chair while putting those damp rags up. We stopped doing that years ago! Even in Spain there are modern conveniences that allow us to deal with the heat! I feel sorry for you,* Lola laughed. *You're no match for me! You've learned to be content with whatever you're given. You silly woman! Haven't you realized that the world belongs to those who are willing to risk everything to gain an advantage? Your foolish attempt to cool down your room has given me access at last. You have let me in!*

Her gazed riveted on the matching side tables that flanked the bed, for she knew that many put their secrets in such a place. She walked to the nearest one, opened each drawer, and rummaged through them. Finding nothing of interest, she walked to its mate, and repeated her search. *Not much here of a personal nature.* She turned and faced the imposing wardrobe. Surprised by its surpassing beauty, she opened one door, looked through Naomi's things, and then shut it. Opening the other door, she resumed her search. She found the garments old fashioned and much too modest for her taste. Just as she was about to close the door, she looked toward the far right and saw a silk-wrapped hanger that held a delicate white peignoir. Aware that she was too short to reach the hanger, Lola stepped into the wardrobe, grabbed the hanger, and stepped out while her eyes caressed the negligee. *Who are you kidding? You're not going to wear this.* Lola laughed sardonically, placed the hanger around her neck, stood in front of Naomi's full-length mirror, and preened. Her eyes glazed over as she said in her most sultry voice, "Like me, Chaz? Come and see what *tu mamá* has for you!"

Startled by the noise of a car pulling into the driveway, she took off the garment, stepped into the wardrobe, and put the peignoir back where she had found it. As she turned to leave, her foot tangled in something. She bent down, pulled it off, took it with her as she got out, and closed the massive door. When she heard the men coming through the side yard she realized, *I don't know where to hide.* She heard the gate close. Their voices grew louder. She knew she was about to be discovered and ran to the dining room. She eyed the drapes and realized that they were so thick no one could see through them. A moment passed. She heard nothing, felt secure, and noticed the fabric clutched in her hand. She held it up and realized it was a skirt. *Schoolgirl garb. I heard Naomi came here as a teenager, and now I have proof.* She ran her hands down the side seams so the material would be flat for folding, felt something, put her hand in a pocket, and pulled out a letter. A sublime smile lit her face. She smoothed the envelope and turned it over to see whose name was on the address. Eyes aglow with malicious delight, she refolded it, tucked it into her waistband, and smiled. *This is what I have been looking for!*

Fearful of being discovered, she chose to stay where she was and looked around the room. *The design of this room was for the table to face north and south, not east and west as it does now.* Her curiosity aroused, she looked at the large gold rug that filled the room. *It's just as I thought,* she said to herself when she spotted the deep depressions where the table had once stood. *Someone moved the table so it faces east.* She stood in front of the massive breakfront and knew the changes accommodated Naomi's rituals. Lola looked at how the table was set and noticed the unusual the pair of candlesticks. *There is nothing else in the house made from this kind of wood! These weren't purchased by any of the previous owners.* The teenager walked to where Naomi would sit, saw the matches, and an exquisite scarf of intricately woven design in various shades of blue and white. *Ah, Naomi, tonight you face east as you light your Sabbath candles. In doing this you ask your husband to forsake the church! But I will show you up for what you really are!* Armed with what she needed, Lola waited for the men to leave and heard them speaking.

"Funny seeing Naomi at Mass today."

"Unusual. Never seen her in church except to light candles and pray."

"Madre says Naomi walks with God in her own way. Even after La Señora died, no one ever saw her pray, yet every one knows she does. She's a private person."

"That's why she needs her Friday evening and Saturday alone times," Lola heard one of the men say as they opened the gate and left.

Once she heard the gate bang shut, Lola breathed a sigh of relief and brazenly entered Naomi's kitchen. "I have won! You don't know it yet, Naomi, but I have beaten you at your own game! Just wait until they find out who you really are!" She took out a Coke, gulped it down, and left through the back door. *I'll enjoy seeing you unmasked before all your friends,* she thought as she reviewed everything she had discovered.

The teenager walked to the lower patio and wondered, *When is the best time to reveal this pretender?* She sat down in the shade. *The problem is that I will have only one chance to discredit her! I must confront her in front of as many of her friends as possible!* She tried to remember something she had heard that was eluding her. Frustrated, she picked up her magazine and entered her place of confinement. *I will remember. After all, there is not much to think about here except this.* She shuddered from a sudden chill. *It's gotten much too cold in here.* She walked to the air conditioning unit intending to turn it off but found it was not on.

"Poor Naomi," Lola purred with malice as she opened the letter. "You've no idea how hot it's going to get for you! There are no rags that will cover up who you are once I'm through with you!"

Then feeling that she had forgotten something important, she told herself, *If I can relax and let my mind drift, the information will come.* She closed her eyes to block out the distraction of the shadows the leaves made on the walls of the grandmothers house. Her mind drifted back in time and she tried to reach that state of awareness that her mother had told her was available to those with special knowledge. A sad sigh escaped her lips when she remembered the child she had been before her mother had left. She heard herself calling into the darkness of the night as she had then, "But how do I get this special knowledge?" while her mother rushed down the street away from her and the responsibilities of her family. Trapped in her memory, she saw her brother and sister, awaken, and roll over to look at her. She saw their wild-eyed hungry stares and said, "Don't worry. She will be back by morning, she always is." She pulled the tattered remains of the soiled bed linen around them and drew them close to her so they could share each other's warmth. Lola remembered it all as she dozed.

Sometime later, she roused herself as if from a drugged stupor. Her eyes still closed, she reached for the linens to cover the children. Unable to find them, she opened her eyes, and looked around her surroundings. *That was a long time ago. They're better off at the orphanage,* she told herself as she tried to remember them. Vince had on a crisp, white shirt and black pants with a crease in them just like a grown-up. Juliana wore one of those silly pleated skirts like the girls who go to the nuns' school. *Do not worry and do not forget me,* she called over the ocean to them with her heart. *I will come for you as soon as I can!*

She drowsed off again and heard herself calling to her mother while she hurried down the street in the dark, never to be seen by them again. "Where is this special knowledge? I need your help! Tell me," Lola screamed as she awoke. Befuddled, she walked to the kitchen and fixed a compress for her head. She returned to the couch, lay down, closed her eyes, and placed the cool compress on her forehead. She sighed and fell asleep. Hermana, my sister, when will you come for us? said the little voice that never left her alone for very long, We are waiting for you, but we are almost too old to stay. If we leave how will you find us? Lola placed her hand on the compress and muttered, "Just wear your little skirt, have Vince wear his outfit, and I promise I will...." She awoke with a start, threw the towel to the floor, and dashed to the door. "Wear your little skirt," she hollered. Where is Naomi's little skirt, she asked herself as she raced toward the house.

Naomi walked onto the patio. "Oh, look, the boys have already delivered it!" She opened the box and looked inside. "But where is the quilt?"

"Your door was open. Perhaps they put in there."

"Probably." She walked to her room and looked in. "Yes, it is on my bed."

"Good." He looked into her bedroom and noticed the stark white walls, not a picture or photo in sight. "That is much too valuable to be left outside. The boys showed wisdom by putting it in there."

"No." Naomi sighed with exasperation. "They are as nosy today as they were when Maria married their father."

"I did not know that you guarded your privacy so tightly."

Naomi closed the French doors and walked to the kitchen. "Chaz, my life has been filled with people who need many things from me. My bedroom has been off limits to everyone. It has been the only place where I could have some privacy. I have gone to great lengths to remember to shut the hall door tight. Otherwise, it would swing open and I knew those boys would see it as an invitation for them to enter. However, since I left the French doors open, they entered my room. They know better than to do that, because when they were younger, I caught them in there many times. I spoke to them about this, but they do not respect even this small request of mine."

"If you like, I will speak with them about this," Chaz offered as he drew her into his circle of love. She looked at him questionly. "Do not worry, remember as your husband, I swore to protect you."

Naomi looked at her husband's unguarded countenance and knew he was unaware of her duplicity. *I should tell him about me.* Just as she was about to speak, Chaz guided her to the back door and drew her into the dining room.

"You need to relax," he said, then added as he looked at her. "I hope you like the wine I bought to go with the special dinner you fixed. I would like to open it now and make a toast to our love and our life together." Aware that twilight was fast approaching, Naomi thought of all she needed to do. She wanted to ask her husband to wait. But as he bent down to kiss her, she felt her will evaporate, replaced with a smile. Chaz smiled and winked at her as he uncorked the bottle of the wine. He poured it into his glass, and began her education by calling it, "A good chardonnay." He swirled the liquid and held it up to the light to checked its clarity. "This allows one to experience the essence of the wine, which connoisseurs refer to this as its nose," he told her as he took a sip, which he held it in his mouth and breathed through his nostrils. "This allows you to sense the body of the wine on your palette." He poured a glass for her. "And this allows your husband to toast his beautiful bride."

Naomi took the glass, assaulted by feelings of longing and fear. Hoping to hide her thoughts, she glanced down and saw the skirt she had placed in the bottom of the wardrobe fifteen years before lying at her feet. Shocked to find it there, she picked it up, felt for her uncle's precious letter, realized it was missing, and drank the wine quickly. "Chaz, forgive me, but I must get the dinner on! Can we have another glass when we eat? I know I will be able to relax and enjoy the experience more then."

Perplexed by her response, Chaz shrugged.

"Good." Naomi ran from the dining room to her bedroom. She scanned the floor as she fled, her eyes searching in vain for the last link she had to her Uncle. When she entered her room, she closed the door, turned on the light, and searched the wardrobe. *Why was this out there? Where is Tío's letter?* She looked around the room and knew someone had been there. *But not the boys. They were curious. Whoever did this was malicious!* Unable to find an answer, she quieted her heart as best she could and placed the skirt in the wardrobe. Trembling with the fear of impending doom, she forced herself to return to the dining room as she silently told herself, *There is nothing you can do about this now.* She picked up her wine glass and walked to the kitchen. "I am sorry I ran out that way. Come keep me company."

"Yes, *Mamá.*" Chaz followed and watched in silence as Naomi took the plate of empanadas from the oven and carried them to the dining room table. Entering the kitchen once more, she returned with two servings of noodle *kugel* and a hearty salad.

As Naomi walked to the foot of the table, Chaz hurried to get there before her, and pulled out her chair. Once she had sat down, he returned to his seat. "*Nomi,* this looks especially good. It has been a long time since lunch."

"I need to bring in one more thing, then we will be ready to eat." She scurried to the kitchen and brought back her Friday night *challah,* wrapped in its embroidered cover. She smiled at her husband. "Now, dinner is ready."

Chaz sat down and began to put food on his plate. "It must be just about twilight I guess."

Naomi stood at the foot of the table.

Chaz glanced at her. "Is there something I can help you with?"

Aware that if Chaz understood what she was doing, he might consider it a sacrilege, she cleared her throat and smiled at him. "No, but will you stand while I light these candles?"

Chaz stood while Naomi covered her head with the scarf in the same way Jewish women have done since the Law of Moses came down from Sinai.

"Naomi, I will stand to honor you all the days of my life." He turned to refill his glass and missed the circling of her hands as Naomi's movements joined with all the women of her heritage through the generations while she silently prayed the litany, which brought her a sense of *Shabbat shalom*, Sabbath peace and freedom from fear.

She sat down and watched as her husband did the same. When he was finished filling his plate, Naomi said, "Please pass the plates down to me. Then tell me about your meeting with the foreman and how the work on your house progresses."

Chaz talked and talked. Every time he thought he had reached the end of his telling, Naomi would ask another and then another question. Finally, their meal concluded, Naomi had them move to the living room where she served espresso-flavored cherries to complement the sweetness of the cookies she had baked for desert accompanied by tea served in the silver service.

When Naomi sat at the baby grand piano, she was aware that a feeling of satisfaction seemed to flow between them, and was glad that she had decided to play the *Moonlight Sonata*. Chaz leaned back on the stuffed sofa, and his chest expanded with pride. He pulled a cigar from his coat pocket and looked in his wife's direction, waiting to see if she would allow him to smoke in the house. "Only on Friday night." She turned her mind to the music and serenaded his heart. Once the concert was finished, the refrain lingered in the air as Naomi rose from the piano to clear the table.

Chaz came up behind her and nuzzled her earlobe. "It is such a romantic night. Let us not waste it, my love."

She turned toward him. "Chaz, remember our arrangement. Tonight and tomorrow belong to me for myself alone." She picked up some dishes, walked into the kitchen, and turned on the tap.

He followed her carrying the *challah*. "Naomi, forgive me, I am a fool driven by desire. Here, let me do this. It is hot and you have done enough. Go, I will see you on Saturday."

"Are you sure?" She handed him the dishtowel. "You know there is no dishwasher here," she added as she handed him the scrubbing pad.

"I will correct that as soon as possible." He hung his jacket on the hook at the back of the pantry, glanced at the dishes, and smiled. "I have done my share of dishes. Do not worry. I will take good care of your special things, but you may find I have eaten the remainder of this wonderful bread you made for me."

"Do you like it?"

He walked to her and attempted to draw her near. "*Sí, mucho.*"

"Chaz, remember you promised! I can have my alone time."

"So I did. Well, if you must be alone, you better leave now or I will not be able to let you go!"

Naomi stood in the middle of the kitchen, stared at her husband, and thought, *God has truly blessed me.*

"Now go. The sooner you go, the sooner I will see you again!"

Sabbath Rest

Naomi overslept, headed for the shower, stood under the cool water, and tried to collect herself. A feeling of impending doom enveloped her. Before she could wonder why she was worried, she seemed to hear her *mamá* say, *"We all have our share of troubles, but if we trust in God, blessed be He, we will always find help, for he will teach you how to lead an honorable life."* Stepping from her shower, she asked her mother as she had when she was a child, *"But,* mamá, *Esther did not lead an honorable life. Yet God blessed her and used her to save the Jewish people!"*

"Oh, Naomi, when will you learn? Sometimes God puts us into situations where we need to survive until he calls upon us to stand up for him."

"When Queen Esther was called to stand up for God, did she?"

Her *mamá* had handed her the wash basket and they walked to the clothesline. *"Daughter, do you think we would be having this conversation if she did not do as God needed her to do?"*

"I see. Then Esther was a hero!"

"No, God was and is the hero! Esther was a servant just as your papá *and I are. And you—you will be a servant also, Naomi."*

"No," Naomi remembered saying as she stamped her foot. *"I want to be a hero!"*

Her mother had taken the wooden clothespin out of her mouth and used it to point at her. *"Naomi, wishing for such things could bring you much sorrow! Better a little quiet life of peace than a noticeable one of stress!"*

Naomi thought about these words as she dressed, opened her door, and listened. *I have not needed to do this for many years,* she thought as memories of her early experiences within the *casa* flooded back to her while she entered the hallway. She was prepared to flee to her room at the first sound but soon realized that the house was empty. Aware that

Chaz was out, she walked to the dining room so she could make certain he had put everything away as he had told her he would. When she entered the room, she felt Chaz's love as if its very essence permeated the walls that surrounded her. She looked at the table with the olive wood candlesticks still in their place, the matches, and her head covering next to them, and a sense of security and permanence she had never known enfolded her.

The unpleasant odor of instant coffee caused her to wrinkle her nose. She knew that smell could only be from Madre Vida's Sanka and assumed that her religious strictures had forced Chaz to rummage around in the cupboard until he found the old can. Hurrying to the kitchen, she set up the espresso machine, so that when he returned there would be good coffee, happily aware that though she loved the coffee, she had only begun to make it to please him.

She reached into the fridge, pulled out her Saturday food stores, and went back to her room. As she closed the door, she remembered her *mamá saying, "Today is a day to cleanse ourselves. Eat only natural things, not cooked food, but foods in their raw state, and drink only water. In this way, you will train yourself to focus on God and not your stomach. And in this way you will be healthier than those who do not follow this advice."*

"But, Mamá, *is this written in God's word?"* her sister Rebeca would whine.

"I do not know," Mamá would answer. *"But is it something we have always done, so it must be important that we continue to do this. Yes?"*

"Sí," Beca would mumble as Naomi watched her sister resign herself to the situation. *Oh, Beca,* it *was always so hard for you and so easy for me to eat this way,* Naomi thought. She laid out her food for the day. *But this thing that is now facing me, I know you would handle it well while I am uncertain what to do should my fears become reality.* Naomi closed her eyes, thanked God for the food, poured a glass of water, and remembered Beca telling her when things became difficult for her bear. "Be brave, like Esther, be brave!" She pulled a ripe plum from her bag and thought, *But Esther was a brave person. That is why God choose her.*

She picked up her Bible, turned to the cover page, and read, "The Holy Scriptures, according to the Masoretic text." Though she had owned it for many years, she still did not understand the significance of these words. However, as she scanned down the page, she saw the words "Published by the Jewish Publication Society of America" and smiled. She knew that only a Bible from this society could be hers. *Only in America can a woman leading a double life find a way to bring this blessed comfort into her home.*

Using the index as a guide, she turned to the story of Esther, read the Word of God, bit into a plum, and studied Esther's story. *It is as if God knew I needed this story and placed it here for me to read for such a time as this.* She smiled after she finished reading and placed her Bible back in its hiding place. *Queen Esther, you were one like me,* Naomi thought while covering her most precious possession with the yellow drapes. *I will use your story as my model and tell Chaz everything.* Aware that she could accomplish nothing without God's help, she did as Queen Esther had, and prayed.

As the suns rays faded, signaling the end of *Shabbat,* Naomi opened her wardrobe in search of a garment that would strike the just the right note with Chaz. *I want to look as if I had gone to a lot of trouble to present myself to him, just as Queen Esther did for her husband, the king. Yet I also need to look as someone who has no ulterior motive.* Her eyes settled on the peignoir, its message of purity spoke to her heart, and suddenly she knew what to wear. She pulled out a white cotton dress with a round neckline and caped sleeves, found her seldom worn scarf of many colors, and tied it to the side. Then placing her high healed huaraches on her feet, she was about to open her door and step out, when she realized her hair needed attention.

While she worked to tame her unruly tresses, she remembered Chaz's delight when he ran his hands through her loose tendrils. Her desire to please him uppermost in her mind, she shook out her hair, placed her hands in running water, worked some moisture through it, and wound her tresses around her finger. *When the moisture is gone, I can shake out my hair and wear it the way mi papá loved me to,* Naomi thought.

When she opened her door and walked into the hall, she thought, *This cool air feels like a caress on my skin.* She walked into the kitchen, noticed that the sun was low on the horizon, and took out the ingredients to prepare her special frittata. Although she had planned to wait until Sunday to tell Chaz her secret, after reading about Queen Esther she hoped the food would relax him so she could share her secret.

Chaz found Naomi in the kitchen and said, "I am glad you are back."

She greeted him with a kiss. "You have missed me?"

He caught her to his chest. "You have no idea what it is to miss someone as I have missed you! Everywhere I went people stopped me and asked why I was out without you. It seems that except for your *niñas* and a few friends, no one knows about your odd habit. I tried to explain them to those who asked but was told was to come home and apologize for whatever I had done to make you kick me out. Do you know what it feels like to be disgraced for no reason at all?"

A look of overwhelming sadness crossed her face. "Yes, yes I do. I know that feeling all to well. I grew up feeling that way. Remember, I told you all about that the other day?"

"Forgive me for making you think that I had forgotten." He inhaled the fragrance of the sautéing vegetables, potatoes, and spices. "That smells good."

Naomi noticed his hungry look. "Did you not eat?"

"Nothing tasted good to me."

"I had a bite or two of a plum and some water, but somehow eating without you was not very enjoyable."

Chaz wrapped his arms around her waist. "Did you know that it would happen like this for us?"

"I did not know what would happen or when, and I had assumed I would have to keep our dinner in the warm oven until you returned. But look, here you are at the very moment it is ready!" She cut the frittata, plated their food, and turned toward the dining room.

Chaz took the dishes out of her hands and looked at her with the full force of his love. "*Nomi*, let us eat in the other room."

"Why there? That is the room with the television."

It seemed to her that he did not hear her because he carried their plates into the den, and set them on snack tables, which she assumed he had set up while she was sequestered in her room. "There is a good ball-game coming on. I know you will enjoy it once I explain the rules to you!"

Naomi brought their drinks in, and sat down while he fiddled with the rabbit ears, his eyes glued to the little box. As the game began, Naomi watched him lose all sense of anything outside the image on the screen. *There will be no confidences shared this evening. I can wait until Sunday as I originally planned,* she told herself as Chaz ate with relish while she settled back and he educated her about the game of baseball.

Two hours later, Naomi yawned. "How much longer will this game go on?"

"That is the beauty of baseball. You never know!"

"What do you mean, you never know?"

"It depends on overtime."

Naomi took their plates into the kitchen. "I understand about over-time. The dinner is over, our desert is finished, we had our coffee, and I am over my desire to spend time watching a game that will never end!"

"But, Naomi, are you not the slightest bit interested in finding out who wins?"

Naomi stepped into the hall and saw her husband facing the television. "No, Chaz, you finish your game. I will prepare for tomorrow's guests."

"All right."

Naomi cleaned up from their dinner and set up for her *amiga* group. She placed the dishes in large woven baskets. The glasses and napkins graced the sideboard. Looking around the room, her eyes assessed her handiwork and she muttered, "Good, everything is ready for tomorrow."

She headed to the kitchen to clear the counters of all unnecessary objects especially the espresso machine, which she put in the cupboard. She knew that if it were left it out her friends would insist on her making a special cup *just for them* and that would cause her to be apart from Chaz whom she hoped would agree to join them just this once.

Tucking a tendril of hair behind her ear, she took her grocery list into her office, picked up the phone, and called her store.

"*Bueno*," said the familiar voice.

"Lana, is that you?"

The older woman chuckled. "*Sí*, Tía."

"I am calling to make certain things are going to arrive here as I requested."

"Don't worry. Everything will be at your house just like always, well ahead of your *amigas*. Haven't I always seen to this for you?"

"Yes. I do not know why, but it is especially important to me that everything tomorrow be—"

"Just so."

"*Sí*, just so."

"I'm finishing your lemon cake now. Desi will be here right after Mass to pick everything up. He will take your order to your *casa* like he always does."

"Good. For some reason I am nervous about tomorrow. I certainly do not need any surprises!"

"Naomi, if you did not want any surprises, you should have remained single. The life of a married woman is full of surprises."

Thinking about the end of her day, Naomi said, "I am beginning to understand what you mean." She placed the receiver in its cradle and walked to the den.

Chaz's eyes were fixated on the television screen.

"Tomorrow is a big day for me, I think I will turn in."

"All right."

When she entered her room and closed the door behind her, she admit to herself, *This has been an odd day. I feel as if our courtship, the past few days, and Chaz's attention were an illusion. Perhaps what I have seen this evening is really the man I married.*

Chaz turned toward the hallway and realized that Naomi was gone. Suddenly aware that he was a poor excuse for a bridegroom, he walked to her room. "Naomi, forgive me. I did not mean to take my thoughts away from you tonight." Hearing no response, he opened the door. Naomi froze, her desire for closeness replaced by her fear of exposure. "Naomi, let us not part this way. Come out and let us spend some time together tonight."

Naomi smiled, entered the hallway, and placed her arms around him. "It is a lucky woman who has a man that will pursue her."

Chaz kissed her brow. "Are you lucky then?"

"Yes."

He guided her to the patio and into the moonlight. "I am the most fortunate woman I know." They sat down by the fountain. He looked at her adoringly. "I will be right back." Breathing in the night, she leaned back in her chair and looked at the stars. *What is it about the night that makes it so magical?* Music enfolded her and she thought, *Chaz is thinking of me.* The words to their song pulled her back to the moment when had he showed her that she was important to him.

Chaz came back carrying a tray with a pitcher of iced tea and two glasses. "This is a lovely way to end our day." He filled her glass, then his, and pulled his chair parallel to hers. He sat down, placed his arm along the backrest, and motioned for her to snuggle with him. Naomi tried to cuddle, but squirmed, unable to find the right spot. "*Nomi,* you stress yourself over things that are simple." He guided her head to his shoulder where he knew she would find comfort.

"My mother used to say that. But I do not know how to be any other way."

"That is why you have me. I am a man who knows how to cut through all of your concerns. Trust me. Everything will be good for us."

Naomi nodded and felt her body relax. "Yes, everything will be good for us." She drifted off.

The soft colors of predawn filled the sky and a lone bird chirped.

"Sweetheart, we need to get to bed," Chaz whispered.

Naomi yawned, opened her eyes, and noticed that Chaz was looking at her strangely. "Did I fall asleep?"

He stood and shook his arm. "We both did."

"What woke you?"

"I noticed a tingling in my arm and needed to move."

"But you were trapped! I had you trapped!" she laughed.

"*Exactamente!*" Chaz helped her to her feet.

Naomi smiled at him. They turned toward the house hand in hand. Naomi noticed that he hesitated and realized that her French doors were open wide in an unspoken invitation for him to enter her room. He grimaced and directed their steps to the kitchen door. As soon as they crossed the threshold, she headed for her room. He followed. When she turned to say good night, she was startled to see the look of wounded pride in her husband's eyes. "I wish that tonight was our first night together, *amor mio.*"

She wrapped her arms around his neck. "Wait one more day. Tomorrow will last forever."

"Promise?"

"I promise," she boldly exclaimed, allowing him to see the yearning in her own eyes.

Chaz pulled her close. Naomi could feel his heart hammering in his chest. Before she knew what was happening, he pinned her against the wall while his hands began to grope her. Then, just as suddenly, he stopped, turned, and walked away. He called over his shoulder, "Tomorrow will last forever. I will make sure of that!"

Secrets and Memories

Sunday, early morning, though not fully awake, Naomi's mind was already at work. *So many things have changed since I was a little girl in Spain.* Mi mamá *used to say,* "*The world keeps getting older and so do I.*" *I never believed her, not until today. Maybe it is because tomorrow I will be thirty-one. Perhaps it is because tonight I will become one with* mi esposo. *For some reason I find myself thinking about the past and wishing my family were with me now.*

She rose from her bed and thought about her future. Her mind turned back to Spain, her family, and she found herself smiling wistfully as she peeked outside her French doors. Certain no prying eyes were watching, she opened them wide so the cool of the morning could enter her room. Walking to the chair, which had stood erect against the wall for more years than she had lived in the *casa*, she picked it up, and placed it along the left side of her wardrobe. She climbed onto the seat, stood on tiptoes, and reached as far as she could, intent on grabbing hold of the handle of her old suitcase. A smile lit her face as she lifted it out of the recessed niche, placed it on her bed, and opened it. Musty smells of her childhood permeated the old moss green silk lining, and greeted her, as she looked within. Her eyes roamed its fabric while she searched through the upper pockets and found what she was looking for. She teared up as she pulled out a picture of her family and gazed at the only tangible link between her and them. *Look at us,* she thought. *I wonder what they are like now.* Imagine as she might, she could not envision her sisters all grown up, and her *mamá* and *papá* older. Sniffling back her tears, she tried to remember the wise words she had heard her *mamá* share with other women as they prepared to wed and found herself sadly admitting, *I never paid attention because I thought I had all the time in the world to hear my mother's words of wisdom.* Not wanting to greet Chaz in a forlorn state, she forced a smile while she searched for and found a small picture with a document and pulled them out. She looked at her hidden identity with the eyes of her husband. *This could be my undoing. There in bold type is my real last name. If my husband knew that my original name was* Baruch, *which in Hebrew means blessed, I would probably lose him.*

Naomi remembered her father had said, "Your name has been given to you as a double blessing because both your first and last names have the same meaning but for different reasons! *The name Naomi was given to you because when the Naomi spoken of in Scripture believed herself forsaken by God, He, blessed her anew! And our last name . . . That to is a blessing! But we dropped one letter in our last name. Those who look for us can find us. But the rest of them, they do not know that our name means blessed since it is a Jewish word used in our Jewish prayer, the* Shema. *Is that not clever? There is only one letter difference!"*

"Yes, Papá." She sighed as if he was standing in her room. Responding as she always had, Naomi felt her old fears enlarge as her stomach and head ached from the strain of always trying to be someone she was not. While she looked at the picture of herself and her family, she fingered the worn edge of the small snapshot. She smiled a smile of longing and remorse. Though she knew the words by heart, she turned the picture over and read, "Naomi Baruch, born June 22, 1937. Named by Rabbi Leiva on June 24, 1937. May God continue to guide her all the days of her life." She searched for the words, which her mother had chosen for her from the book of Esther for her life verse and read, "But who knows? Perhaps you have come to this position for such a time as this."

She tucked the picture and the condemning birth certificate back in its envelope, closed the lid, and returned her suitcase to its hiding place. *Chaz will never know! He believes he has married Naomi Blanco because that is my adopted name. It is the name on my citizenship papers and this name is on our marriage license.*

Though she tried to distance herself from her premonition of disaster, she found she could not. Aware that there would be nothing gained by succumbing to fear, she headed for a refreshing shower and planned her day. *What could go wrong?* she asked as she dressed for the day, and opened her bedroom door. As she crossed her bedroom's threshold, she though about her life within a life while she, stopped, and reverently touched the little unobtrusive box affixed to the inside lintel of her bedroom. Wishing, as she always had, that it held the scriptures Jews hung on their lentil, she kissed her fingers, pretending that they had touched the place where God's holy words lay hidden, and prayed, Adonai, *allow me to gain favor in my husband's eyes when I share with him my faith and heritage.*

Satisfied that she had begun her day as her *mamá* had insisted she must, she hurried to the front door, picked up the paper, and tucked it under her arm. Sunday's paper was one of her pleasures because by reading it she found out what was happening outside her world of safety and seclusion. A smile lit her face and she sighed with anticipation as she walked into the kitchen, brewed a cup of tea, and glanced at the clock. *It is quite early,* she realized, hoping to have uninterrupted hours to peruse the paper.

With her tea in one hand, paper in the other, she sat down by the fountain, and pulled the sections apart. Naomi enjoyed her interlude as she sipped her tea, and read about everything that was going on in the city. She noticed that there was a revival of *Kismet,* remembered Lucinda telling her about seeing the musical, and admitted to herself, *That is something I would like to see. I have heard it is very romantic and I am beginning to realize that I yearn for such things now that I am in love.* She took out the funnies, remembered the previous night, and her failed attempt to have Chaz focus on her. Realizing that it was absurd of her to expect him to know what she needed without telling him, she scolded herself. It had been years since she had done that. But this morning that is exactly what she did when she thought, *If you had told Chaz that you wanted to speak with him about important matters, he would have turned off the game.* She realized how foolish she was to upbraid herself that way and chuckled.

Chaz smiled as he came up behind her and placed a kiss on her damp hair. "Good morning, my heart. It is good to hear you laugh. You were up early. Did you sleep well?"

She turned toward him and noticed his haggard appearance. "Yes, *y usted?* How did you sleep?"

"Not so well." He sat down across from her. "This waiting takes a toll on a man."

"On a woman too."

"You look as if nothing had caused you a moment's frustration."

Naomi saw him scrutinizing her. "Chaz, do you not realize that the work I have been called to do for the *niñas* made it necessary for me to hide my thoughts?"

"I know that you are guarded, but you do not need to be this way with me."

"If I learn to be less guarded with you, I may reveal something at immigration that would jeopardize my work." She picked up her paper. Her eyes scanned the text while she offhandedly added, "I do this as a means of accomplishing my goal. It has nothing to do with you."

"It has everything to do with me!"

"You are making too much of my reserved nature. I am certain you will come to appreciate it as we grow together. After all, I have seen what happens in some homes when a woman tells her husband her every thought."

"What happens?"

Naomi glanced at the comics and laughed. "Well, the poor man never has a moment's peace!"

Chaz's face flushed with anger. "If you want me to have peace, then why do you laugh?"

Naomi looked up from the funnies and burst out laughing. When she was finally able to control herself, she said, "My laughter is not aimed at you, but this comic I am reading! Come over here." She patted the seat next to her. "I will show you why I laughed."

Chaz sat next to her. Naomi pointed to the cartoon. "See, is that not funny?" He looked at the drawing of a cat, a dog, a goldfish, and tried to figure out what made Naomi laugh. When Naomi realized that he did not see what she did, she said, "Sweetheart, each one of them is trying to think like the other one does."

"Why is that so funny? Trying to understand someone is a sign of respect!"

"Yes, but look, they do not do this because they like each other. They are trying to take advantage of each other. Now look at the last box. See what has happened?"

"All I see is a big hovering cloud and feet."

"Right! They have gotten into a fight! They are just like people. If we do the right thing for the wrong reason, we may get the wrong result! Is that not funny?"

"Naomi, you have a strange sense of humor!" He stood, walked to the kitchen, and noticed that she had prepared nothing for them to eat. "Naomi, are you planning to cook breakfast?"

"I am reading the paper. I will make you something in about an hour."

"You will cook for me in an hour!" He crossed the threshold. "I do not need you to cook for me! Better, I should cook for you! Then you will be put in your place!" He fumed as he fixed them a hearty breakfast. A short while later, he carried a serving tray laden with food onto the patio. "Permit me." His pronunciation was curt and his stance ridged.

Naomi stared at him for a second then beamed. "Why, Chaz, how very kind of you." She put the paper aside. "I will clear the table." While Chaz placed their meal on the table, Naomi looked at the food he had prepared. "No one has ever cooked for me like this." She tasted the eggs. "These are very good. How did you learn to make them?"

Chaz took a fork full of eggs. "My *madre* insisted I know how to take care of myself. 'Chaz,' she would always say, 'you may marry a girl who does not know how to do anything. You may need to teach her!' So I let her teach me these things when the men of my family where not around to make fun of me."

"Yes, it feels awful when someone makes fun of you."

"Not just someone! Your family. It feels bad when the people you look up to tell you that you do not measure up, even if they tell you that whatever you have not done well they will keep a secret! Yes?"

"*Sí*... a secret." Naomi winced and teared up.

Chaz noticed her reaction and took her hand in his. "Naomi, I feel as if I have put a wall between us."

She brushed her tears aside. "There is no wall between us, nor will there ever be, if I have anything to say about it."

"Good!" He gulped down the last of his breakfast. "How fast can you be ready to leave?"

"Are we going someplace?"

Chaz held up two tickets. "It is a surprise."

"I see that you have tickets for a ferry ride. Where are we going?"

Chaz carried the remains of their meal inside. Naomi followed on his heels. "That is for me to know and for you to find out! Get your jacket and hat. Then meet me on the porch in five minutes."

"But, Chaz, I have to clean up from our breakfast and we have company coming this afternoon. I cannot leave now!"

"Yes you can!" He set the tray down, picked her up, and carried her to her bedroom door. "*Nomi* from now on Sunday, before your *amiga* group comes, is our time. You are to have the store deliver what you need and ask Florita to come and help you as she did yesterday. That will allow us to get away! It will be good for us to have time together and what better day than when everyone is in church or pretending to be too sick to go to there. Immigration will never call on Sunday. It is the perfect day for us to be together without you feeling guilty because you were not available to help someone!"

"You are right and I love you for thinking of this!"

"Good, you have just five minutes to get ready!"

Five minutes later, Naomi was on the front porch, ready to go, her face flushed with excitement. When Chaz walked onto the porch, she looked at her watch. "It seems to me that you are a minute late!"

He gazed upon his lovely bride, was glad that she wore the outfit he had bought for her, took her by the hand, and twirled her around so he could get the full effect of the glorious hat and scarf, which framed her face beautifully.

He heard a noise and glanced at the curb. "Come, our cab has arrived."

"A cab? I have never used a cab except for an emergency! Money should not be squandered needlessly!"

"I agree. We do not want to throw away money, but our Sundays are precious. I do not care how much it costs for us to have the pleasure of these few short hours together. This time belongs to us and us alone."

"Yes, Chaz."

They walked to the curb, Chaz opened the door for his bride, and she slid in. He joined her on the bench seat. She snuggled close and looked into his clear brown eyes. "I have planned this day especially for you." He smiled, wrapped his arms around her, and gave the cabbie the address. "I hope it will be meaningful and help to heal some of your hurts."

Every fiber of Naomi reacted to Chaz's words as their cab sped away. *God, does my husband now want to fix me? Or is he trying to be thoughtful?* She glanced at him and he smiled at her. *Be calm,* she told herself. *The people who hurt you before did not care about you. No one who cares for you would willingly cause you pain. Relax! Relax! Relax!* She repeated the words to herself as the ride and the security of Chaz's nearness lulled her into a sense of peace.

As the cab neared the wharf, she felt conflicted and thought, *I have felt this way before.* She was leery of what might await her but forced herself to silently reprimanded her fears. Finally, the cab stopped. Plastering a smile on her face, she stepped onto the same wharf where she had stood years before.

Chaz glanced her way.

Naomi teared up as she looked at the harbor. She remembered the official taking her from the ship she was on. She remembered arriving at Ellis Island. She had known an interview and subsequent deportation were the only possible outcomes to her story. The fears she had experienced engulfed her as if the past fifteen years no longer existed and she was again that frightened teenager. She looked at the wharf where the ferry she and Madre Vida had taken all those years before had docked and shivered.

Chaz noticed and put his arms around her. "Are you all right?"

She did not respond.

He smiled. It seemed to Naomi that he was certain he understood her problem when he said, "You are here legally. No one has the right to take you away." Taking her hand in his, he led her up the gangplank of the ferry and coxed her up the stairs to the top deck. Unbeknownst to Chaz, he seated her in the same place she had sat in fifteen years before. "Today is a good day for facing fears. I will help you rid yourself of some long-standing demons, and since your *amiga* group comes today, you will help me feel comfortable in a house full of women. Yes?"

Forcing herself to remain calm, she looked at Chaz. She realized he understood more about her than she had assumed. "Yes," she said, her voice constrained. She sat down and closed her eyes. "Tell me when we get there."

"But, Naomi, the boat ride is lovely. Do you not want to see the harbor and watch the birds?"

"I will face this and never go back to that place again."

"You will feel different afterwards."

"How do you know how I will feel? You have never had America denied you! You have never needed to sneak around like an unwanted thing! Can you really believe that you understand what I felt or what will help?"

"I know that the things we do not make peace with haunt us." He drew her close. "You are not that fifteen-year-old girl. You are loved, have a full life, and you are an American citizen. No one can take those things away from you."

She pulled away and looked into his eyes. "Are you so certain about that?"

"Yes, I am. But I do not know how to help you believe that what I say is true."

She forced a smile. "I will try to borrow some of your ideas and try to believe as you do."

The boat stopped at Liberty Island. "Good." Chaz turned his attention toward the statue and stood. Naomi did likewise.

Her gaze followed his. "I never saw that the last time I was here."

"But why?"

"When I discovered Abuela Sosa had died, we were outside the harbor. With everything that happened, I missed seeing the statue. When the immigration official took me to Ellis Island, I kept my eyes shut. I knew I would not be allowed to enter the land and did not want to see the statue."

"What happened when your *tía* rescued you from immigration?"

"By then, I was so scared, hungry, and alone that I accepted help from someone I did not know. She seemed nice, but I was so concerned about discovering what I had agreed to that I forgot to look at the statue." She looked at 'The Lady,' as her uncle had called the statue, while both of them took a moment to collect their thoughts. Chaz moved away from her. Although it was only a slight separation, his movement was not lost on Naomi. *This was to be a special outing, just for the two of us. How can he have chosen something so painful?*

"Would you rather stay aboard the ship?" She nodded and looked at him beseechingly. They sat down. The time ticked by as they waited. Naomi stared ahead, dry-eyed, while she tried to forget all that had occurred and how the situation had forced her into a life she thought she had fled. Finally, the passengers returned from their tour. The boat pulled away from the dock. When the boat docked again, they tried not to look at each other, fearful of what they might see. They stood, not quite knowing what to do. A young man walked by with rock 'n' roll music blaring from his transistor radio. Chaz noticed Naomi's reaction. "Can you put on another station?"

"Why should I?"

"That is hardly music for a honeymoon."

"Don't worry! I know just the station." He turned to a station playing romantic music. "My mom likes this."

The announcer said, "And now, from the Broadway musical *Kismet*, we bring you, 'And This Is My Beloved.'"

Naomi smiled. The music swelled around them. She looked up at Chaz and admitted, "That is the musical I wanted to see."

> *Dawn's promising skies*

Chaz reached for her hand.

> *Petals on a pool drifting*
> *Imagine these in one pair of eyes*
> *And this is my beloved*

Naomi decided to trust him as he had asked her to and placed her hand in his.

> *Strange spice from the south*
> *Honey through the comb sifting*

The music engulfed them. If anyone had asked Naomi, she would have said it created an unspoken bond between them. *I do not care where he takes me*, she admitted to herself, *I would follow him anywhere!* As the music crested around them, they looked at each other, remembered the divide that threatened to cost them their happiness, and smiled at each other. Chaz drew Naomi toward him and gazed onto her eyes. "Trust me and do not fear."

"I will." They walked to the visitor's center and into the day that lay ahead of them.

Later, as they were about to head back to the ferry, Chaz asked, "Is everything all right now?"

"*Sí*, everything is fine." The young man with the pocket-sized radio walked past them. "I think I have gotten my bearings right for the very first time." Turning toward the dock, they looked down on the little jetty where their boat was docked and heard the music swell.

Chaz placed her hand in his. "This song speaks of you and our love."

Naomi blushed. "Will you be thinking of me this way for always?"

"Yes." His eyes caressed hers. "You see, there is nothing here to fear, just new things to experience."

Lola looked out her window, watched the *casa,* and waited. *This is boring,* lamented the teenager. Since her windows were open, she had heard Chaz ask Naomi to spend the morning with him. "How sweet of him to give me the opportunity I needed to get that suitcase from where Naomi hid it!" she cooed. "I don't even have to worry about being discovered!"

After they left, she entered the kitchen. She hoped to find fresh brewed espresso but finding none, she settled for a Coke. *This will do for a pick-me-up,* she thought. She sat down at the kitchen table, savored the soda, and the freedom of being in the *casa. Poor Naomi, you'll never know what happened to you, you poor, stupid, unsuspecting child! You may be older, but I'll prove I'm wiser!* Finished, she walked into Naomi's room, saw the chair her benefactor picked up, and placed it where Naomi had. Since she was shorter than Naomi, she placed a pillow from the bed on the chair, stood on it, and grasped the handle of the old suitcase. "Now we'll see who you really are." She put the suitcase on the bed, opened the latch, and rummaged through its pockets. When she found Naomi's secrets she smiled to herself, and carried it to the grandmother's house. *You'll be so busy when you get back you won't have time to miss this!*

Satisfied that she had everything she needed to unmask that pretender, Lola lay down in the midmorning heat. *I will not be able to rest until Naomi is exposed!* Feeling agitated, her sense of destiny almost realized, she tried to quiet her thoughts. When she was almost asleep, the house phone rang. She put a pillow over her head and hoped it would stop but soon realized that the caller would continue to let it ring until someone answered. She ran to the kitchen intending to take the receiver off the hook.

When she lifted the phone, Lola heard a nasally female say, "*Hola.*"

This could be a godsend, she realized. *Find out what the woman wants!* "Can I help you?" she asked in a sweet voice. She heard voices in the background coaxing the woman.

"Wait. I'll find out," the woman whispered to the others.

Lola waited impatiently while the woman conferred with her friends. Finally, she asked, "Is Naomi in?"

"No, Chaz and Naomi are out."

The silence that followed gave Lola time to devise a plan. Using her most ingratiating voice she asked, "How can I help you?"

"I am calling for some of us who made squares for Naomi's quilt."

"What a lovely gift. Naomi really likes it!"

"Well, good … Is it possible … well, you know how it is."

"Well, yes," Lola said while she tried to understand the woman's unspoken request. "Do all of you want to stop by and see how beautiful it looks now that it's put together?" She heard a sigh of relief from the woman. "Come today about one thirty. I know Naomi will want to thank all of you for what you have given her."

"Oh, that is very good," the woman said. She repeated the invitation to her friends.

"But this is Naomi's afternoon with her *amiga* group," one of the women objected. "We can't barge in!"

Lola listened while the women debated among themselves. Frustrated, she finally asked, "Would you deprive her of the pleasure of thanking you herself? You know how busy she is with her work and now a husband. It would be better for all of you to come here than for her to try to thank you each, one at a time."

"That is true," she heard the women say.

"Now, I'm not going to tell her you're coming. I think this should be a surprise. Otherwise, she will worry about not having enough food for everyone."

"Don't worry. We'll call the others and make it a big surprise for Naomi. We'll bring the food and drinks. It'll be a real *fiesta*."

The women who had been speaking in the background chimed in, "Yes, a *fiesta* for Naomi!"

"What a wonderful idea!" Lola smiled, happy to know that she would be able to reveal Naomi for who she was in front of the entire community. A malevolent grin contorted her face into a grotesque mask. "I'll look forward to seeing you all this afternoon!"

"Yes, we'll see you this afternoon!"

Lola hung up the phone and thought, *This is coming together better than I had hoped!*

She sauntered back to her place of confinement, opened the door, and realized, *I don't mind being forced to be here. After all, what's a few hours more when I'll soon have it all? Besides, being here gives me time to plan everything.* She raced to the suitcase, opened its lid, found, and reviewed the evidence. Then she planned how to use the bits and pieces to build her case. Hoping she had saved the best for last, she opened the letter, and smiled to herself, a smile of pure malice as she read:

Dear Sister,

Things go well for me here, but I miss all of you. I pray that in time you will be able to join me here in a free land where we can practice our faith openly. I am sending you some money towards the sea voyage. Perhaps one of the older girls can get a job with someone who is coming to America in exchange for the rest of their fare. Once they arrive, I will be able to show the government my ability to take care of them and America will let them in. Then the two of us can work, and save, and so that eventually, we will all be here together. Until then may God, blessed be He, continue to watch over all of you.

All of my love,
Your brother, Abraham Cohen-Scali

Lola gloated silently. *This proves that I was right! If I only had this, it would be enough to condemn her because everyone with the name of Cohen is a Jew! If her uncle is a Jew, then so is she! Hidden Jews have called themselves by different last names for centuries and I am certain Naomi has as well! Everyone knows that no one does that unless they have something to hide. And adding Scali, again a Jew trick. Many of them added a Spanish name before or after theirs. However, I haven't been fooled, I was never fooled! I knew she was a Jew from her curly hair, to her arrogant features, her attitude of superiority... all I have uncovered proves it! Chaz will get rid of her and he will thank me!*

Her head filled with dreams of unquenched longing, Lola lay down and drifted into a fitful sleep. Although she did not wake, she wondered about her restlessness. *I haven't thanked God for helping me find what I needed to unmask this deceiver.* She called out to God in her delirium, "God, thank you for allowing me to show everyone who Naomi really is. I have done what you have asked me to do! I have earned my reward!"

Hoping to be able to sleep, Lola turned over so the full light of day was behind her. Still she found no peace. Eventually she got up more worn out than she had been before. Groggy, she walked to the bathroom and stripped off her sodden clothes. She set the water to its coldest setting, stepped into the shower, and let the full force of the water hit her body. Shaking uncontrollably, she emerged, and dried herself. Thinking her body was reacting to cold air, she hurried to turn the air-conditioner off and was surprised to find it was not on. "Come on," she commanded her body as a wave of shivers hit her so hard she found it difficult to stand. "You can't get sick now! Tomorrow you can rest. Tomorrow everything will be sorted out as it should be!"

She knew she had to look her best for the unmasking. So she walked to the little closet and assessed each outfit. *I must look pure, virginal, as one who has nothing to gain but is doing this out of a sense of duty to God.* She held up a pure white shift. *I will appear to them as an angel, a bearer of God's wisdom to them*, she thought. *I'll tell them what I know and they'll react as only those in the church know how. They'll be free of Naomi's tricks and Chaz will be mine.*

An hour before Naomi's *amiga* group was to meet, Desi pulled the truck into her driveway. Unlatching the side gate, he walked across the patio, and opened the kitchen door, keeping it ajar with an old Spanish tile used for that purpose. It always took him four trips to bring in Naomi's Sunday order.

Lola heard him walk back and forth and observed his every move. When she saw him close the side gate and return to the *casa*, she realized he had more to take care of inside the house. *Now's my chance*, Lola thought as she walked unhurriedly across the patio and into the kitchen. She smiled at Desi. "*Hola*, it's a hot day. Isn't it?" She turned on the faucet, reached over, cupped water into her palms, and used her hands to place it on her neck. The liquid ran down her torso in rivulets that drew the young mans eyes to the curves it brought into sharp focus. Batting her eyelashes at Desi, Lola cooed, "Do I know you?"

Caught off guard by her pure attire, Desi assumed she had not meant to stir him the way she had. Gulping and sputtering he answered, "I haven't seen you here before, or anywhere else for that matter!"

"Because that Naomi keeps me hidden!"

"But why?"

"Ah, that's a good question." Lola smiled. "I wish I had a good answer for you, *señor.*"

"Do you mean that you're not here of your own freewill?" Desi tried to focus on the work he needed to complete,

"*Sí,* Naomi holds me captive and won't let me go." She pointed to the grandmother's house. "If she knew that I'd come out from the little house down there, I fear it wouldn't go well for me."

"She's never treated anyone like that before. Why is she treating you this way?."

Lola smiled at him, leaned over the sink, cupped water into her palms, and moistened her neck while the water made her upper body visible through the wet material. "I am sorry to say I do not know."

Desi drank in the soft perfection of her frame. His gaze followed the rivulets of water to where they merged and noticed that she wore nothing under her flimsy shift. Startled and repulsed, yet aroused and excited, he headed outside. "I'm certain there's a good reason."

Lola laughed at his remark and followed him to the side yard. "Don't be scared, little man. No one will ever know besides you and me. You'll see. Being bad can feel so very good."

Shocked, Desi turned to look at her, repulsion and desire visible in the set of his jaw. "Never will I want a woman who acts like you!"

She walked toward him, arms open wide to enfold him. "Oh, but you do want me." Mesmerized by her sinewy walk, and the way the light played on her skin, Desi stood transfixed. Lola continued to use all that she knew to bind him to her. "Come to *mamá,*" she uttered in her most sultry voice.

Naomi entered the kitchen and saw boxes on the countertops. "Desi, Desi, are you here?" Her voice escalated with concern as she repeated her question.

Chaz followed her. "I heard you calling. What is the matter?"

She pointed to the boxes of perishables. "I came into the kitchen and found things were not set up."

"Today it is taking him a little longer. After all, his truck is here, so he is here somewhere. Do not worry."

"But, Chaz, Lola may have seen him!"

"Calm down." Chaz motioned for her to sit down. "After all, what would Lola want with him? He is just a boy."

"Chaz, listen to yourself!" Naomi shouted. "You told me not to keep her here and now I have endangered Flora's son!"

When Lola heard Naomi and Chaz yelling at each other, she turned her attention toward the kitchen. Desi took advantage of the opportunity and fled. "Good, they are fighting," Lola murmured to herself. She turned back to complete the young man's education and saw him latch the side gate as he left. "I'll take care of you later," Lola whispered. She moistened her lips with her tongue. "There'll be plenty of time later!"

A moment later, Desi walked through the front door, saw Chaz, and nodded. "I've been checking your build-out across the street."

"Naomi, Desi is here." Chaz pulled him into the kitchen. Upon seeing Desi, Naomi fled in tears.

"Women, I'll never understand them!"

"That makes two of us. Come, I will help you finish."

While they set up the food, Chaz tried to get Desi to talk but found him tense and on edge. Finished with the work, he offered Desi a Coke. They sat on the front porch and gulped down their sodas, enjoying the slight breeze. Chaz eyed the young man. "Anything unusual happen today?" Desi stared at the older man and thought about the young woman he had seen. Chaz watched as Desi's face revealed what Naomi had feared. "So you met Lola."

"I saw her. She spoke to me. She tried to entice me. I felt drawn to her. I would've done whatever she wanted, but I didn't meet her. No! If you are wondering if I met her, I did not! And I don't ever want to meet her. She is *indecent!* You know what I mean. She is filth! Why does Tía have her here?"

"That, my friend, is a question for the ages. Why does a woman do what she does? If you find out, be sure to tell me. I would really like to know. I told Naomi the girl was no good. She had her stay here anyway. But she goes tonight and good riddance!"

"How has Naomi put up with this, this thing in her home?"

"Desi, when someone is as pure as Naomi, they do not see the evil in this world."

"Yes, that sounds like Tía all right!"

"Tell me, Desi, why do you also call her Tía? She is not your aunt or relative and you are not one of her *niñas*."

"Oh, you're wrong about that, my friend." Desi laughed. "Once Naomi has extended any part of herself to you or your family, you become part of her family. I think it's because when she came here, she had no one. Now most of the *barrio* is indebted to her. But she never lets us feel that way. She lets us feel like family by making each of us part of her life."

"I did not know that Naomi had such a large family."

Desi stood and walked to his truck. "If all of us got together, I think even this house with its large patios wouldn't be able to hold all of Tía's family."

Chaz walked into the kitchen, his desire for his bride heightened by his realization of just how much her caring ways had changed so many lives. Naomi heard him enter and turned toward him. Chaz nodded. "That boy was caught off guard by Lola. If we had not come home when we did, I do not know what would have happened."

Naomi ran to her husband. "Please forgive me for not listening to you when I brought her home. I did not understand what you were saying."

"Of course you could not understand."

"I should have trusted your judgment. If anything happened to him, it would have been my fault!"

"Naomi, how could you have known? You never met anyone like Lola. Anyway, forget it. She can do nothing to any of us. We all know she is no good. Besides, the boy is safe. Go freshen up. Your *amigas* will be here in a few minutes and you do not want them to see you like this. Go get ready. I will finish here."

Naomi looked around the kitchen. "Well..."

"Tell me what to do and I will do it. Trust me!"

"You mean like I did today?"

"Yes, just as you did earlier today."

Naomi rushed over and kissed him. "Chaz, I never knew how to face down any of my fears until today." She ran toward her bedroom. "With you here, I can do it all!"

"Do you not mean that together we can face anything?"

She turned to look at her husband and smiled. "Yes, that is exactly what I said!"

Daughter of Zion

Naomi studied her reflection in the mirror and realized that the haunted look around her eyes and the tightness in her jaw had disappeared. Aware that she liked the woman she was becoming, she smiled at herself. She placed her lovely new hat on her head and draped the colorful scarf around her neck, allowing it to flow artfully over her shoulder. Feeling loved, she almost danced into her office as she thought about the song Florita had gotten for her. She shut the door, retrieved it, stepped into the parlor, and smiled to herself, pleased that she had a surprise for husband. Taking her place at the piano, she put the sheet music in the stand, and lifted the keyboard cover while she hummed the tune that had so deeply affected her. As she placed her fingers on the keys, she hoped the song would speak to Chaz. She wanted him to experience the music, as she had, a gift from *Adonai*. The melody filled the air. Naomi's mind drifted back to the tender way Chaz had helped her overcome her fears, and his loving concern for her. She smiled and admitted to herself that although she had loved him before, she had never understood the fullness love could be until then. Her fingers seemed to fly across the keys while she found herself praising God for she knew that this love was a gift from him that could weather any storm. Then as if layering memory upon memory, Naomi remembered how Chaz's gift of music had touched her heart and knew it could not have happened if he had not become her husband.

Chaz entered the parlor and watched his wife, content to revel in her presence and the magic the music evoked. Naomi saw him and nodded. He studied her and saw a woman who had acquired a sense of self and an inner peace. *I have won her and with God's help, I have gentled her. She is mine and by her own admission she is sorry she did not listen to me.* He remembered his discussion with the priest and the counsel he had received as a young boy from his *padre* and *abuelo*. He thought of Bridgette's words and knew that what she had said was true. Then he winked at Naomi, pointed toward the suit, smiled, and saw her color heighten. She inclined her head toward what one would describe as *the listening chair* since it faced the piano. Chaz nodded, and sat down where she had directed, pleased that she wanted him close. The music's tempo changed, surprising him with a rendition of a song that she knew held special memories for them both.

"This is from me to you, *cariño*," she whispered. Her soft alto voice seemed to fill the room as she sang, "You ask me how much I need you, must I explain?"

Chaz realized that their two hearts were finally one and brought his baritone to accompany her in singing, "I need you, oh, my darling, like roses need rain," as he stood, and crossed to the piano. Finished with their rendition, Chaz clapped his hands. "That was marvelous, *que maravilloso!*"

"Yes! We agree," female voices called from the vestibule as those gathered there applauded.

The couple turned and looked at the crowd. "Why are you here?"

"We called to speak with you, but the two of you were out. A young woman—"

"Yes, this woman Lute speaks of, she invited us to come and see how lovely your quilt looks now that it's finished."

One of the women noticed Naomi's look of surprise. "We should leave."

"It is all right." Naomi motioned for them to come in.

"We didn't come empty handed," Stella said. She carried in a seven-layer dip large enough to feed twenty.

"Yes, we all brought something for your *fiesta!*" Susanna motioned for those behind her to enter.

Chaz eyed the chichén asado that Nicco carried in for Lucinda. "I think a *fiesta* for Naomi is *una muy buena* idea!"

Naomi pulled Chaz aside. "We were to have a small group here today. Who could have arranged this?"

"I do not know, but let us take advantage of this outpouring of love. After all, who better than you to have a *fiesta* in her honor?" He smiled at the petite woman bringing in a large watermelon. "Let me help you with that."

Aware that her husband's lack of concern should put hers to rest, she greeted the women, excused herself, and returned with the memory quilt. She draped it over the couch and watched as the women crowded around.

Evelyn bent over and touched one of the finer needle-worked pieces. "I didn't know it would be so large."

Naomi smiled at her. "Which square is yours?"

"This little ordinary one over here."

"It is one of my favorites."

"It is? But why?"

"You captured what it was like for me when I first came here." She pointed to the embroidery at the bottom of the square. "This prayer is one I prayed often when I first came to the *casa*."

Evelyn smiled and turned to the women. "I knew it would be all right for us to come!"

"Look at mine next," the women seemed to say in one voice. Chaz pulled up a chair for Naomi to sit on while one by one they came to look at the quilt and show her their work. Chaz stood by, beaming as he watched his wife and heard the women's words of appreciation. With every comment, he marveled that of all the men who had sought her hand, and he had that heard there were many, she had chosen to marry him.

"Everything is ready! Let's eat," someone called from the kitchen.

"But, *mis amigas*," Naomi said as she stood. The crowd pressed forward, pushing her ahead of them.

"We're all here," Justine called from the front porch. "The crowd was so thick we have been unable to come in but now that everyone seems to be moving to the patio, we can enter the *casa*."

Naomi turned back hoping to see Justine and her *amigas*. Unable to spot them, yet wanting them to feel her love, she remembered that Madre Vida had taught, when not certain what to say, say something positive and said, "Good."

Upon reaching the patio, the throng dispersed and Naomi saw the transformation that had taken place in her backyard. There were festival lights, long tables covered with orange table clothes, chairs, a buffet ready to eat, and a small group of musicians playing the songs of her youth.

Naomi walked toward an inconspicuous chair. Flora noticed and pointed with pride to the one belonging to La Señora. "Naomi, you must sit in the set of honor!"

"I cannot sit there!"

Chaz took her hand, led her to the chair, and explained, as one would to a child, "Naomi, it is time for you to take your rightful place in the community, and own who you are. Sit in the chair they have brought for you."

"Yes, Chaz." She sat on the chair of authority and smiled while a woman brought her a plate of food. Then everyone sat down and began to eat.

Chaz's gaze swept the throng. He saw Nicco kiss Lucinda good-bye and leave. "Am I the only man here?" He turned to leave.

"No, do not leave. You belong here with me."

"But, Naomi, I had not planned on all these women. It is overwhelming!"

"That is why I need you to stay."

"Yes, stay, Chaz," the women said. They pointed to the place next to Naomi, which they had draped with a blue ribbon that said, "Reserved for Chaz."

A familiar voice from the far end of a long table said, "You should always share in the joy and blessings of each other."

Scanning the unknown faces in search of the one that belonged to that voice, Chaz spotted her, and smiled. "Naomi, look, my friend Teresa is here!" He walked toward the old woman.

Naomi realized who it was and snarled, "I do not want you—"

"You don't want her here?" Lola emerged from behind the large tree. "Of course you don't want her here. What's the matter, Naomi? Afraid that old Jew would reveal your secret? Don't worry about her. I have all the proof anyone will ever need about you and your deceptions! Look," she said as she held up the telling evidence. "This is who you have chosen to honor, a Jew! Here is her birth certificate, a letter from her uncle. It's all here. Look!"

"Lola, leave Naomi alone," Chaz bellowed. "She is not what you think she is!"

"She is exactly what I know her to be! If you doubt me, go into the dining room and look. You will see that everything has been moved so that when Naomi lights her Friday night candles, she faces east as all

Jews do." A curious silence fell. Everyone stopped what they were doing and looked at Naomi, their gaze riveted upon her. As Naomi searched their faces, she could almost hear their hateful thoughts. Lola stared at Naomi with unmasked contempt and cleared her throat. Once the teenager was certain she had everyone's attention, she continued, "Go to the dinning room and look at the marks on the rug and the dimensions of the room." Naomi could hardly believe what she was hearing. As she watched, she saw everyone look at her as if none of them had never known her. It seemed to her that Lola snarled with disdain when she added, "Look at her head covering and then come back and read this letter. Then you will know that what I say is true."

Naomi rose from La Señora's chair. She wondered if it was her sitting on this seat of honor, which did not belong to her, that had brought about her downfall. She searched Chaz's face and knew the fault was hers alone and that alone she must face the situation. She had chosen the path that brought her to this event for she had known all those years ago that doing as Madre Vida asked, she might experience this painful ending. Rent with grief, she forced herself to look at Chaz with all the love her heart held.

He saw her look at him and turned away.

She gulped back her tears and began, her voice barely a whisper, "You do not have to look at those things. I was going to tell you about myself later today, Chaz, but I might as well tell you now. She is right. I am a Jew, a daughter of Zion."

Chaz stood and walked away.

Naomi scanned the crowd. She knew this would be the last time she would lay eyes on these people whom she had come to love more than her own family. For the first time in fifteen years, she thought of her needs rather theirs and said, "And now, if you will excuse me, I have had enough excitement for one day." She stood and walked away.

"Naomi, why did you deceive me? How could you do this?" Chaz hollered.

Naomi heard the hate-filled words. She felt their painful sting as her one and only love, a love that had pledged to be true to her throughout her whole life, shattered before her. Yet she forced herself to say nothing, for there was nothing to say. Had there been something to share, she knew there was no one who would listen, not even if she could bring herself to tell them everything. She reached the threshold of the kitchen, turned, and smiled at them. Tears ran down her face. She nodded as she turned away. She knew that she must leave quickly for Chaz had affirmed her worst fears when he exclaimed, "I can never trust you again!"

Now there is no more hiding, for you have told them you are a Jew, Naomi thought when she reached the threshold to her bedroom. *Even your husband despises you.* She sobbed though no tears fell. Retching, she entered the room, closed the door, and prostrated herself. "God, what is it that my people have done that no matter where we go or what we do, we are always caught in the middle of this turmoil? I never intended to have such a visible life," she said, glad that no one could hear her. "I planned to be a servant for you and hoped you would shelter me. Now there is nowhere for me to hide. You asked me to work here for you. I believed you sent me to help Tía. She chose, trained, and adopted me so that I could do what she entrusted to me. I have become what I needed to be so that I could do what my American *madre* asked me to do. I believed you me sent here for such a time as this. Dear *Adonai,* now my time has ended. Help me have the strength to leave. Allow me to do this quietly and with dignity. And help them to, sometime in the future, remember that I loved them."

Naomi, a voice seemed to call, *have you forgotten so quickly that which you knew at your mother's knee?*

"What is that, Lord?"

Do not fear, the voice that was more than a voice soothed *Remember, wherever you go, whatever you ask of me, which aligns itself with my Word, I have promised to fulfill it, for I know the plans I have for you, plans to prosper you and not to harm you, plans to give you hope and a future.* Aware that *Adonia* had given her a promise from the scriptures that her mother had taught her and her sisters, Naomi believed him. She tore her heart away from all that mattered. The Lord credited her belief in him as righteousness and silently affirmed to her that in his time everything she yearned for would become her reality.

I did not mean to love you so, Naomi thought as she resigned herself to the fact that Chaz no longer loved or wanted her. *There is nothing to lament,* she told herself. She walked to her bedside table, took off her wedding band and hat, set them down, and reminded herself, *You showed him an illusion rather then your real self. Your deceit created this situation. Remember, when you are hurting, so is he.*

She took out notepaper and a pen. *You do not deserve him, an honorable man*, she silently upbraided herself as she wrote,

> Chaz, Dearest One,
> Annul this marriage. The church will be happy to do this for you. I know you will be happier without me in your life.
> May Adonai bless you,
> Naomi

She folded the paper in half, placed it alongside her hat and wedding band, and turned away with a sense of finality. She walked to where she had hidden her Bible and picked it up. Sitting on her bed, she looked around her room, and drank in the security and comfort she had experienced there. She remembered Madre Vida's words to her the first day she had come to this house and to this room. *"This will become a place of comfort for you. You will see. It will be good for you. I will hide you and protect you until it is time for you to bloom. When it is your time, you will be revealed a lovely flower!"* Thinking it decidedly odd that God would promise the fulfillment of these things only after the bright promise of her hopes were dashed, Naomi heard Justine's voice at her door.

"Naomi, open the door! Let me in!"

Since Naomi did not respond, another woman said, "She is not answering."

"No more, *Adonai*," Naomi prayed. "Please no more of this. I cannot take the look of recrimination I know will be on their faces."

Using her stern parental voice, Justine insisted, "If you do not open this door, I will have Bobby break it down!"

Naomi gulped back a sob. "Go away! I cannot face you!"

"I understand. Just let me in. This is not as bad as you think. People did not know how to act. They asked me to apologize to you."

"This is exactly what I experienced in Spain. No matter where a Jew goes within the Spanish community, this always happens. It is what the church has taught that has created this problem! But I did not kill your God!"

"I know you believe what you are saying is important, but what you are speaking about has nothing to do with me." Justine opened the door wide enough for her to peek in. "Besides, I have something to show you and things you need to know."

Naomi grabbed her belongings, intending to flee, but realized that Lola had her immigration papers. She knew she could not leave without them and the things she had taken from her parents' home. However, never wishing to appear needy again, she said, "There is nothing I need to see or to know that will change my mind."

Justine turned toward the other woman. The door to Naomi's bedroom opened. They heard Naomi gasp, turned, saw her, and seemed to freeze. She thought it odd that they did not force their way into her room but instead turned to each other as if she was not there while Justine said, "It is bad enough that she feels alone. Do we really want to force ourselves on her?"

The old woman looked at Naomi. "We must."

Justine nodded to the old woman, who turned toward Naomi. "Let us help you. You are not as alone as you think you are."

"It was a woman's help that got me into this situation. I do not think I need another woman to help ever again!"

"Oh, but you are wrong," the old woman said. "You do not know me, but I have known you since your first bus ride to this *casa*. I know that when you arrived here, you had to remain in this house. Then upon Vida's death, you faced many choices that led to freedom and responsibility or self-alienation through hiding. In both your doing and hiding, you have been so busy that you have missed some very important things that we need to share with you. Let us in!"

"You stay where you are!" Naomi stood and slammed the door shut. "I will only open this door to get back my things. Then I will leave and none of you will see me again!"

As much as she wished she could not hear the women speaking with each other, Naomi leaned towards the door and heard the women's conversation.

"It is just as Vida feared," the old woman said.

"Yes, it is, but what can we do?"

"I know. Listen, daughter of Zion, did you not wonder at the *Mezuzah* on your door lintel? Did you not notice Vida never went to church but chose to isolate herself during *Shabbat*? Have you been so wrapped up in your own fearful deceptions that you did not realize that she also was as we are?"

Naomi opened her door and glared at the women. "What do you mean, she was as we are?"

Justine and Teresa hurried into her room and closed the door. "Naomi, we are of Jewish heritage just as Tía was!"

"That is not true. If it were, I would have known."

The two nodded in unison. "Why would you have known? Two women in the house each pretending to be something they were not!"

"But, Justine, you prayed to the Virgin Mary."

"Yes, Naomi and you light votives at the church every *Erv' Shabbat*."

"I would have seen the evidence."

"You did. But you were so busy hiding who you were that it never registered with you!"

"What evidence?" Naomi advanced on them, intending to open the door, and push them out.

Justine looked at her friend and smiled. "Naomi, where did the jar come from that you put the *schmaltz* in?"

Naomi stopped. Her mind raced back to the first time she decided to render chicken fat and found the small jar at the back of the refrigerator. *Yes, I guess I should have figured it out from that,* Naomi thought to herself. "It makes no difference!" She saw the look of disbelief on their faces. "I need to get out of here now!"

"Can we not help you then?" Teresa asked.

"Yes, help me to leave. Now, this very minute. I cannot bear the thought of looking into the eyes of any of these people again." She turned away from them and picked up her things.

"But what about Chaz?'

"I have left him the ring and a letter telling him to get an annulment. I know the church will be happy to do this. Since I am, according to them, a heretic." She walked over and touched the scarf that had so recently framed her face. "Besides, we never consummated our union. I could not bring myself to be with him until I told him who I was. I had planned to do that tonight. I told him yesterday that tonight we would be together and that our togetherness would last the rest of our lives. What a fool I was to think that I could snatch happiness out of a lie no matter how well intended it was!"

"But, Naomi, he does love you!" Justine insisted. "That is why he reacted as he did!"

"It is too painful for me to believe that to be true. He shared what he felt. I am out of his life. After all, how can there be any relationship without trust? Besides, it is of no importance to me." Naomi eyes filled with tears. "I am as my *padre* and *madre* always taught me, only able to associate with my own kind. With them I will be safe and safety is better than love. Safety is worth everything!" Naomi looked from Justine's face to the weathered face of the old woman. "Now, if you would help me, help me to leave! I must go before I hear any of their recriminations or see their faces again!"

"All right, let me see if I can get your things from the patio and find Lola to see if she has anything else of yours," Justine said. "This may take some time. I will come back once I have gotten everything and found Alex."

"Why Alex? I told you I do not want to see anyone. I just want to leave!"

"I understand," Teresa said. "But we cannot let you wander the streets at night."

"That is right." Justine hurried out of the room and returned with her pocket calendar. She pointed at her notes. "Our family reunion begins on Tuesday. Ruth and the children are there now. I will have Alex drive you there. You need to be among others who are of the seed of Abraham. You will see. This will be good for you," Justine called over her shoulder as she walked into the hall and closed the door.

Teresa sat on the bed and motioned for Naomi to join her. "Come, child, sit here and we will talk for a moment before you leave. This has been a hard day for you. I was concerned it might go this way because I overheard Lola speaking with Rita, the girl who cleans house for us, about her plans for you. That is why I came. I know Vida wanted you to bloom and believe me, you will. Your growth has not taken place in season because you have tried to live a double life. This terrible thing that has happened to you will become your greatest blessing!"

"I am through with thinking about or wishing for a blessing."

Teresa picked up Naomi's Bible and nodded. "Then you are ready to listen."

She opened to Isaiah 53 and read:

"He was pierced for our transgressions, he was crushed for our iniquities; the punishment that brought us peace was upon him by his wounds we are healed. We all, like sheep, have gone astray, each of us has turned to his own way; and the Lord has laid on him the iniquity of us all. He was oppressed and afflicted, yet he did not open his mouth; he was led like a lamb to the slaughter as a sheep before her shearers is silent, so he did not open—"

"But," Naomi interrupted in a reverent whisper, "that sounds like—"

"Yes, it sounds like our *Messiah.*"

"No, you must be tricking me!" Naomi spat the words at the old lady. "You are pretending to be Jewish. But you are reading from your book, the *Catholic Bible!*"

"Naomi, look, it is your own book I am reading from." She handed Naomi's Bible back to her.

Shoving it aside, Naomi screamed, "This is a trick! You are a deceiver! Get out of my room!"

Warding off the younger woman's blows, Teresa stood and prayed, "May our God, blessed be He, the God of Abraham, the God of Isaac, and the God of Jacob, guide and protect you all the days of your life, *daughter of Zion.*"

As Teresa walked to the doorway, Naomi sank to the bed, her energy spent. The old lady saw the wooden box, placed her fingertips on it, turned to Naomi, and nodded good-bye. Then lifting her fingers to her lips with a reverence Naomi had not seen since she had left her family years before, Teresa closed her eyes and prayerfully kissed the fingers that had touched the blessing of *Adonai* while she silently prayed to him who is unseen. Then she left.

Naomi wondered if her wild imaginings could be true and ran to the box. She opened the lid and found that what she had wished was in fact true for inside were God's words. Suddenly aware of the wisdom of the old woman, she thought, *Why is she able to live here and openly proclaim her faith?* She picked up her Bible. *How is it that a Jew knows where to look in our Scriptures to find words that speak so clearly of Christ—their God—words written in our Jewish Bible? Am I so vulnerable that I will believe whatever anyone tells me?* She opened her Bible and by happenstance found the words she had heard. She sat down and tried to read them, but her tears blurred the words.

A few moments later, Justine pushed Alex into Naomi's bedroom and closed the door. "Look who I finally found."

Naomi looked up, tears obscured her vision, so she asked, "Yes, who is it?"

"It's me, Tía," Alex answered in his quiet, reassuring way. "I have come to take you away from all of this."

Naomi motioned for him to come closer as she shivered. "Good. I must confess my strength has left me. I am not certain I will be able to walk on my own."

"Don't worry, Tía. My mother is packing your things. When everything is ready, I will wrap you up and carry you out in this blanket." He held up the memory quilt. Hearing his comforting words, Naomi closed her eyes and seemed to drift off.

For a brief moment, all was serine. Then Justine looked at the quilt and exclaimed, "No, not that! She will not want to see that!"

Worried that his mother's words would awaken Naomi, Alex glanced in her direction, but she slept on. He smiled reassuringly and whispered, "I know what I'm doing." He took a blanket from Naomi's wardrobe and watched as she roused herself to see him lay it on her bed. Justine asked Naomi about what she wanted done with some mementos. As she turned to speak with Justine, Alex turned her quilt over, placed it on top, and turned toward her. "This is like hide and seek. However, unlike that game, no one will find you. I will cover you up from head to toe. Everyone will think I am taking something back to the store. Since I always help Desi do this after your Sunday lunch, no one will stop us. Trust me."

"No, Alex," Naomi said with her last bit of strength as she lay down in the blankets as he directed. "I am through with trusting anyone, even you."

Alex wrapped Naomi's frail frame in the blankets. "Then trust in this," he said as Justine tucked Naomi's Bible in the blankets. She kissed Naomi, prayed over her, and sent her on her way. "Take good care of her."

"Don't worry. I will not leave her until she is settled. Then I will bring the car back so we can all go to the reunion later this week."

"Alex, you are a man after God's own heart, but I was not talking to you. I was praying to *Adonai*."

Rumor and Reality

"What did you think?" Xavier giggled while in a drunken stupor. "Did you think you were marring a saint?"

Chaz held his empty shot glass out to his friend. "Yes, I did." He motioned for Xavier to refill it.

"But, *amigo*, you've drunk your fill. Besides, you told me to never let you near the hard stuff again!" He held the bottle to the florescent light so that he could see how much tequila remained. "Here, let me help you keep your pledge." His hand shook as he struggled to bring the bottle of Cuervo Gold in line with his glass and he giggled.

Chaz stared at him. "Xavier, if you want to present yourself to your wife later tonight as a man, not a mountain of raw flesh, you had better pour that into my glass!" He grabbed Xavier's hand, forced him to release his grip on his shot glass, picked it up, and hurled it against the wall. When it shattered, he smiled. "Forget what I told you before. I need to drown my sorrow and not think about the shame that woman has brought upon my name!"

Staggering to the kitchen in the back of his tobacco shop and back again, Xavier held a shot glass in his right hand, in his left some more beer. He sat down and refilled their glasses with tequila. "To your health, *amigo*." He moistened the back of his hand with saliva, and followed the machismo ritual of lick, shot, lime, adding beer as a chaser. The men matched each other round for round. "Just like the old days, *amigo*," Xavier said with a sigh. "I have missed those days!" He looked at Chaz to see if he understood what he meant. His friend's cold icy stare greeted him. "And you? Have you missed those days, my friend?"

Chaz stood. "No, I have been pleased that I was able to overcome my bad habits, alcohol, and all it brought my way, a degrading life with no hope of bettering it!" He downed another shot, followed with lime and beer. "And more than that, I was amazed that she would have me! Even when I was a bum, she never judged me. Yet at the moment I learned who and what she was, I judged her—most harshly!"

Xavier stood and clamped his arm around his friend's shoulder. "Don't worry. Women always forgive. It is their nature. You will see!"

Chaz removed Xavier's arm and staggered toward the door. "Naomi is not like other women and our situation is not like the ones married couples have."

"But what is the problem, my friend?" Xavier asked. He walked to the door and opened it to let some fresh air in. "You still love her, don't you?"

Chaz averted his eyes. "I still love her. But, I cannot have her. She is without honor and has lied to me, to all of us!"

"Remember my friend, did not Christ say we are to forgive?"

"That is what I have heard. But I do not know how to reconcile her behavior with the fact that she comes from the people that killed Christ!" Chaz stumbled from the shop.

"When we first met, you told me about your family and the *rancho* they work on. They may be able to help you deal with this. Go visit them. Leave and let the gossips find no target for their wagging tongues."

Chaz waved good-bye and wove his way back to the *casa*. His feelings surfaced. Since he had always kept his inner thoughts at bay, this was a strange and uncomfortable experience. Seldom one to admit fear, he had always known that if he looked at who he was for too long, he would not like himself. Yet he did not know why. Instead of trying to find the solution to this dilemma that had plagued him since before he could remember, Chaz thought about everything that had happened and his feelings of betrayal intensified. Although he wished it were a lie, it was true that he felt cheated, and it was true that he was trying to fight off that feeling. But he could not. For the truth was, he felt lied to by the one he had chosen to give all he was, heart and soul, to. All the long, winding way home, he allowed his mind to replay everything that had happened. Acutely aware of being humiliated, he became enraged.

By the time he reached the *casa*, his anger had grown beyond his ability to stifle it.

When he discovered that the front door would not open, he used the full force of his rage and thrust it open. The door banged into the wall and he guffawed. He grinned, pleased with his accomplishment. "No one can put anything over on me," he slurred as he staggered in. He smiled to himself as he looked around the front rooms. "Nothing matters anymore." He wove through the dining room and into the kitchen. Stopping at the espresso machine, he drained the dregs as he remembered Naomi taking it from its hiding place and saying, "*If our guests smell this, they will all want some, but no one else is to have any. I am making it especially for you!*"

His cup in hand, he walked to dining room and thought about what Lola had said. He pulled out a chair, sat, bent over, and ran his fingers though one of the indentations in the rug. His eyes glazed over with loathing. Righting himself, he looked across the table to the place where Naomi had stood to light the candles on Friday night. He wondered how he could have missed her ritual.

Lola emerged from the shadows. "You see, it is just as I told you. You should have listened to me. I could have saved you from all this pain and humiliation."

Chaz gazed at her with longing and repulsion. "Yes, that is true."

She walked toward him with demure steps so as not to arouse his suspicion. "I have been waiting for you all of my life. I know I didn't make a good impression on you when we first met, but it was because of her, that deceiver, Naomi. She was the one who caused the trouble between us, just as she has caused the community to feel pity for you." He listened to the girl, transfixed by what she said as she walked up to his chair. She lifted her flimsy nightgown to her thighs, spread her legs apart, straddled his, and sat down. She rubbed her body suggestively against his and aroused him. "Come, I love you. Let me help you forget this humiliation." He looked longingly into Lola's eyes and realized how wonderful the oblivion she offered would feel. Intoxicated by her nearness, he stood and pulled her fiercely to him

She took his hand, led him to Naomi's bedroom, and pointed to his wife's virginal bed. "Come. Take me there." She began untying the series of bows on the white peignoir he and Naomi's *niñas* had chosen for his bride to wear on her wedding night.

Noting the finery, he turned away from her. "I want you out of here before sunrise tomorrow! If you are not gone when I get up, I will call immigration to come and get you. You remember how it feels to be there waiting to be deported. I know you are too smart to find yourself in the same fix again. Remember, they will never let you stay here if you are brought back to them a second time, believe me, everyone here knows what you are. No one will come to help you this time!" He turned and walked away.

"You think you've won, you drunken lout! Well I've got news for—"

"I have lost everything that mattered to me. But you, Lola, have not won. Perhaps someday you will learn that this not a game. Heaven help those poor unsuspecting fools who meet you before that day comes! Now leave! I will not tell you again."

He walked into the suite of rooms Naomi was to share with him and slammed the door shut. The bed they were to have shared mocked him. Sadly aware that he was again becoming what he despised, he walked to the bathroom, turned the shower to its coldest setting, and stepped into it fully dressed.

When the late afternoon sun filtered into his room, Chaz groaned and got out of bed, groggy from the previous night's drinking. He vaguely remembered the night, Lola's call to cast his body into eternal torment for one night of sexual pleasure, and moaned. Ruminating on what he had almost done, he felt sick, ran to the bathroom, and vomited into the shower. He turned, caught a glimpse of himself in the mirror, and saw the effect his one night of drinking had wrought. "I cannot become this person again!" He turned the water to its coldest setting and stuck his head under the faucet. While he dried his head with the scented towel he had used the day before, Chaz realized what a stark difference there was between the two days. He glanced at his reflection in the mirror, and admitted, *I do not know what to do. Without Naomi, nothing matters.*

"Hello, anyone home?" said a voice that Chaz assumed was coming from the front door.

"Come in," he said. Then thinking of the damage he had done the night before, he sarcastically added, "The door is open." He dressed and walked to the vestibule. Startled to see the priest standing in the dappled light of the porch, he forced a smile. "Padre, what brings you out so early?"

"My son, I came as soon as I could. Many have called me. Some have visited asking for penance because of their behavior in this whole affair."

"What did those asking for penance think they needed to seek forgiveness for?"

"Many things. Most especially allowing themselves to be misled. You know how that is."

Chaz looked at the man, who, except for the wedding and his counsel beforehand, had never involved himself in Chaz's affairs. His first inclination was to ask him to leave. However, knowing it was not wise to discount the man's visit, he said, "*Sí*, I know how that is."

The priest walked to the dining room and sat down at the table while his eyes searched for the telltale signs of Naomi's duplicity. "What do you intend to do?"

"Nothing." Chaz picked at a hangnail on his index finger. "What is there to do? She deceived me. No, let me correct my statement; she lied to me, to all of us."

"Yes, she did. But have you always told the truth?"

"I thought she was a saint. But I found out differently. She is just like everyone else."

Padre Paul glanced toward the kitchen and saw Lola walking toward the house wearing a bikini. "Do you really believe that?"

Chaz followed the priest's gaze and hollered, "I told you to be out of here before dawn today!"

The girl smiled and blew him a kiss.

The priest looked at the teenager's ripe body then back at Chaz. "Get her out of here!"

"Padre, I have tried but she will not leave."

"She will go once she realizes you will not be back."

"I cannot leave and miss the opportunity of speaking with Naomi when she returns."

"She will be gone all this week, perhaps longer."

"Who told you this?"

"I cannot tell you. It will have to be enough for you to know that the people she is with love our Lord and her. They will make sure that no harm comes to her. Though you have not sought my advice, I believe it would be best for you to go home and come back in a week."

"I cannot leave. I am in the middle of building my office space across the street and the men begin the renovations on Naomi's *casa* tomorrow!"

"Bobby and Justine are concerned for you and Naomi. They offered to step in and manage things for you and the *niñas*. Since Justine has helped Naomi as she did La Señora, the work would be in good hands. Because Bobby is a foreman in the building trade the same thing is true of him. With their eldest, Alex, now a man, they feel comfortable leaving their children in his care. They offered to live in the *casa* until either you or Naomi return. And of course, we all pray you will be able to come together again as husband and wife. They agree with me. Both of you should be out of the area so those of us who love you can deal with the fallout from the unfortunate affair."

Chaz furrowed his brow. "This unfortunate affair is my life!"

"Just so."

"Hello, can I come in?" As Chaz turned to see who was there, the priest whispered, "It is Mr. Martinez. Be careful what you say to him. He has been trying to get his hands on the estate since La Señora gave it to Naomi."

Because the priest's words validated what Naomi had said, Chaz was uncertain whether he wanted to invite the man to enter the *casa* or not. Before he could make up his mind, Padre Paul greeted the man and ushered him into the dining room. "Here, my friend, is a man of much importance," he said by way of introduction. Chaz smiled at the barrister. He choose to keep his thoughts to himself, but he if he were to voice them, he thought he might have asked the priest if he had forgotten that the attorney had contacted him and asked that he bless Chaz's first meeting with Naomi. However, since all had gone well with his plan until yesterday, Chaz had no reason to believe Padre Paul had anything to gain by aiding someone who he thought might have ulterior reasons for visiting. Yet, having discovered how wrong he could be where his wife was concerned, he decided to watched and listen to both of them.

Mr. Martinez nodded at the priest's compliment, smiled ingratiatingly, and extended his hand to Chaz. "I am here to see how I may be able to help." Chaz took the offered hand to shake and was surprised to discover that the attorney had not intended to shake hands but give him his business card. The attorney sat down at the dining room table. "This problem can be easily rectified. Of course, you never consummated your marriage, so the church can have your union annulled. I will make the arrangements. And since I feel badly about this situation, there will be no charge."

"That is very gracious of you." Chaz walked to the sideboard and set the card down. "I do not know what course of action, I will pursue. Now if you will excuse me, I have some packing to do. Business calls me away. I should be back within seven to ten days. I will call on both of you when I get back." He walked away.

Padre Paul nodded and the attorney stood. They turned and headed toward the front door.

"*Un momento.*" Mr. Martinez motioned for the priest to wait while he turned, examined the placement of the furniture in the dining room, and checked the rug for the telltale markings.

"I see the story has gotten out already. This poor couple. How will they ever be able to withstand the gossip and slander?"

The attorney joined the priest and motioned for them to exit the house. Once they were on the porch and the door closed, he said, "Padre, this marriage should be annulled. You know the church would have them lead separate lives. How can a Jew and a believer in Christ and the Holy Sacraments ever have a life together, let alone honor God?"

"That, my son, is a very good question. But let me ask you a better one. What would you have been willing to do in order to keep the one thing that means the world to you?"

"I would do anything!"

"Really? Would you be willing to give up something you value to get something you desire?"

"Yes! Yes! I know what it is to want something and have to wait for it for a very long time. I understand how the desire for that unobtainable thing can color all of your life and cause you to feel cheated though you have been blessed with fortune, recognition, and position. The reality for a person like that is without their object of desire their world is desolate, bleak!"

The padre looked at the attorney with sympathy. "Then, my son, you understand the situation between these two." He hurried away.

"But, Padre, you cannot be serious. She is only a woman!" He hurried after the priest.

Padre Paul heard him running to catch up and waited. When the attorney joined him, he opened his mouth to say something, but before he could the priest said, "My son, she is his woman. Though she deceived him, he has bound her to his heart, and I believe he will not let her go."

"Then we must help him! Remember we talked about her unsuitability once before. Now we have proof! With your help, we can both profit from this affair and help our friend Chaz as well!"

"I will have no part of this!" the priest insisted as he walked away.

"Then I will have to report you to the bishop!"

Padre Paul turned around. "Do that and I will be certain to leak information about some of your activities to the press."

"You threaten me!"

"I am not threatening you. I am telling you that Christ taught, *'Let the one amongst you who is without sin cast the first stone!'*"

"So this is the woman you wanted me to be like," Florita yelled at her parents. She ran to her bedroom, pushed her sister out, and slammed the door.

"Florita kicked me out of my own room!" Alicia yelled.

"I'll go," Flora told her husband. "This is a problem that needs a woman's touch."

Dominic shook his head and motioned for his wife to sit down. "Flora, a girl celebrating her *quinceañera* should not need to rely on us when it comes to matters between her and her sister."

"Yes, you are right."

"Imagine the commotion this information about Naomi will cause throughout El Barrio. I was afraid for my job when La Señora died and left control to Naomi but she proved to be a good choice. Now, if we need to, will we be able to make it on your salary?" She took out the few dollars she had from her purse and looked to her husband. He dug deep into his jeans and pulled out all he had left from the previous week's wages. They prayed and counted their money.

"Dominic, we only have forty-four dollars and fifty-three cents, not enough to pay our bills and make it until your next payday!"

"The store always pays on Tuesday, which is tomorrow. So we will be fine."

"We will be fine if there is a store to work at and someone has the authority to sign our checks!"

Dominic took her work-worn hands in his. "Someone will step in."

Flora looked into her husband's eyes. "I remember when the kids were young and I got so sick that you had to work an extra job. You came home so tired that all you did was sleep."

"We got by then, if we have to tighten our belts again, we can!"

"But Alicia's *quinceañera*—we still owe money for her dress!"

"Don't worry. We will find a way. We always have."

Alicia overheard the end of their troubled conversation and stepped into the kitchen. "What's going on?"

They did not answer. She waited, still no answer.

"You don't tell me anything! First, Florita kicks me out of my own room and slams the door in my face. Then I come in here and you both look as if someone just died!" Alicia noticed their sorrowful faces and saw the few dollars. "Money troubles?" She nodded toward the paltry sum.

Her parents looked at each other. Dominic nodded to Flora. "If she is old enough to ask the question, she is old enough to know the answer."

Flora put the teapot on to boil. "*Sí*. It's too late for coffee. Would you like some tea?"

"That would be good." Dominic motioned for Alicia to join them and told her about Naomi's sudden departure from Spanish Harlem.

Alicia ran to her room as she called over her shoulder, "Don't worry!" She banged on the door. "Let me in!"

"Go away!"

"Florita, this is no time to think about yourself. Our parents are in a bad way. I need to get to my savings so I can help them! Now let me in!"

When Florita opened the door, Alicia ran in and out again, slamming the door shut behind her. She sniffled and flopped down on her bed. A second later, Alicia barged in and grabbed her hand. "You're coming with me! I need you by my side when I speak with them!"

"You've never needed me for anything," Florita said as she stood.

Alicia pulled Florita into the hallway and whispered her plan as they walked to the kitchen.

"This can work!"

"I know!" Alicia guided them into the kitchen. They sat down next to each other.

Their mother looked from one daughter to the other. "This is an unexpected blessing. I never thought I would see you two together, happily choosing to be so until one or both of you had moved out of the house."

Dominic eyed them. "So, what's on your mind?"

"Well…" Alicia tried to press her money into her sister's hand.

Florita pushed the money away and whispered, "No! It's yours. You do it. I'm only here for moral support!"

Alicia forced a smiled and put the money on the table. "This is for you." She stood to leave.

Her father looked at the money. "Come back here immediately!"

Alicia shook her head. "Only if you promise not to yell at me."

"Dominic, let's not fight. Alicia means to help us. Let's be thankful we have a resourceful child in our home."

"But where did this money come from?" He picked up the roll, undid the rubber band, and fingered the bills.

"There must be over two hundred dollars here."

"No, Papá, there is exactly three hundred and fifty-two dollars there."

"*Pero, hija,* where did this come from?" her mother asked.

"I've been trying to tell you for almost a year. I sold some of my songs to a recording company! I had hoped to perform them but have been unable to audition because of the plans you've made for me. But anyway, here's all that's left of the money I earned."

Dominic stared at her. "All that is left!"

"Alicia, we are very grateful for your help. But we need to know what you have been up to and why you have been sneaking around behind our backs."

Her father scowled. "I couldn't have said it better if I had tried!"

"I can explain it to you better if you will just listen, all right?" Alicia raced to her room, grabbed the record player, her demo records, and returned. "I know this isn't your kind of music, but it's popular. I can make a living writing and singing songs like these. The producer said he wants me to go on tour with the group that recorded these. I can start as a backup singer. If someone gets sick, I'll fill in. It could be a big break for me."

She plugged in the record player, put her demo on, and watched her parents as the music played. Though she knew their every gesture and facial expression, she could not figure out what they were thinking. While she listened, she remembered the producer saying, "*You, young lady, have an amazing voice. That coupled with your ability*

to conceptualize new musical forms will allow you to have quite a career!"
She could still hear herself say, "Wonderful! Now all I need to do is
get my parents to approve!" However, when he answered, *"That's easy.*
Bring them down here I'll speak with them. I am certain they will see the
advantage of having you represented by our company. We will make certain
they are satisfied with your contract," she knew they would never agree.
Now she hoped she had a chance to get them to agree to her plans.

The song ended. Before they could say no, Alicia said, "I have a letter of intent from the music producer. He would like all of us to come
down to his office and talk over the possibilities available for me!"

Her mother took the letter from Alicia. Her father nodded. "We
will read what this man has to say. Then we will see."

"Have you heard?" Lucinda's clients asked her repeatedly as she escorted
them to her station and draped them for their haircut, perm, color, or
weave, then the gossip would start. Everyone had their ideas about
Naomi and Chaz. Many were upset about Naomi's duplicity. "After all
this time, imagine, a Jew! Well, it just shows how deceptive *those* people
can be!"

After a few hours of listening to the nasty things the women said,
Lucinda put the seldom used back-in-one-hour sign on the front door
and called a staff meeting.

Everyone grabbed their lunch and sat down in the back room.

"What are you hearing from your patrons today?"

"Everyone's upset," Cassia said between bites.

"Yes," said the others. A few of the stylists exchanged whispered
excuses as they tired to figure out why Lucinda had closed the shop.
None of them could remember a time when Madonna Elegante had
closed during business hours.

Lucinda looked at her girls—Cassia, Marie, Jackie, and Estella.
"You need to know that this personal problem of Naomi's could affect
our bookings. Naomi helped me get my cosmetology license and this
shop. I wouldn't be here if it weren't for her."

"What does Naomi's situation have to do with the shop?" Jackie asked.

"Oh, come on, are you blind and deaf?" Estella asked. "It's all over
town. Everyone has come in and said derogatory things about Naomi's
situation. Her marriage, her faith; even her work in the community has
been called into question."

Marie took out her pink nail polish and applied another coat. Since she never voiced an opinion, they were surprised to hear her say, "That's true. But all we have to do is say nothing one way or the other. It's easy."

"Naomi was good to me. I'm not going to turn my back on her now. If someone speaks about Tía and her situation while they're here, I will ask them to leave."

"But that would mean we'd lose our clientele!"

"That's why I've called this meeting. I'm not going to allow Naomi's personal affairs to be talked about as if she were dead. If any of you want to be involved in gossip, or if you're afraid of losing your clientele, then you need to find another salon to work in!"

"But where can we go?" Estella asked.

"That's not my problem." Lucinda grabbed her purse and hollered to the receptionist, "I'll be back at one. If anyone calls and wants to book an appointment here, make certain you tell them once they enter this establishment, there will be no discussion of any sort about Naomi. Is that clear?"

"Yes, Lucinda," Corrine replied.

Estella watched the backdoor close behind the proprietor. "What could Lucinda be thinking? We rent our stations. Without our rental payments how long could she stay in business?"

"Even if we wanted to go, it would take weeks to find the right place, negotiate a rental agreement and notify our clients," Jackie said.

"And Lucinda is asking us to leave today or stay under her guidelines," Cassia said.

"She … didn't … say that."

"It was implied," Estella said. "Corrine will tell our clients about Lucinda's ban on gossip when she answers the phone."

"I don't want to stay where someone tells my clients what they can and can't talk about," Maria said. "There's a shop on Twenty-Third Street that's advertising for stylists. Their salon is newly renovated, I've heard they have several stations open."

"Good," Jackie and Cassia said.

"Corrine, could you bring us the phone book?" the girls asked.

Corrine was certain that the staff was causing themselves unnecessary grief. But she picked up the phonebook and walked to the back. "Here you go." She handed the book to Jackie.

Estella pulled it out of Jackie's grasp. "Let's call them now!" She walked to the back phone and dialed the salon's number.

Corrine followed them. "What can you be thinking? Each of you came here with no clientele. Now the moment Lucinda makes a rule—a good rule—you are afraid and want to leave! Shame on you, Jackie," she said as she looked at the girl. "You came here with a license and a baby. Lucinda set up a nursery for you in the back room so you would not have to pay for daycare that you could not afford. Estella, no one thought you would be able to handle the work with all of your health problems," Corrine continued as she looked at the overweight woman who held the phone in mid-air. "You told Lucinda you had no clientele because you bounced around from shop to shop. You came here as a last resort. She allowed you to work rent free for three months so you could get back on your feet. Everything you have accomplished here is because of her help!" Corrine's gaze swept over the staff. "Do you want me to continue?"

"No," they said in unison. They were afraid to meet her gaze because everything she said was true.

She walked to the front desk. "I thought not!"

The girls talked amongst themselves and nodded toward Corrine. "She's right." They walked to the reception desk. "Don't tell her we were about to leave. It's embarrassing enough that you heard us!"

"Girls, I only needed to remind you about what you know to be true. Lucinda is a recipient of Naomi's gifts. She passed them on to you. Now it is your turn to pass them on to someone else."

The women looked at each other. "Yes, that's true."

"Perhaps the gifts you have been given will be poured out on Naomi."

"Why would we give *that* woman anything at all?"

"Did you not realize that in order for her to do what Tía asked of her, she postponed her life, and put all of her plans away so she could be as we needed her to be?"

"But she hid who she was from us," Jackie said.

"True. But how could she accomplish what she was asked to do in this community if we all knew her to be a Jew? Wouldn't we have treated her differently?"

"I suppose so," Estella and Marie said.

"You see, sometimes unusual requests make us act in unusual ways. Since Naomi never harmed anyone, can we not forgive her as she, most of all the people we know, surely needs forgiveness?"

"Yes. That's right," they all said. "God tells us to forgive, so we must forgive her."

"But we cannot forget that she's a Jew!" Cassia spit out her words.

"Yes, let us never forget that a Jewish woman came here, gave her life over to our needs, and served us as God in Christ told us to serve one another."

"But you're making her sound like a saint!" Jackie shouted.

"Oh, is that how you have heard what I said?"

"Yes," they answered.

"If all of you think that what this woman did makes her sound like a saint, who am I to argue with you?" Corrine smiled and picked up the phone. "Madonna Elegante, how can I help you?"

Lucinda entered her salon a few moments before one. She was pleased to see her stylists relaxing in the back room. "Is everything all right?"

"Yes. We've talked it over and think your rule is a good one."

"In fact, it might be a good idea for us to stop gossiping altogether," Maria said.

"Yeah," Estella said. "What I remember most and really appreciated best when I first got here was that no one talked behind my back."

"Do you all feel this way?"

"We discussed it and agreed that we'd like this to be a salon where people would be able to feel good about themselves instead of being worried that something they shared with us would be repeated to someone else."

"Good." Lucinda headed to her station. Corrine turned and smiled at her. "Corrine, I want to talk to you."

"Coming." Corrine got up and walked to the first chair.

When she arrived, Lucinda whispered, "Did you do this?"

"I was at the front desk waiting to answer the phone. If the girls did not leave, it is because of you. After all, this is a good salon. Ask anyone in the area. They all want to come here! Right?"

"Right." Lucinda grinned at her mother.

A Sign

Corrine got into her daughter's car. "It was a good day after all."

"Amazingly so." Lucinda put her car in gear. "I thought they'd leave."

"So did I. But they are smarter than we have given them credit for."

"I guess they are." Lucinda turned out of the parking lot and drove the few blocks to Naomi's street. Finding the house, she parked in front, and looked its façade.

"Why are we here?"

"Just thinking about Naomi and how much her help meant to me. I owe her a lot, but I never thanked her."

"Is that what you think she wanted from you?"

"No. I know she wasn't that type of person. That's why this situation is so hard for me understand. To think that she has been shamed when all she did was meant to bless us! It is very hard for me to hear," she cried.

As her mother moved to draw her near, she glanced out the widow and handed her a tissue. "Here, better mop up, and blow your nose. She pointed to an approaching figure.

Lucinda looked up. "Oh, it's only Nicco."

Corrine dug in her daughter's purse and handed her daughter's lipstick to her. "It's only Nicco." She pulled down the visor so Lucinda could apply some fresh color. "You say that every time you see him. What's the matter with Nicco? Do you think you are too good for him?" She reached across her only child, opened her door, and pushed her out.

"I've known him forever. There's no chemistry!"

"I don't want chemistry! I want grandchildren!" Corrine closed the door and pulled out her crossword puzzle. Lucinda leaned against the car, hoping he would not embarrass her by walking by without saying a word.

Nicco stopped, looked her up and down said, "Hi." He took off his work gloves and leaned against her car.

Lucinda looked him over appraisingly, noticed how trim and fit he was, how open and charming his smile was, and remembered why she had set her heart for him. She took every opportunity to deny her feelings for him because she would never admit to anyone how she longed to be his wife. Averting her gaze, she looked across the street to the build-out. "This looks promising." She shifted her gaze to look at him.

"It's okay." Then before he thought better of it Nicco asked, "What are you doing here?"

"Just looking."

"Oh, for heaven's sake," Corrine hollered as she got out of the car. "You two have been having this conversation for five years!"

"So?" Nicco asked.

"So, nothing! You like her and she likes you. When are the two of you going to get together?"

"Mother!"

"Mother, what? What am I doing that's so terrible? I want grandchildren before I am too old to enjoy them! Now, listen, you two, I am running out of patience. I've waited a long time—what are the two of you waiting for?"

Nicco turned to the fiery redhead who had captured his heart before he was old enough to understand such feelings. "What are we waiting for?"

"I don't know . . . a sign maybe."

"A sign. You're waiting for a sign?"

"What kind of sign do you want?"

"Oh," Lucinda answered playfully as she got back into her car, started the engine, and motioned for her mother to get in. "I don't know . . . something about a blessing," she called back to him as she drove away.

"A blessing." He looked at the house where the blessings had overflowed. *What kind of blessing does a woman who has everything want?* he wondered as he watched her drive off in a brand-new red Corvette.

He forced himself to think about the job, walked across the street, and ticked off his list of must-dos so he could tell Derrick the site was secure for the night. When he came, Derrick spoke with Nicco, who was acting as site manger, walked the site, and signed off on the work. As the men left, he nodded to them. "Looks good. See you tomorrow." When the last man left, he took Nicco aside. "Tomorrow we start the work on that house." He pointed to Naomi's *casa*. "Are you up for the challenge of taking on this project?"

"Me?"

"You got your license so you could oversee projects like this, right?"

"I can handle it!"

"I believe you." Derrick handed Nicco the keys. "Just remember the front gate gets taken care of first.

They rolled the architect's elevations out on the long workbench and reviewed the project together. "That sounds sort of backwards. Why do it that way?"

"Something about making certain that all the *niñas* that have been here and their families can find the old place."

Nicco looked at the notations on the ledger and pointed to one that was obscure. "What does this mean?"

"That's about this." Derrick motioned for Nicco to follow him to his truck. "Help me with this." He dropped the back end. While they struggled to pull out the sign, he explained, "Chaz had it commissioned to hang above the front door. It's heavier than it looks." The two of them wrestled the sign out of the flatbed and leaned it against the old *casa*.

Nicco looked at the sign and read *A Place of Blessing*, which Chaz had selected for a plaque. He measured the sign. "Where is this supposed to go?"

Derrick referred to the notations on the architect's blueprint. "See the arch over the front door? This will hang above it."

Nicco measured the dimensions of the sign, compared them with the architect's measurements, and scratched his head. "Boss, it's not going to fit."

"You sure?" Derrick scribbled down the dimensions, joined Nicco at the front door, measured the arch and sign, and rechecked the measurements against the ones annotated by the architect. "It's off by seven inches." Derrick returned to the table and flipped through the additional elevations and drawings. He waved Nicco over to look at the original information about the front exterior and pointed to a notation almost obliterated by a dark water stain. "I see the problem."

Nicco looked at the notation. "I see. The door is one-of-a-kind. They probably wanted to bring in double doors but the structure of the house wouldn't let them. It seems that they had this door done, custom."

"We're trying to complete this on deadline, and this is a problem we don't need!"

"No problem. I can manage it!"

"But the sign took two weeks to make."

"You asked me to take over this project. Do you trust me?"

"Of course I do, with the regular stuff, but this is unusual. I'll have to speak with the architect and Chaz about this."

"Derrick, give me some time and let me handle this. You won't be sorry."

"What do you have in mind?"

"My uncle's a retired woodcarver. He'll make up a new sign without relying on blueprints. He lives in the neighborhood and knows about this house, even its history. He'll make certain it's done right."

"All right. But what about this sign? We went with the wrong dimensions. Our boss isn't going to be happy about the wasted money. It'll come out of our profits! That may affect our bonus."

Nicco rubbed his stubble. "I have a use for it."

"How much will you pay me for it?"

"I said I could use it. I wasn't planning to pay for it!"

"I can't give it to you!"

"Okay, boss. How about we trade?"

"Trade?"

"I'll take this sign off your hands and my Uncle will make another that will fit above the door. We'll call it a trade."

"All right." Derrick got into his truck and turned on the motor. "But don't complain to me when your uncle asks you to pay for the materials."

"I won't!" Nicco re-measured the sign aware that he might be able to win Lucinda after all. He got in his truck and drove to a payphone.

"*Bueno*," Juan said as he picked up the phone.

"*Amigo*, can you help me with a project tonight before it gets dark?" Nicco asked.

"Yes. Where are you?"

"At the site."

Juan reached for his keys. "I'll be right there."

"Good." Nicco smiled as he hung up the phone. He called back.

Juan picked up the phone and said, "*Bueno?*"

"And bring your pickup truck!"

"Okay." Juan told his wife, "Nicco needs me. Go ahead and have dinner with the kids. I may be home late."

When Juan turned into the construction zone, Nicco pointed to Naomi's house and hollered, "Pull over there!"

Juan parked in front of Naomi's house, hopped out of his truck, looked at the house, and grimaced. "What are we doing here?"

"This is my first job as foremen. Nice, huh?"

"Old. Is this why I'm here?"

"Nope, you're here to help me give Lucy a sign."

"What are you talking about?"

"Lucy's mother told us she's tired of waiting for us to get together. She wants grandkids now—*pronto!*"

"What did Lucinda say?"

"Not much. Just that she's waiting for a sign."

"That makes sense to no one but Lucinda."

"I thought so too! But look." He showed his friend the beautifully carved sign. "It belongs to me. I want to hang it over the door to Lucy's salon. It will just fit and cover up the one she has."

"How do you know that?"

"I painted it for her. Do you think I've forgotten the dimensions?"

"Nicco, what if she doesn't like it?"

"Juan, if this isn't the sign she's been waiting for, then she is not the woman for me."

"After all you've done to get her attention, you're going to let a sign determine if you'll be together or not?"

"Look, the lady asked for a sign," Nicco said as he and Juan picked up the cumbersome sign. "I'm giving her a beautiful sign. If this doesn't reach her heart, nothing will."

"Okay, for a moment I was worried."

They hefted it into the truck bed, closed the tailgate, and sped down the street to Lucinda's shop. "Now I understand. Lucinda has finally caused you to lose your head!"

"*Sí, estoy loco en la cabeza!*" Nicco smiled to himself. "My friend, you're absolutely right!"

They pulled up to the back door, and Nicco felt along the top for the key. Holding the key up for Juan to see, he shouted, "We're as good as in!" Juan smiled, gave him the okay sign, and drove the car around front while Nicco unlocked the back door, and walked to the reception desk. He picked up the phone, dialed his uncle's home, and heard his cousin answer, "James, I'm at Lucy's shop. Tell Uncle Ricky I need him here *pronto!* Ask him to get some of his friends and to bring the ladders we used here last time. And ask him to hurry!"

Nicco hung up the phone, walked out of the front door, and surveyed the activity on the street.

"Not much going on tonight." Juan put on his work gloves.

Nicco smiled, reached into his back pocket, and pulled out his. "Remember the first day on the job when we showed up without these?"

"Boy, do I ever!" Juan laughed. They wrestled the bulky piece from his pickup. "I thought my hands would be scarred from all the blisters I got!"

"Good thing we've learned a thing or two since then!"

"I'm not sure what you learned. It's been eight years since you painted that sign for Lucinda. Now you seem to think this new sign will do the trick for you in the romance department."

"Juan, did you read what the sign says?"

"Not really."

"I couldn't put it into words until I saw this sign today, but I've always believed that because of Lucy's friendship with Naomi, she's been looking for a sign that our marriage would be a blessing. When I saw this sign my thoughts made sense."

Juan had heard all of Nicco's lovelorn musings before so instead of commenting, he looked at the sign. "Will it fit?"

"It's just the right size!" Nicco exclaimed, glad that Juan didn't remind him of his failed attempts to win the fiery redhead. "And I believe it's the sign she's been waiting for!"

"Good," Juan said as the rest the men pulled up. "But you haven't asked her if she wants to change the name of her business. What if she doesn't like it?"

"If that happens, well then, I'll give up!"

Just as Juan was about to say, *I heard that before,* the men hefted the ladders out of the truck and someone hollered, "Hey, watch what you're doing!"

While Nicco directed the activity, Uncle Ricky greeted him, and then Juan with a slap on the back and scowled. "What do you mean by calling the house and leaving a message for me with the boy? What would have happened if we had been out?"

"Can we talk about this after we hang the sign?" Nicco showed his uncle the sign.

His uncle ran his hands over the intricate woodwork. "Nice, almost as nice as that *mi bisabuelo* made!"

"I got this because the dimensions were wrong for the location. I believe it was fate because Lucy asked for a sign."

"Not again! Why don't you just get married like normal people do?"

"I will, Uncle, I promise! But don't you think this is a nice way to propose?"

"You're finally proposing to her?"

"Yes! I am!"

"Then what are we waiting for?" his uncle hollered. "Nicco needs this done before sundown. He is proposing to Lucinda!"

"Okay," Nicco said, hands outstretched, ready to do whatever was needed. "How can I help?"

"You, you can help by getting some flowers, a box of chocolates, and a lovely card for your intended." His uncle pushed him out of the way.

"All right. I'll be right back!"

"Take your time."

"I will." Nicco hurried to the florist's shop.

"Nicco, don't forget the ring."

"I won't!"

"You think he'll remember the ring?" Uncle Ricky asked no one in particular.

"Are you kidding?" Juan said. "He has had an engagement ring for her since he was eighteen."

"Well, what's taken him so long?" one of the other men asked.

"Who knows. All I know for sure is that by now that ring has become quite an investment."

"What do you mean?" Nicco's uncle asked.

"About once a year his friend, the jeweler, lets him upgrade his purchase. Over the years Nicco has dragged me down there to look at new rings. He usually upgrades his choice."

"You're kidding," the men said.

"No, I'm not. I bet he has laid out over eight hundred on that ring!"

An hour later, the men stood in front of Lucinda's salon and eyed their handiwork. "This looks real good," Uncle Ricky said. "Lucinda may be getting more of a blessing than she ever expected!"

"I hope this ring doesn't make all our wives jealous," one of the men said as they got back into Uncle Ricky's truck and waved good-bye to Juan.

When Nicco walked into the barbershop, Ted said, "Hey, Nicco what brings you here?"

"I need a shave and a haircut, *pronto!*"

"You'll wait your turn." Ted nodded toward the patron in his chair. "I have to finish here. Take a seat and I'll be with you soon."

Nicco watched the barber remove a hot towel from his patrons face. He saw Chaz and said, "I thought you'd gone."

"I had planned to. Then I took a look at myself and realized I did not want my family to see me looking like a bum. They have spent enough time worrying about me."

"It's good that I ran into you." Nicco walked to the barber's chair, leaned over, and said, his manner conspiratorial, "I'm planning a little surprise for Lucy. I could use your help!"

"No." Chaz stood and paid Ted. "I have to get going."

"I really do need to talk with you."

"All right." Chaz looked across the street. "Meet me at the barista's when you finish here, but hurry up! I am not planning to hang around here tonight."

By the time Nicco walked to the barista's, Chaz was seated at one of the outside café tables.

"Just a sec." He entered the barista's and ordered a coffee and two cookies. When he returned, he unpacked his tray, put a cookie on a napkin, and placed it in front of Chaz.

Chaz eyed the sweet, grimaced, and pushed it away.

"Not a sweet lover?" Nicco sat down and took a big bite of cookie, followed by a gulp of espresso.

"Only once did sweets appeal to me." Chaz turned away so Nicco could not see his pain. "What do you need from me?"

"Tomorrow, I begin a new project. I'm the site foreman on Naomi's house."

"That is of no importance to me."

"I heard that the two of you were quits."

"Since you know that why pester me about something that no longer concerns me?"

"I had to talk with you because there's a problem with the sign you ordered."

"What about the sign?" Chaz extended his legs to their full-length, tilted his chair back, and put his hands behind his head.

Nicco saw his friend relax and continued, "It was made to the wrong specifications. I'm having another made."

"I already told you, I am not involved with any of this any more."

"I know. But since you commissioned and paid for the sign, I need you to okay a different concept."

"Why different?'

"The sign would overhang the arch and dwarf the scale of the front door. Though you aren't going to be living there, I knew you'd want to know the reason why your instructions were altered."

"So, fix it!" Chaz drained the dregs of his cup, stood, and turned to walk away.

"It's not that easy," Nicco explained as he stood. "We need it to say something different, something with fewer letters so it will fit over the door as you wanted. I was thinking of something like...like calling it *Casa Naomi,* or *Casa de Naomi,* if there's room enough. Do you like either of those ideas?"

"Why would you call it *The House of Naomi?* She will never come back here again!"

"Of course she's coming back!" Nicco noticed Chaz's pained expression. "The work she was entrusted to do will call her back! Besides, her heart is here, with you, with all of us! She can't stay away any more than you can try to convince yourself that you don't love her anymore!"

"You are wrong, Nicco." Chaz picked up his valise and turned to walk toward the bus terminal. "I will always know that I love her. I just cannot be with her!"

"But Chaz, what about the sign?"

"Do whatever you want, but I do not think she will be back. If she does come here again, she will not want people staring at her!"

"Chaz, I think when she comes back, the fact that the house has her name on it will mean something to her!"

"You could be right." Chaz quickened his pace. "Do whatever you think is best. Only keep my name out of it!"

"I am so certain the two of you will come back, that I commit before God that Lucinda and I will not wed until both of you are standing up for us at our wedding!" Nicco exclaimed so loudly that people turned around and stared at him.

Chaz turned back and insisted with equal fervor, "Nicco, do us both a favor and leave God out of this!"

BIBLIOGRAPHY

Footnote: Paris, Erna, *The End of Days*, pg 306–306, Amherst, NY: Prometheus Books, 1995.

Cohen, Dr. Martin A. *The* Martyr-*The Story of a Secret Jew and the Mexican Inquisition in the Sixteenth Century*: The Jewish Publication Society, 1973.

Columbus, Christopher: *The Book of Prophecies*, Edited by Christopher Columbus, Repertorium Columbianum, V. 3 Hardcover.

Gitlit, David M., *Secrecy and Deceit, The Religion of the Crypto-Jews Philadelphia*: The Jewish Publication Society, 1996.

Gitlitz, David M. and Linda Kay Davidson, *A Drizzle of Honey-The Lives and Recipes of Spain's Secret Jews*, New York: St. Martins Griffin, 1999.

Lazarus, |FCO|goog_qs-tidbit goog_qs-tidbit-0Emma, The New Colossuss, written in 1883, in 1903, engraved on a bronze plaque and mounted inside the Statue of Liberty|FCC|.

Liebman Jacobs, Janet, *Hidden Heritage-The Legacy of the Crypto-Jews.* Berkeley: University of California Press, 2002.

Sanchez, Dell F., *Aliyah! The Exodus Continues*, San Jose: Authors Choice Press, 2001.

Wiesenthal, Simon. *Sails of Hope*, Macmillan Publishing Co., Inc., 1973.